Tracy was forced to give up working due to a severe chest illness in 2006 and began to write her first novel 'Steel to Muck' which was published in August 2013. She is kept busy with her eleven grandchildren but has still found the time to write her second novel 'Above and Below the Clouds'. This novel tells the story of a Bomber Command station in WWII. Tracy also finds time to ride her horse, Nutmeg and knits for her loved grandchildren.

Dedication

I would like to dedicate this book to my Dad who has fought and won many battles of ill health. His courage and bravery has inspired me to be who I am today.

CONTENTS

CONTENTS

A Better

Home

Pages 4-18

Reducing noise nuisance

Inconsiderate neighbours, traffic, or noisy teenagers can be a headache in every sense and although complete sound-proofing is seldom possible, but much can be done to reduce the nuisance.

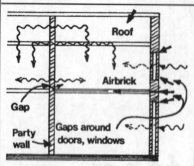

First try to decide how the noise is reaching you; it may be airborne or transmitted through solid materials. Some of the possible paths are indicated.

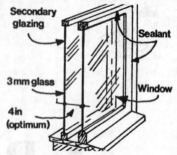

Noise passing through a window can be minimised by fitting secondary glazing, with gap in 4in. between panes; even 2in. is helpful, but narrow gap gives good thermal insulation only. Use thicker glass (e.g. 3mm.) for secondary pane. Seal any gaps around frame.

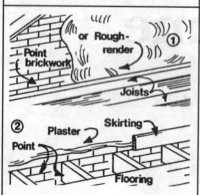

Reduce noise through party wall in roof space (1) by pointing any open brickwork with mortar-mix; or rough-render whole wall. Deal with noise through boarded floor by sealing all gaps and/or removing skirting, few floorboards and pointing exposed brickwork below plaster (2).

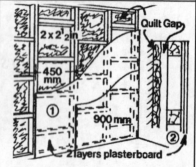

When all else fails, it should be helpful to insulate a party wall (1) though space consuming and rather expensive. Hang glass-fibre, mineral-wool quilt down wall, fix framing to walls, ceiling, floor, leaving about 1/2in. gap, and cover with two layers plasterboard (2).

NOTE: It is always best to reduce/prevent noise at source. Remember that any draught-sealing - around doors, windows, through floors, walls - can reduce noise transmission.

Preventing cold floors

Despite modern central heating systems, cold floors can still send a chill through a room. Simple to afix draught excluders may be all you need for warm toes and smaller bills.

Cold floor may result from floor-level draughts rather than actual floor coldness especially when there is an open fireplace. Draughts can come under door-bottom (1), between floorboards (2), under skirting (3); also from single-glazed window without radiator under (4).

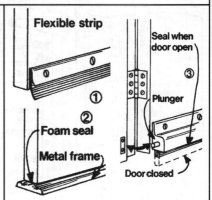

Door-bottom draught seals: (1) has flexible strip which sweeps over floor/carpet; (2) is threshold seal with rounded foam seal in aluminium frame; (3) automatically causes seal to be pressed down, through plunger, when door is closed. It will clear carpets.

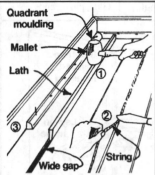

To fill wide floorboard gaps drive in wedge-shaped lath coated with glue (1); fill narrower gaps with soft string coated with filler (2). Use wood quadrant pinned to floor to prevent draughts under skirting (3).

Check concrete floor for damp by fixing polythene sheet (1); if damp under sheet after few days apply a damp-proofer. Make dry floor less cold with foil-backed building-paper underlay.

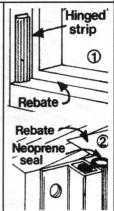

Stop window, door-frame draughts with self-adhesive hinged' strip (1) or neoprene sealer inside frame (2).

Building an airing cupboard

An airing cupboard in a spare room can provide ideal storage space, not only for bed linen and towels but also for your fermenting home-brew.

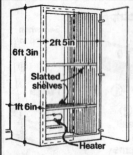

Cupboard has 2 x 2in. framing, covered top, sides with 1/2in. chipboard. Two lay-on doors can be in 3/4in. chipboard/blockboard. Slatted shelves take linen; base, with airing-cupboard or small tubular heater, can take wine-making jars.

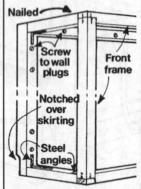

Make front frame first, with lap-halving joints secured with glue and 3in. nails. Mark wall positions and fix two uprights and top rail. Fix top, bottom rails with 3in. steel angles.

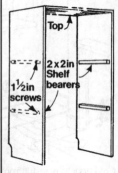

Fix chipboard top with glue, 11/4in. panel pins. Trim edges, prepare chipboard ends. Hold in position, mark for bearers; fix them with glue, screws. Glue, pin on ends.

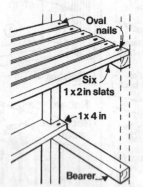

Space and nail six slats to upper bearers; have 1 x 4in. back slat for lower shelf - to prevent linen falling over heater, connected direct to socket or through time switch.

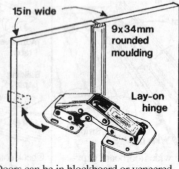

Doors can be in blockboard or veneered chipboard 15in. wide and overlapping frame front 1/2in. Self-closing lay-on hinges shown are suitable and obviate need for door catches. An overlapping rebate on one door is formed by gluing and pinning on double-rounded moulding.

Ranch-style swing doors

A door you just push against to open and which closes behind you can be a boon in the kitchen if you have to carry plates and food from room to another. Ranch style doors are the answer.

Double or single swing doors convenient for a kitchen can be short ones hung on double-spring hinges. Doors can be made from kits or from basic materials; narrow ones can often be mock window shutters about 3ft. 6in. high in wood about 1-1/8in. thick to suit lightweight spring hinges.

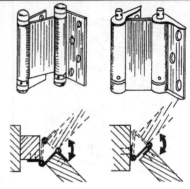

Two types of double-spring hinge, showing method of operation. Springs in cylinders are tensioned with rod supplied. Choose hinges and doors together, ensuring door thickness matches hinge width. Doors finished to 1-1/8in. thick are generally suitable.

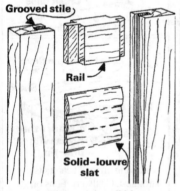

Attractive lightweight solid-louvre doors can be built up to size, as shown, by using ready-made stiles, rails and louvre-shaped boards. Tongues of rails, and ends of boards, are glued into stile grooves and door cramped up till glue sets.

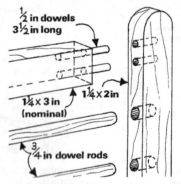

Simple doors can be made as shown. Rails are dowelled and glued to stiles, while 3/4in. dowel rods at 3in. centres are glued into well-fitting holes 1-1/2in. deep in stiles. Store all wood in warm room for fortnight before use, to minimise later warping.

Fixing shelves in an alcove

To avoid alcoves become wasted areas of a room, shelves can be put up quite easily. There are several methods of fixing shelves depending on the level of expertise and the weight of the load.

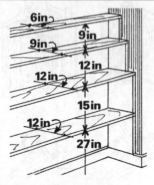

Shelves can be in veneered chipboard, 3/4in. blockboard or 1in. softwood. Heights are suggested but can be varied as required. Top shelf could be 1/4in. glass resting on foam draught strip.

Simple method, without drilling walls. Each shelf is pinned to upright below; next upright is pressed over sharpened ends of pins previously driven through shelf. Uprights could be fixed to walls with masonry nails.

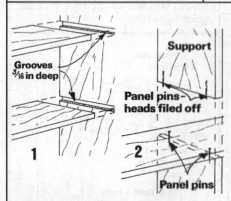

1 Alternative method of mounting, especially when shelves are all same width, by using uprights grooved to receive close-fitting shelf ends. Again, masonry nails could be used to make firm. 2. For shelves over 3ft. long and heavily laden, central supports are desirable. Pins in base of uprights have heads cut off and ends filed sharp.

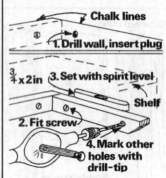

Mounting on wall bearers is strongest. Chalk positions on wall, drill and countersink bearers and drill wall for one plug with masonry drill. Insert plug and temporarily screw on bearer. After sequence shown remove bearer, drill and plug wall and make final screw fixing.

Making a small serving hatch

A serving hatch from the kitchen to your eating area could prevent accidents as hot food and crockery is carried from one room to the other.

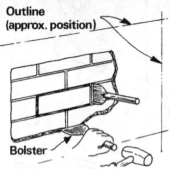

Outline (approx. position)

Bolster

To make hole in half-brick or breeze-block wall first mark approximate position in chalk, both sides. Chip away plaster with bolster (wide cold chisel) and hammer (1). Cut mortar around one brick, both sides, and drive out.

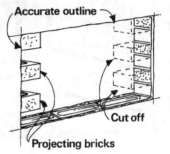

Accurate outline

Cut off

Projecting bricks

Now mark hole accurately, even number of bricks high and wide. Chip away plaster and remove whole bricks. Cut around remaining projections with sharp bolster and break off. While driving out bricks have assistant support wall on other side with heavy baulk.

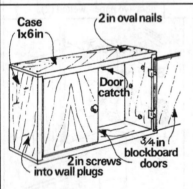

Case 1x6 in

2 in oval nails

Door catcth

3/4 in blockboard doors

2 in screws into wall plugs

Make case to fit opening; it may project slightly. Set it square on mortar or plaster bed and fix to wall plugs. Make-good plaster around case - or set flush to wall and nail on moulding. Make and fit doors after plaster has set.

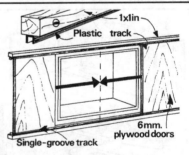

1x1in

Plastic track

6mm. plywood doors

Single-groove track

For simple sliding doors fit single-grooved track to 1 x 1in. battens more than twice hatch width and screw to wall plugs. Make doors to fit in 6mm. plywood, glass or acrylic sheet. Folding table can be fitted to other side of wall; or use ordinary table/sideboard on either side.

NOTE: It is generally unwise to put even small hatch in a load-bearing wall. If in doubt, seek advice of local surveyor or a builder.

Glass/acrylic cabinet doors

Simple shelving can gain from the fixing of glass doors to enable your displays to be seen and not touched.

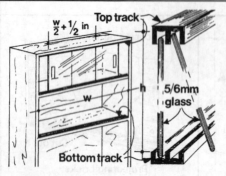

Simplest are sliding doors, running in fibre or plastic tracks. Doors can be in 5 or 6mm. glass or clear/tinted acrylic sheet. Fix tracks before having doors made to fit; take measurements as shown. Glass doors can be ordered with edges ground, but are more expensive. Finger grips in glass, acrylic, or wood can be attached with clear adhesive.

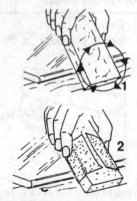

Edges of glass can be rounded by laying on newspaper on bench edge and rubbing with circular motion, using oilstone, with oil (1) or wet-or-dry abrasive paper, wetted (2).

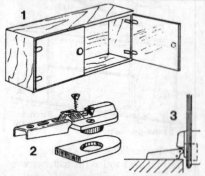

Lay-on hinged doors (1) are popular, using spring-closing glass-door hinges (2). Fit in hole about 1-3/8in. diameter following instructions supplied with them; but holes in glass must be made by glazier with special tool. Circular projection goes through glass/acrylic (3), and outside plate is held with two screws.

Acrylic doors can be bored with woodworker's expansion-bit or saw-bit (shown) after drilling central hole. Grip door in vice with hardwood behind it. Round edges with wet-or-dry paper.

Adding extras to kitchen units

A few easily assembled fixtures can help provide more storage space at accessible levels in your kitchen.

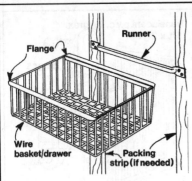

Coated wire baskets and plastic drawers, with side flanges, can be fitted in cupboards by screwing runners to sides. Runners may need packing out, as shown, to take standard drawers or to clear edge of door. Drawers come in widths from about 13.5 in. to 18in.

Basket shelves can be fitted inside a door for storage of small jars. Type shown in mounted on a solid door after fitting screw eyes (1). For hollow doors, special clips are fitted after drilling two small holes (2 and 3).

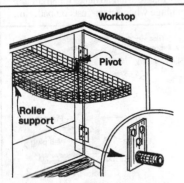

Corner cupboards between worktops can have semi-circular shelf baskets to make better use of space in the corner. They fit on pivot baskets screwed to frame. A roller bracket screwed to other side gives additional support.

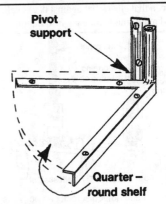

A quarter-circle shelf from, say, half inch plywood can be mounted on a steel pivoting-bracket assembly that allows the shelf to open through 90 deg. for easy access.

NOTE: If these fittings are not stocked by DIY stores you may be able to get them by mail order. Check out DIY magazines for addresses.

Installing a bath/shower screen

A ready-made screen to stop your shower water from flooding the bathroom can be easily installed what ever shape or size is needed.

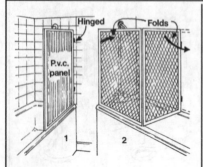

Two types of hinged screen: (1) Single, can be hinged or lifted off hinges to simplify cleaning of bath; this pattern can be brought ready-made, as kit, or can be made up with suitable double-glazing components. (2) Double-folded screen that closes flat against back wall; sold ready-made for easy installation.

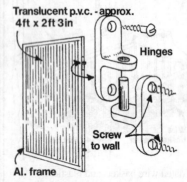

Outline details of screen made with hinged-type double-glazing components. Representative hinge is shown, where one part fits in aluminium frame section; pin portion screwed to wall. Arrange for slight gap at hinge when screen rests on bath rim.

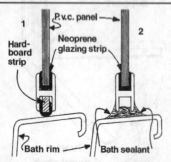

Home-made hinged screen can be sealed against bath rim (1) if weight of screen just falls on bath. If fixed screen is preferred, it can be secured to wall with aluminium angles and to bath rim with bath seal, white or coloured.

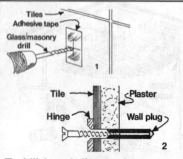

To drill through tiles, use sharp masonry or glass drill, with adhesive paper tape to prevent 'wander' (1). Use hand drill or power drill at very low speed. To avoid cracking, end of plug must be beyond back of tile (2).

NOTE: For heavy fittings on plaster and building boards it is best to spread the load by fixing battens to wall and screwing fitting to these.

Wardrobe fittings

The fittings you require in your wardrobe is a personal choice and the best way to mix and match to suit your taste is to fit them yourself.

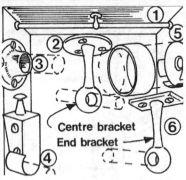

Centre bracket
End bracket

First requirement is hanging rail (1). Use plated steel tube about 3/4 in. diam., with centre support (2) if more than 30in. long. End supports can be plain sockets (3); hanging bracket for either end or top fixing (4); slip-off socket (5); top/shelf-fixing bracket (6).

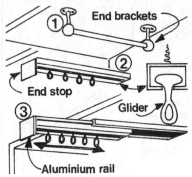

End brackets

End stop

Glider

Aluminium rail

For wardrobe less than 20-21in. deep, it is better to use front-to-back rail. Among types are: (1) normal tubular rail carried between two end brackets; (2) aluminium rail with nylon gliders; (3) extending rail - of which one of several patterns is shown.

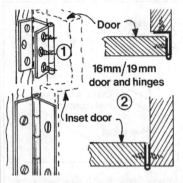

Door

16mm/19mm door and hinges

Inset door

Hinged lay-on doors in chipboard look well hung on brass cranked hinges (1); use three for 6ft. door. Inset doors can be securely hung on 25mm. or 32 mm. piano (continuous) hinges (2) using only small-say 1/2in./5/8in.x4 screws. Or have three or more skeleton hinges.

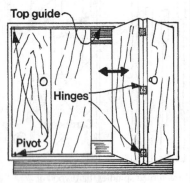

Top guide

Hinges

Pivot

Folding doors are easy to hang and can be bought as complete kit; or set of all fittings (door gear) can be obtained for use with home made/ready-made door leaves. Double (Four-leaf) doors are shown, but you can use a single pair for width up to 3ft. or so.

Staircase improvements

It has was fashionable in the '60s to cover in old balusters. Now they - or turned spindles - are again popular and not difficult to expose, renovate or replace.

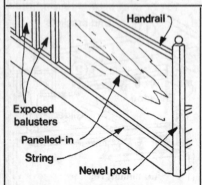

Removal of panels (hardboard, plywood etc.) might reveal sound balusters. If softwood, they can be stripped and varnished for 'pine' finish; hardwood sanded and re-varnished.

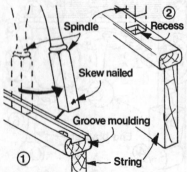

When they are to be paint-stripped, spindles are often best removed. In most cases they can be driven out with a mallet, as at (1); the upper end is removed in the same way. If spindles fit in shallow recesses (2) drive them free at the top and lift them away.

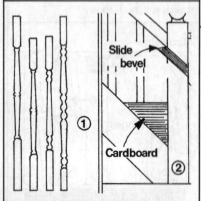

New turned spindles, hardwood or softwood, come in various styles and lengths (1). Choose length rather greater than height to handrail and mark ends, for sawing, against slide bevel or card cut to fit angle of staircase (2); or use old balusters as guide for end-sawing.

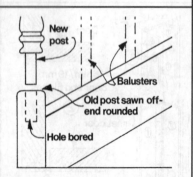

New newel post, matching spindles, can be fitted without dismantling stairs. Saw off old post, true end and bore accurate hole to receive post. Slightly round sawn end and, when post is good fit, glue and fix it along with handrail. Complete kits (post, spindles etc.) are available.

More shelves?

Shelves are a relatively easy storage and display option, but ensure you chose the right design for the objects they will have to carry.

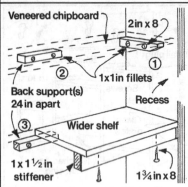

An economical recess shelf is easily mounted on two fillets screwed to wall plugs (1), with support at back (2) for shelves more than about 24in. long. Longer shelves, especially over 6in. wide, may need a stiffener (3) along front edge to prevent sagging.

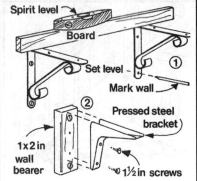

For flat wall, shelf brackets of various types can be chosen. Have them with horizontal arm 1 - 2in. less than shelf width. Fix brackets 24in. apart, 6in. from shelf ends; set against spirit level (1) and screw to wall plugs. Better, screw bearers to wall, brackets to bearers (2).

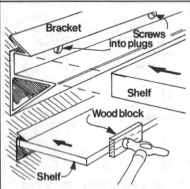

Mainly for shelves up to 6in., very neat fixing is obtained by using special full-length profiled brackets. Bracket is screwed to wall plugs and grips shelving hammered into groove. Use wood block to avoid bruising. Check shelf against bracket before purchase.

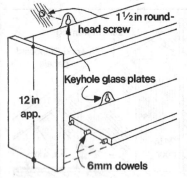

Neat pair of removable shelves can be made as shown from standard veneered chipboard up to 9in. wide. Corners are dowel-joined, and keyhole glass plates at 24in. centres slip over round-head screws into wall plugs. File shallow slots for glass plates.

Under-stairs storage

As space is often a valuable commodity in family homes, why let the area under the stairs go to waste? There are options to utilise the area which will suit all level of skills.

A usual and rather 'ordinary' arrangement which is practical and easily made. The board for the 'alternative' position coat hooks could be made longer, placed lower, to take children's outdoor clothes. It would be better, of course, to cover-in the triangular opening with door/curtains.

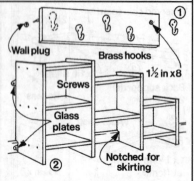

Brass coat hooks can be screwed to length of veneered chipboard over countersunk screws driven into wall plugs (1). Shelves could easily be mounted on aluminium brackets. Better is to make shelf unit, which can be fixed with glass plates and screws (2).

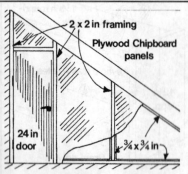

Whole under-stairs area can be covered-in with plywood/chipboard panels after making a framing. Standard 2ft. x 6ft. 6in. door is shown, but wider one can sometimes be fitted, depending on space available. Or 'concertina' type door - or curtains - could be used.

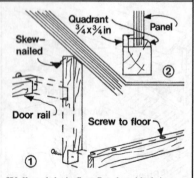

Wall upright is first fitted and halving joint made for rail; it is then screwed to wall plugs. Other joints are shown (1). Uprights are fixed under stair string with skew nails/screws after forming joints. Panels are pinned to 3/4in.x3/4in. softwood and edges finished with quadrant (2).

Moveable room divider

A room divider is make a useful and attractive feature to have in any large room. Not only does it separate areas for privacy but it can also act as a draught excluder.

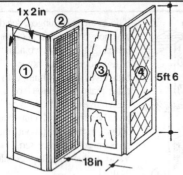

Four-leaf room divider, or folding screen, is made up with softwood or hardwood frames (1). They can be covered with fabric (2), panelled with thin plywood (3) or expanded metal, perforated hardboard etc. (4). Choice governs weight and degree of draught-restriction.

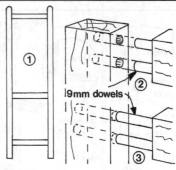

(1) Alternative frame, suitable when draught-screening is not important. (2) Dowel joint, with dowels about 1 1/2 in. into both upright and rail. (3) Easier through-dowelling joint: drill holes through upright and use as template when drilling rail. Fix with glue, lay frame flat.

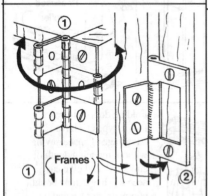

Special brass folding-screen hinges (1) are best because they allow folding in either direction. For folding in one direction only, brass flush hinges (2) can be used without need for recessing frames. Use at least three 2in. hinges between each pair of frames.

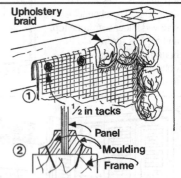

Frames can be covered with fabric (1), edges turned in and fixed with cut tacks. Braid can be secured with fabric adhesive/tacks. Any panelling can be sandwiched between lengths of, say, 3/8in. moulding (2), mitred at corners and pinned to the inside edges of frame members.

Wardrobe doors

Your choice of wardrobe door could make all the difference to the look of your bedroom, but be careful your expertise is up to fixing the type of door you pick.

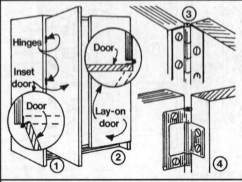

If doors are to be hinged, decide whether you prefer inset (1) or lay-on (2) type; both would not be used together, as shown. Either type is easily hung with either piano (continuous) or flush hinge (3, 4). Piano type gives best fixing with chipboard doors. Flush hinges (about 2in.) do not need to be recessed. Various other hinge types could be used.

Suitable gear for sliding doors weighing up to 23kg. (50lb.) and not less than 19mm (3/4in.) thick. Two recesses are cut in each door to take bottom rollers; nylon top guide is recessed into door edge. Top channel is screwed under wardrobe top, and track is screwed to bottom. Neater finish can be obtained by forming groove to receive top channel.

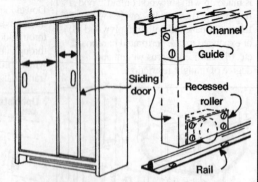

Folding doors, shown as louvre type (1), have advantage of space-saving without reducing depth of cupboard, and give easy access. They can be bought complete, or gear can be bought separately; it is generally suitable for 1 1/8in. (30mm.) minimum door thickness. In both cases, full instructions are supplied. Representative top (2) and bottom (3) pivots are shown.

Painting &
Decorating

Pages 20-60

Easy-to-hang wallcoverings

Wallpapering is a job that can daunt quite a few people, but here are some tips into making light of it.

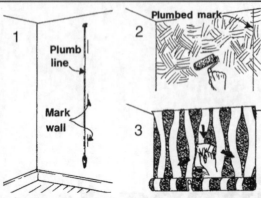

One type of vinyl can be hung direct from the roll, or in lengths, after pasting wall. First drop plumb line width of vinyl from starting point; mark wall and join marks with pencil and straight-edge (1). Apply paste with brush or roller (2); set vinyl to line and smooth out from centre with damp sponge.

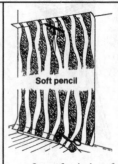

Leave few inches of waste top and bottom, press into angle, mark with soft pencil, pull away slightly, trim with scissors and smooth back.

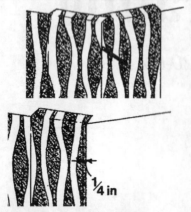

At internal angle press into corner and mark (1); cut vinyl to leave $1/4$in turning on to second wall (2). Then hang cut length to overlap after marking a plumbed line.

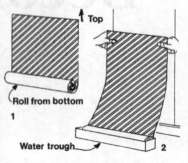

Cut ready-pasted vinyl to lengths, with pattern matching, to allow for top and bottom trimming. Roll length (1) and put into water trough (supplied free with this vinyl). Leave a minute or so before drawing up (2) and applying to wall. Smooth down with damp sponge and trim.

NOTE: 1) Plumb each wall before commencing to hang. 2) Use special 'vinyl' paste. 3) Do not paste wall for paper-backed vinyl. 4) Vinyls shown can be peeled off for redecorating.

Rendering exterior walls

Rendered walls can not only look very attractive in themselves, but can also protect against damp attacking brickwork

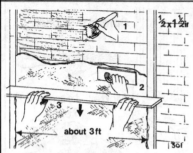

Brick wall can be faced using ready-mixed rendering mortar, made up with water. Brush down old wall and, if green treat with fungicide. Rake out pointing, damp wall (1) and apply mortar with steel trowel (2). Laths may be nailed to wall and removed as work proceeds. Board (3) is used to level off.

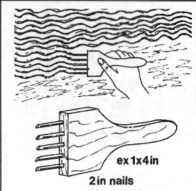

ex 1x4in
2in nails

Before rendering is hard scratch about $^3/_{16}$in deep with tool made as shown. Nails about 2in long are driven in $^3/_4$in apart and heads nipped off with pliers.

For pebble-dash finish throw washed shingle against soft second coat and lightly press with board or wooden float. Cover ground at foot of wall to catch falling pebbles-which can be used again.

Tyrolean (fine rough-cast) finish is obtained by using plain or coloured prepared mix containing small chippings. It can be spattered over first coat by throwing from scoop, or, with hired Tyrolean machine shown.

GAIN EXPERIENCE on small, garage or garden, wall. Check at your DIY store for booklets giving guidance on external renderings. Manufacturers should have free publications available.

Wall-cladding with slate

Cladding in random, coloured slate around $1/2$ in thick can give a warm, rustic finish to walls (interior or exterior) fireplaces, etc.

The slate can be fixed to most sound, firm surfaces, but not to soft or loose wall plaster. Ceramic tiles are best removed from fireplaces surrounds before cladding with slate.

Spread over back

Mortar: 1 cement/ 6 sand

'Butter' slate with mortar made from one part cement, six of builders' sand. Make up with one part p.v.a. bonder in three of water instead of water alone. For use around open fire or heating stove add one part hydrated lime to dry mix. Press slate against wall.

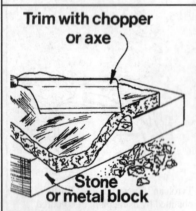

Trim with chopper or axe

Stone or metal block

When slate needs to be trimmed or shaped hold it over straight edge of stone or metal and hack away with wood chopper or axe. Trimming is not difficult after a little practice.

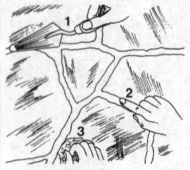

After fixing slate fill gaps with grouting (often supplied with slate). Press in with small trowel (1); slightly hollow by drawing finger tip along (2), or level off with damp sponge; carefully remove excess after completion of grouting with clean sponge damped with clean water. (3).

NOTE: Coloured slate for cladding is supplied by various firms; they can often also supply special adhesive for use instead of mortar, along with instructions.

Painting without brushes

Some find it easier to paint with a pad than with brush or roller.
Here's how to get the best out of them.

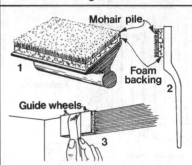

Pad tools, in various sizes, are made as shown (1). For window frames etc. there is a small one (2). Cutting-in to corners can be done with a brush but a special edging tool (3) may prove more convenient.

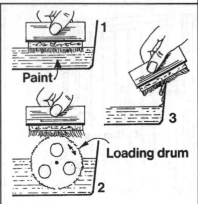

After slightly thinning the paint, charge pad by dipping pile only into paint (1), or by using a special tray with loading drum (2). Draw charged pad lightly across edge of tray to remove excess paint (3). Try to avoid getting paint on foam backing.

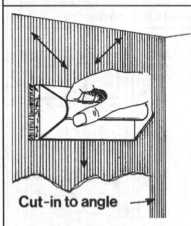

Use large pad (up to 7in) for walls, and apply paint in random overlapping strokes, as with a roller; with oil paints finish with light strokes in one direction. For narrow surfaces use pad in similar way to a brush.

Clean water-based paints under running tap, squeezing pad, until water runs clear. Then dry by pressing against newspaper. After oil paints, use brush-cleaning fluid before rinsing and drying.

Redecorating a hardwood door

Hardwood doors are a very pleasing feature of any property, and it is not too difficult a job to bring them back into a good condition.

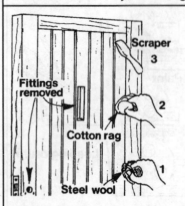

With boarded oak door which has been oiled but since neglected, remove old oil by lightly scouring with medium steel wool wetted with white spirit (1) and immediately wiping off with rag (2). If necessary, finish with scraper (3).

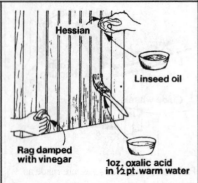

To remove weather stains: (1) brush with oxalic acid, leave $1/2$ hour; (2) wipe with vinegar-damped rag and rinse with water. When dry rub linseed oil into whole of door (3); thin first application with white spirit. When soaked in apply neat linseed oil, repeating after four and ten days. Buff with coarse rag.

For varnished door in oak or other hardwood, flat down with wet-or-dry abrasive paper, well wetted, rubbing in direction of grain. Use mask to prevent scratching across end of adjacent rail (1). If varnish is cracked or blistered remove with chemical paint stripper and knife (2) before rubbing down.

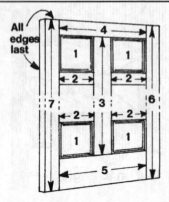

When re-varnishing use same type varnish as before; eg. pale exterior or exterior polyurethane. Give one full coat, following sequence indicated.

Follow same procedure with new or stripped door, giving two coats pale exterior, four coats polyurethane.

24

Dealing with rust and rust stains

Rust can be both unsightly and very expensive in the long term if it is not checked on ferrous fitments, like metal window frames.

Remove all surface rust with wire brush and scrape out corners with pointed tool. Easier than hand-brush (1) is to use electric drill with wire cup brush (2). Protect eyes with goggles when wire-brushing.

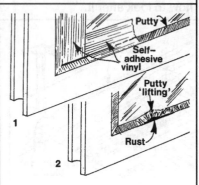

With steel window frames fix strips of self-adhesive vinyl over putty and edges of glass to prevent scratching (1). If putty is being forced away by rust (2) chip it out; re-putty after rust treatment.

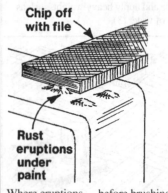

Where eruptions occur due to rust formation under paint chip off with tip of file before brushing.

Remove rust stains from concrete/stone by sponging with solution of salts of lemon or oxalic acid. Leave few minutes, then rinse with water containing a little ammonia. Some rust removers can be used instead.

AFTER RUST REMOVAL there is choice of methods: 1 – Apply liquid rust 'killer' according to makers' instructions and then paint. 2 (better) – Remove old paint, rub down to bare metal with emery cloth, apply 'self-galvanising' primer and finishing paint. 3 – If semi-matt black finish is suitable, simply apply bituminous.

Renovating a parquet floor

If you are lucky enough to live in a house or flat with laid with parquet, you have one of the most beautiful floors possible. Here's how to look after it.

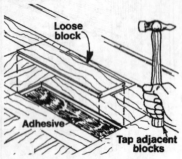

With block-type parquet refix loose blocks after scraping off old adhesive and applying new bitumen/rubber flooring adhesive. Immediately remove, with rag damped with white spirit, any adhesive squeezed out. Before replacing, check adjacent blocks by tapping; if sound is 'hollow', lift and refix.

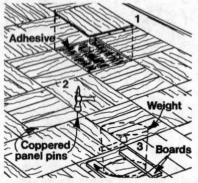

Loose thin parquet tiles or panels can also be fixed with adhesive (1). If warped, secure to wood floor with few coppered panel pins (2). On solid floor lay boards over tile and apply heavy weight, such as bucket of water (3).

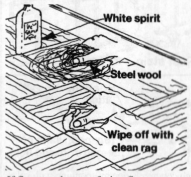

If floor needs re-surfacing first remove all wax polish by scrubbing with medium steel wool and white spirit. When wax has been softened, wipe off immediately with coarse rag or hessian.

Repeat if necessary before applying new floor seal, polyurethane varnish or plastic finish.

Where floor is rough or pitted, sand down after removing all wax and before re-surfacing. By hand, use No 6/0 garnet paper around cork sanding block (1); rub only in direction of grain.

Easier to use is a power-tool finishing sander, working in any direction.

Fixing acoustic ceiling tiles

Acoustic tiles could be essential if you like loud music, but live in a flat below someone who prefers peace and quiet. But the wrong sort can be a fire risk. So make sure you use fire-proofed tiles.

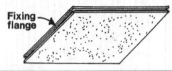

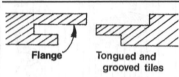

Flange   **Tongued and grooved tiles**

Acoustic tiles – not to be confused with ordinary ceiling tiles – give a good measure of sound insulation and are favoured by hi-fi enthusiasts. They also provide thermal insulation.

Light in weight and made from wood or other fibres, they are tongued and grooved to lock together.

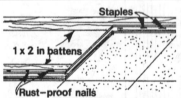

To provide air-space, fix 1 x 2in sawn battens across ceiling with centres one tile width apart; 12 x 12in tiles are usually preferred. One flange of each tile is fixed to batten with stapling gun – bought or hired – or non-rust flat-head nails, each set about 4in apart.

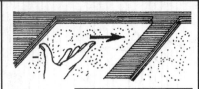

Simplest method of fixing to ceiling is with special acoustic-tile adhesive.

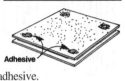

Trowel four blobs about the size of a walnut on the back of each tile and slide it into place. For more efficient result, though, there should be a 1in air-space between tiles and ceiling.

Battens can be fixed to joists, through plaster, with 3in nails or $2^1/_2$in screws. Screwing is better if plaster is not very sound. On concrete ceiling, fixing can be done with panel adhesive or a mastic adhesive. Take care that battens are securely bonded.

NOTES: If tiles are not of non-flam grade they can be treated with fire-retardent emulsion paint first. Always store in room few days before fixing.

Repairing exterior wall renderings

Damaged and cracked rendering can trap water and lead to a damp wall, which then starts to crumble. Here's how to fix it.

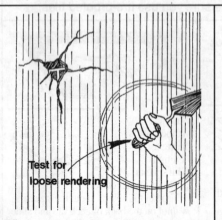

Test for loose rendering

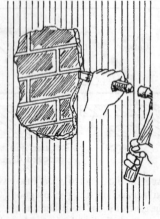

Where cracks or bulges occur, tap with end of trowel handle: if there is hollow sound rendering should be removed over the 'hollow' area by chipping with hammer.

Cut back to solid, firm rendering with cold chisel and heavy hammer to bare bricks in approximate shape of rectangle. Be sure that rendering is firm around the cut edges.

Wire brush

1:3 p.v.a. bonder and water

Scrub bricks with wire brush (1) and remove dust with soft brush. Paint over bricks and mortar edges with p.v.a. bonding agent, mixed one part with three of water (2).

1:4 cement : sand

Make mortar with one part cement, four sand, mixing with the 1:3 diluted bonding agent (instead of with water). Smooth on with large trowel – in two coats if more than $1/4$ in thick.

Hessian tacked on board

If rendering is stippled, match up patch, while still wet, by pressing against it and slowly withdrawing a square board, with simple handle, covered with a piece of hessian.

Replacing damaged floor tiles

When floor tiles become loose, or damaged, it is not too big a job to replace tiles. Just follow these diagrams step-by-step.

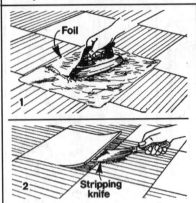

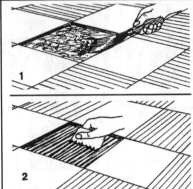

A vinyl tile can usually be lifted after heating with a hot laundry iron, applied over a sheet of cooking foil (1). When the adhesive has been softened, prise up with a decorator's stripping knife (2). Vinyl-asbestos (brittle) tiles can be chipped out with a cold chisel.

While the adhesive is soft it can be scraped off the floor with a stripping knife (1). Remove as much as possible and smooth the surface. Then apply a coating of floor-tile adhesive with a serrated spreader (2) and press the new tile into place.

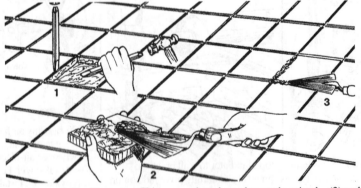

Quarry tiles are laid with mortar. Chip out a broken tile with a cold chisel.

After removing a broken or loose tile chip out the mortar with a cold chisel and hammer. (1); also chip away grouting around tile.

'Butter' back of new tile with mortar – bought as dry, ready-mixed – (2) and tamp into place, seeing that it is level with others.

Use same mortar for re-grouting (3). Work into joint, smooth off, and wipe excess from tile surfaces with damp rag.

Painting a radiator – and behind it

This is not a very appealing job, but one that is worth doing properly to keep your radiators looking good – and corrosion free!

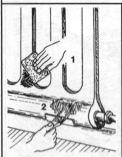

First rub down any rust patches (1) with wet-or-dry abrasive paper. Apply a rust-inhibitor fluid (2); leave for 20 minutes, then wipe dry and apply metal primer.

Wipe radiator with rag damped with white spirit and, when dry, give two thin coats of gloss paint, working in sequence indicated.

To paint back of radiator and wall (when heating is off!) put rags to catch water drips at each end and slightly slacken the gland nuts shown.

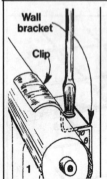

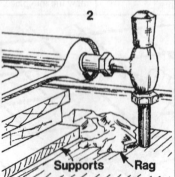

Remove clips holding top of radiator to wall brackets; representative type is shown (1). Carefully pivot radiator on bottom brackets on to boards or other supports previously arranged in position (2), and then temporarily tighten nuts. Reverse the procedure to replace radiator after paint is dry. Check for water leaks, and re-tighten nuts if necessary.

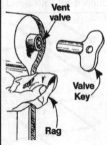

In case any air has entered system, slowly open air-bleed (vent) valve with key provide with installation. After a 'hissing' noise, water will drip; immediately close valve.

NOTE: Radiators vary in shape and method of fixing to wall. If in doubt seek advice of heating engineer before attempting to move them.

Replacing wall & fireplace tiles

Damaged tiles nearly always catch the eye, particularly in they are of a fairly plain design. Replacing them is no big deal.

First scrape all grouting from around damaged tile with broken hacksaw blade or pointed tip of old knife. Scrape down to full thickness of tile without cutting into wall.

Break tile with smart hammer blows, preferably on a part of the tile that sounds 'hollow'. If tile does not break away, make a few holes with masonry drill across a corner.

Remove any remaining fragments with cold chisel, or old wood chisel. Tap chisel smartly with a hammer.

Chip off old adhesive and make surface as smooth as possible. Then spread wall-tile adhesive thinly over back of tile and press firmly into position. Wipe off adhesive squeezed out.

(1) If tile does not have spacing lugs insert strips of card; remove before adhesive sets. (2) Next day, rub grouting into joints with rag and smooth along joints with moistened finger tip.

NOTE: Obtain matching new tile(s) before commencing work, checking that thickness is same as that of old ones.

Repairing wall coverings

Wallpaper and other wall coverings can so easily get damaged, especially if you have young children or pets. The damage can often stand out like a sore thumb. So here's how to deal with it.

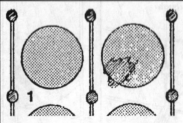 

Where wallpaper has been scuffed (1), tear off loose edges and smooth with glasspaper. Then cut a spare piece of

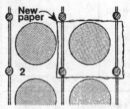

wallpaper as patch so that pattern matches (2). Tear edges of patch irregularly, tearing away from patterned side (3). Paste back of patch and smooth into place with clean, soft duster (4). Outline of patch should scarcely show when the paste dries.

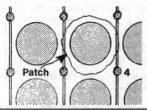

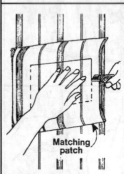 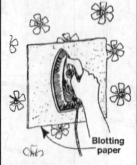 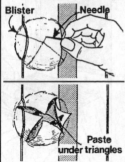

With vinyl wall covering, lay patch over damaged area and cut through both thicknesses with sharp knife. Peel vinyl from wall to sides of square. Paste and smooth on patch.

Grease marks can be removed from paper by damping with a fabric – or clothes-cleaning fluid, laying clean white blotting paper over and applying warm iron. Repeat if necessary.

A blister in paper is dealt with by making 'star' tears from centre with point of sharp needle (1), pasting back of paper (2) and smoothing down.

With vinyl make star cuts with knife.

Fixing stone-effect wall panels

An alternative to slate or tiles around fireplaces and other features, or even on a complete section of wall, is stone-effect wall panels.

Stone-effect panels in rigid moulded plastics can be obtained in a variety of patterns and 'stones'. They can be fixed to clean walls, simulated fireplaces etc. with adhesive. Shown are: wall, Georgian Stone; fireplace, Roman Stone.

Panels (sizes and patterns vary with make) usually have serrated sides so that joins will not show. Above are Rustic Brick and Random Stone. They can be cut when necessary with fine-tooth saw, scissors or sharp knife.

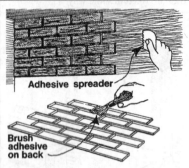

Adhesive spreader

Brush adhesive on back

When doing a wall start at one top corner and work across. Apply a contact adhesive (preferably type with 'delayed bonding') to wall and to all ridges on back of panel. When adhesive is touch-dry press panel to wall.

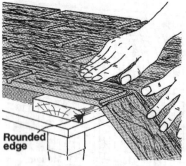

Rounded edge

Some panels (see makers' instructions) can be bent as shown after warming in front of electric fire. For a sharp angle do the bending in stages, re-warming between each. Do not apply undue force.

PANELS MUST NOT: be subject to temperatures above 150 deg F (warm to the touch); be used near open fire; be within 2 in of gas-fire flue.
   Follow makers' instructions with panels and adhesive.

33

Giving a new look to old tiles

An effective way to freshen up old tiles is to fix some self-adhesive tile prints, mosaics or mirror or metal tiles, at strategic points.

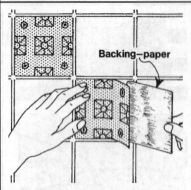

Apart from enamel paint, which is inclined to chip, easiest way is to apply a few self-adhesive tile prints, available in a range of colours and patterns, and in either 6 in. or 4$^1/_2$in. Peel off backing while smoothing on to cleaned tiles with fingers and soft duster.

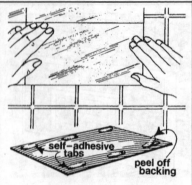

Another way is to cover whole or part of area with mirror tiles (in sizes from 4 x 4in to 18 x 12in.). Use kind with self-adhesive tabs, and press firmly into place after removing protective backing. Reflection is distorted if original tiles are irregular. Thin metal tiles are fixed in same way.

New tiles can be laid over the old, using ceramic-tile adhesive. Alternatively, lay squares of mosaic tiles. With either, start at bottom against skirting board or a lath, which gives support to first course. Fill joints with grout day after tiles or mosaic panels have been laid.

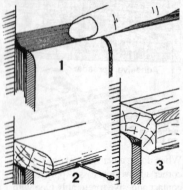

On a part-tiled wall cover top edge after overlaying new tiles, by: (1) applying filler or grout and smoothing with moistened finger tip; (2) fixing wood strip with contact adhesive and/or steel pins. Where two sets of tiles do not quite align, fit a rebated cover strip (3).

Decorating stairway & landing

Actual decoration is similar to that for other walls and ceilings – the only difficulty is in gaining easy, and safe, access.

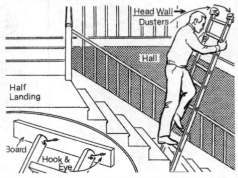

Upper part of head wall is reached from short ladder, as shown. Tie dusters around top of ladder; or, if wall sounds hollow when tapped, fit a temporary board, as inset, to spread weight.

Head Wall → Dusters
Hall
Half Landing
Board
Hook & Eye

Ceiling and top of well wall are reached from strong scaffold boards which do not bend unduly.

Arrangement shown is applicable to usual staircase with wind (bend) near top. If window sill is not available use short ladder or steps leaning against wall as support. Nail temporary board to half-landing to prevent foot of steps or ladder from slipping.

Head Wall
Scaffold Boards 1¼ x 9in.[min.]
Strong Box
Well Wall

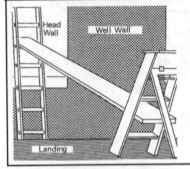

Head Wall
Well Wall
Landing

When stairs are straight, or wind is at lower end, a single scaffold board can be supported between ladder and steps on landing. Be sure that all is secure and steady before standing on scaffold.

Laying tile mosaics

Tile mosaics were popular way back in Greek and Roman times. They make a wonderful alternative to ordinary tiles. Here's how.

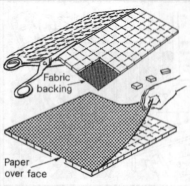

Buy mosaics in sheets (about 12in. square) and fix as single large tiles. When necessary, cut to size with scissors or razor blade. One type has fabric backing; the other is faced with paper, which is removed after laying.

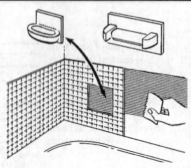

Mark tiling area on wall, spread tile adhesive evenly with serrated spreader over area of three sheets and press mosaics into place. If tile-type soap dish, toilet-roller etc is required, cut out hole for it; press if against adhesive and hold firm for few minutes.

After laying three mosaic sheets, firm and level them with rolling pin or length of broomstick. Leave for 12 hours till adhesive sets, when joints can be filled with grouting.

If there is paper facing, remove this first by damping and peeling off.

(Top) Fill joints by rubbing grouting well in with muslin pad; remove excess with damp rag. Polish with tissue when dry.

(Bottom) Cut single mosaics to fill in around wall fittings etc. with tile cutter, or sharp end-cutters as shown. Press them into the wet adhesive.

NOTE: Buy adhesive and grouting when buying mosaics; mix according to makers' instructions.

Fixing ceiling tiles & mouldings

Cove moulding and ceiling tiles can create an elegant effect in almost any room, and the job is not that daunting.

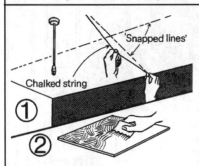

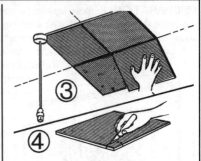

First clean ceiling thoroughly, washing off water-soluble distemper or stripping paper, and make good any faults.

When dry, make two lines at right-angles: simplest method is with chalked string, fixed at one end, held taut and 'snapped' (1). Where convenient, make each line approx $10^1/_2$in (for 12in tiles)

from centre of light fitting.

Coat back of each tile in turn with ceiling-tile adhesive (2) and firmly press first four into position (3). Mark and cut tile to fit ceiling rose (4) with really sharp knife or special hot-wire tile cutter.

Work outwards and into corners, trimming last tiles to fit to walls.

Internal-corner pieces

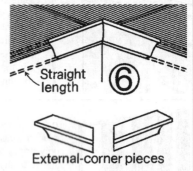

Straight length

External-corner pieces

Cove moulding in expanded polystyrene (same as tiles) can be used with or without ceiling tiles. Clean surfaces and fix with ceiling-tile adhesive. Start with special, mitred, corner pieces; coat flat sides and mitred ends with adhesive and

carefully press against ceiling, wall and each other (5). Use different mitred pieces for any external angles (6). Fill between corner pieces with straight lengths, cutting last with very sharp carving knife or hot-wire tile cutter.

NOTE: Preferably use flame-resistant tiles or coat, before fixing, with flame-retardant paint.

Repainting a panelled door

Taking that extra bit of care with a panelled door, particularly a front door, means a really good-looking result.

PREPARATION: Remove handle; lay newspapers on floor; lightly scrub with weak sugar soap, using old brush, from bottom upwards. Sponge down from top with clear water and allow to dry. Rub down any rough spots with wet-or-dry abrasive paper while door is wet.

PAINTING: Working from top downwards, paint moulding around each panel, then the panel itself. Next paint muntins (short uprights). Then do rails, door edge and stiles in that order, Paint door casing last. A $1^1/_2$in brush can be used throughout, or use a $^3/_4$in for mouldings.

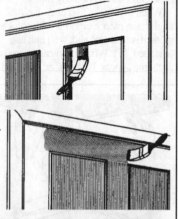

To paint panels or larger areas, apply stripes of paint vertically; brush out backwards and forwards across the stripes. Smooth by laying-off vertically with the tip of the brush.

38

Stripping old paint

This is a job that can seem a real drag to many people, but the right approach and the right tools makes it much easier.

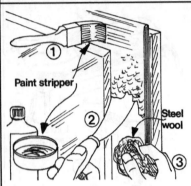

Paint stripper

Steel wool

Chemical paint stripper is often best on steel window frames and for small areas of woodwork; it can be expensive for large areas.

Brush on liberally (1), wait till paint softens, wrinkles, then remove with scraper (2). Rub down with steel wool damped with white spirit.

Keep flame moving

Bucket of water

Blow-lamp quickly softens paint, but must be used (outdoors only) with great care. Keep flame moving 'ahead' of scraper: drop hot scrapings into bucket of water.

Small gas blow-lamp shown is suitable for small jobs. Larger ones, with gas cylinder, can be hired.

Metal sheet as guard

Hot-air paint stripper is easier to use and less likely to char wood than a blow-lamp, but might require long electrical extension lead. When stripping window frames, avoid over-heating and so cracking glass. One way is by holding a sheet of metal, shown as guard.

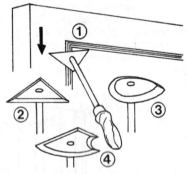

No matter what method of paint-softening is adopted, special scraper-called a shave hood-is useful for corners and mouldings (1).

Triangular (2) serves most purposes, but pear-shape (3) and straight/curved (4) are often helpful; (2, 4) also used on flat surfaces.

Hanging wallpaper and vinyl

Covering, or recovering, your walls is a fairly big job, but one well-worth doing. Here's how to organise it.

First ensure that wall is clean and sound. Then 'size' with thinned cellulose paste; use special paste for vinyls. (1) With improvised plumb line of chalked string, 'snap' a guide line for the first length.

(2) Cut off a few lengths 4-6in longer than wall, lay all on table and paste top one. Fold paper from each end and carry over forearm.

(3) Undo first fold and smooth paper (or vinyl) on wall with paperhanger's brush, pressing into angles. Undo lower fold and brush down to skirting.

(4) Crease angle at top with scissors tip, draw paper away, cut off waste and brush back; repeat at bottom, but using soft pencil to mark trimming line. Repeat for other lengths, butting all edges.

(5) Some vinyls are ready-pasted and supplied with water trough and instructions; cut length is put in trough and drawn out.

(6) To clear a flush switch, turn off main electricity supply, remove switch plate, make diagonal cuts and trim off triangles. Switch plate will cover cut edges.

Never turn more than 1in

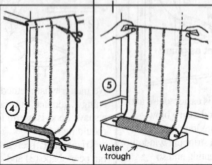

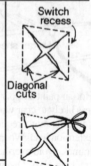

around corners. On each other wall 'snap' chalk line 21in from corner.

Rejuvenating old wall tiles

What to do when old wall tiles begin to look tired and uninteresting?
Well, there are quite a few alternatives. Here are some of them.

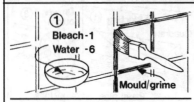

When grout has moulded/mildewed
(usually because of condensation)
lightly scrub with old paint brush dipped
in dilute bleach (1) or so-called tile-and-
grout cleaner. Shabby grout can be
freshened by applying special cleaning
grout (2); remove surplus with damp rag
after every square yard.

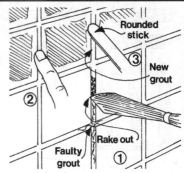

When grout is cracked, broken it is best
to rake out with, eg. putty knife (1); then
rub in new grout with sponge. Smooth
with moistened finger tip (2) or rounded
stick (3) and remove excess with damp
cloth. When dry, polish whole tiled
surface with clean muslin pad or tissue.

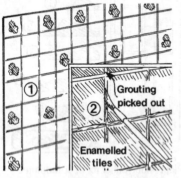

Give new appearance to tiles by applying tile transfers – to suggest border or in
random pattern (1). Or clean tiles with
detergent and paint with good enamel-
lacquer (no undercoat). Grout lines can,
if desired, be picked out in white or
colour with artist's pencil brush (2).

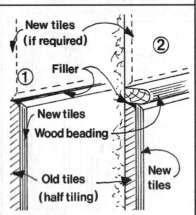

Perhaps best is to lay new tiles over old,
using standard tile adhesive. With half-
tiled wall, fill gap (1) and, if preferred,
fix wood beading with contact adhesive
(2). If whole wall is to be tiled, tiles
above the 'step' could be of a different
colour/pattern.

Choice and use of mouldings

Mouldings and beadings can enhance the look of any room when used in conjunction with doors, skirting boards and furniture.

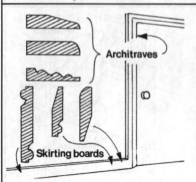

Some typical softwood mouldings for use in carpentry. The skirting boards shown are reversible so that each can be used for alternative patterns.

All the mouldings can be used for various other purposes. In buying softwood mouldings, seek those free from large, loose knots.

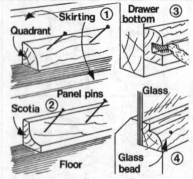

Four useful small mouldings or beads:
  (1) and (2) softwood beads suitable for draught-proofing between skirting and floor; they are pinned to skirting;
  (3) drawer-bottom moulding to receive hardboard or plywood bottom;
  (4) bead for securing glass panes, especially in cabinet work.

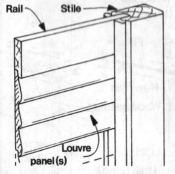

Louvre-effect panels, doors can be made from ready-made mouldings in hardwood or softwood. The moulded panels are glued and pressed into grooved stiles, while rails are fitted top, bottom and, if required, in middle.

Check assembly 'dry' before applying glue and pressing together.

Plain doors (either room or furniture) can often be made more interesting by the use of mouldings; these are usually mitred, glued and pinned.

Among suitable types are:
(1) astragal; (2) double astragal;
(3) broken ogee; (4) barrel; (5) cover;
(6) one of many embossed patterns.

Painting outside walls

Painted outside walls can make an attractive feature, but care is necessary if you are not to trap damp in the wall, under the paint.

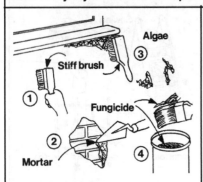

First check wall surface, remove dust, loose rendering, etc. (1) and, if necessary, make-good rendering, pointing (2).

Then, if there is any mould, green algae, brush off with stiff brush (3) and apply a fungicide (4) – following makers' instructions– to kill mould spores.

Next, especially if any making-good was necessary, check porosity of wall in various places: apply damp sponge to brickwork, rendering; if water is absorbed within about 30 seconds, treat whole wall with the stabilising solution recommended by makers of the paint to be used.

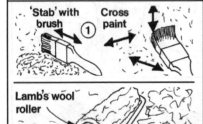

Paint (exterior emulsion, masonry, stone, etc.) can be applied to textured or Tyrolean finish with 3-4in brush or 6-7in roller. Use (cheaper) wall brush with stabbing action; then brush criss-cross (1). If using roller choose 'shaggy' lamb's wool pattern (2).

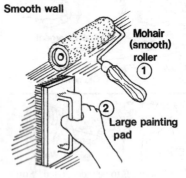

Painting of smooth (non-textured) wall can be done with brush in normal way. Or you can use a mohair or foam (smooth) type of roller (1); or a painting pad (2). No matter which tool is used, apply paint in criss-crossing strokes to ensure good, uniform finish.

Preparing for room decoration

Good organisation is one key to making decorating easier. And the first step is to prepare the room well beforehand.

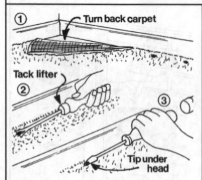

For whole-room redecoration, first remove as much furniture as possible; put rest in centre and sheet-over.

If skirting is to be painted, fitted carpet should be turned back (1), after removing tacks with tack-lifter (2), claw hammer; or with hammer and plastic-handled screwdriver (3).

Easy, safe access is important. For ceiling, upper walls use stout steps and, eg. sawing horse(s) to support proper scaffold board, preferably reaching nearly across room (1); have supports not more than 5ft apart. Even better is portable scaffold (2).

Scaffold boards can be hired.

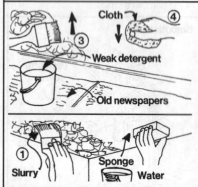

Wash surfaces to be redecorated. 'Soft' ceiling distemper (now little used) must be fully removed; lightly scrub with wetted wall brush (1), then wipe off slurry and clean with sponge (2).

Wash walls, woodwork with weak detergent, from bottom up (3); rinse downwards from top and wipe clean (4).

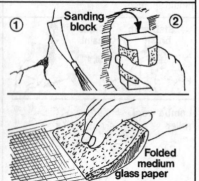

Fill cracks, plaster faults in ceilings, walls with plaster filler (1); slightly over-fill and smooth with medium glasspaper when hard (2).

Cracks in wood are best filled with stopping or 'fine-surface' filler. Lightly sand sound paint to 'flat' surface and provide good key for new paint (3).

44

Long-life exterior paintwork

Careful preparation of exterior surfaces, particularly wood, will mean that your paintwork looks good and lasts, with no defects.

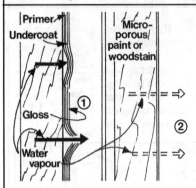

Customary three-coat paint system (1) gives excellent results but can fail through dampness in wood; when warm, it vapourises and may cause blistering, peeling.

Newer (single coat) microporous paint or a preservative-stain allows vapour to escape (2) while preventing entry of water; but they lack high-gloss.

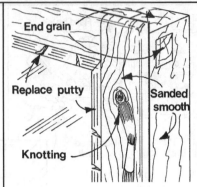

Strip cracked, flaking paint before repainting-and sand down to smooth, bare wood for other than three-coat painting. Treat any knots with knotting and replace defective putties.

When redecorating, take special care to seal end grain. Before re-coating, allow wood to dry out as much as possible; best done in warm weather.

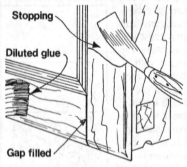

While preparing woodwork for re-coating, press flexible filler/stopping well into any open joints. If wood is slightly rotted, cut away soft surface and apply several coats of diluted woodwork glue. When last coat is hard, level off with stopping and sand whole surface. Paint by following either single-or three-coat system.

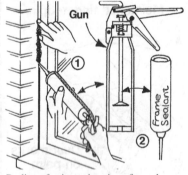

Peeling of paint and rotting of wood (which further damages paint) is caused by entry of moisture. Paint, preservative stain or varnish is effective but gaps around frames should be sealed (1), preferably using sealant gun and cartridge sealant (2). Fill, then smooth with moistened finger tip. Seal when wood is dry.

Problems on exterior walls

Good preparation of surface is secret of successful finish – whatever decorative coating is to be applied.

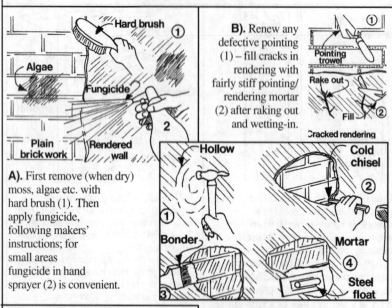

A). First remove (when dry) moss, algae etc. with hard brush (1). Then apply fungicide, following makers' instructions; for small areas fungicide in hand sprayer (2) is convenient.

B). Renew any defective pointing (1) – fill cracks in rendering with fairly stiff pointing/ rendering mortar (2) after raking out and wetting-in.

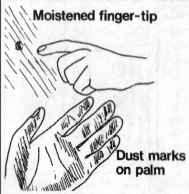

D). If brickwork/rendering is very porous or dirty is should be sealed with eg. stabilising solution.
  Check with moistened finger tip (porous surface dries in few seconds); rub with flat hand and see if palm is dusty.

C). Rendered walls should be checked carefully, because any fault may cause wall dampness. Tap lightly with hammer, listening for 'hollows' (1). If found, break and chip out rendering, (2); next scrub clean and coat with diluted bonder, (3) before filling with stiffish mortar, (4) like ready-mix rendering/point mortar.

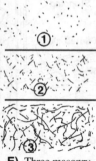

E). Three masonry-paint finishes: smooth (1), sand-textured (2), full textured (3). Apply most with brush or roller; some with spray-gun.

Decorating uneven walls

There are many ways of decorating over uneven walls, without fully stripping surface and replastering. Here are some of them.

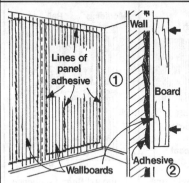

When wall is only slightly irregular, good surface can be obtained fixing decorative wallboard, or hardboard (for painting/papering) with wall-panel adhesive (1). This mastic-like adhesive is for gun application. Press wallboard down with edge of straight board (2).

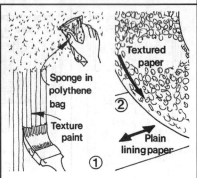

If you can't beat 'em – disguise irregularities by applying texture coating (1) or textured paper such as Anaglypta (2).

Hang lining paper horizontally before heavy wallcoverings. Both texture paint and textured papers, in white, should be emulsion-painted when dry.

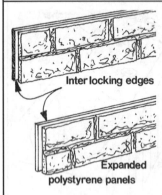

Yet another method is to fix interlocking stone-effect panels of expanded polystyrene. Fixed with ceiling-tile-type adhesive, they hide unevenness and give insulation/anti-condensation. Finish with emulsion paint.

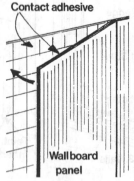

It is not practicable to paper over tiles, but surface can be soothed with wallboard/ hardboard fixed with contact or panel adhesive.

'Hinge' boards carefully into position.

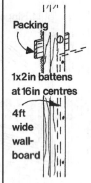

If using battens to receive wall-boards, insert packings where required to ensure firm, flat face for boards.

Painting sequences

Different surfaces and different shapes need different techniques with your paint brush for the best results. Here are some.

Large vertical area, as flush door, is the most difficult surface to gloss-paint well. Paint in slightly overlapping rectangles, in sequence indicated. Do next rectangle while edge of previous one remains wet.

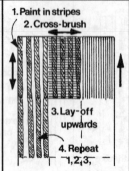

For each rectangle, first apply paint liberally in stripes; then brush across them without recharging brush. Finish by laying off with light upward strokes, Using only very tip of brush

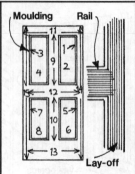

Quite a different sequence is followed for, eg., panelled door, although each panel is treated as separate rectangle. Object is to paint in grain direction and to lay-off across rails ends.

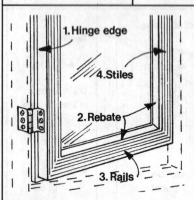

Casement window frame is easy, following same principles. Do hinge-edge first; paint outer frame last. Allow paint to run full $1/8$in on to glass, to form moisture seal. If there are glazing bars, paint these before rebates, treating them in same way as mouldings.

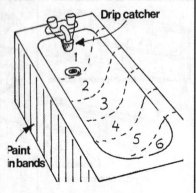

When brush-painting bath (with bath enamel only) it is best to work in a series of bands around bath, as indicated. Work quickly to ensure 'wed edge'. Follow instructions supplied with enamel. Hang small jar/tin under tap(s) if there is any risk of drips.

Laying quarry tiles

Unglazed quarry tiles are harder-wearing and more slip-resistant than glazed tiles. They are also less expensive and suitable for both indoor and outdoor use.

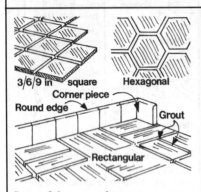

3/6/9 in square   Hexagonal
Corner piece
Round edge
Grout
Rectangular

Some of shapes are shown; square or rectangular are easiest to lay.

Round-edge tiles can be used for step-edges, skirtings; use corner pieces with latter.

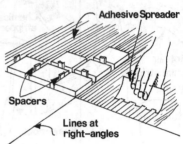

Clean, solid floor
Adhesive Spreader
Spacers
Lines at right–angles

Lay in same sequence as vinyl tiles, after first' snapping' two lines at right-angles across floor. Spread cement-based flooring adhesive with notched spreader, about 1sq yd at a time, then press tiles over it.

For attractive grout lines, temporarily insert plastic tile spacers.

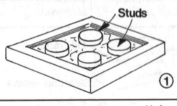

Studs
①

Check with board
②

On reasonably flat solid floor-which must be clean-apply adhesive about 3mm ($^1/_8$in) thick. If floor is slightly uneven or tiles are deeply studded (1) use thick-bed (about 6mm) adhesive.

Especially with thick-bed, check level often with board edge while laying proceeds (2).

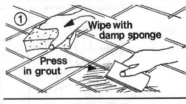

① Wipe with damp sponge
Press in grout

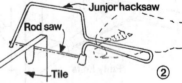

Junior hacksaw
Rod saw
Tile
②

(1) At least 24 hours after tiling, press grout well into joints with squeegee; wipe off excess before it sets with damp sponge, then clean cloth. (2) Make shaped cuts with saw file (not saw) in junior hacksaw frame. Straight cuts can usually be snapped after scoring deeply.

Exterior repainting hints

Painting outside surfaces can seem a daunting job. But the reality need not be that bad. Here are some useful tips.

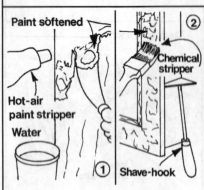

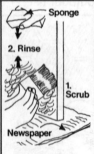

Badly cracked, flaking, blistered paint is best stripped. Easiest is to use hot-air stripper and stripping knife (1); drop hot, stripped paint into bucket of water.

Near glass, especially with metal frames, chemical stripper avoids risks of cracked glass.

Strip rebates with shave-hook (2).

Prepare merely shabby paint by scrubbing, from bottom upwards, with solution of paint cleaner/sugar soap; then rinse off downwards; wipe dry.

When softwood has been stripped, sanded, treat all knots with knotting. Then apply primer, undercoat, gloss- or three, four coats varnish to hardwood.

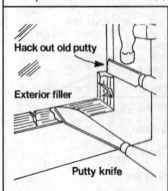

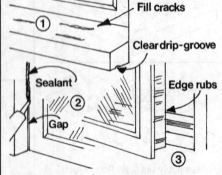

Do not paint over cracked, loose putty. Fill simple cracks with exterior cellulose filler (1).

Remove and replace all putty when condition is bad.

Hack out with, eg., old, broken-off table knife.

(1) After stripping/rubbing down, fill open cracks with stopping or resin paste; also check that sill-grooves are clear. (2) Fill gaps around door/ window frames with silicone sealant, applied with 'gun' or using applicator tube. (3) Sticking or rubbing doors/windows may result from build-up of old paint; strip and repaint.

Dealing with rust

Rust can appear in all sorts of places. But there are several different techniques for dealing with it. Here are some of them.

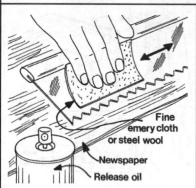

Rusty saw may be best treated by first spraying both sides with release or penetrating oil. Leave few hours, then clean with fine emery cloth or steel wool. Repeat if necessary and finish by sawing across pieces of waste wood. Saw will probably need sharpening.

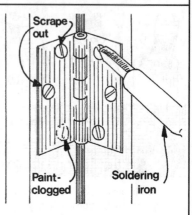

Rusted-in screws, such as those in door hinges, can be loosened by scraping paint and rust from around them and across slots, applying release oil.

If necessary, apply hot soldering iron before using well-fitting screwdriver.

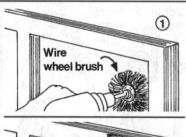

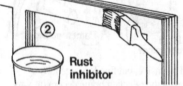

Remove rust from steel, iron with wire brush, either hand or (1) power-operated, wearing protective goggles.

Next brush on rust inhibitor (2). Later, wipe with rag, brush on metal primer and two coats gloss enamel.

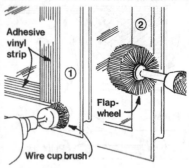

A wire cup brush, in power drill (1) is sometimes preferred for rust removed. If either this or other power-tool brush is used on window frames, it is wise to protect glass from scratching with, eg., strips of self-adhesive vinyl. A flap-wheel (2) is another alternative; glass protection is not necessary with this.

Painting methods

What to use when – paintbrush, roller or paint pad? It all depends on the job – and on what suits your working methods best.

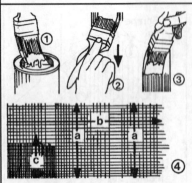

When brush-painting, dip half into paint press against inside of tin and lightly wipe off excess (1). Lay-on (apply) paint under fair pressure (2); then lay-off, drawing brush-tip lightly upwards. Do wider surfaces in overlapping rectangles about 2 sq ft each in sequence shown (4).

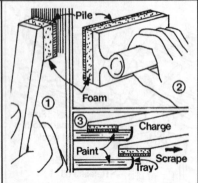

Some workers get better results with paint pad, in patterns/sizes such as (1,2) for, eg., window frames and wall. Rub pile of new pad across hand to remove loose pile, and use first for non-gloss paint. Dip only pile into paint, in flat tray, and lightly scrape off excess (3).

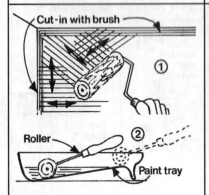

Roller is generally liked for walls, ceilings. Buy good quality, in lambswool or in mohair pile.

Paint with criss-crossing strokes (1), after cutting-in to angles with small brush. Charge from special roller tray (2) unless using newer 'solid-block' emulsion that comes in its own tray.

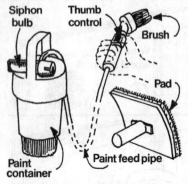

Expensive, but fine for large jobs by even the reluctant home decorator, was Paintmate. Paint container, pressurised by soda-siphon bulb, was clipped to user's belt and had flexible feed pipe, handle with thumb-operated valve into which choice of range of brushes, pads, rollers is inserted. Anyone still have one?

52

Wall-tiling pointers

Wall tiles laid well look great. But if they are all over the place, you have got a visual horror on your hands. Here's how to avoid that.

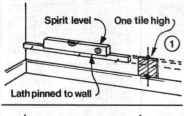

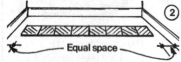

(1) First step is to pin lath, set true against spirit level, temporarily to wall, one tile high (max) at highest point.

(2) With plain wall, lay tiles along floor and move them as necessary until they are centred on wall – equal gap each end.

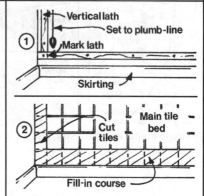

(1) Temporarily fix vertical laths to marks made on horizontal one, setting true against plumb-liner or spirit level.

Lay main bed (area) of tiles. (2) Remove laths when adhesive has set and fill in bottom course, then corner tiles cut to fit – cut edges against wall.

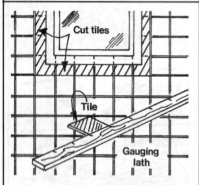

With window or feature wall, tiles should be centred on feature, with cut tiles or equal width each side; lay these after completing main area.

Setting-out is best done by using lath marked out in tile widths for use as a measure or gauge.

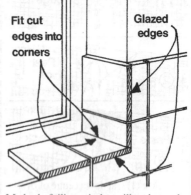

Method of tiling window sill and reveal, using 'universal' tiles, some of which in each pack have either one or two edges glazed. Select and arrange tiles so no unglazed edge is seen in finished work.

Hanging wall fabrics

No, not wallpapering, but hanging fabrics. There's quite a difference, and here are some of the things you need to know.

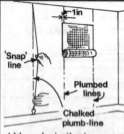

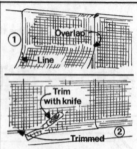

Although similar in some ways to paperhanging, there are important differences - largely because unbacked fabrics (eg. hessian) tend to stretch. Start by plumbing series of lines on wall 1in. less than fabric width apart. Hang paper-backed fabrics as heavy wallpaper.

Brush heavy-duty paste evenly over wall to 1/2in. short of line (1). With length of fabric 2in. longer than 'drop', rolled (face-in) on broomstick/tube carefully smooth to wall with clean paint or felt roller, or soft paperhanger's brush (2).

Overlap lengths at least $^1/_2$in, as shown (1).

Then press fabric into angles of ceiling and skirting, and carefully trim with really sharp craft knife (2), without cutting into plaster.

Finish by pressing ends well into angles.

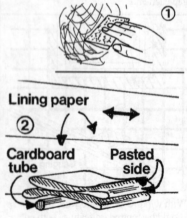

Trim joins: (1) Cut down centre of overlap with knife, straight-edge; (2) peel away both edges; (3) carefully roll back cut edges and apply paste down exposed wall. Then smooth back fabric to produce perfect join. Avoid overpasting.

If wall is oil-painted, first wash with sugar soap and 'key' with coarse glasspaper (1). Then (as with any heavy wallcovering) line, horizontally, pasting and 'concertina'-folding paper (2).

Smoothing uneven walls

If you want a nice smooth wall surface – for covering, painting, tiling or whatever – here's how, and how to dodge the problem.

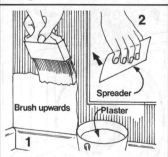

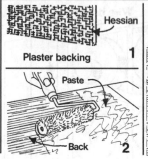

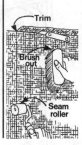

Rough or uneven wall can be smoothed by applying a heavy coat of special 'skim' plaster (bought ready-mixed) with a wall brush (1). Work upwards and, after well covering, smooth and level with spreader (2) supplied with plaster. Detailed instructions given on container.

Easy, though not inexpensive, way to 'plaster' and decorate plain (eg. brick, breeze block) wall is with special plaster-backed hessian (1) in choice of colours. Soft plaster becomes hard when adhesive (supplied) dries. Apply to back of sheet, after trimming selvedges, with medium-pile paint roller (2).

Offer sheet to wall, as wallpaper, smoothing down with soft brush and pressing joins with seam roller. Then trim top and bottom (3).

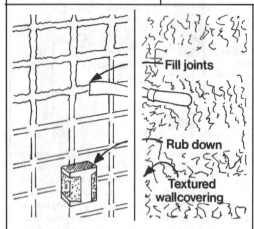

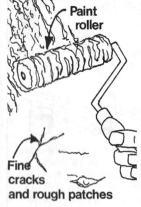

If tile joints are slightly over-filled with plaster filler and then sanded down, a surface can be produced that will be suitable for, at least, a textured wallcovering. Or the tiles can be covered with the plaster-backed hessian without joint-filling.

'If you can't beat 'em, join 'em' – by coating a rough, uneven wall with ripple-finish paint, simply applied with roller.

Preparing metalwork for painting

How to remove rust and old paint from different types of metal –
when it's time for a new paint job.

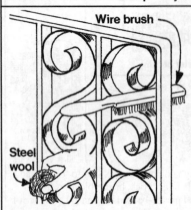

Before repainting wrought iron, remove
paint and rust with wire brush and coarse
steel wool, working well into all corners.

The better this is done, the longer will
the later painting last.

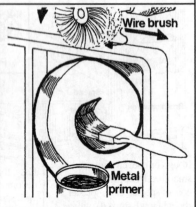

Rust and paint removal may be more
easily done on accessible parts with wire
brush or flap-wheel in a power drill.

Immediately after cleaning, apply a rust
inhibitor or anti-rust metal primer.

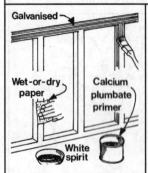

New, galvanised metal should
first be cleaned with white
spirit, rubbed on with wet-or-
dry abrasive paper; then wipe
clean and apply appropriate
primer. 'Weathered' gal-
vanising can simply be primed.

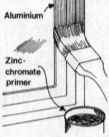

Aluminium does not
normally need to be
painted but if it does
treat with white
spirit/fine wet-or-dry
paper, as galvanised
iron, and apply
appropriate primer.

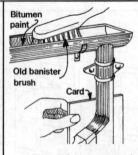

Prepare iron gutters and
down-pipes externally in
same way as wrought iron.
But wire-brush inside of
gutter and give two coats of
bitumen paint. When
priming, painting down-pipe
protect wall with card.

NOTE: Always protect eyes when using any wire brush. After preparation
as above, apply undercoat and finishing coat in usual way. Same applies
to ready-primed metalwork.

Texture painting walls & ceilings

Texture paint can make an interesting surface effect on walls and ceilings, and enhance the decoration of suitable rooms

Masking tape
or gummed paper

Adhesive
tape

Newspaper

Texture 'paint' (not unlike wall filler) is bought ready-for-use. Stir, and apply evenly with 4-6in brush.

Draw brush down, then back; do not brush out. Masking of woodwork, shown, helps – or use small brush around edges.

After covering area about 18in wide and 3ft long, texturing can be done in a variety of ways; three are shown.

(1) For veined or bark effect draw plain wood roller slowly over the paint.

(2) Stippling can be done by using board with hessian fixed over it; press lightly against paint and then withdraw it.

(3) Make swirls with sponge

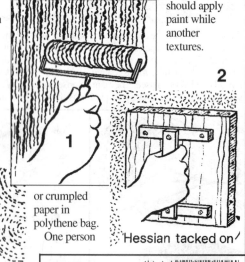

should apply paint while another textures.

2

or crumpled paper in polythene bag. One person

Hessian tacked on

1

Sponge in polythene bag

3

If preferred, a neat finish around edges can be obtained by lightly drawing a chisel-ended stick along. Wipe stick after each stroke.

NOTES: First prepare surfaces as for other decorating; if porous apply primer-sealer. Practise texturing before starting on room. Observe maker's instructions. The white textured finish can be emulsion-painted, if desired.

Removing ceiling tiles

Some older ceiling tiles can be a fire hazard. Removing them is definitely the best answer. Here's how to do it.

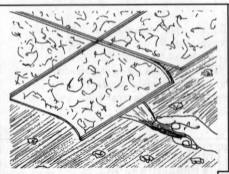

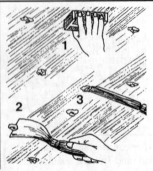

Expanded polystyrene ceiling tiles of ordinary (not self-extinguishing) type can present a fire hazard, especially if they were fixed with blobs of adhesive rather than a full surface coating – which is nowadays always advised. They can be prised off, with care, using a broad stripping knife, as shown.

Removing adhesive blobs is more difficult. They can be rubbed down with medium glasspaper held around a cork block (1); scraped off with a knife (2); or chipped off with a sharp chisel (3).

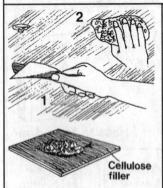

Cellulose filler

When blobs are chipped off plaster is usually damaged. Fill holes with cellulose filler, pressing in with knife (1). Leave slightly 'proud' and, before filler is quite dry, smooth by lightly wiping with damp rag (2).

Sugar soap   Paste Powder

Water

Old adhesive can often be softened, so that scraping is easier, by brushing on a paste made by mixing equal parts sugar soap and wallpaper paste with water; leave for two hours. Mixture is caustic, so keep off skin and all other surfaces. Wear protective gloves. Rinse ceiling after scraping.

NOTE: When fitting new polystyrene ceiling tiles it is wise to use those of self-extinguishing grade or/and paint with special flame-retardant emulsion paint. Coat whole of back with adhesive.

Stripping exterior paintwork

A good rule of thumb is: 'Strip paint only when it is blistered or cracked' – otherwise you are making unnecessary work for yourself.

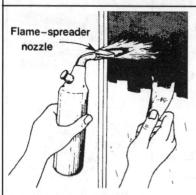

Flame–spreader nozzle

Soften paint with chemical stripper or blowlamp, taking care to avoid burning; then remove with stripping knife.

Liquid-gas blowlamp is best type for amateurs. Keep it moving slowly over paint, ahead of knife.

Put hot scrapings into metal bucket.

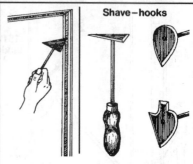

Shave–hooks

Mouldings and angles are scraped with shave-hook after paint has been softened with blowlamp, or with chemical stripper used according to instructions on container.

Triangular shave-shook is suitable for angles, but one of other two shapes shown is better for curved mouldings.

All are sold by tool merchants.

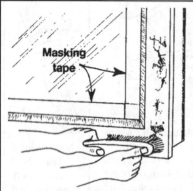

Masking tape

Flaking paint and rust on metal window frames can be removed with wire brush, followed by emery cloth.

Do not brush putty, but masking tape avoids risk of scratching glass.

Protect eyes with goggles.

After stripping to bare wood, rub down with glasspaper; then paint knots with knotting varnish.

Apply priming, undercoat and gloss paint. For metal, use a 'zinc-rich' primer.

Exterior decorating – in safety

Method is similar to interior work but involves use of ladder. Using it effectively and safely is vital to your well-being.

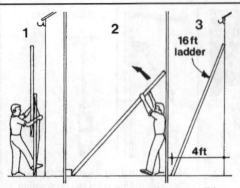

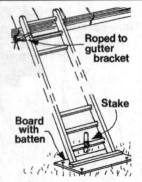

An extending aluminium ladder with rope pull is best. Erect near to wall (1) with foot on bottom rung.

Raise long ladder by walking under it (2); base is against kerb or supported by helper. When erected, move base out quarter length of ladder (3).

Support base by roping to stake. Instead, on soft ground, use board with batten fixed and long nails as spikes. Lash top to firm gutter bracket.

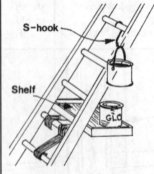

Clip-on stand-off stay is useful when painting gutters or to avoid ladder crushing plastic gutter. It grips wall without need for roping.

Moveable footrest allows comfortable working.

Have both hands free when working from ladder.
Paint kettle can be hung from home-made S-hook or, better, shelf that clips over rungs can be used. This will hold paint cans, brushes and other tools.

In mounting a ladder hold sides loosely with crooked fingers. Do not grip the rungs.

LADDERS and most fittings shown can be hired from tool-hire shop by the day or longer. Especially when painting walls, a moveable scaffold tower – also to be hired – is very desirable.

Handyman
in the
Garden

Pages 62-94

Building a low garden wall

Bricklaying is rightly seen as a craft skill. But, while you may not be able to match the speed of the professional, here is how to achieve a result a craftsman would be proud of.

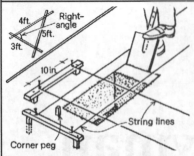

First set out trench for foundations, using pairs of string lines at right-angles. Right-angle can be set with three laths nailed together as shown. Dig between lines to a depth of at least 9in, removing top soil and going into firm ground.

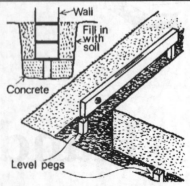

Make bottom of trench level and drive in pegs (projecting about 3in) so that tops are all in line when checked with spirit level. Put in rather sloppy (not watery) concrete to tops of pegs.

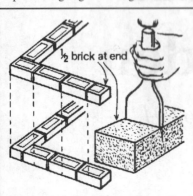

Lay alternate brick courses as shown after concrete has set, making mortar joints about 3/8in thick. Put bedding layer on concrete for first course. Use bolster (very wide) or ordinary cold chisel and heavy hammer to cut half-bricks.

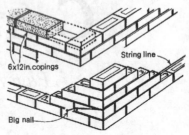

Lay first course, then build up corners or ends, with taut string guide for each course. Check verticals often with spirit level or plumb-line. Place mortar bed for each brick in turn and trowel mortar on one end. Tap brick down to maintain level. When wall is 18-24in high lay pre-cast slabs as coping.

WHAT TO USE: CONCRETE: Ready-mixed or use 1:2:5 mix of cement, sharp sand and gravel. MORTAR: Dry ready-mixed is convenient; or use 1:1:6 mixture of cement, hydrated lime and washed sand.

Garden steps

Another job that may look harder than it actually is. You can build attractive and practical garden steps with this step-by-step guide

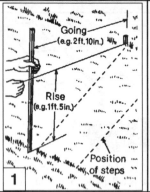

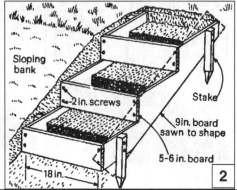

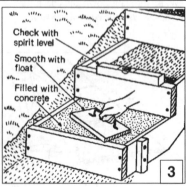

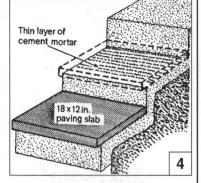

The proportions of steps are largely governed by the angle of the bank they are to climb. Seek to make them 'easy': risers not more than 6in; treads not less than 12 in. Measure the distances – 'rise' and 'going' (1).

Then divide each equally and construct a simple form of frame based on these dimensions (2). Make it from boards at least 1 in thick and use screws to fix parts together.

Using form as guide, roughly dig out steps in the bank. Fix form with stakes, and fill each step to within 2-

$2^1/_2$in of top and front with soil and small stones rammed well down.

Now fill with slightly wet (just pourable) concrete made from 1 part Portland cement, 2 parts sharp sand, 3 parts shingle or gravel. Tamp well down and smooth surface with simple wood float (3). After 5-6 days, dismantle and remove form, trowel on thin layer of cement mortar (1 part cement to 4 parts sand) and lay paving slabs to overhang about 1 in at front (4).

Paving a garden path

In any garden, an attractive paved path not only makes a practical feature, but can greatly enhance its design. You can also use this method of paving a drive-way (see note, below).

Remove turfs and soil to the width of the paving slabs and a depth of 1in more than slab thickness. Lightly rake and then roll firm and flat.

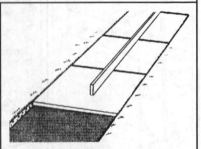

Spread $1/2$in thickness of sand or fine, dry soil. Place slabs, leaving $1/4$in gaps. 'Walk' the slabs down and check for evenness with the edge of a board.

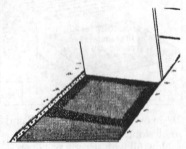

If any slab rocks, 'hinge' it up and put extra sand around the edges to leave a slight hollow in the middle. Then 'walk' the slab down again until firm.

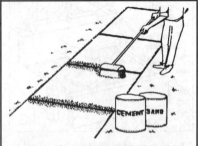

Leave for a week to settle; then brush a dry mixture of equal parts of sand and cement into the gaps. Remove all surplus. The cement will set with normal atmospheric and ground moisture. Or sprinkle lightly with a watering can in very dry weather.

NOTE: If subsoil is not hard and firm, excavate an extra 2in (or at least 4in for a drive) and ram in rubble or small, broken stones to the extra depth. Then proceed as above.

Repairing a tarmac drive or path

Nothing looks worse than potholes disfiguring a tarmac surface. But it's not a big job to put the matter right

Potholes and hollows in tarmac can be filled with cold macadam, sold in paper sacks. First sweep clean, then cut away loose edges around hole with cold chisel and heavy hammer, slightly undercutting by holding chisel at an angle.

PRIMER

Brush out hole and apply primer (by makers of macadam) with an old brush; for larger areas an old yard broom is more convenient. If primer is not available, use proprietary bituminous waterproofer of kind used for concrete floors.

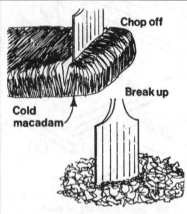

Chop off

Break up

Cold macadam

Remove paper bag from macadam and chop off a lump with a spade. Then break up into small pieces with edge of spades and rake until it resembles rough soil. Fill hole with this, raking it well into edges and leaving slightly 'proud'.

Rammer

Sprinkle with chippings

Ram down with board nailed to end of heavy bulk, or beat down with back of spade, after sprinkling chippings. If garden roller available, finish with that. For holes more than about 1.5in deep fill in layers, priming between them.

Making a stepping-stone path

Stepping stones look best - and add length to the garden - when laid to an irregular winding line.

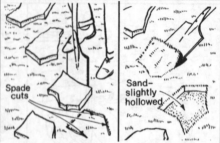

Lay the stones loose, move as necessary and check that they are easy to walk along. When satisfied, commence to fit them.

Cut cleanly around each stone in turn with a sharp spade, keeping close to outline of stone.

Lift the turf and then remove earth to a total depth of about 1in more than stone thickness.

Spread sand in hole, making it slightly hollow. Fit stone and 'walk' it down. Lift and put in more sand if necessary.

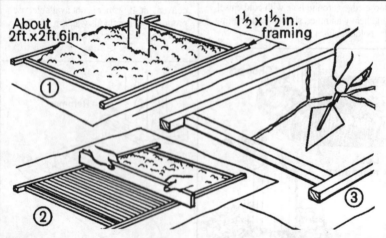

If suitable stones are not available make concrete slabs.

Form a simple nailed frame, place over polythene sheet on flat surface and tamp in a 1:3 cement-sand mix (1). Level with edge of board, used with sawing motion (2). After two-three hours cut random shapes with trowel (3). Two days later, knock frame apart and stand stones on edge for a week before use.

CARE OF PATH: Stones should be at exactly soil level. If any sink, lift and put a little more sand in hole.

Making garden gates

An attractive garden gate can make the approach to your home, all the more welcoming when you return after being away.

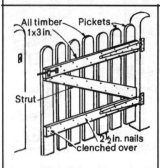

A simple picket gate is easiest to make. Nail rails to end pickets; mark strut to shape, saw and nail on. Fix other pickets about 1.5in. apart. Nail from front of gate, clenching at back.

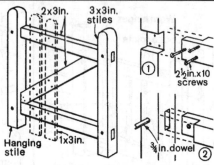

More substantial picket-style gate with simple jointing of rails and stiles. Easiest joint is halving (1), which should be glued and screwed. Mortise and barefaced tenon joint (2) is very much better, but needs more skill. Joint is locked with well-fitting dowel through stile. Strut is made to fit and skew-nailed.

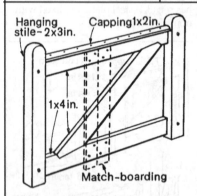

Wider gate (up to 4ft) with frame joints as for picket and match-boarded front; boards are nailed and top ends protected by capping nailed to rail. Could be in hardwood, and oiled or varnished.

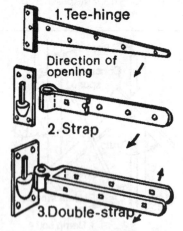

Hinge (1) is suitable for light gate only. Use (2) or (3) for heavy gate. Bolt through square holes, screw through others.

MATERIALS: Planed softwood or hardwood. Use galvanised nails and screws, and galvanised hinges.

Repairing a garden gate

**How to cure a common problem found on many gardens gates –
sagging so that the toe snags on the ground**

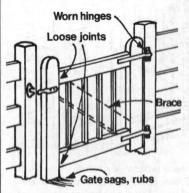

Common fault with garden gate is
sagging so that toe rubs. It can arise
because of loose joints, worn or rusted
hinges, or the lack of a diagonal brace
(shown dotted). Or the post may be
loose or broken.

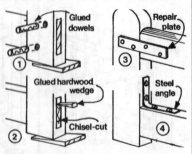

Four ways of treating loose joints,
after wedging under toe of gate: (1)
holes are drilled through joint and
dowels smeared with glue are driven
in; (2) tenons are split with chisel and
thin, glued hardwood wedges driven
in - trim dowels/wedges after glue
has set; (3,4) steel plates are fixed with
non-rust screws.

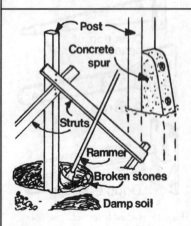

To secure loose gate post, dig hole
around it, set vertical with temporary
struts and ram small broken stones
and damp soil into hole (1). Or fill
with concrete; or fix concrete spur (2).

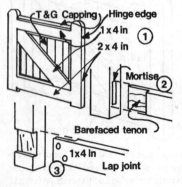

Outline details of sturdy gate up to
40in wide (1). Frame corners are best
jointed with mortise and barefaced
tenon (2) but lap joint (3) could be
used. Fillets of 1in x 1in carry t & g
boards fixed with galvanised nails.
Coat joints with waterproof glue.

Building a screen wall

Screen walls are an ideal way to create privacy, even 'rooms' in the garden, sometimes with a touch of mystery illuminated by patterns of shifting light and shade.

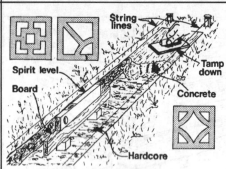

Use concrete blocks in wide choice of patterns; three are shown. First set out foundation trench with string lines 12 in part. Dig 9 in deep and ram hardcore (broken stones etc.) to half depth. Drive in pegs and set level, then fill with concrete to top of pegs and tamp down.

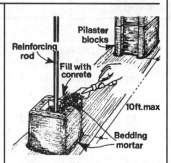

Build piers at ends, with concrete pilaster blocks. Pass blocks over iron rod driven in before concrete sets, checking against string line and spirit-level. Fill with wettish concrete.

After building three blocks high lay screen blocks, working from each and after checking spacing.

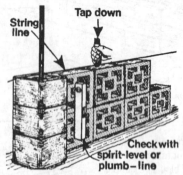

Keep other courses to level of string line, tap down with trowel and check frequently with spirit-level or plumb-line. Clean off mortar joints. After two courses build up pilasters and continue.

NOTE: Get instruction sheet when buying blocks, and follow it, especially for blocks other than 12in square. Top caps can be brought for pilasters and wall. For convenience use standard concrete mix and bricklaying mortar mix, which need only be mixed with water.

Easy-to-build 'stone' walls

If building a wall out of real stone seems too demanding, there is an attractive alternative. Why not try using reconstituted stone? It is as easy to lay as brick-work. What's more it can look very good indeed.

Cast reconstituted-stone blocks are very easy to lay and give a good representation of real stone walling. Blocks are usually in two sizes, one half the length of the other, and typical dimensions are given.

Coping stones are also available; plus larger flat stones for use as pier caps, etc.

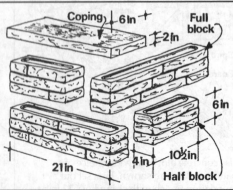

Lay blocks on solid base of concrete foundation with mortar of proportions shown, or with ready-mixed bricklaying mortar mix made up with water. Spread mortar over 'frog' with trowel and tamp next block on to it. Procedure is similar to bricklaying. Mortar should be made shade of blocks – by choice of sand of colouring.

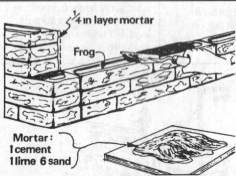

Work out dimensions to eliminate or minimise need for cutting blocks. Example shows simple dustbin screen, with holes for decorative effect. Block outlines, shown in heavy lines, are not seen as such in finished wall. Similar, larger construction could be built to enclose a fuel-oil tank. Use blocks also for low garden walls.

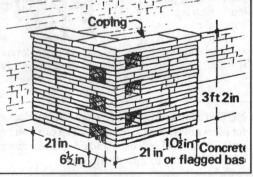

70

Patio-laying hints

When it comes to laying a patio, the final effect can easily be spoilt. So, here are some tips on how to get a really good look.

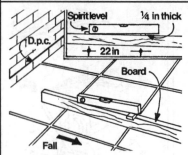

Paving slabs, in choice of colour, size, shape, are easiest to lay. They should be given 'fall' (especially away from walls) of 1 in 80-100. This can be checked with straight 6-8ft board with two small blocks, shown, to support builders' spirit level.

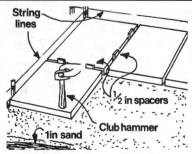

On firm ground, excavate 3in deep. Compact with heavy roller, making level in one direction, providing 'fall' in other. Lay 1in sand/fine ballast and set slabs to string lines, spacing with pieces of about $1/2$ in wood. Tamp firm with eg. handle of club hammer.

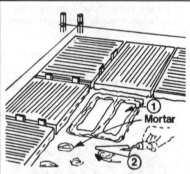

Good alternative to sand, giving firmer support, is weak (1 cement: 5 sand) mortar. Lay as 'box-and-cross' (1) or, less strong, five dabs (2). Tamp slabs down well, checking levels and flatness with board/level in all directions. Insert spacers between slabs.

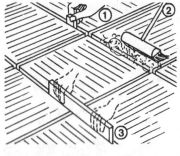

Day after laying: 1. remove spacers (if not taken out previously); 2. brush dry mortar mix into open joints; 3. press down with board to leave $1/4$in deep recesses. Remove surplus mortar. Alternative is to point with stiff mortar mix, again ramming with board.

NOTES: 1. Have patio in warmest sheltered spot available. 2. First draw plan on squared paper, seeking to avoid need to cut slabs. 3. Excavate 4-6in on softer ground and lay well-compacted hardcore bed.

Laying a paved patio

A paved patio is an asset to any home, or even a holiday caravan, but it's worth taking trouble with the job to get an attractive result.

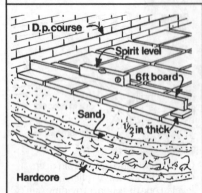

Lay slabs over 2in layer of sand raked to even thickness over firm base. Unless ground is firm, first put down 2-4in of hardcore. Have patio 6in below level of d.p. course in house wall and ensure 'fall' away from house wall, using board, spirit level as shown.

Consolidate hardcore, earth with rammer (1), heavy garden roller (2) or – easiest and most effective – a special plate vibrator (3). Vibrator has its own motor and can be hired from tool-hire shop. Go over whole area two or three times in different directions.

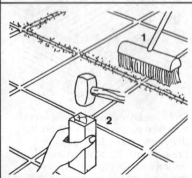

Put down sand and lay slabs 2sq yd at a time. Vibrator will lower slabs about $1/2$in, nearly filling joints with sand. Brush more sand into joints (1) and use vibrator again. Alternative is to have 1in sand, tamp down with wood block and club hammer (2).

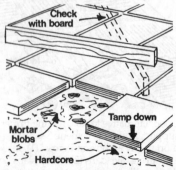

Instead of using sand, on really firm hardcore base, slabs can be laid on five blobs of mortar (one cement: five sand) and tamped down with wood block and club hammer.

Check often with edge of board and tamp down upstanding edges or corners, to make flat.

Fencing repairs

Replacing a fence that has suffered damage, either from wind, rot or wear and tear, is expensive. Often a repair is much cheaper.

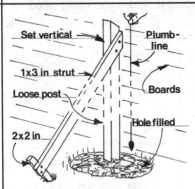

Posts usually 'go' first. If just loose, set upright and fix strut (temporary or permanent). Dig hole around post and fill with damp soil and broken stones, ramming firm; or with dry concrete mix – which will set in day or two without added water.

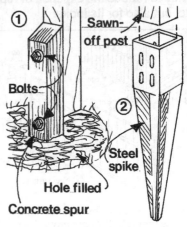

Concrete spur

With post rotted at ground level, saw to sound wood, make hole and set concrete spur upright, then fill with wet concrete. When set, drill and bolt post (1). Or use special steel post spike (2).

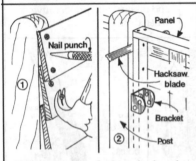

(1) Rotted, broken feather-edge boards can be removed after punching nail-heads through or by using claw hammer to withdraw nails.

(2) Fencing panels come in standard sizes. Remove damaged one by prising out nails, or cutting through them with broken hacksaw blade. New panels are easily fixed by sliding through U-brackets shown.

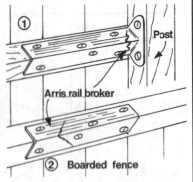

Arris rails broken at (tenoned) end (1) or along length (2) can be made good with special repair plates. In fencing work treat all new wood, broken/sawn ends with preservative.

All nails, screws and fixings should be non-rusting; e.g. galvanised.

Protecting outdoor timbers

Timber out of doors can greatly enhance any garden, or even a simple backyard, but it is essential to keep it in good condition, not only to reduce the expense of replacing it before you really need to, but also for its looks.

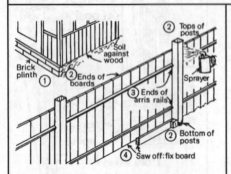

(1) Minimise decay by keeping timber clear off the ground. (2) Apply proprietary wood preservative liberally with brush when timber is dry. (3) Drench with preservative, preferably using pressure sprayer. (4) Saw off rotted ends and fit horizontal board after treating with preservative.

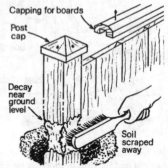

Posts and boards can be protected by nailing on cappings treated with preservative. Scrape soil from base of posts, scrape decayed wood with wire brush and drench with preservative when dry.

After treatment, drive in angle irons to give extra support. If badly weakened by rotting, saw off base of post, dig hole and fix special concrete spur.
Fill hole with broken stones and concrete.

Char ends of rustic poles (for pergolas etc). in embers of bonfire. Preservative can also be applied to charred part.

NOTE: Many of the treatments below are unnecessary if timber has been vacuum-impregnated with preservative before purchase. Some merchants can supply such specially treated timber at extra cost.

Erecting a garden fence

Today there are proprietory systems for erecting fence posts (you can get details from many DIY stores or garden centres), but here is one well tried method for putting up your garden fence.

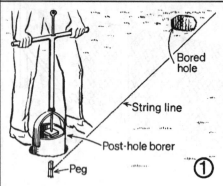

Bored hole

String line

Post-hole borer

Peg

①

4x4in. oak post (top sloped)

Broken stones ②

1. Fix length of string parallel to line of intended fence and about 6in away. Make post holes at 6ft intervals – 2ft deep for 5-6ft fence; proportionate for other heights, but not less than 1ft. Holes can be dug about 12in square, or made more easily (except in stony ground) with special post-hole borer, which can be hired or bought.

2. Put 2in layer of broken stones in bottom of hole, insert post, and fix it upright with struts as shown. Gradually fill hole to within 2in of top with broken stones, ramming firm with heavy pole.

3. Fill hole with dry mix of one part cement to three sand and pour on water to wash mixture into stones. When set, remove struts and fill hole with fairly stiff 1:2:4 mix of cement-

Filled with dry sand-cement mix

③

sand-gravel concrete. Take it above ground level and slope top away from post.

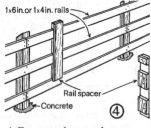

1x6in.or 1x4in. rails

Rail spacer

Concrete ④

4. For popular ranch-type fence fix softwood rails with 2-3in rustproof nails. Make a simple spacer as shown to set rails parallel and at equal distances.

NOTE: General procedure shown applies to almost any type of fence, but if fencing is bought as a kit observe additional instructions supplied with it.

Erecting chain-link fencing

An attractive alternative to wooden fencing nowadays is chain link, which is usually plastic coated to give an extra dash of colour

Plastic-coated chain link is supported by straining wires and stapled to posts – end ones with angled struts. Hardwood is best but good-quality softwood can be used. In either case give three liberal applications of wood preservative before use. Chain link can be in sections, as shown, or in full length, carried over face of posts.

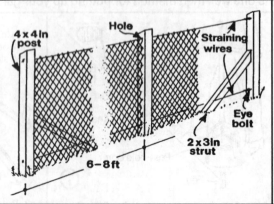

Sink posts 18in into ground for fence up to about 4ft high; 2ft for higher fence. Then fix struts; method shown at (1) is simpler, but method at (2) stronger. In firm soil ram gravel and soil into holes; in light soil concrete made from one part cement, three sand and five aggregate is to be preferred.

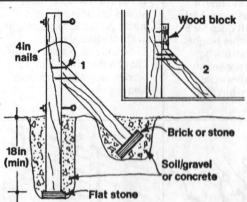

Bore posts for eye bolts, fix straining wire to eye at one end, pull really tight and bind to eye at other end. Drilled steel plate simplifies twisting of wire ends. Tension wires finally by tightening eye-bolt nuts. If in sections, thread mesh over straining wires after fixing at one end, or secure it with twists of wire.

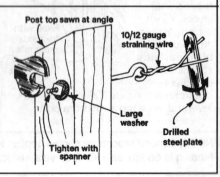

Building a barbecue

A permanent, brick-built barbecue is a delight on warm evenings when meat cooked over a proper fire can take on the aroma of charcoal and/or woodsmoke. Much better than bottled gas.

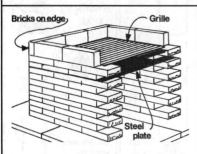

Suggestion for simple barbecue made from spare bricks or blocks. It can stand on concrete base of paving slabs and be built as temporary structure, without mortar joints. Grille may be from old cooker; steel plate, for fire, could be replaced by fire bricks over loose brick base.

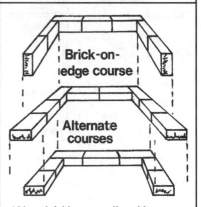

Although laid temporarily, without mortar, it is best and easiest to 'bond' the bricks as shown. To avoid brick-cutting, side walls are left toothed in front.

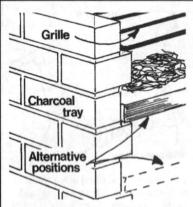

Simple permanent barbecue can be built on sound base with bricks on edge, but placing few on side to support grille and charcoal tray (better than flat steel).

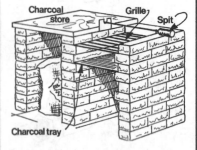

Permanent barbecue in reconstituted stone can form attractive garden feature. Kits are available with stones dressed to size. That shown is more sophisticated than some and kit comes complete with chromium-plated grille, battery-operated rotating spit and a charcoal tray.

NOTE: Site barbecue in sheltered spot. It could be helpful to experiment with temporary construction before building a permanent one.

Installing a garden water tap

Not every house has a tap in the garden, even when it would be really useful for a keen gardener. Here's how to install one.

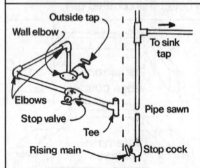

Outline diagram of pipework for outside tap. New fittings are to left of broken line; existing pipework on right. Fittings can be bought separately or as a kit, complete with instructions. Turn off stop cock, sink tap and cut rising main with hacksaw to receive Tee section.

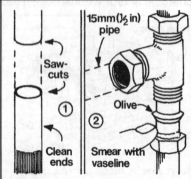

Make saw-cuts to allow pipe ends to be 'sprung' into Tee; trim ends with file and clean 1in of pipe with steel wool.

(1). Fit nut, olive (from Tee) over pipe, smear vaseline into nut threads.

(2); screw on nut with fingers and then carefully tighten with spanner.

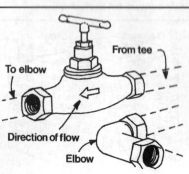

Brass compression fittings are shown for stop valve (to cut supply from tap in winter) and elbows.

All are fitted in the same way as Tee, and all should be for 15mm. pipe; they also fit $1/_2$in imperial pipes, which may have been used in the original installation.

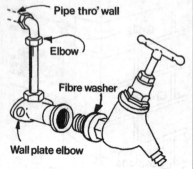

The tap itself is screwed into a wall-plate elbow screwed to wall plugs and mounted below a 15 or 16m. hole made through wall with masonry drill.

All pipes can be cut to length with a hacksaw; sawn ends should be trimmed and cleaned as for Tee.

NOTE: Although the fittings shown are referred to are of metal, others can be had in pvc, some with push-in fittings. See makers' literature for details.

Decorative concrete blocks

It's easier than you think to make concrete blocks for your garden – and in a variety of colours too!

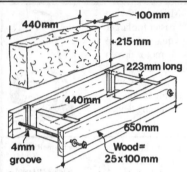

Concrete blocks can be made in many sizes; that shown is a metric block nearest equivalent to imperial 18 x 9in. Blocks are cast in 'knock-down' wooden mould made as shown, secured with long bolt or threaded rod each end.

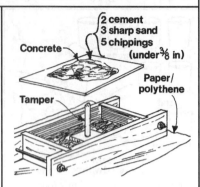

Mix concrete to proportions shown, using only fine chippings as aggregate. Paint inside of mould with old engine oil or ceiling white (to prevent sticking) and lay over paper or polythene. Gradually put in concrete and tamp down with home-made tool.

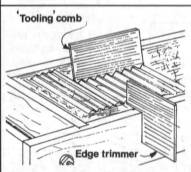

Tooled stone finish is produced, after leaving few hours, with comb made from hardboard, metal or plastic. Smooth surround can be formed with edge trimmer made as shown. Remove mould after 48 hours; then leave blocks to 'cure' for several weeks under polythene sheet.

'Tree-bark' effect can be produced by drawing wooden roller over concrete. Rather similar appearance is by lightly drawing stiff brush over surface – again a few hours after casting

COLOUR of blocks is governed by that of sand used, but many other shades can be obtained by using coloured cement or adding special cement colouring to concrete when mixing.

Mixing and laying concrete

Many DIY jobs around the house and garden will need concrete. Here's how to go about mixing and laying your own.

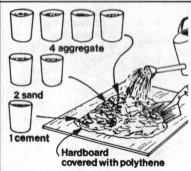

4 aggregate

2 sand

1 cement

Hardboard covered with polythene

For most purposes a 1:2:4 mix (one Portland cement, two washed sand, four aggregate) is best. Mix well together, dry. Then add water gradually while continuing to mix. For small jobs bags of 1:2:4 dry mix are convenient; re-mix before adding water.

Mixer makes job easier for larger quantities. Hire motor-driven mixer or use hand tool as shown; mixing is done by wheeling device after loading.

'Tyre'

Edge (forme) boards

Tamping board

Before laying set up 'forme' with boards. Slightly over-fill between them and then level with tamping board made as shown. It is used by two people with sawing action while moving slowly along.

Small areas or rough patches can be smoothed with wooden float simply made as shown (1). Apply light pressure to avoid bringing much water to surface. For non-slip finish draw soft yard broom (2) over a few hours after laying. Concrete should always be slightly sloped for drainage; preferably make scratches in direction of slope.

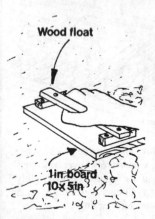

Wood float

1in board 10 x 5in

Direction of slope

2

NOTE: Avoid adding too much water, which weakens concrete. Correct mix will just hold together when handful is lightly squeezed. As rough guide, use about 3 gal per 1/2cwt (25kg) cement.

Making concrete paving slabs

Concrete paving slabs have all sorts of uses around the home. And they are not that difficult to make.

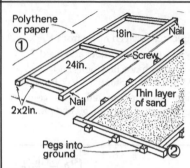

Make a simple frame, or form, to hold the concrete. For small batches make as (1) and lay on a flat floor or other hard, level surface. For larger batches and bigger frame, fix with pegs on level surface and lay smooth layer of sand in bottom (2).

Fill frame with cement mix, gently pressing down with spade to avoid air pockets. Then level off by tamping with edge of board. Work from one end with sawing motion of board, so as to form a series of shallow ridges and hollows.

NOTE: If coloured concrete is preferred, use ready-coloured cement or mix special colouring with the water. For crazy paving cut irregular slabs with trowel or old knife.

Well mix dry cement and sand with shovel or spade; sprinkle on water and continue mixing. Make a fairly stiff mix – a squeezed handful should just hold its shape.

About four hours after laying, cut to slab sizes required with trowel against a straight-edge. Leave five or six days before removing frame. With frame (1) remove screw and knock off side with hammer. Keep slabs another week before use.

Garden Screen and Pergola

A trellis, whether as a simple screen or developed into a pergola, offers the gardener all sorts of possibilities.

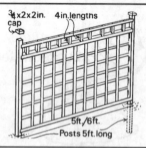

Simple trellis screen made from $1\frac{1}{2}$ x $1\frac{1}{2}$in rough sawn timber and fixed together with notched joints and galvanised nails. Standard $\frac{1}{4}$x 1in sawn laths are used for the trellis; these come in lengths of 3ft, 3ft 6in, 4ft, 5ft and 6ft.

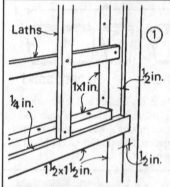

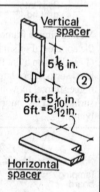

① Lengths of 1 x 1in sawn timber are nailed inside main frame to receive laths. Note that the vertical ones are set-in-twice thickness of laths (1). Nail on horizontal laths first; a shaped piece of wood simplifies equal spacing, which varies with width covered (2).

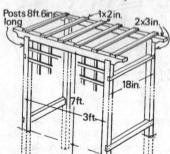

Construction of strong pergola for climbing shrubs. It consists of two inverted U-shaped frames with cross rails, also boards nailed across top to support blooms. Trellis at sides can be nailed to 1 x 1in bearers in the same way as for the screen. Decorative corner trellis sections are optional and may be preferred for their appearance. Notched and halving joints can be used as shown.

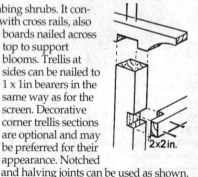

TIMBER: Oak is ideal for posts but expensive and not easily found. Softwood is suitable if well treated with preservative before screen or pergola is fixed in ground.

Building a car port

Whether you have a house without a garage, or a garage with room for only one car, when your family has two – or more, there is often room beside a house to build a car port.

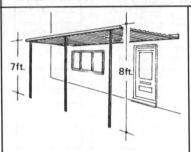

7ft.

8ft.

Port is made to abut house side and will take a medium-size car. Dimensions allow for use of six standard (30in x 8ft) 3in-corrugation pvc sheets for roofing. Planning permission should be obtained from local authority surveyor before ordering materials. PVC gutter and down-pipe could be fitted at lower end.

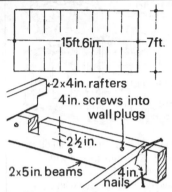

15ft.6in. — 7ft.

2×4in. rafters
4 in. screws into wall plugs
$2\frac{1}{2}$ in.
2×5in. beams
4 in. nails

Roof frame is made from preservative-treated timber, using notched joints as shown. Assemble loose on ground; then fix wall plate. Posts and other main beam are then made up and positioned before attaching rafters.

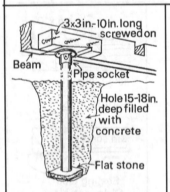

3×3in.-10in. long screwed on
Beam
Pipe socket
Hole 15-18in. deep filled with concrete
Flat stone

Steel pipes about 2in OD, with flanged sockets, support open side. Dig holes, put flat stone in bottom, temporarily fit rafters and check whole assembly. Fill holes with concrete; when set, nail rafters permanently.

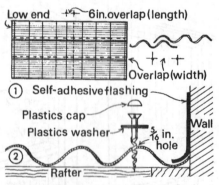

Low end — 6in. overlap (length)
Overlap (width)
① Self-adhesive flashing
Plastics cap
Plastics washer
$\frac{5}{16}$ in. hole
Wall
② Rafter

How roof sheets are overlapped (1). To fix sheets drill $\frac{5}{16}$in holes and secure to rafters with special $1\frac{3}{4}$in screws, sold in packs complete with plastic washers and caps (2). Screw well down, but without distorting corrugations. Use about 10 screws a sheet. Special aluminium flashing tape can be bought as complete kit.

Making a small greenhouse

Nowadays many gardeners buy a small greenhouse, either ready-made or in kit form, but building your own is quite simple.

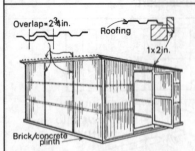

Framing is best in red cedar, but other softwood, if liberally treated with branded preservative, can be used. Roof, ends and door are covered with clear box-section PVC sheet 30in wide in 6ft and 8ft lengths. Sheet can be cut with fine saw. For better insulation, fit special moulded foam under ends of sheets.

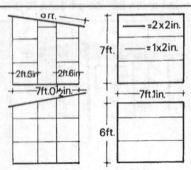

Make four separate frames to (outside) dimensions shown, using 2 x 2in and 1 x 2in timber. Dimensions allow for 2-3/4in overlap of sheets. All joints can be simple halvings, secured with synthetic (waterproof) glue and galvanised nails/screws. Lengths of 1 x 2in cover open tops of sheets on ends.

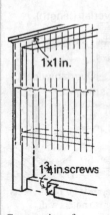

Construction of door, showing 1 x 1in cover strip for top of box-section sheet.

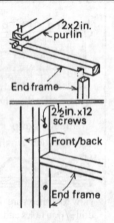

Joints for three roof purlins (below). Fixing of end to side frames with galvanised screws.

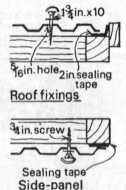

How box-section sheet is fixed, using screws with plastics caps and washers sold in packs especially for this purpose.

Small greenhouse – in polythene

When it comes to building a simple, small greenhouse, all your need is wood, polythene, glue, tacks, screws – and some skill.

Suited to more experienced woodworker, the greenhouse is covered with heavy-gauge (preferably 'horticultural' grade) polythene sheet. It consists of two end frames with four frames for roof and sides screwed to them. Latter frames touch at corners but need not be angled to fit.

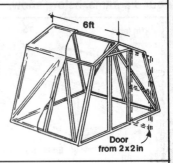

Door from 2×2 in

Similar end frames (1) are set out on garage floor over outline drawn in chalk; or use string lines on smooth lawn.

Lay members over outline and mark out corner joints (2) against sides of meeting members. Make joints with saw and fit halved-in door posts, securing with waterproof glue and 3in nails. Assemble

and fix corner joints with glue and screws. Leave frame flat until glue has set.

Make door, with halvings similar to (2) after final assembly.

Waterproof glue

1¼ in×8 screws

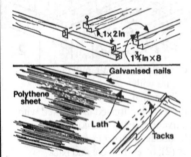

1×2 in

1¾ in×8

Galvanised nails

Polythene sheet

Lath

Tacks

(Top) Side/roof frames have halving joints, glued and screwed. Side-frame diagonals are glued and nailed.

(Bottom) Polythene sheet is fitted after removing all sharp corners from framing. Keeping taut, secure with tacks and cover with wood laths. New sheet is needed every few years.

Making a small garden frame

There are many uses for a simple, small garden frame that can be easily moved when needed. Building it is really quite simple too, as our diagrams, below, show.

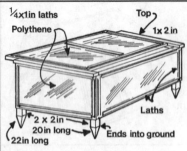

¼x1in laths
Polythene
Top
1x 2 in
Laths
2 x 2in
20 in long
22in long
Ends into ground

Main frame is in 2 x 2in, top in 1 x 2in, softwood covered with long-life polythene secured with laths. Uprights project 6in and are pointed to press into ground. Use pre-preservative-treated wood or – before final assembly – treat all sides, ends, joints with clear or green wood preservative, which is non-toxic to plants.

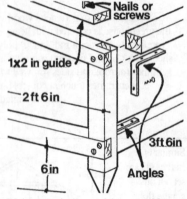

Nails or screws
1x2 in guide
2ft 6 in
3ft 6in
6 in
Angles

Make two similar end frames with corner-halving and T-halving joints secured with zinc-plated screws. Fix front and back members with strong metal angles, screws. Fix 1 x 2in top guides with galvanised nails, non-rust screws.

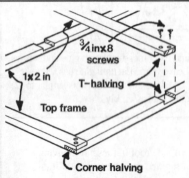

¾ in x 8 screws
1x 2 in
T–halving
Top frame
Corner halving

Frame for top is made to fit freely between 1 x 2in guides and to project 1in. at front and back. Again, corner- and T-halving joints are used to form rigid structure. Fit together temporarily; then treat with preservative and assemble finally.

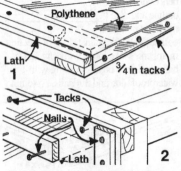

Polythene
Lath
1
¾ in tacks
Tacks
Nails
Lath
2

Cut polythene to fit, pull taut and secure with a few cut tacks.

Then make good fixing with preservative-treated laths, fixed with galvanised nails. Do not fit lath at front edge of top (1), but fit all round, as (2), on ends, front and back.

Making a garden frame

You only need fairly basic woodworking skills to build this garden frame – with a sliding top for ventilation.

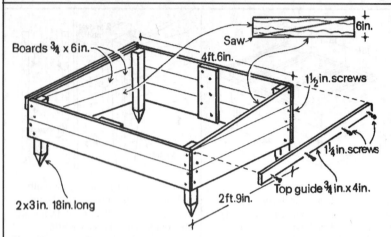

Boards ¾ x 6in.
Saw
4ft.6in.
6in.
1½ in. screws
1¼ in. screws
Top guide ¾ in. x 4in.
2x3in. 18in. long
2ft.9in.

Frame base is built around four pointed legs. Dimensions could be modified so that an old window may be used for the top light. This runs between two guides and will slide upwards to provide ventilation. Red cedar, which is rot-proof, is best timber.

If any other kind is used, treat it thoroughly with garden-grade wood preservative.

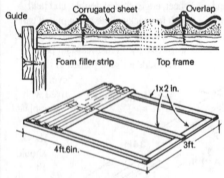

Guide
Corrugated sheet
Overlap
Foam filler strip
Top frame
1x2 in.
4ft.6in.
3ft.

Make top frame as shown and, for lightness, 'glaze' with clear corrugated pvc sheet. Use shaped foam filler strip across the three rails and fix sheet with non-rust screws and soft plastics washers. Drill ample clearance holes for screws. Buy special foam, screws and washers from

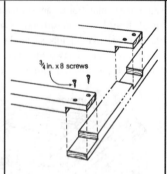

¾ in. x 8 screws

Use half-lap joints for top frame, and secure with synthetic-resin (waterproof) glue and non-rust screws. Mark out joints with try-square and gauge. Form end joints with saw only; other two with saw and chisel.

Garden frame with sliding lights

Here is another garden frame with a different system of sliding lights for ventilation

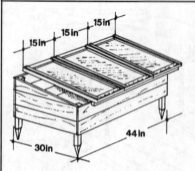

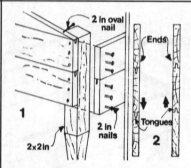

Sides and ends are in $3/4$ x 6in. tongued and grooved boards, with corner posts which press into ground. Three sliding frames are 'glazed' with heavy-gauge polythene sheet – preferably of horticultural grade. All timber should be treated with a proprietary 'clear' preservative before assembly; it may then be painted later.

Boards are fixed to corner posts with galvanised wire nails (1). One board, for top of both ends, is sawn diagonally to provide slope. This means that tongues must point upwards in one end; downwards in the other (2). Tongues/grooves are planed off bottom boards and also top boards at front and back.

All three sliding frames are similar and made from 1 x $1^1/_2$in softwood. Corners are simple halving joints, secured with waterproof glue and two zinc-plated screws. Top is covered with polythene sheet, edges folded double, and held with few tacks while being pulled taut. Three edges are then covered with wood strips fixed with rust-resistant panel pins. Guide rails are planed to slight bevel and fixed with zinc-plated screws. They should fit closely against front and back.

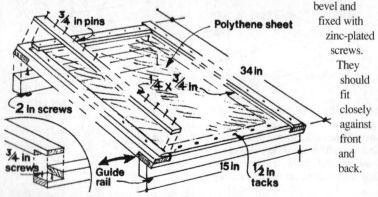

Building a garden pond

A pond makes an attractive feature in any garden, and can also nurture all sorts of interesting plants, and even wildlife

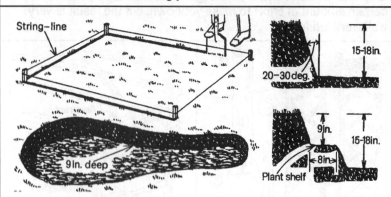

First mark out the shape on a level site. Use pegs and string for rectangle and a length of stiff rope for other shapes. Then nick around the outline with a spade and excavate 9 in deep.

Slope sides about 20 deg. – or 30 deg. in loose soil. It is best to make a plant shelf at least part-way round. Continue excavation to full depth: 15in for up to 20sq ft.

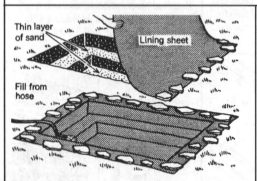

Remove all sharp stones and put down a thin layer of sand. Place one end of lining sheet in position and weight it down well with stones. Draw it over the hole, placing further stones. Fill with water, which will stretch and shape the sheet to the hole.

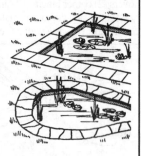

Trim off irregular edges of sheet and lay stones or slabs just over-lapping trimmed edge. Use square slabs for formal pond, crazy for informal.

LINING SHEET: Cheapest but least durable is blue polythene; use double thickness. Permanent and best is special 'pond' sheet of pvc – reinforced terylene. Required size is maximum length (over surround) plus twice depth, by maximum width plus twice depth: ie. for pond 8ft x 5ft x 18in, use sheet 11ft x 8 ft. Cut sheet before commencing work.

Rustic carpentry

Rustic furniture and trellis work look good in any garden, and the latter makes a wonderful climbing frame for many plants. It takes a certain amount of effort to make your own, but the result is very well worthwhile.

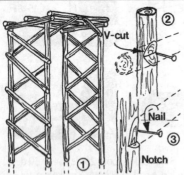

Rose-arch (1) is a good example of rustic archwork. Strength is obtained by triangulation, where possible, and only simplest of joints are used. For cross-overs (2) corner bracing (3) and also for first set of side diagonals, make saw-cut, them remove waste with chisel.

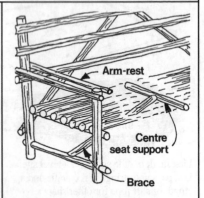

Garden seat up to 4ft 6in long can be made with 2in rustic poles. The diagonal braces at back, also arm rests can be in $1^1/_2$in poles. Have seat 17in high and 18in deep; make back total height of about 38in.

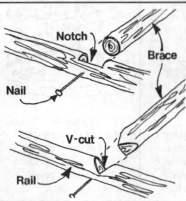

Two methods of making a T-join, as for, eg., seat brace: you can make two saw-cuts and chisel out waste (1) or make V-cut in rail and form V on end of brace (2) using saw and chisel or sharp hatchet.

Pointed wire nails can cause splitting (1), so blunt end (2) by driving against stone; or use floor brades (3). With 2in poles use 3-4in nails.

Larch is best, but always choose poles with thin, smooth bark rather than bark that is thick, rough and loose (2)

Rustic patio furniture

Once you have gained confidence on the simpler pole-based rustic garden items, it's not too difficult to move on the this more sophisticated rustic patio pieces. If you already have good wood-working skills, these should present you with few problems.

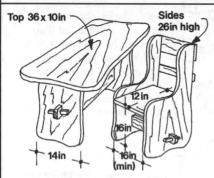

Both table and chair (or seat) would ideally be made in full width wavey-edge elm 1in or more thick. In practice, though, it will generally be necessary to make up widths with boards edge-glued together. Elm, oak, ash, are best, but softwoods such as red cedar, even pine, could be used.

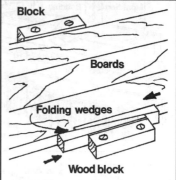

Boards can be glued together with waterproof glue after truing edges and scratching (to form 'key',), then wedging between blocks screwed to bench top/rigid board. Shape with coping/jig saw when glue has set.

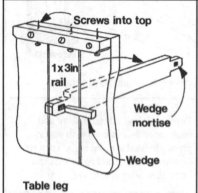

Table leg

Table leg is mortised to receive wedged tenon on end of rail, while fillet is glued, screwed to leg and top after making rail joint. Work calls for sharp tools and fair experience in constructional woodworking. Make wedge tight; do not glue.

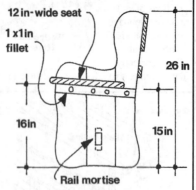

Rail mortise

Chair has shaped sides and wedge-mortised rail – similar to table. Back boards are fixed with glue and zinc-plated/brass screws, as is fillet supporting chair-bottom. As elsewhere, dimensions are approximate, according to timber available.

Making a window box

If your house has little or no front garden, or if you live in flat, a window box can bring a touch of the garden to any room.

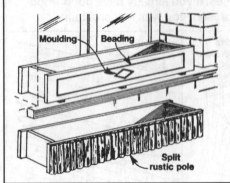

Box can be left plain, or simple decoration can be added. Two forms are shown: upper, wooden mouldings are fixed to front with waterproof glue and panel pins; lower, lengths of split or sawn rustic pole are attached with galvanised nails.

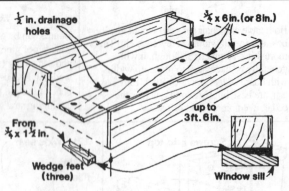

All main parts are from planed softwood board $3/4$in thick; it can be 6in or 8in wide according to sill width available. Saw to lengths, mark positions of ends and bore drainage holes in bottom. Check that all will fit correctly.

Three wedge-shape feet are made to allow for slope of sill and permit drainage.

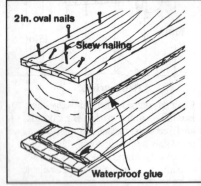

Drill small holes through front and back for nails. Fix ends with waterproof glue and skewed nails. Then fix bottom with glue and nails. Box can be painted after glue has set.

FINISH: Treat inside and outside liberally with green (not brown) wood preservative. Or leave front untreated and prime and paint. Or give three thin coats varnish.

'Wheelbarrow' plant trough

One of the more attractive features you can place in your garden is this 'wheelbarrow' plant trough – but first make your 'wheelbarrow'.

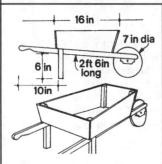

Half-size barrow, with shingle in bottom, is suitable for plants in soil or pots. Make in softwood and treat liberally with clear wood preservative before priming and painting.

Wheel can be bought, or made from 1in timber; fit on steel spindle with tubes to hold central spindle.

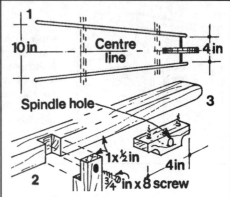

Plan of shafts with wheel in place (1). Box is screwed over shafts and holds them in position. Fix legs with halving joints (2) secured with waterproof glue and zinc-plated screws. Blocks for wheel spindle (3) could be in hardwood, and are drilled half through for spindle and screwed to shafts.

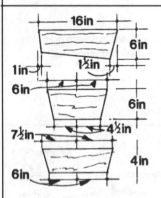

Approximate dimensions for sides, front and back, in $^1/_2$in to $^3/_4$in timber or 8mm waterproof plywood. Ends of sides are slightly bevelled to butt against front and back. Mark front/back from centre line.

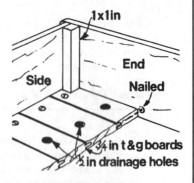

Make box by gluing and nailing sides to 1 x 1in wood planed to fit corners. Tongued-and-grooved boards are made to fit bottom and secured with galvanised nails through sides. Bore drain holes and screw box to shafts.

Easily made garden chair

If you're only just starting to build up your woodworking skills, this simple garden chair, with no joints, may be just the place to start.

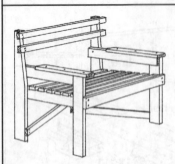

Chair is made without any joints, the parts being fixed together with resin (water-proof) glue and zinc-plated screws. Elm is best, but red cedar is good alternative; both may be finished by oiling. Or use red deal and treat with 'clear' preservative and paint.

These elevations give principal dimensions and show method of setting out end frames which are made first.

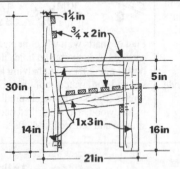

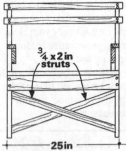

Note that the rails come inside the uprights and that seat and back slats are made to overhang about $1/2$ in at each end. The chair is strengthened by fixing diagonal struts as shown, one at back and other at front. Outside edges of slats should be rounded over with plane and glasspaper. Drill and countersink clearance holes for screws.

When using deal, all members should be liberally treated with preservative before assembly.

Construction of each end frame. Mark slope on back upright and saw outside line before planing smooth. Screw frames together temporarily and check that they match. Then glue and screw – except arm-rail, which must be left until seat slats have been fixed with glue and screws.

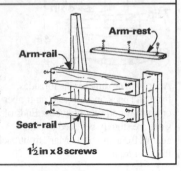

Problems
Around
the Home

Pages 96-128

Condensation with double glazing

All the benefits of double glazing can be undermined if it develops condensation problems between the two panes of glass.

With single-glazed window, steam or heavier condensation forms on cold glass when warmer, moist air from room strikes it.
Use of ventilator will usually reduce condensation, but wastes heat.

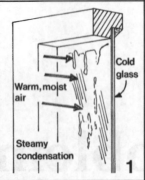

Cold glass

Warm, moist air

Steamy condensation

1

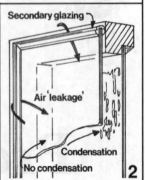

Secondary glazing

Air 'leakage'

Condensation

No condensation

2

Secondary/double glazing reduces condensation, but if not fully sealed to frame warm, moist air can 'leak' into space between panes, causing condensation on outer pane.

Good seal is important.

Trouble is reduced if new glazing is fixed or re-sealed when weather is warm and dry.

Alternative is to admit some outside air through plastic tubes fitting closely in inclined holes as shown. Lightly stuff ends of tubes with, eg., glass fibre.

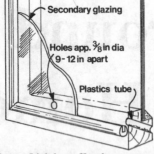

Secondary glazing

Holes app. $\frac{3}{8}$ in dia
9 - 12 in apart

Plastics tube

3

Another method is to make muslin 'sausage' bags and fill with silica-gel, from chemist; this absorbs moisture.

Remove bags from time to time, and dry out in a warm (turned off) oven.

Secondary pane

Muslin bag with silica-gel

4

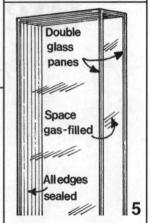

Double glass panes

Space gas-filled

All edges sealed

5

Most reliable method for new windows is to have special d.g. panels; space between glass panes is filled with inert gas and edges sealed.

Curing door and window rattles

A door or window that rattles can be infuriating if your are trying to read or watch TV – and may be a source of heat loss too.

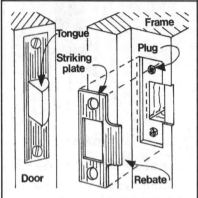

Door can rattle if not fully closed by latch tongue. To correct, remove striking plate and refit further into rebate after widening recess and, if necessary, mortise – as indicated by dotted lines. Plug original screw holes with wood splints and make new ones.

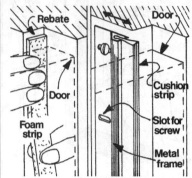

Rattle can often be prevented by using draught strip. Self-adhesive foam strip can be applied down edge of rebate (1); or another type of draught-strip (2) can be fixed to outside of frame so that door 'cushions' against it when closed.

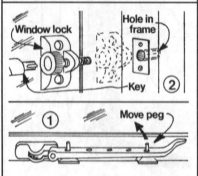

Hinged wooden casement windows can sometimes be made to close more firmly by slightly moving one stay peg (1); by moving catch plate for the handle; or, best, by fitting a window lock (2), which also gives increased security; it is operated by a special key supplied.

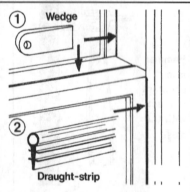

Sash windows may rattle because of looseness in frame, indicated in heavy lines and arrows.

The noise can be stopped by inserting rubber wedges (1) or, better, by pressing in replaceable rubber draught-strip (2); this is removed when window is to be opened.

Replacing a broken window pane

Even in the best run households, windows do get broken. It is much cheaper to replace glass yourself.

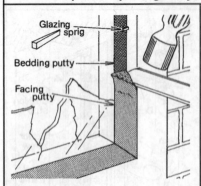

Hack out hard facing putty with an old knife and a hammer. Remove any glazing sprigs (used in wood frames only) and carefully remove and sweep up all broken glass; it is a good plan to wear gardening gloves for this.

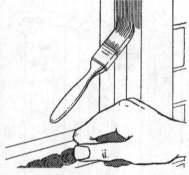

Chip out the bedding putty and coat the rebate with primer. From a ball of well-kneaded putty, press in a thin, even layer (use special putty for metal frames). Fit the new pane, which should be $1/8$in shorter and narrower than the opening.

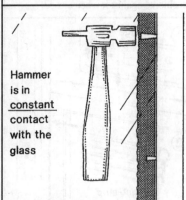

Press the glass firmly and evenly on to the bedding putty, with the palms of the hands, squeezing it to a thickness of $1/8$-$1/16$in.

Insert glazing sprigs about 18in apart; when driving them in, "slide" the hammer so that it is always in contact with the glass.

Press in the facing putty with a sweeping movement of the thumb. Then draw a putty knife firmly and slowly over it to leave a smooth surface.

Finally, trim off the bedding putty around the inside of the window.

Draught-proofing a door

With heating bills what they are today, any draught is worth tackling for the comfort of yourself and your bank balance.

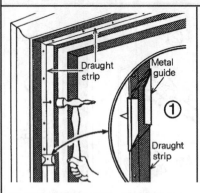

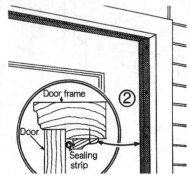

(1) Fixing hinged plastic draught strip to side of frame rebate. Keep it taut and set it straight with metal guide supplied with most makes. Slip guide over strip, drive in one pin, then temporarily fix strip by spiking guide into door frame.

Drive in a few more pins, then move the guide further down.

(2) Outside fitted draught seal, used mainly for exterior doors.

There are variants of the seal shown; all are fixed with door closed and with flexible sealing strip very lightly compressed against the door.

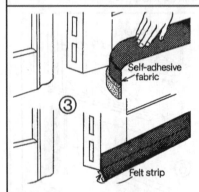

(3) Simplest type of door-bottom draught excluder (for interior doors) is self-adhesive fabric band edged with hard felt. Fix it, with door closed, so that felt presses lightly on floor.

Hinged 'mechanical' excluders on same principle, in wood or plastic, are fixed with screws.

(4) Threshold excluder, consisting of arched flexible plastic strip in aluminium frame; it is screwed or nailed to floor.

(5) Aluminium interlocking weather seal, for exterior doors. One member is screwed to threshold, other to inner side of door.

Draught-proofing a window

Windows, even if they are double glazed, are a great source of heat loss if they are a pathway for draughts. Here's how to stop them.

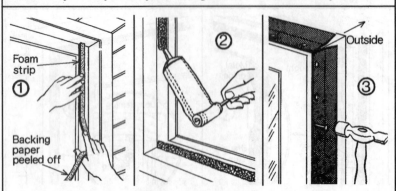

Three methods of treating a hinged casement window: 1 and 2 are suitable for either wood or metal frames; 3 is applicable to wood only. Shown are:

(1) Fitting self-adhesive foam strip around rebate on the outside. Window closes against the foam.

(2) Applying a special draught-seal mastic in place of foam. After laying a strip of mastic, wet inner face of window frame with lather and close window to compress the mastic; then open until mastic 'sets' – it remains flexible.

(3) Pinning hinged draught strip around the outer edge of the window itself.

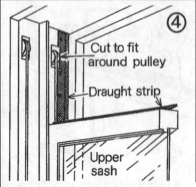

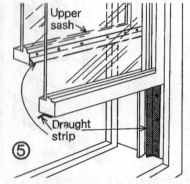

To seal a sliding-sash window use hinged plastic draught strip, following instructions supplied with it. Plastic is easier to fit; metal types possibly more effective.

(4) First pin strip down both sides of window case to full length of upper sash. Also pin a length to top edge of upper sash.

(5) Treat sides of case for lower sash in the same way, and pin a strip to bottom edge of lower sash. Also pin a strip to the inside face of the bottom (so-called 'meeting') rail of the upper sash.

Replacing broken sash cords

Sash windows are well worth looking after. They are often of an attractive design in themselves, and provide varied ventilation.

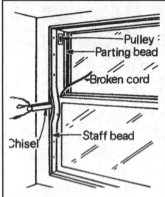

Prise off side staff beads, from centre to each end. Lower sash is then free and can be drawn forward. To remove upper sash, next prise out the parting bead.

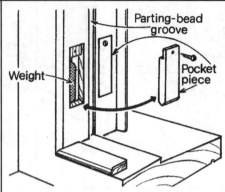

Prise out pocket piece (sometimes there is one for each sash, as shown) after removing any securing screws. Weight and end of cord can then be withdrawn. Remove other end of cord from sash and cut new piece to original total length.

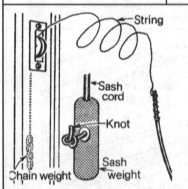

Bind length of string to end of new cord and tie small weight (eg. piece of chain) to end of string.

 Pass weight and string over pulley and use to pull cord through pocket.

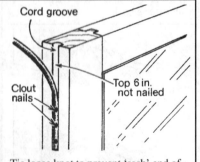

Tie loose knot to prevent 'sash' end of cord slipping over pulley, attach cord to weight, un-do loose knot and, with helper to support sash, fix cord to lower end of groove in sash with clout (large-head) nails.

NOTE: It is best to renew both cords of either sash if one is broken. If cords to upper sash are to be replaced do these first; then fit parting bead. Next do lower sash, and re-fix staff beads with new nails.

Repairs to rotted window frames

You can save yourself the cost of a new window frame by catching any rot in time and making good the damage.

The lower rail of a casement window is most prone to rotting due to water seeping in past loose or cracked putty.

If not treated soon enough repair is difficult, or a new frame may be required.

First scrape out all defective putty with a shave hook.

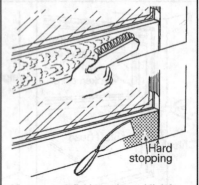

Next remove flaking paint and lightly scrub with a wire brush. If wood is soft and partly rotted liberally brush in p.v.a. (the milky white) wood adhesive when the wood is quite dry.

Repeat; then fill hollows and all open joints with hard stopping (from paint shop or ironmonger).

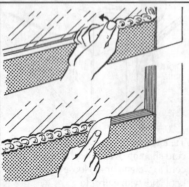

Holding a ball of putty in hand, press it well into the glass rebate with a sliding motion of the thumb.

Next level off with putty knife. When putty is hard (after week or so) give undercoat to putty and frame. Whole window can then be painted in usual way.

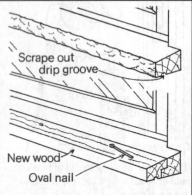

A partly rotted wood sill can be treated in same way as window frame. See that drip groove is clear; if not, water will seep under sill. When sill is badly rotted at front edge, cut off and fit new wood with waterproof glue and nails.

Remember to have a drip groove.

Repairs to leaded-light windows

If leaded windows are showing signs of wear and tear, you can do various things before considering a complete replacement.

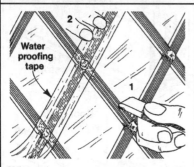

When rain enters, emergency repair can be made by carefully pressing down lead on outside with smooth knife handle (1), and then sealing with waterproof adhesive tape (2); tape is tough and transparent and not to be confused with ordinary adhesive tape.

Always have a helper support window on inside while working.

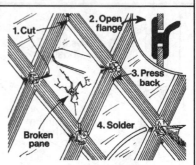

Remove a broken pane by cutting lead at each corner and carefully opening flange with knife blade. Fit new glass with mastic around the edges. Then press back lead and solder joints; use large, hot iron and resin-cored solder, taking care not to melt lead.

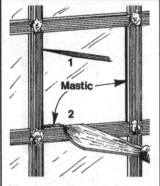

More permanent repair for water leakage is by raking out old mastic from channel (1), pressing in mastic with putty knife (2) and slightly pressing back lead.

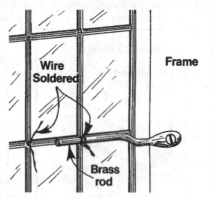

If window 'bows' under wind pressure, support can be given by fixing a shaped brass or steel rod across frame, inside, soldering lengths of copper wire to lead and binding these around rod.

When lead is perished and cracked, new window (plain or leaded) is required.

MASTIC can be a sealing compound or one made by well mixing metal-glazing putty with a little linseed oil to form stiff paste.

Weatherproofing a door

If bad weather can get past any of your outside doors, your home will not be all that cosy, and heating costs will probably soar.

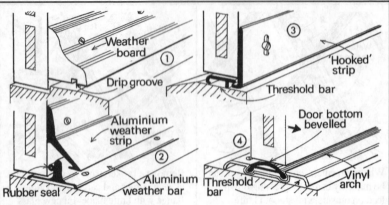

Rain is often prevented from driving under a door by the use of a conventional weather board (1), but see that the drip groove is not choked or damaged.

An aluminium weather strip is more effective when used with a threshold seal, of which one type is shown (2).

Another effective device is an aluminium interlocking seal with one element screwed to the threshold, the other to the inside of the door (3).

When using a threshold bar (external-door type) with arched vinyl seal (4) a separate weather strip is not required.

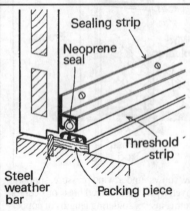

When the sill has steel weather bar and door is rebated, fit a strip-wood packing to support a threshold strip.

The type shown is used with alumin-ium/neoprene sealing bar screwed to outside of door.

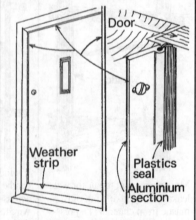

Having sealed door bottom, edges should be sealed against wind and weather.

Of many types of seal available, that shown is very effective and is adjustable after fitting because of slotted screw holes.

Treating rusted window frames

If you are planning to paint metal windows, it's vital that you first tackle any rust that has developed. Here's how.

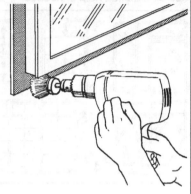

Rust and flaking paint must be dealt with before repainting.

Use a wire brush to remove it, but protect the glass, inside, with strips of self-adhesive plastic sheet; it can be re-used.

Glass protection is not needed on the outside, but avoid scratching the putty.

A wire cup brush in an electric drill makes the job easier, but wear goggles.

The flanges of hinged casements are best done from outside – with window wide open – where possible.

Do not apply too much pressure and move the brush in steady strokes.

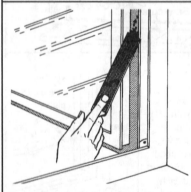

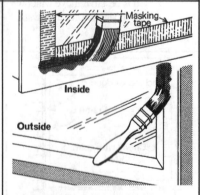

Use the tip of a file to scrape off hard rust patches; this is especially useful down the flange at the hinged edge of a casement.

Rust or thick accumulations of paint can prevent proper closing of the window and put undue strain on the hinges.

After rust removal, smooth with emery cloth and give a coat of special metal-priming paint. Go well into the shallow internal rebate, using masking tape around the glass. Follow with undercoat and gloss paint. You can paint the outside without masking.

Replacing window frames

Window replacement is job for more experienced workers. Carefully study the procedure and makers' catalogues and instructions to decide if skilled help is needed.

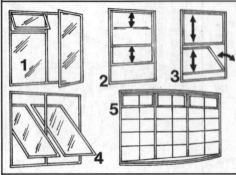

Five of many available types: (1) casement; (2) sliding sash; (3) sliding and pivoting sash; (4) pivot-hung; (5) Georgian bow.

Many come in choice of aluminium/steel, plain or anti-condensation treated; softwood, plain or plastic-encased; hardwood; or u.p.v.c. plastic. U.p.v.c. and plastic-coated frames need no maintenance. Pivoted types can be cleaned from inside.

To remove old window frame, remove hinged/sliding frames, take glass out of fixed frames. Make inclined saw-cuts in each frame member, including sill, and prise out with crow-bar. It is best to remove window board before sawing sill.

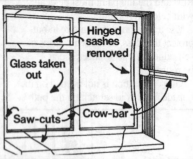

Hinged sashes removed

Glass taken out

Saw-cuts

Crow-bar

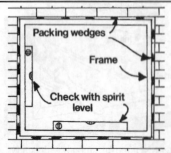

Packing wedges

Frame

Check with spirit level

After taking out old frame and cleaning opening, fit new frame, setting it square against a builder's spirit level, and packing with thin wood wedges. After frame is secured, fill gap with mortar or, if narrow, with flexible mastic.

Secure frame in opening with 2½-3in screws, set about 18in apart at each side, driven into wall plugs.

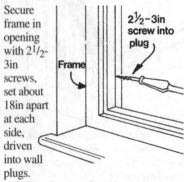

2½–3in screw into plug

Frame

Drill and counterbore for screws so that they come between wedges. Fill counterbored holes with wood pellets.

Dampness: doors & windows

When dampness appears around a door or window, it is time for some remedial action. Here's what to do.

Dampness which appears in a window reveal or beside the frame of an exterior door points to defective mastic on the outside; water seeps through the gap and soaks into the wall plaster.

Dampness under a window indicates faulty mastic and/or 'choked' drip groove in outside sill.

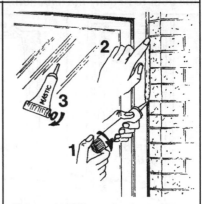

Rake out old filling and replace with flexible mastic. Apply with self-dispensing container (1), filling the gap. Then smooth off with moistened finger-tip (2).

For small jobs, small tube with turn-key (3) is convenient.

Test for rot with knife

Drip groove

Drip groove may have become choked after repeated painting, so that water runs under sill and into wall. If so, scrape out groove and apply new paint, leaving groove clear.

Check woodwork for rot (softening) with knife point.

Putty knife

When rotting is not severe treat by stripping paint, brushing in two coats 1:1 diluted woodwork adhesive: water; (1); make good with exterior filler (2) before rubbing down and repainting.

Treat only when wood is dry.

Dealing with twisted doors

Twisted doors can leave gaps through which draughts whistle. Fortunately, it is not always necessary to replace, or even remove the door to remedy the situation.

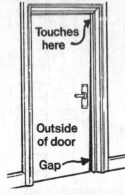

Twisted door leaves gap, usually at bottom (shown) or top of closing edge. Correction may be possible without removing door.

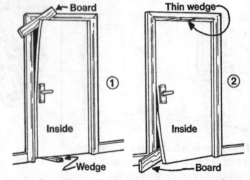

Thin (often old panelled interior) door can sometimes be trued as shown; where gap is at bottom (1); and at top of door (2). Objects is to twist door slightly in opposite direction; it will spring back a little when wedging is removed. Correction may take a few days, so method is usually applicable only when there is another exit from room.

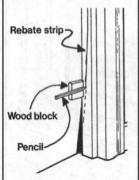

Another way is to scribe rebate strip to shape of (slightly curved) door. Mark as shown with pencil against wood block and then cut away along, or parallel to pencil line.

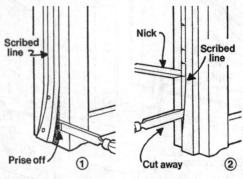

When rebate strip is nailed on (usual with modern doors) it can be cut to shape with spokeshave/chisel after carefully prising off (1). When rebate is moulded in framing (2) cut with sharp chisel: first make a series of nicks, to prevent splitting, and then cut to line. Finish by paring with chisel. rebate strip at top of frame may also need attention.

Lifting floorboards

It is sometimes necessary to lift floorboards to replace faulty ones or to gain access to the floor space. Make sure you employ the best method to avoid damaging good boards.

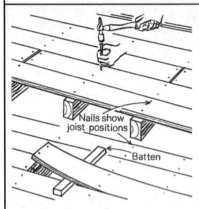

Nails show joist positions

Batten

To replace faulty board or gain access to pipes or cables, first remove board. With square-edge board, punch all nails through, prise up end, insert a batten and gradually lift whole board.

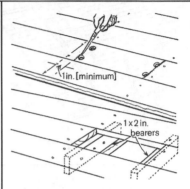

1in.[minimum]

1 x 2 in. bearers

When not convenient to lift whole board, bore 3/4in. holes as shown and saw across with keyhole, or pad, saw. Trim board end to side of joist and nail on bearers to which new board can be fixed.

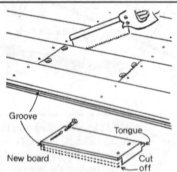

Groove

Tongue

New board

Cut off

With tongued-and-grooved boards, saw across ends, then saw off tongue. Lever out board and remove sawn tongue. Make new length of board and cut off shoulder of groove. Fix to bearers with nails or screws.

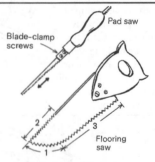

Pad saw

Blade–clamp screws

2

3

1

Flooring saw

A pad saw, or keyhole saw, is generally used by handymen, but a flooring saw is better if available. Start at centre of cut with curved end 1; then pierce with 2 and complete with 3. Holes are not required.

CAUTION: Turn off main electricity switch before starting, and saw with care to avoid damage to any cables or pipes under boards.

Replacing roof tiles

Replacing lost or damaged tiles is not a particularly difficult task, if you have a head for heights.

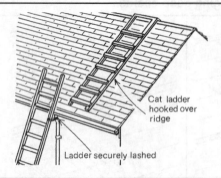

Cat ladder hooked over ridge

Ladder securely lashed

Attempt roof work only if you have a head for heights; and work from a ladder when possible. Ladder should project above eaves and be secured at both top (to down-pipe or other firm fixture) and bottom. Before climbing on to roof have a cat ladder, which hooks over the ridge.

If many tiles are loose or broken re-roofing may be necessary. A single plain tile can be replaced after gently wedging up the adjacent ones. Cut off nail heads where necessary with ripper, shown or thin strip of steel with sharp edge slid under the tiles. Secure new tile with strip of aluminium or zinc, bent to form a clip, fixed to a lath with galvanised nails.

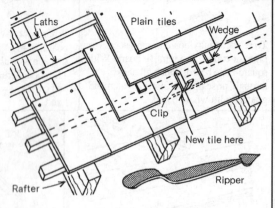

Laths

Plain tiles

Wedge

Clip

New tile here

Ripper

Rafter

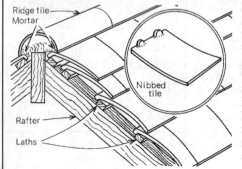

Ridge tile
Mortar

Nibbed tile

Rafter

Laths

Nibbed tiles are hooked over the laths, and a single tile can be replaced by easing up adjacent tiles and pushing the new one into place. Nails are generally used only at every fourth course and can be cut if necessary. Broken or loose ridge tiles (a half-round one is shown) can be replaced on a bed of mortar made by mixing cement, lime and sand in proportions 1:1:5.

Repairs to lath-and-plaster

If you live in an older house, sooner or later you'll have problems with lath-and-plaster work. If large areas are damaged, it is usually better to have work done by a plasterer.

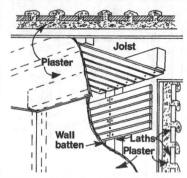

With this finish (usually only in older houses) laths are nailed across the joists, or wall battens, and plaster is pressed through the laths so that it forms a 'key' behind them as shown in insets. It breaks away if laths are faulty.

Cracks and small areas of damaged plaster can be filled with cellulose filler. But where laths are broken, first pack hole with crumpled newspaper soaked in thin filler (1). When dry, apply filler, mixed to a thick paste, with small trowel (2).

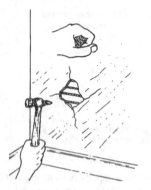

All cracked, loose plaster (test by tapping with knuckle) should be chipped away until a firm and 'solid' area is reached. Take care to avoid damaging laths.

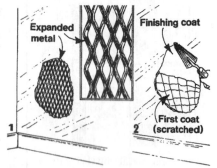

Where laths are broken over larger area fix expanded metal over them (1), after coating cut edges with paint to prevent rusting. Then apply two coats of wall plaster. When first is nearly dry, scratch with tip of trowel; then apply second coat with large trowel or float to finish flush with existing plaster (2).

Stop draughts and save fuel

In these environmentally-aware days, one of the most effective ways an individual can make a difference is by burning less fuel in the home. Draughts therefore, have to be eliminated.

Most draughts come in around outside doors and opening windows, but they can also come through gaps between floorboards and between floor and skirting. Trace them with lighted candle or cigarette smoke.

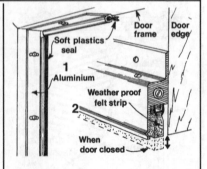

Fix draughts strip to top and sides of door frame (outside) and around casement window frame (inside). Adjust type shown (1) on screw slots so that seal touches closed door/window. Automatic draught excluder (2) seals bottom when door is closed; felt strip rises when door is opened.

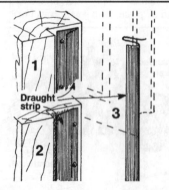

V-shape spring metal strip (1) is easy to fix; 'hinged' strip in spring metal or plastics (2) is simple and inexpensive. Special spring strip (3) can be clipped or slid on metal window frame.

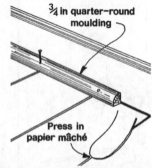

Seal floorboard gaps by pressing in paper mache with knife blade. Quarter-round moulding closes gap between floor and skirting. Fix with pins into floor.

NOTE: Fittings shown (chosen mainly for ease of fixing) are typical, but not necessarily best in all circumstances. Examine makers' leaflets to decide on most suitable cases.

Curing stair faults

Stairs in a state of disrepair can be very dangerous, but ensure you are not creating more problems as you work on them.

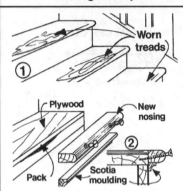

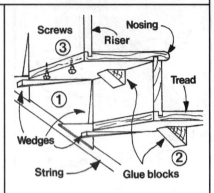

Carpet should not be laid over badly-worn treads (1). Trim off tread nose, fix 6/9mm. plywood to tread with flooring adhesive, packing near centre to ensure plywood cannot 'spring'. Fix new nosing (ex 1 x 1/2in.) with glue and screws (2). Then glue and pin Scotia moulding.

When underside of stars, shown, is accessible, creaks can be stopped by: (1) replacing and tightening any loose wedges, after coating with glue; (2) re-fixing or replacing loose glue blocks-usually three per step; or (3) by screwing through rear edge of tread into riser.

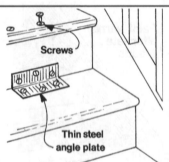

When it is not feasible to work on underside of stars, creaking can often be overcome by screwing through a 'springy' tread into the edge of the riser below (two, three screws should suffice) and/or by screwing thin metal angle plate in centre between tread and riser.

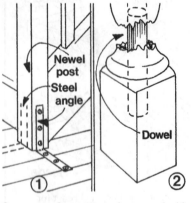

Loose newel post (1) can be secured with one-perhaps two-strong steel angle(s) recessed into floor and post. Broken baluster rail is best replaced but if matching rail not available, glued dowel can be used after accurate boring.

Dealing with worn stair treads

Uncarpeted stair treads can become worn after long use and can be dangerous, so early action is recommended.

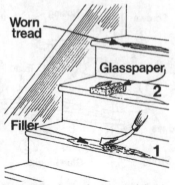

Scrub the stair treads clean and then make good with hard adhesive filler (1). Smooth off with glasspaper (2), after which treads can be covered and/or painted.

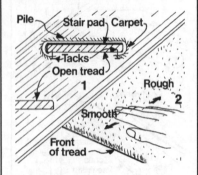

Normal stairs can be carpeted in usual way after fitting stair pads (felt or foam). Open treads can be carpeted with short lengths, bound if necessary, fixed as shown (1). In all cases, pile should point down stairs. Check by stroking with hand (2); carpet feels smooth in direction of pile.

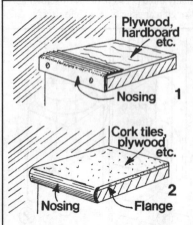

Instead of carpeting - and better for open treads - cover with plywood, sheet vinyl, etc. and fix aluminium/plastic nosings (1). Better appearance is obtained by fitting aluminium nosing shaped as (2). Covering (cork tiles, plywood etc.) is fixed over flange.

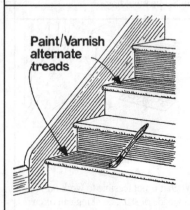

When steps are to be painted or polyurethane varnished do alternate steps so that stairs can still be used, striding over two steps at a time. When dry, do remaining steps. Apply subsequent coats in same sequence.

Using metal repair plates

Metal repair plates can bring new servicable life to all sorts of household furniture and fittings. As usually, though, make sure you use the right type.

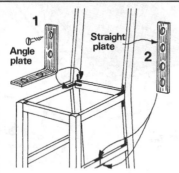

Angle plates (1) in steel or brass will strengthen loose joints of furniture in such positions as shown. Straight plates (2) can be fitted, one each side, to secure a break, after gluing. Do not use plates on antique or high-grade furniture, though; repair by traditional methods.

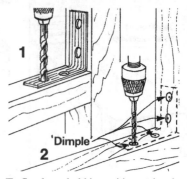

To fix plates, hold in position and make shallow 'dimples' with tip of drill diameter of screw hole in plate (1). Next make pilot holes, about 2/3 diameter or screws, in centre of each 'dimple' (2). Secure with screws that just fit holes in plate.

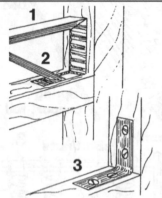

Appearance is improved by recessing plate. Draw around it and make series of chisel cuts (1), before scooping out waste (2). Fix plate as before, when it will appear as shown (3).

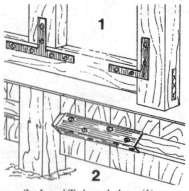

Large flat L and T-shaped plates (1) are useful at joints for frames of, for example, gates and doors; they can be recessed for better appearance if preferred. Long angle plates (2) are made for repairing broken or cracked arris rails of a fence.

Repairing a divan that sags

A sagging divan bed is not necessarily fit only for the rubbish dump. It can be retrieved without too much difficulty.

Deep sag near centre

When a divan bed is seen to sag badly near the centre, a satisfactory repair can often be made if the bed is other-wise in sound condition.

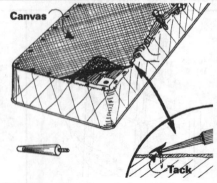

Canvas

Tack

Remove headboard, turn bed upside down, unscrew legs and take off canvas; do not disturb cover material, edge of which will be found underneath. Drive out each tack by holding screwdriver under head at low angle and striking with side of hammer.

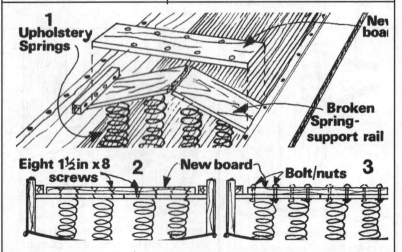

1 Upholstery Springs

New boar

Broken Spring-support rail

Eight 1½ in x 8 screws 2

New board

Bolt/nuts 3

When canvas is removed you will probably find a broken rail similar to that shown (1). Make a strong board to fit across broken one and drill/countersink for screws (2); press down over break and drive in screws, checking that springs are aligned. better, if access can be gained to underside of broken board, is to fit bolts, nuts and washers (3).

Rainproofing a roof

A leaky roof can cause all sorts of problems inside the house if not quickly dealt with. Prevention is better, obviously, than cure, so regularly check for loose tiles.

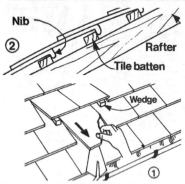

Loose or broken tile (1) can allow entry of rainwater. Slightly raise two tiles above broken one insert wedges; then raise faulty tile so that nibs (2) are clear of batten, and draw tile out. Slide in loose/new tile, pressing until nibs lock over batten.

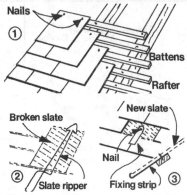

Slates are nailed at top or centre (1). To remove broken slate, cut nails with ripper (2) which can be hired. New slate can be slid in and secured with lead/zinc strip previously fixed with galvanised nail, then bend over bottom edge of slate (3).

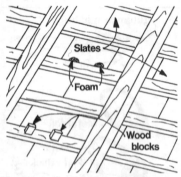

If roof is unlined, a loose slate can be fixed from inside. Ease slate upwards, clean both the slate and edge of batten and then fix small wood blocks coated with a quick-setting epoxy-resin adhesive. Or apply blobs of an adhesive-foam aerosol sealant.

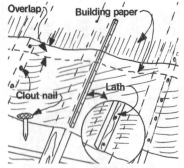

While working in loft is good time to line roof with foil-backed building paper or felt. Work downwards from ridge, overlapping lengths at least 3in. Secure with galvanised clout nails or, better, tack in place and secure with thin laths, using galvanised nails.

117

Keeping the weather out

The elements can play havoc with the structure of your house and the roof with all its fittings is the first place they will find an ingress.

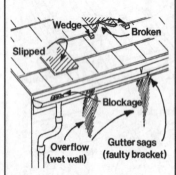

Check roof and gutters. Slipped tile can usually be pressed back into place. To replace broken tile, insert thin wedges, remove broken and slide in new tile. Overflowing gutter (causing damp in walls) can be caused by blocked down-pipe, sagging gutter.

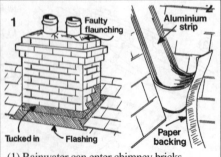

(1) Rainwater can enter chimney bricks through cracked flaunching - replace with mortar; defective pointing - re-point; cracked flashing - temporary repair by coating with bituminous mastic; flashing not tucked into horizontal brick joints - press in, re-point. Flashing can be replaced with sheet zinc; easier is to use adhesive aluminium flashing strip; similar can also be used (2) to seal leading valley gutter, between roofs at angle.

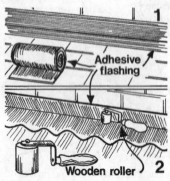

Leaking joint between wall and lean-to roof (tiled, slated [1], felted corrugated [2]) can be sealed with adhesive flashing of lead or aluminium foil. Make surfaces clean, dry and press down with, e.g. wooden roller.

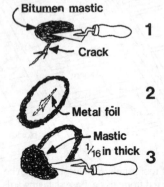

Fill cracks, holes in (well cleaned) flat felted, asphalt or concrete roof with bitumen mastic (1); press foil, canvas over it (2); apply more mastic (3). Whole roof can then be coated with bitumen waterproofer.

Treating mould

Mould - which may be greyish-green, black, brown - can form in any room where there is moisture, and especially if ventilation is not adequate.

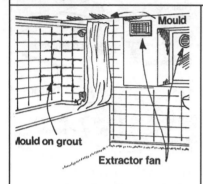

In a bathroom, trouble often occurs where steam from bath and/or shower can condense. Installation of wall or window extractor often effects a cure.

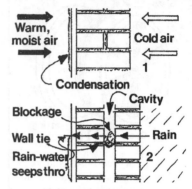

Condensation forms when warm, moist air strikes a cold surface (1); good ventilation soon dries the air. Dampness may cause mould when rainwater can seep through solid wall (1) or cavity wall with defect (2).

Mould is best removed, and further growth reduced/prevented by applying special fungicide (from builders' merchant) following makers' instructions. Or apply diluted household bleach, leave two hours, then wipe off.

It is sometimes better to rake out moulded tile grout (1), treat with fungicide/bleach, then press in water-resistant grout (2); smooth with wetted finger-tip (3). Polish tiles with tissues when dry.

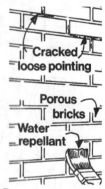

Prevent seepage through wall by replacing faulty pointing, brushing on water-repellant solution or applying masonry paint.

Room ventilation

Proper ventilation in your house will not only prevent the growth of mould but will also help to create a healthier atmosphere.

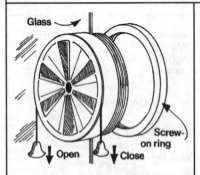

Simple type of open-close ventilator fixed through circular hole in window pane. In clear plastic, it has internal 'fan', operated by air-flow, which indicates when open. Though suitable for living-rooms, bedrooms, it may not suffice for steamy kitchen or bathroom.

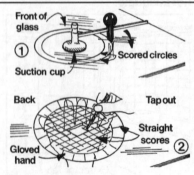

To install ventilator (or extractor with similar mounting) fix new pane, with hole cut by glass merchant. Or (not easy!) hole can be cut as shown: first score two circles with radial glass cutter (1); score series of straight lines (2); tap out over gloved hand; trim edge with pliers.

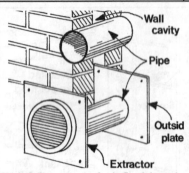

Wall-fitting extractor fan is fixed through hole made in outside wall, through which is passed plastic tube (sawn to correct length) or telescopic metal pipe. Hole is cut out with cold chisel and club hammer, preferably after drilling central hole through wall from inside.

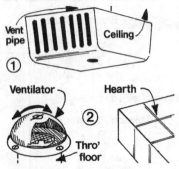

(1) Ceiling-mounted extractor for lavatory/shower operates from light circuit; remains on for set time after switching off light. (2) Open-close ventilator for draught-free air to open or gas fire, takes air from under wooden floor.

NOTE: Different brands of extractor fan vary quite a bit in shape and installation method. Study makers' instructions carefully - preferably before purchase.

Waterproofing a felted shed roof

Worn or damaged roof felting can be easily replaced without have to completely re-roof the shed.

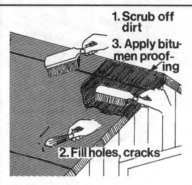

1. Scrub off dirt
3. Apply bitumen proofing
2. Fill holes, cracks

If felt is not badly worn it can be renovated by removing dirt and moss (1), filling any holes and cracks with bitumen mastic, using putty knife dipped in paraffin (2) and then coating all over with bitumen waterproofing paint (3).

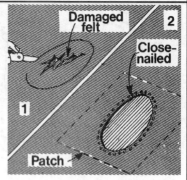

Damaged felt
Close-nailed
Patch

Repair any damaged area (1) by cutting around with sharp knife and inserting large piece of roofing felt as patch (2). Apply bitumen water-proofing under edges and secure with galvanised felting nails about 25 mm. apart. Paint roof with bitumen proofing.

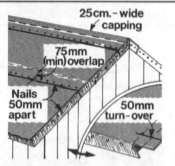

25 cm. - wide capping
75 mm (min) overlap
Nails 50 mm apart
50 mm turn - over

Badly worn/perished felt can be stripped and replaced. Lay lengths of felt along roof, starting at eaves. Cut out corners, turn 50 mm. over edges, keep taut and fix with galvanised nails. Lay next length overlapping first and finish at ridge with capping strip.

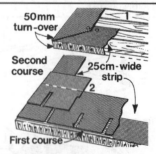

50 mm turn-over
Second course
25 cm- wide strip
First course

If slope is 30 deg. or more re-covering can be with strips of slate-effect felt. First fix plain felt along eaves and verges (1). Lay first course and start second with 1 1/2 tiles, as shown. On exposed site put dab of mastic under tab of each slate.

NOTE: Felt should be laid flat 24 hours before fixing. Slate tiles come in cartons to cover 5 sq. metres; study directions enclosed or get maker's instruction leaflet.

121

Dealing with woodworm

Woodworm, whether in your furniture or floorboards, will soon make a meal of your house unless you take immediate action.

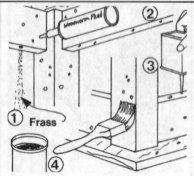

Furniture woodworm is often on underside (1). Examine, especially if 'frass' (fine white dust) is seen. Simple treatment is with special Aerosol of woodworm fluid (2). Or turn piece upside down and apply fluid with can having special nozzle (3); and/or brush fluid into wood (4).

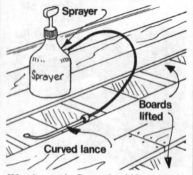

Woodworm in floors should be treated both on top and underneath. Take up a few boards - say every third - and use garden-type 'pump-up' sprayer with curved lance, as shown. Spray affected timbers in loft in same way, but wear face mask, goggles in such confined space.

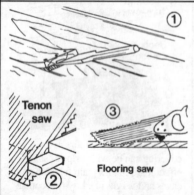

Prise up square-edge floorboards with, e.g., wide cold chisel (1) at a board end. When tongued-and-grooved (2) it is usually necessary to saw through tongue along one edge. It can be done with tenon saw, but i is easier with a flooring saw (3), if available.

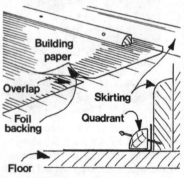

If vinyl flooring is to be relaid (not recommended) over floor treated with preservative or fluid first put down foil-backed building paper as protection. Give good overlap at joins and, preferably, turn paper up wall at least 1/2in. and cover with quadrant moulding.

Avoiding condensation

Condensation not only causes the problem of steamy windows but the moisture can cause untold damage unless checked.

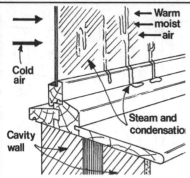

Cold air

Warm
moist
air

Steam and
condensation

Cavity
wall

Condensation is caused when warm, moist air strikes a colder surface - as on a window pane, or even a cold wall or plain metal window frame. Better ventilation, to reduce moisture, is best remedy but can be costly in heat-loss. Double-glazing often reduces the nuisance.

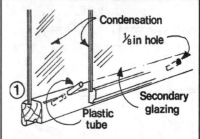

Condensation

⅛ in hole

① Plastic
tube

Secondary
glazing

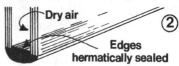

Dry air

②

Edges
hermatically sealed

Secondary (double) glazing (1) may prevent condensation of inner pane, but not between panes - where removal is difficult. Two or there small holes to outside air usually reduces trouble. Sealed d.g. units (2) prevent it because between-glass air is always dry.

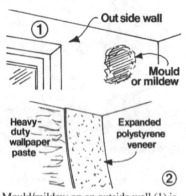

① Out side wall

Mould
or mildew

Heavy-
duty
wallpaper
paste

Expanded
polystyrene
veneer

②

Mould/mildew on an outside wall (1) is probably caused by condensation. Dry out (with e.g. hair drier) then apply fungicide as makers direct. Avoid further trouble by lining wall with polystyrene veneer (2); this gives thermal insulation and can be papered or emulsion-painted.

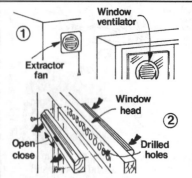

Window
ventilator

① Extractor
fan

Window
head

②

Open-
close

Drilled
holes

Opening window helps but wastes heat. Extractor fan/ventilator in kitchen, bathroom should be fitted as high as possible in outside wall/window opposite door (1). For bedrooms open-close ventilator in window head (2) may suffice.

Treatment for damp walls

Never redecorate a wall without first dealing with any damp patches. Where possible, treat them at source - outside.

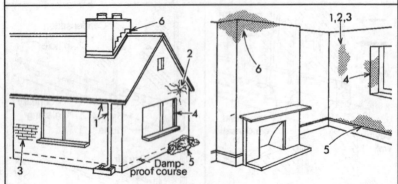

Some main causes are shown, with the effects they produce. These are (with basic cures): 1, overflowing or leaking gutter or downpipe (clean out, repair or replace); 2, fault in rendering (hack off and replace damaged rendering); 3, faulty pointing (rake out and repoint) and/or porous bricks (give two coats of silicone water repellent); 4, seepage between window frame and brickwork (fill with mastic); 5, earth etc. heaped above damp-proof course (remove) or faulty damp-proof course (call in a builder); 6, damaged lead apron around chimney stack (have replaced).

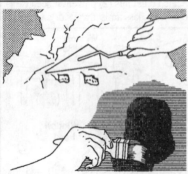

After curing fault, strip paper from damp patch and 2-3ft. around it; better still, from whole wall. Rake out and replace any badly damaged plaster. Smooth wall and well brush in a fungicide or household disinfectant. Then paint on a waterproof sealer, following makers' instructions. Both preparations are stocked by builders' merchants.

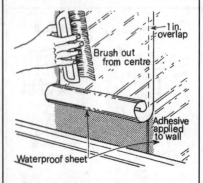

For an even better result, next cover the area or the whole wall with special waterproof sheet. You can get rolls of metal foil, plastic-laminated sheet or treated paper from a builders' merchant. It must be fixed with the special water-resistant adhesive recommended for the particular sheeting used.

Fitting a wall ventilator

A ventilator is often the best cure for kitchen condensation and is not too difficult to install.

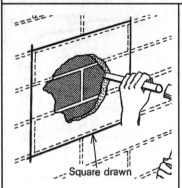

Square drawn

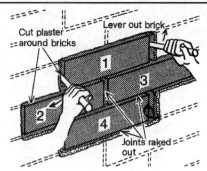

Cut plaster around bricks

Lever out brick

Joints raked out

A ventilator can be fitted near the cooker, through an outside wall; the method shown applies to the usual cavity brick wall. Mark approximate position of 9 x 9 in. ventilator on wall and back out plaster in centre to find positions of bricks.

Adjust position of opening so that there is a whole brick across top and bottom and cut away plaster to shape shown. Chip and rake mortar joints and lever out bricks in the sequence indicated. Repeat on outside wall, finding position by measurement or by drilling through a joint from inside. First brick may have to be broken.

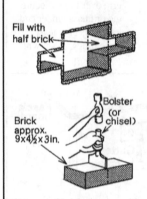

Fill with half brick

Bolster (or chisel)

Brick approx. 9x4½x3in.

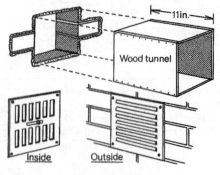

11in.

Wood tunnel

Inside   Outside

Cut one of bricks in two with cold chisel, or with 'bolster' (wide chisel); wet exposed bricks and replace two half bricks with mortar made from 1 part cement to 4 sand.

Make simple wood box tunnel to fit hole and reaching from inside to outside of wall. Fix tunnel with mortar and repair wall on inside with plater filler. Screw 'open-close' ventilator plaster on inside and louvre plate on outside. For still better ventilation, fix extractor fan in hole (following maker's instructions). Most extractor fans are supplied complete with a metal tunnel.

Correcting roofing tiles/guttering

Slipped or fallen tiles (1) should be dealt with as soon as possible; neglect can result in further damage.

Widely used tiles (2) have 'nibs' which fit over the tiling battens (3). A loose tile can be carefully pressed back into position. A fallen one can be replaced by pressing new one under overhanging tiles; if necessary, slightly raise latter by inserting wood wedges.

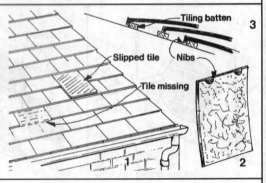

When damage is not close to eaves use (hired) roof ladder of type with hooks and wheels at one end. Wheel up roof, then turn over so that hooks grip over ridge. Secure the ordinary ladder and let it project at least three rungs, as shown.

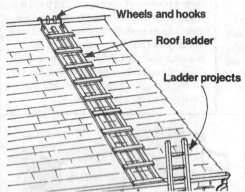

Gutter should be in straight line, free from debris, and have slight 'Fall' towards down-pipe (1). If it sags (2) or is blocked overflowing can cause damp wall. Check with bucket of water. Replace any faulty gutter bracket (3).

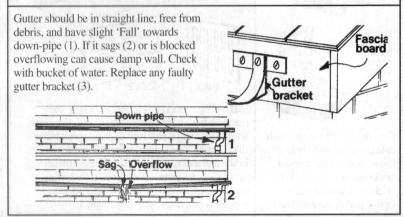

Repairs to wood block flooring

Beautiful wooden floors can be marred by just one damaged block, but fortunately they are relatively easy to replace.

Take out loose blocks and tap adjacent ones with a hammer. Lift any that sound 'hollow' because they would probably become loose later. When there are loose blocks over a large area suspect rising damp; if any traces remove blocks and allow to dry slowly.

Bitumen-rubber adhesive

Re-fix blocks with bitumen-rubber flooring adhesive or waterproofer adhesive of similar type. Pour a little on floor and spread evenly with old brush or fine-tooth spreader (shown). Allow it to become just tacky and fit each block in turn, pressing firmly down.

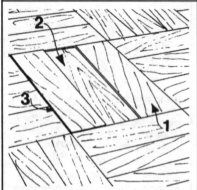

Ideally, new block should lie exactly flush (1). If it tends to be 'low' (2) lift and apply adhesive to base of block; fit when adhesive is tacky. Should a block be very slightly 'proud' (3) it can be levelled by sanding after adhesive has set.

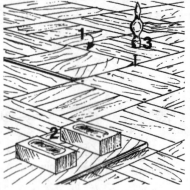

(1) Plywood panels or tiles simulating blocks sometimes tend to curl (e.g. after installing central heating). Lift and apply thin coat of adhesive. When tacky replaces panel and (2) cover with weighted board or (3) secure to wood floor with panel pins.

Dealing with damp

One chore which should never be put off for another day is treating damp, if left it can become a serious hazard.

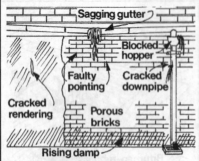

Some exterior causes of interior dampness which should first be checked and, if necessary, corrected. After curing overflow faults, defective pointing, porous bricks can be treated with two coats of a colourless water-repellant or with masonry paint. Cracked, loose rendering should be removed, replaced. Rising damp calls for other treatment.

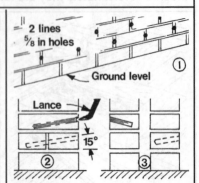

Rising damp in a wall, through absence of (in old house) or defective damp-proof course is best treated by specialist, but can be done by drilling 5/8-3/4in. holes into brickwork (1) and injecting damp-proofing fluid with lance of pressure sprayer (2). Cavity wall (3) needs to be treated from both sides.

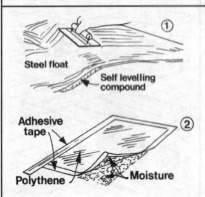

Slight rising damp in solid floor can be cured by brushing a special damp-proofer over floor. Alternative is to use damp-proofing self-levelling compound, spread with steel float (1). In doubt, fix polythene to floor; if underside is damp when lifted two days later, damp is confirmed (2).

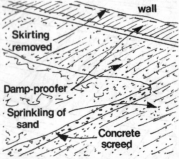

For more serious rising damp, remove skirting, spread two coats of bituminous damp-proofer over floor and up wall to level of d.p.c., sprinkle sand over it and then lay concrete screed at least 2in. thick. (This raises floor level). Before using any proprietary damp-proofer study makers' literature for detailed instructions.

Things to Make

Pages 130-184

Making adjustable toy stilts

If you have adventurous children – or grandchildren, nephews or nieces – here's how to make them a toy with a long history.

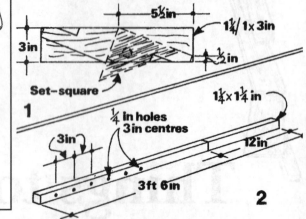

Stilts can be adjusted over a wide range by moving foot blocks, secured with coach bolts and wing nuts.

Hardwood such as beech is best, but sound, knot-free softwood will serve. Both blocks (1) are made from 12in length of $1^1/_4$-1in x 3in (nominal) planed timber. Set out side slopes by measurement and mark end at right-angles against set-square. Saw and plane both to shape before sawing in two. Mark and drill handles (2).

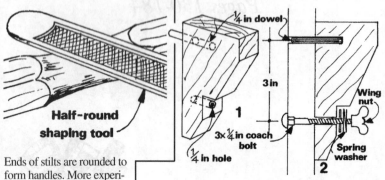

Half-round shaping tool

Ends of stilts are rounded to form handles. More experienced worker would use chisel or spokeshave, but half-round shaping tool can be used, followed by flat shaping tool and glass-paper. Make really smooth.

Drill two $^1/_4$in holes exactly 3in apart in blocks, as shown, and glue length of dowel in upper one (1).

Coach bolt passing through stilt handle goes through lower hole and is fitted with large washer, spring or locking washer, and wing nut (2). Dowel plugs into next hole above, so holding block firm and rigid.

Making a nursery chest/toy box

Here's a chance to use your woodworking skills – or at least improve them – with a useful item for young children.

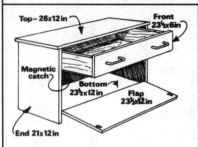

Unit can conveniently be made in white plastic-veneered chipboard 12in wide.

One 6ft board will make both ends and top; another, bottom, flap and drawer front. Sawn edges are covered with matching iron-on edging strip.

Blockboard 3/4in thick could be used instead, and painted. If ready-made or kit drawer is used, some measurements may need slight modification.

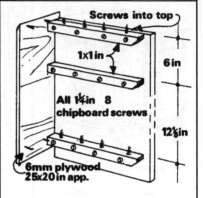

Parts are fixed together, and drawer runner provided, with 1x1in planed softwood fillets glued and screwed to ends, top and bottom as shown.

First assemble without glue and check fit of flap and drawer front.

Secure plywood back with glue and 3/4in panel pins 3in apart.

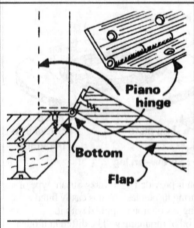

Flap front is fixed to bottom with piano hinge 1in-1 1/4 in. wide (when open) sawn to 23 1/2in long. Fix to lower edge of flap first, making small starting holes for 1/2in chipboard screws.

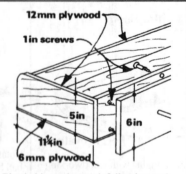

Plastic kit can be used, following makers' instructions, or drawer made to fit opening as shown; dimensions given are approximate. Fix parts together with woodworking adhesive and 1 1/4 in panel pins. Fix drawer front with adhesive and eight 1in screws.

Making revolving bookcase/table

Here's an attractive and useful piece of furniture on which to develop your woodworking skills. Have a go!

6in legs

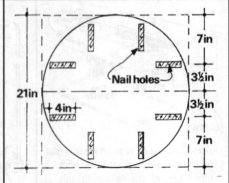

7in

Nail holes

21in

3½in

4in

3½in

7in

Circular bookcase is carried on turntable fitted between book-case itself and matching leg base.

After assembly, top could be covered with laminate, edges with edging strip; or whole could be painted/varnished.

Cut out three discs of $^3/_4$in blockboard with coping saw after marking two, as shown, for positions of uprights. Mark accurately and drill $^3/_{32}$in holes for nails. Smooth sawn edges with shaping tool and glasspaper. Then prepare uprights in blockboard, making ends square and rounding over outside edges.

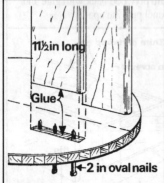

11½in long

Glue

2 in oval nails

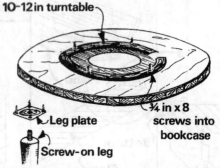

10-12in turntable

¾ in x 8 screws into bookcase

Leg plate

Screw-on leg

Fix uprights with woodworking adhesive and 2in oval nails.

Slightly recess nail heads with punch and fill holes with plastic wood.

Set true, leave overnight until adhesive sets, and then smooth with fine glasspaper.

Rotation is provided by a 'Lazy Susan' type of ball bearing turntable, which is easily fitted following instructions supplied with it.

Method of mounting will be different if other type of turntable is used; follow makers' instructions, taking care that turntable is accurately centred.

Screw-on legs are fixed with plates and screws provided.

Making spice jar shelves & racks

If you want to make your woodworking skills useful in the kitchen, how about trying one of these simple racks or shelves?

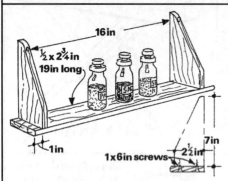

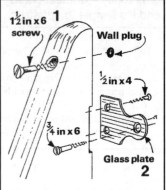

Simple shelf for wall mounting made in hardwood (eg. elm, oak, beech) and finished in polyurethane varnish. It will take eight jars 2in diameter. Saw ends to shape, round over corners and edges, and smooth with glasspaper.

Make shelf, drill and countersink for screws, and fix to ends with chipboard screws.

Alternative methods of fixing to wall plugs. (1) bore $5/16$in hole through centre for screws. (2) Make shallow recess with chisel or file and screw on 1in glass plates.

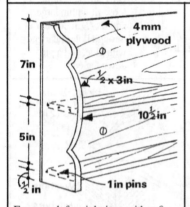

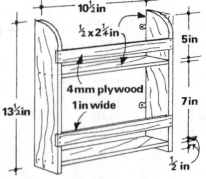

Fancy rack for eight jars, with softwood ends and shelves, plywood back. Shape ends with coping saw and smooth with glasspaper.

Glue and pin shelves and back, punch down pin heads and fill holes. Screw through back into wall plugs.

Rack for eight jars, made to screw on inside of a cupboard door. Could be in softwood, painted to match door.

Strips of plywood (clear plastic is better if available) recessed into ends support jars, which should fit snugly; modify dimensions for larger, smaller jars.

Making a toy ironing board

Here's a useful toy to help get the kids – boys as well as girls today – domesticated, and it's simple to construct.

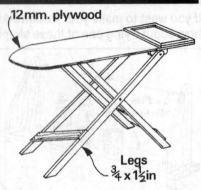

12mm. plywood

Legs
³/₄ x 1½in

Top is made from 12mm plywood and has simple iron tray at end. Shaped portion can have cover of cotton material, fixed on underside with drawing pins. Legs are in ³/₄ x 1½in nominal planed wood, which will actually measure about ⁵/₈ x 1¼in.

5in
6 in
5in
Dowel
11in
10in
30in
Ply-wood
3in
6in
8 in
7in
10in

Shape plywood top with coping saw and smooth with shaping tool and glasspaper. Form tray with ³/₈ x ³/₈in strips secured with panel pins.

Make larger leg frame first, gluing and pinning on 3mm plywood brace. Have smaller frame loose fit within larger, and fix ³/₈in dowel rod through holes near end with glue, and a pin down leg end.

Larger leg frame is pivoted on wood blocks (1) glued and screwed on top.

Small block with piece of plywood (2) serves as hook for end of smaller frame. All pivot fixings are with screws fitted with large washers; leg frames are pivoted together as shown (3).

Blocks
³/₄ x 1½in
3in long

3mm. plywood
3x2 in

2 washers
washers
³/₁₆in hole
1¼ in x 8

Clearance hole is made through outer frame and screw grips firmly in inner one. After assembly, mark and saw off legs so that table stands level.

Making a lady's dressing stool

Now here is an elegant piece of furniture that will look well in any bedroom, whether the lady herself or her partner makes it.

For more experienced wood-worker, stool can be made in hardwood, varnished; or soft-wood, painted.

Deep cushion, 18 x 12in, can be made with fabric or up-holstery-vinyl case stuffed with foam chips and 'buttoned'; buttons, both sides, are sewn together with linen thread.

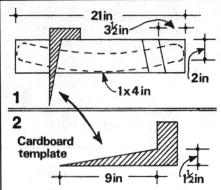

1 21in 3½in 1x4in 2in

2 Cardboard template 9in 1½in

Mark out side rails on 1 x 4in planed timber (1).

Draw on leg positions against cardboard template (2). Do all marking-out before sawing curves with coping or keyhole saw.

Keep outside lines and then smooth with shaping tool and glasspaper, or with spokeshave.

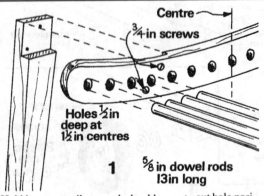

Centre ¾in screws

Holes ½in deep at 1½in centres

1 ⅝in dowel rods 13in long

2 19in ex 1x2in 1in

Hold legs over rails to mark shoulder lines for joints. Set marking gauge to half wood thickness and mark depth of all halvings.

Cut out halvings and fit joints; when correct, taper legs (2) and fix to rails with glue and screws (1).

Trim ends after glue has set and mark out hole positions from centre outwards.

Bore holes in which dowels are good fit, slightly radius dowel ends, brush glue in holes and assemble.

Stand on level surface till glue sets.

Building a toy Jeep

Even in this age of video games and TV for kids, this is one toy that should go down well with most younger boys and girls.

Popular toy is made from oddments of softwood and plywood, and fitted with ready-made tyred wheels. Length of bent wire serves as windscreen frame, and is a tight fit in holes in bonnet. After well sanding, apply undercoating and grey-green eggshell paint before fitting wheels.

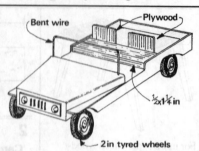

Cut out chassis from 1 x 6in planed softwood (which will measure about $^7/_8$ x $5^3/_4$in).

Make bonnet-wings unit from 12mm or $^1/_2$in and 3 or 4mm or $^1/_8$in plywood; wider end of bonnet overhangs chassis by the thickness of the plywood sides.

Cut back and sides, shaping with coping or fret saw.

Fix parts together with glue and panel pins: $^1/_2$in for thin plywood, $1^1/_4$in for the rest.

Attach bonnet-wings assembly to base, then axle beams and plywood side.

Fix wheels, using screws with push-on domed plastic caps (1).

Use thin plywood, lined as grille, for radiator, and capped screws as headlamps (2). Make and fit seats last, using strip of wood with plywood rectangles for backs.

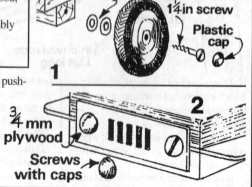

Making a drop-side dolls cot

This could be just the ticket for a daughter, granddaughter or niece – or even a young male relative in these days of political correctness.

Toy is a scaled down version of child's cot and has ready-made scale drop-side fittings.

One side and base are fixed to ends; other side slides up and down. Cot can be painted with lead-free enamel and transfers applied to ends.

Ends in 9mm plywood are sawn and smoothed to shape. Then bearers for plywood base are glued and pinned on as shown; base is glued and pinned to bearers after fixing one side with glued dowels.

Drop-side is fitted after securing other side and base.

Labels in upper-right diagram: Fixed side; 9mm plywood 20×12 in; ¼ in dowels 1½ in long; ¾ in pins; ¾ × ¾ in 10¼ in long; 9mm plywood base

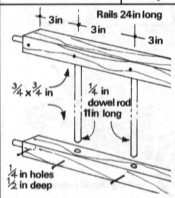

Labels: Rails 24 in long; 3in; 3in; 3in; ¾ × ¾ in; ¼ in dowel rod 11 in long; ¼ in holes ½ in deep

Both sides are made in same way, but drop-side is ¼ in shorter and rail ends are not dowel-jointed. Bore holes ½ in deep in softwood rails and insert dowels. Adjust if necessary, then re-assemble with glue, lock dowel ends with pins and punch down heads.

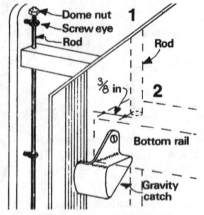

Labels: Dome nut; Screw eye; Rod; **1**; Rod; ⅜ in; **2**; Bottom rail; Gravity catch

Drop-side is carried on steel rod passing through three screw eyes, near top, bottom and centre, ends secured with dome nuts (1).

Gravity catch (supplied with fittings) is screwed on inner face of each end and automatically holds side in raised position (2).

Make a waddling, pull-along duck

Here is another delightful child's toy that you can make for a young family member, and hone your woodworking skills at the same time.

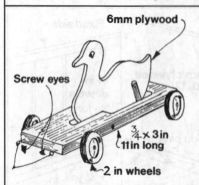

6mm plywood

Screw eyes

$\frac{3}{4} \times 3$ in 11 in long

2 in wheels

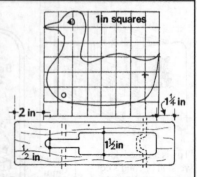

1in squares

2 in

$\frac{1}{2}$ in $1\frac{1}{2}$ in

$1\frac{1}{4}$ in

Mark out plywood and cut with coping saw. Form slot in base with coping saw after boring five $\frac{1}{2}$ in holes.

Drill hole near front of duck and through base to take $\frac{1}{8}$ in wire pivot; tight fit in base, loose through plywood. Have washer each side of duck.

Duck is made to pivot, and rocks as toy is pulled along. Movement is obtained by using a simple crank-axle for rear wheels, along with a strip of metal/plastic as push-rod.

Duck can be painted yellow, with base in red or blue.

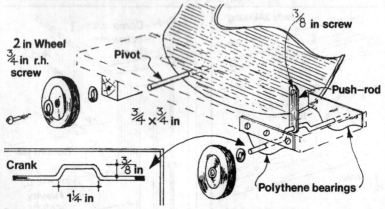

2 in Wheel
$\frac{3}{4}$ in r.h. screw

Pivot

$\frac{3}{8}$ in screw

Push–rod

$\frac{3}{4} \times \frac{3}{4}$ in

Crank $\frac{3}{8}$ in
$1\frac{1}{4}$ in

Polythene bearings

Screw 2in plastic wheels to block at front. Rear wheels are made tight fit on ends of cranked axle; use soft wire bent to shape shown and serrate ends with cold chisel to grip in wheel – or secure with epoxy glue.

Make push-rod from strip metal/plastic.

Then make two bearings with pieces cut from heavy-gauge polythene container and screw to sides of base. Screw push-rod, with washer each side, to duck.

As toy is pulled, crank and push-rod cause duck to move up and down on the front pivot.

Build a wall-unit for a teenager

Before setting to on this job, it would probably be best to discuss its design with the teenager who is going to use it.

Unit shown is 8ft long, but could be shorter. It provides central dressing table with mirror, one end that serves as a writing desk with bookshelves above, and the other as hi-fi accommodation with record rack above.

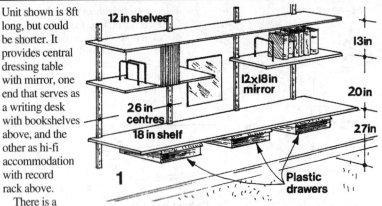

12 in shelves

13in

12x18in mirror

20in

26 in centres

18 in shelf

27in

1

Plastic drawers

There is a moulded plastic drawer (about 15in wide and 16in long) for each section. All shelves are in vinyl-faced chipboard, which may be plain white or wood-grain.

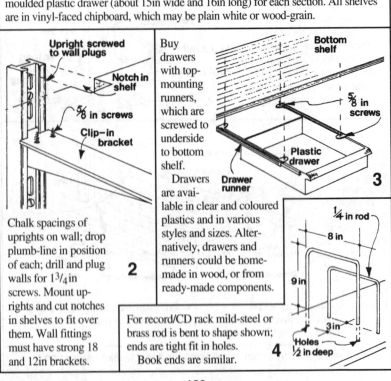

Upright screwed to wall plugs

Notch in shelf

$\frac{5}{8}$ **in screws**

Clip–in bracket

Chalk spacings of uprights on wall; drop plumb-line in position of each; drill and plug walls for $1^3/_4$in screws. Mount uprights and cut notches in shelves to fit over them. Wall fittings must have strong 18 and 12in brackets.

2

Buy drawers with top-mounting runners, which are screwed to underside to bottom shelf.

Drawers are available in clear and coloured plastics and in various styles and sizes. Alternatively, drawers and runners could be home-made in wood, or from ready-made components.

Bottom shelf

$\frac{5}{8}$ **in screws**

Plastic drawer

Drawer runner

3

For record/CD rack mild-steel or brass rod is bent to shape shown; ends are tight fit in holes.

Book ends are similar.

$\frac{1}{4}$ in rod

8 in

9 in

3 in

Holes $\frac{1}{2}$ in deep

4

Build a refectory table in pine

This makes an ideal breakfast table for the kitchen, or even a corner of some living rooms or in a modern conservatory.

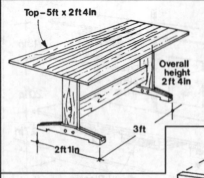

Top – 5ft x 2ft 4in

Overall height 2ft 4in

3ft

2ft 1in

Table is made without joints, leg frames being built up from separate pieces of timber . Top is planed, tongued and grooved boards 1in (nominal) thick; $4\frac{1}{2}$ in boards – which 'make' 4in when fitted together – are preferred but wider ones could be used.

Timber is yellow pine or prime northern pine (red deal), varnished or waxed.

Details of leg frame, which should be 2ft 3in high for chairs with seats 18in high.

Cross-arms are glued and dowelled to upright and rail is fixed with glue and dowels.

Feet blocks are glued and nailed to base. Take care that leg assembles are identical and stand exactly upright.

$2\frac{1}{2}$ in x 8

1x 2in
2ft 3in long

$\frac{1}{2}$ in dowels

1x6in rail

foot block

1x6in

1x3in

2ft 1in long
1x3in
4 long

Plane tongue or groove off edge boards and pull together with two cramps.

Temporarily nail batten near each end until top is glued and screwed to legs.

Cramps can be improvised from stout boards with blocks screwed on.

Apply pressure by driving in folding wedges made by sawing down hard-

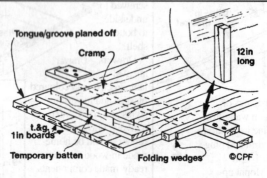

Tongue/groove planed off

Cramp

t.&g. 1in boards

Temporary batten

12in long

Folding wedges

©CPF

wood batten and planing sawn edges.

Plane and/or glasspaper top after assembly.

NOTE: Keep timber in 'room' conditions for a few weeks before use.

Making a drop-side cot

A labour of love for a new baby in the family is certainly a hand-made cot. This one is not complicated to make.

Ends are made as simple frames, with hardboard glued and pinned to both sides. Cut top to approximate shape and then finish after fixing hardboard.

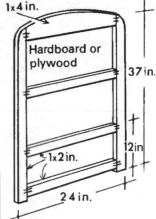

1x4 in.

Hardboard or plywood

37 in.

1x2 in.

12 in.

24 in.

Cot takes 46 x 21 in. mattress, but could be modified for other size. It is painted with (lead-free) lacquer and ends decorated with transfers. Set of metal cot-side fittings could be used for sides (then of similar length) but newer plastics fittings are shown.

For sides (1) bore holes one and quarter inch. deep in rails and fix eleven dowel rods with glue.

Remove all sharp edges after glue has set. Fixed side is secured with threaded nylon bushes and matching screws

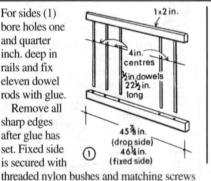

1x2 in.

4 in. centres

½in dowels
22½ in. long

45⅞ in. (drop side)
46¼ in. (fixed side)

①

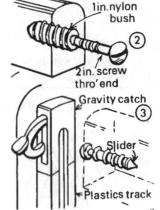

1 in. nylon bush

②

2 in. screw thro' end

Gravity catch

③

Slider

Plastics track

(2). Drop side has sliders which run in plastic track, with matching gravity catches at top (3). Bushes and sliders are tight fit in holes and secured with resin glue.

Plywood 46x21 in.

¾ in. panel pins

1x2in.

13 in.

13 in.

2in. dowels

1x2in. bearer screwed

Base is wood frame with halving joints glued and screwed. It is positioned on end bearers by short dowels with rounded ends glued in frame holes only. Top is covered with 4mm plywood, glued and pinned.

Build a child's easel & blackboard

Have you a budding teacher in the family? Then how about this junior easel and blackboard to test your woodwork skills?

Easel consists of two frames made from 1 x 2in softwood, with simple halving joints. Board rests on adjustable pegs from half inch. dowel rod, slightly tapered with plane or file.

First draw chalk lines (on floor or back of sheet of wallpaper) to full size of frame, measuring from a centre line.

Lay uprights against lines and temporarily nail rails across them. With pencil, draw lines across uprights against rails and, from other side, across rails.

Carry lines around with try-square and mark joint depth with gauge (1).

Saw and chisel out joins and fix with glue and screws (2).

Trim rail ends when glue has set. Make back frame similarly, 3in shorter.

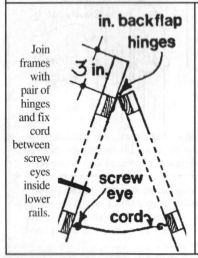

Join frames with pair of hinges and fix cord between screw eyes inside lower rails.

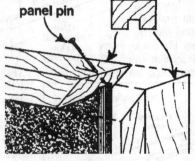

Blackboard can be $3/8$in plywood treated with special blackboard paint.

Or use two backing sheets of matt-enamelled hardboard (one white, one black) framed with single-groove moulding. Mitre, glue and pin corners.

Make corner seating for a dinette

If you only have limited space for a dining room table, this dinette seating could be the answer.

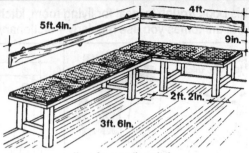

Suitable for corner of kitchen or small living room, seat takes six 16in square, or two 4ft x 16in, box cushions.

These can consist of $1^1/_2$in thick foam interiors, covered with upholstery vinyl; punch a few holes in vertical sides to allow foam to 'breathe'.

Backrest can be $^3/_4$ x 4in boards, padded if preferred. They are fixed to wall with glass plates and screws.

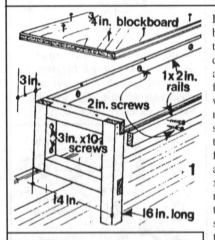

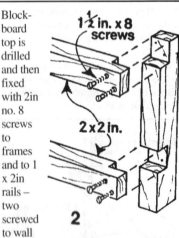

Blockboard top is drilled and then fixed with 2in no. 8 screws to frames and to 1 x 2in rails – two screwed to wall plugs, two to front of frames (1).

Frames are made to fit over skirting board and constructed with halving joints (2) secured with glue and screws.

Fix frames and rails to walls in correct positions and then fit lockboard.

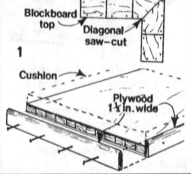

Top can be made from whole or separate pieces of blockboard 16in wide (1).

One piece is sawn diagonally to make two corner pieces. Glue and pin strips of plywood, or laths, to front and ends of top to hold cushions in place.

Constructing a book trough

This book trough is ideal for living room, kitchen or study to keep to hand the tomes you use regularly – dictionary, cookbooks etc.

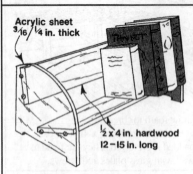

Acrylic sheet
$^3/_{16}$ / $^1/_4$ in. thick

$^1/_2$ x 4 in. hardwood
12 – 15 in. long

The trough could have ends in acrylic plastic which can be clear or tinted. But $^3/_8$ in plywood could be used if more convenient.

Shelf and back rail are in hardwood, not less than $^1/_2$ in finished thickness.

Brass or chrome raised-head screws give decorative touch.

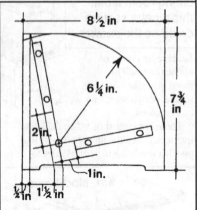

8 $^1/_2$ in

6 $^1/_4$ in.

7 $^3/_4$ in

2 in.

1 in.

$^1/_2$ in   1 $^1/_2$ in

Setting-out of ends. Marking can be done with wax (Chinagraph) pencil.

Cut to shape with coping saw, and smooth edges with medium, then fine wet-or-dry abrasive paper.

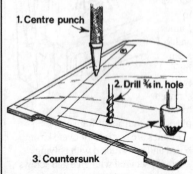

1. Centre punch

2. Drill $^3/_{16}$ in. hole

3. Countersunk

Mark centres of screw holes with centre punch.

With end laid over spare wood, drill four holes; then recess with special countersink bit or with larger drill.

Remember that ends are 'handed', and that countersinking should be on outside of each.

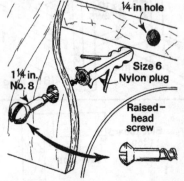

$^1/_4$ in hole

1 $^1/_4$ in. No. 8

Size 6 Nylon plug

Raised–head screw

Smooth ends of rails and, using trough ends as templates, mark positions of holes. Drill to full 1in.

Deep and lightly tap in nylon plugs as shown, with 'wings' along shelf width.

Varnish wood and assemble with raised-head screws.

144

A tea trolley to make

A tea trolley is useful on many occasions other than at tea time – for a television supper, perhaps, or a coffee morning.

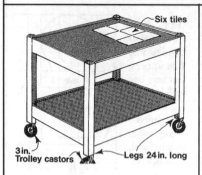

Made in knot-free planed softwood, with plywood shelves, it measures approximately 18 x 27in overall.

Optional tiles in top are useful for hot dishes or teapot. After completion, sand all surfaces, undercoat and paint.

If using tiles, set these in sheet of enamelled hardboard. Castor sockets fit in holes bored in base of legs.

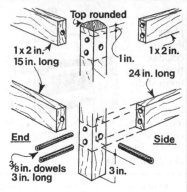

Rails are dowel-jointed to legs. Mark positions on legs and bore 3.8in holes; use these as jig when boring into rail ends. Use woodwork glue on all meeting surfaces and on dowels. Assemble both ends first.

Wipe off surplus glue and, when set, plane off dowel ends.

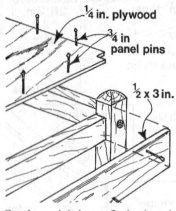

Cut plywood shelves to fit closely and fix with woodwork glue and pins.

Then glue and pin on $1/2$ x 3 in side strips, which form shelf lips.

Punch down all pin heads and fill holes.

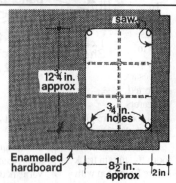

For tiles make enamelled hardboard to fit, then draw around tiles. Bore holes inside corners, cut out with fine-tooth keyhole saw and smooth sawn edges.

Fix hardboard with glue; apply weights till set. Use wall-tile adhesive for tiles, and grout joints.

A kidney-shaped dressing table

Construction of dressing table is simple, and the base provides good storage space. Here's how to make it.

If desired, plastic drawers could be fitted under upper shelf.

A frill hides the interior and is carried on an ordinary curtain track fixed under the $1/2$ in plywood kidney-shaped top.

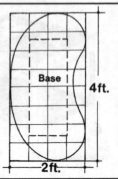

Draw shape of top after dividing into 6 in squares. Cut near line with keyhole or coping saw; smooth edges with shaping tool, glasspaper.

Base unit is made with $3/4$ in blockboard ends, $1/2$ in plywood shelves and hardboard back.

Top boards fit notches sawn in ends, and shelves are supported on bearers.

All fixings are glued, and nailed or pinned.

Ensure that there is room for curtain track before fixing top with glue and screws through boards.

All can be painted – or stained and varnished.

1 x 2 in.

2 in. oval nails

Hardboard back 2 ft 8 in. x 1 ft 8 in

$5/8$ in. panel pins

1 in. panel pins

1 x 1 in. Shelf bearers

$1/2$ in. plywood shelves 2 ft 6½ in x 1 ft 1 in.

$3/4$ blockboard 2 ft. 3 in. x 1 ft 1 in.

Glides

Screws into top

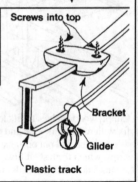

Plastic curtain track is suggested and is fixed after painting/varnishing. Form to shape in hands and fix with mounting brackets similar to type shown. Overlap at centre, front.

Bracket

Glider

Plastic track

Magazine rack-cum-table

This glass-topped table allows ready access – by eye and hand – to the magazines stored underneath. Here's how to make it.

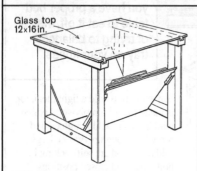

Glass top
12×16 in.

With glass top, rack also serves as chair-side table.

It consists of two dowel-jointed end frames, with open-ended plywood 'through' between them. Looks well painted with satin-finish paint; leg frames could be in white, plywood in bright colour. Frames are made from $1^1/_2$ x $1^1/_2$ in planed softwood.

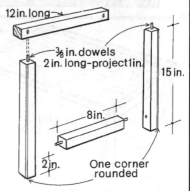

12 in. long

$^3/_8$ in. dowels
2 in. long–project 1 in.

15 in.

8 in.

2 in.

One corner rounded

Each frame consists of four members fixed together with dowels and glue.

Drill holes for dowels and insert in ends after coating with glue.

Glue ends and projecting dowels, press firmly together and leave on flat surface until glue sets.

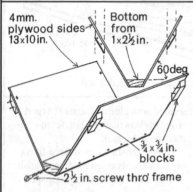

4mm. plywood sides 13×10 in.

Bottom from 1×2½ in.

60 deg

$^3/_4$ x $^3/_4$ in. blocks

2½ in. screw thro' frame

Plane edges of trough bottom to 60 deg; glue and pin on plywood after checking for fit against end frames.

Make wood blocks as shown, glue and pin to end frames.

Glue and screw through to blocks and to frame rails.

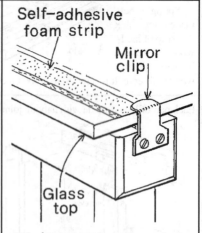

Self–adhesive foam strip

Mirror clip

Glass top

Order $1/3_2$ in float glass (cheaper than plate), with polished edges. Fix tightly with mirror clips after sticking foam draught-strip across top of frames.

Folding-leg bed table to make

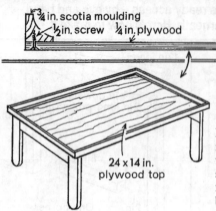

¾ in. scotia moulding
½ in. screw   ¼ in. plywood

24 x 14 in.
plywood top

Breakfast in bed is even more of a treat when you have a proper bed table to eat it off, instead of trying to balance a tray on your knees.

Big enough to hold a light meal, top is made from ¼in plywood edged with Scotia moulding, glued and screwed through plywood. Legs fold away and are self-locking in both open and closed positions.

Two pairs of legs are hinged to ³/₄ x ³/₄in battens well glued, and pinned through top; slightly recess pin heads with punch and fill the holes.

'Spring' is best made from a ¹/₄ x 2in. strip of hardwood, such as ash, but stiff ¹/₄in plywood will serve. It is screwed to wood block, glued and pinned to top.

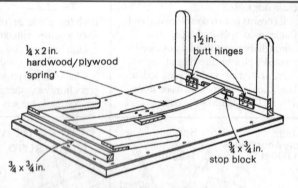

¼ x 2 in.
hardwood/plywood
'spring'

1½ in.
butt hinges

¾ x ¾ in.

¾ x ¾ in.
stop block

Each pair of legs is made with halving joints, secured with glue and screws; expert woodworkers may well prefer to mortise-and-tenon.

Hinges are shown as surface-fixed, but could be recessed for neater finish.

Smooth all edges with glasspaper.

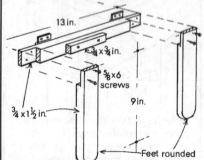

13 in.

¾ x ¾ in.

⅝ x 6
screws

9 in.

¾ x 1½ in.

Feet rounded

NOTE: Finish with polyurethane varnish, or undercoat and gloss paint. Top could be covered with self-adhesive plastics sheet.

Use place mats for hot dishes if top is painted or plastic-covered.

148

Making a turntable TV shelf

This shelf is just the ticket for a small TV in, say, a bedroom or kitchen. It is not advised for a very large or heavy television set.

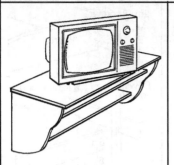

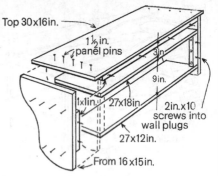

Top 30x16in.

1½in. panel pins

3in.

9in.

1x1in. 27x18in. 2in.x10 screws into wall plugs

27x12in.

From 16x15in.

Fitment has two shelves (upper one for pro-gramme magazines) and is screwed to wall.

Depth of top should normally be about 2in more than overall depth of TV, but check by measurement.

Make with good-quality ¹/₂ in plywood, with 1 x 1in wood fillets. Shape ends with coping saw and smooth with glasspaper. Fix to shelves with woodwork glue and 1¹/₂ in panel pins. Glue and screw fillet to top and fix top to ends. Fix short fillets.

Recess pin heads, fill holes and check assembly is square. Rub down and paint after glue has set.

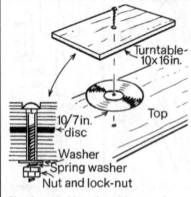

Turntable-10x16in.

10/7in. disc

Top

Washer
Spring washer
Nut and lock-nut

Simple turntable, using old gramophone disc as bearing; enlarge central hole and rub both sides with soap to reduce friction.

Secure whole to shelf with coach bolt, fitting washer, spring washer, nut and lock-nut, as shown inset.

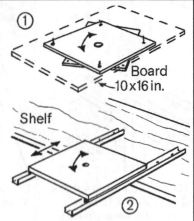

①

Board 10x16in.

Shelf

②

Ready-made steel turntables with ball bearings (1) is screwed direct to shelf; (2) slides on runners, which can be fixed to any strong shelf.

Screw plywood board to turntable top.

Making bunk beds

Bunk beds are a great space saver, either in a children's room or in a small spare room for guests that won't easily take a double bed.

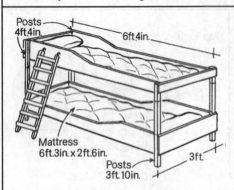

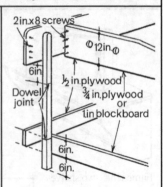

Frame, which takes standard mattresses, must be strong and rigid. Joints are not used, fixings being made with woodwork glue and screws.

If desired, the hardwood posts can be dowelled, so that beds can be taken through a doorway or used as twins.

Cut four shaped sides from two 18in wide boards and fix to posts. Then fix plywood head and foot boards.

If post are dowelled, assemble them before doing construction.

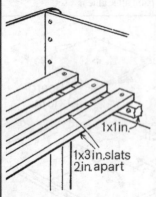

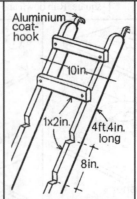

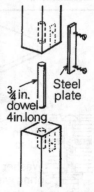

Mattress is carried on softwood slats fixed to 1 x 1in bearers glued and screwed to sides.

Attach bearers before fixing sides to posts.

Ladder rungs fit in shallow V-notches and are secured with glue and screws. Coat hooks go through holes made in bunk side.

Method of joining posts with unglued dowel – steel plate locks connecting sections.

FINISH: Rub down well with glasspaper, carefully rounding all edges and corners. Varnish posts and ladder; paint boards.

An audio-cassettes storage unit

Are those audio-cassettes always scattered all over the place, or in an unsightly pile. Well, here is one answer.

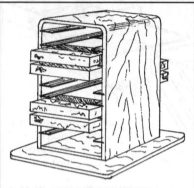

As shown, the unit will hold 20 cassettes in their plastic cases – ten on each side. It is made from 9mm ($\frac{3}{8}$in) plywood, with strips of laminate to form partitions, and a central dowel rod as separator. Base is screwed to bottom of rack.

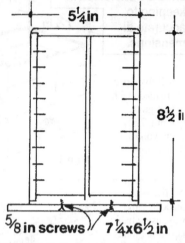

$5\frac{1}{4}$in

$8\frac{1}{2}$ in

$\frac{5}{8}$ in screws / $7\frac{1}{4}$x$6\frac{1}{2}$ in

Principal dimensions, for spacers at $\frac{13}{16}$in centres. Four corner joints are simple halving and dowel fits in holes drilled half-through top and bottom.

Saw cut

Using seven-ply plywood, make halving by sawing through four plies and cutting down glue line with sharp chisel. Allow ends to project slightly and trim after assembly.

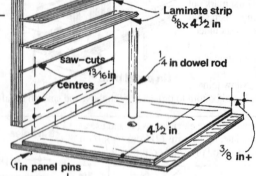

Laminate strip $\frac{5}{8}$x $4\frac{1}{2}$ in

Saw–cuts
$\frac{13}{16}$in
Centres

$\frac{1}{4}$ in dowel rod

$4\frac{1}{2}$ in

$\frac{3}{8}$ in+

1 in panel pins

Make saw-cuts three plies deep, smear in cuts with adhesive and press in strips. Thin (1.0-1.2mm) laminate is most convenient and will fit tenon-saw cuts; for thicker laminate use land saw. Laminate can be cut by scoring deeply with 'laminate' blade in craft knife and snapping by bending upwards. File edges smooth. When adhesive is dry, assemble as shown, gluing and pinning joints.

Making hold-all storage boxes

Suitable for hobbies or needlework materials, this unit is not difficult to make – if sufficient care and patience are exercised in keeping to accurate dimensions.

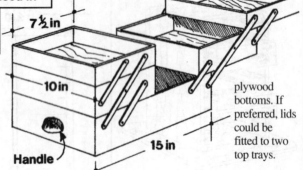

All five boxes are made with first-grade 9mm, 7-ply plywood sides and 4mm plywood bottoms. If preferred, lids could be fitted to two top trays.

7 ½ in

10 in

15 in

Handle

All five boxes made in same way, using half-lap corner joints (1), glued and pinned.

Plywood bottom is also glued and pinned.

First mark out joints; then saw down shoulder line and chip out down glue line (2).

Allow joint ends and bottom to project very slightly, and smooth off after glue has set.

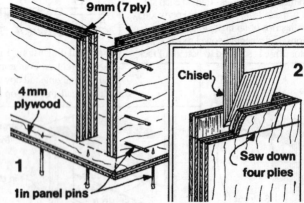

9mm (7 ply)

4 mm plywood

1in panel pins

1

Chisel

Saw down four plies

2

Draw full-size elevation as (1) and use as template. Make arms (2) from $1/4$ x $1/2$ in beech, good plywood or, for heavy

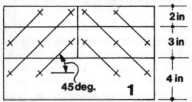

45 deg.

1

2 in

3 in

4 in

$1/8$ in holes

$1/2$ in

4 ¼ in   **4 ¼ in**

2

contents, strip metal such as Meccano. Attach with $5/8$ in, no. 6 round-head screws with washers under heads. Fix long arms to centre of middle tray first.

152

Constructing a chess table

For anyone keen on the game, a purpose-built chess table is a luxury indeed. If you don't play yourself, how about a present for a friend or relative.

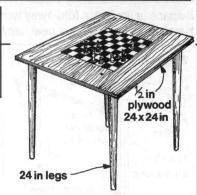

½ in plywood
24 x 24 in

24 in legs

Table has ¹/₂ in plywood top, centre marked with 1¹/₂ in squares, and either ready-made or home-made legs. Plywood faced in light oak gives good appearance when border and edges are stained. Dark squares can be masked and painted.

Plane edges of plywood and mark squares in pencil.

Then score along pencil lines with sharp knife and smooth top with fine glasspaper.

Fix masking tape exactly inside chequered square and brush, say dark oak, wood dye over border.

Leave 24 hours, then wipe with coarse cloth and remove tape before filling in dark squares.

1. Mark out squares

2. Score lines

3. Fit masking tape

6 in

12 in

64 – 1½ in squares

6 in

4. Apply wood dye

Give three coats clear polyurethane varnish over-all after fitting legs.

Instead of ready-made, use legs made in either of ways shown.

Glued/screwed to top

1½ in

1 in hole

1 in square

1 x 3 in 23 in long

1½ x 1½ in leg

'Broomstick' leg

For 'broomstick' leg, make shallow saw-cut and work down to 1in with shaping tool or chisel.

Square legs have stub tenon to fit 1in-square mortise.

Glasspaper legs, glue into 1 x 3in rail and fix both assemblies to top with glue and 1¹/₄in screws.

NOTE: Imperial dimensions given. Now we're officially metric, expect timber merchants to supply in this measure.

Making a fold-away work bench

If space is limited, a fold-away work bench can be very useful. Here's how to make this neat item and fix it to a convenient wall.

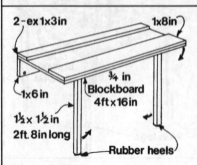

Though not heavy, bench is made rigid by using strong self-locking drop-leaf brackets to support blackboard top, stiffened by gluing and screwing on 1 x 8in softwood.

With narrower board at back, this forms shallow well for tools in use.

Legs, fitted with rubber-heel feet, fold under top.

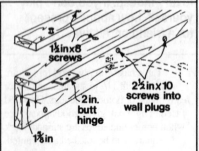

First make inverted-L wall fittings, as shown, reducing width of top board to give correct projection.

Board is glued and screwed to wall board, which is fixed with seven screws into wall plugs.

Top is carried on three hinges as well as two brackets; these are fitted abut 9in from each end.

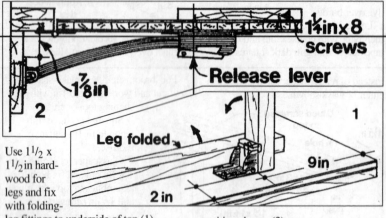

Use 1¹/₂ x 1¹/₂ in hardwood for legs and fix with folding-leg fittings to underside of top (1).

Legs are fitted to lie side-by-side when folded and to be tight against floor when open.

Screw the drop-leaf brackets into the position shown (2).

Dimensions given for bracket mounting apply to one type of bracket about 14in long – but check makers' instructions if other pattern is used.

An artist's folding easel to make

Whatever sort of painting you or a valued friend enjoy, a folding easel lets you take your art to your subject, wherever that may be.

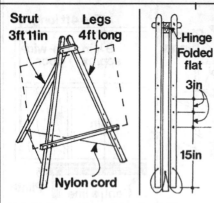

Strut
3ft 11in
Legs
4ft long

Hinge
Folded
flat
3in
15in
Nylon cord

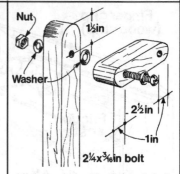

Nut
Washer
1/2in
2 1/2 in
1in
2 1/4 x 3/16 in bolt

Suitable for amateur artist or for children, easel is strong and rigid. For transport or storage it folds flat, as shown.

Legs are held by board-support rail, which can be adjusted for height, and strut by length of nylon cord.

All timber is 1 x 1in (finished size) planed hardwood such as beech or oak; but knot-free softwood could be used.

Legs pivot on bolts passing through short cross-piece; place washers where shown and rivet over end of bolt after fitting nut.

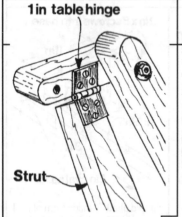

1in table hinge

Strut

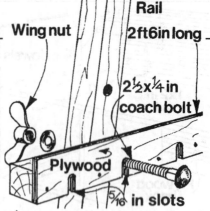

Wing nut
Rail
2ft 6in long
2 1/2 x 1/4 in
coach bolt
Plywood
5/16 in slots

Strut is hinged to cross-piece, using so-called table hinge, which has one flap longer than the other. Secure it with 3/4in ,No. 6 screws.

Front rail, which supports board, is 1 x 1in wood with strip of plywood glued and pinned on to form a rebate. Secured with coach bolts and wing nuts, it can be folded along one leg after slackening wing nuts.

Making a hi-fi storage cabinet

Although both design and dimensions are governed by the actual units to be used, the cabinet shown will serve for most.

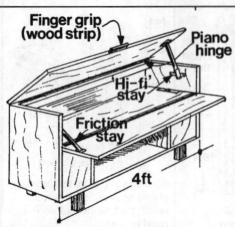

Made in wood – or p.v.c.-veneered chipboard – it has lid controlled by 'hi-fi' (cushioned) stay and front flap with friction stay.

Lower cupboard compartments will take tapes or CDs or speakers.

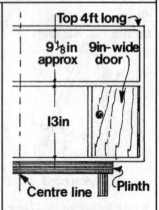

Front view with dimensions.

Flap is 9in board so opening must be slightly deeper than this to accept thickness of closed hinge. Flush hinges can be used for cupboard doors.

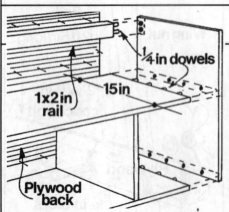

All boards are joined with $1/4$in dowels and glue.

Make bottom, shelf and vertical partitions first so that, with ends, cabinet is 4ft wide.

Make 1 x 2 in hardwood rail, which is dowelled to ends; it is set down by thickness of closed piano hinge. Plywood back is glued and pinned.

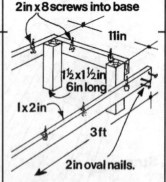

Simple plinth is made from planed softwood and painted flat black. Rails are nailed and glued to legs, nails punched down and holes filled. Counterbore for screws so that they will project $1/2$in, and screw plinth to base of cabinet.

Making a table/bedside lamp

This lamp is easily made from five pieces of hardwood, to be varnished; or softwood, painted. Here's how.

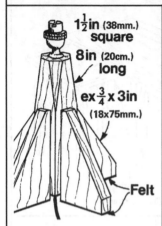

1½in (38mm.) square
8in (20cm.) long
ex ¾ x 3in (18x75mm.)

Felt

Lamp holder is screwed on a flange plate fixed to top of drilled central pillar with three small screws.

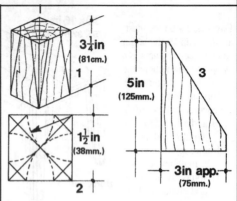

3¼in (81cm.) **1**

1½in (38mm.) **2**

5in (125mm.) **3**

3in app. (75mm.)

Top of pillar is tapered by planing off corners after marking out (1). Octagon is marked on end by drawing diagonals and setting off half length of these from each corner with compasses (2).

Each leg is marked out on ¾ x 3in (18 x 75mm) planed timber (3); then slope is sawn and planed smooth.

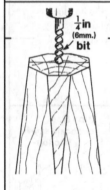

¼in (6mm.) bit

Drill hole for flex through pillar, from each end, with twist bit.

If bit is too short, complete hole with red-hot steel rod.

Legs are fixed to pillar with glue and short dowels.

Drill holes, cut dowels and check assembly before brushing glue over dowels and edge of leg.

Glue strips of felt or thin foam to feet to prevent them scratching.

¼in (6mm.) **dowels**
¾in (18mm.) **long**

Making a set of nesting tables

These meet the dual needs of having enough side tables for guests, yet being able to store them away when not needed.

Two smaller tables 'nest' in slides under the larger one; a back rail acts as a stop and strengthens the larger table.
Tops are in hardwood-veneered chipboard, in standard 15 and 12in widths, and the leg frames are made from matching timber.
All joints are dowelled and glued together.

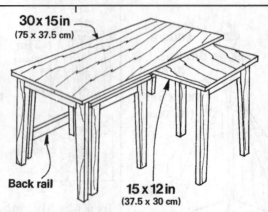

30 x 15 in
(75 x 37.5 cm)

15 x 12 in
(37.5 x 30 cm)

Back rail

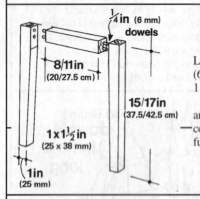

¼ in (6 mm) dowels

8/11 in
(20/27.5 cm)

15/17 in
(37.5/42.5 cm)

1 x 1½ in
(25 x 38 mm)

1 in
(25 mm)

Leg frames are jointed with 2½in (62mm) long dowels going about 1½in into rail ends.
Frames are fixed to tops with glue, and with screws through holes countersunk so that screws go a full ½in into top.

Smaller tables, when not in use, run on slides made as shown. Strips of wood with ends rounded are glued and screwed across leg frames and to central rail glued and screwed to top. Back rail is dowel-jointed between legs before fixing frames to top.
Tables can be finished with three/four coats of polyurethane varnish.

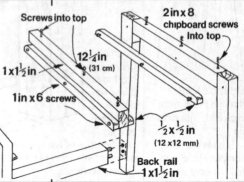

Screws into top

2 in x 8 chipboard screws into top

12¼ in
(31 cm)

1 x 1½ in

1 in x 6 screws

½ x ½ in
(12 x 12 mm)

Back rail
1 x 1½ in

Making a military-style chest

Based on the campaign chests used by military officers of earlier days, this chest makes unusual, but very practical storage today.

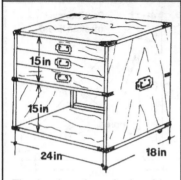

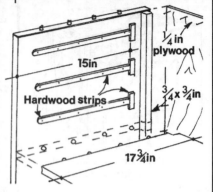

The chest is made to take three 24 x 15 x 5in self-assemble wood drawers.

Assemble these first and then make chest to fit.

Add cupboard doors at bottom if preferred.

Sides, top, bottom, shelf can be made from veneered chipboard (oak or pine suggested) or high-grade blockboard. Joints are glued and dowelled, and hardwood strips are used as drawer runners and stops.

Matching plywood back is glued and pinned to $3/4$ x $3/4$in fillets fixed as shown.

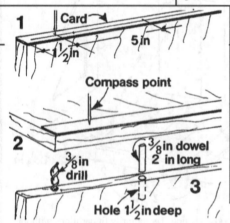

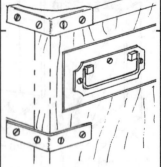

In absence of dowelling, jig, simplest way to mark dowel positions is with strip of thin, stiff card set out as shown (1). Mark on end, turn card over and mark side (2). Drill holes $1^1/_2$ and $1/_2$in deep and insert glued dowels (3). Glue ends of boards.

Brass corner plates, angles and handles are sold as military-chest fittings. Fix them with $5/_8$ x 4in countersink-head brass screws.

Four rubber feet can be screwed to bottom; or fit small castors.

Making a record rack

Even in the age of the compact disc, many people still have prized record collections. So this rack could be a useful present.

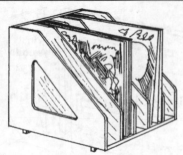

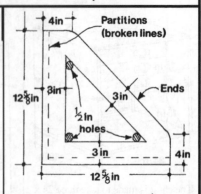

Made entirely in plywood, rack will easily hold up to 50 records, in their sleeves.

Ends and partitions are in $1/4$in (6mm) plywood; back and base in $3/8$in (9mm).

Four small rubber feet are screwed under base.

Mark out ends as shown, bore $1/2$in holes and cut out triangle with coping or keyhole saw. Smooth swan edges. make partitions in same way, but $3/8$in smaller. Trim edges with all pieces held together in vice.

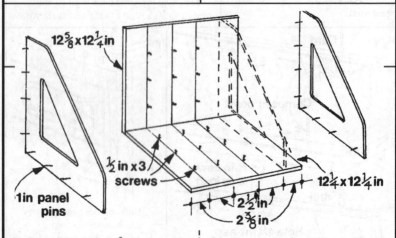

Cut back and base from $3/8$in plywood, true edges, mark on centre lines for partitions and fix together at right-angles with glue and panel pins. glue and pins on ends. Then drill $5/64$in holes for screws and deeply countersink on out-side. Temporarily fit partitions without glue; remove, apply glue and refix, tightening screws. When glue has set, punch down pin heads, fill all holes with stopping, smooth overall with fine glass-paper and finish with varnish or paint.

A folding leg table to make

Primarily intended as a card table, this item can have many other uses. And it is not difficult to construct. Why not try it?

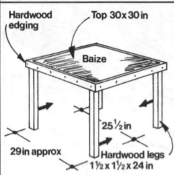

Hardwood edging
Top 30 x 30 in
Baize
25½ in
29 in approx
Hardwood legs 1½ x 1½ x 24 in

A plywood top is covered with baize (which can be replaced) and is carried on simple framing and fitted with edging strips.

The legs fold, one pair within the other, on special hinged fittings.

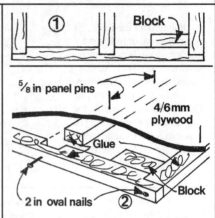

① Block
⅝ in panel pins
4/6mm plywood
Glue
2 in oval nails
② Block

Top has softwood frame covered with 4/6mm plywood. Frame is made with halving joints (1), while 5in-long blocks are fixed in corners at one end, for the inner leg fittings.

Joints are glued, nailed and blocks are glued, then pinned through plywood (2).

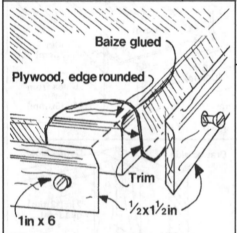

Baize glued
Plywood, edge rounded
Trim
½ x 1½ in
1 in x 6

When glue on framing and plywood is hard, trim with plane/glasspaper, rounding-over edges of plywood.

Baize is next fitted, drawn taut while fixing with fabric adhesive along frame edges.

Edging strip is then prepared, corners mitred, and screwed in position.

1½ x 1½ in hardwood leg
Fitting
Catch release

Hardwood legs are used with special self-locking folding-leg fittings shown, these are sold in pairs for left- and right-hand.

They are firmly screwed to legs, then to frame at one end, blocks at other, so that legs from opposite ends lie alongside when folded.

Under-bed blanket drawers

When space is at a premium, that gap under the beds can be put to good use with these 'skid draws'. Here's how.

It is seldom feasible to fit conventional drawers under modern divan bed, but those shown are on 'skids' of half-round moulding so that they will slide over a carpet. Drawer shown is suitable for 'single' divan bed when there is minimum clearance of 6 $1^1/_4$in – if less, narrower boards could be used.

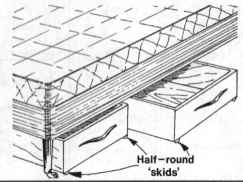

Half–round 'skids'

Drawers are made from four boards and strengthened with corner blocks.

Glue and screw ends to the blocks, then fix sides in same way. Next glue and screw $^1/_2$in square fillets around inside at base; cut plywood bottom to fit, notching out corners.

Secure with quadrant moulding pinned to sides.

Finally glue and pin half-round moulding along bottom edges of long sides.

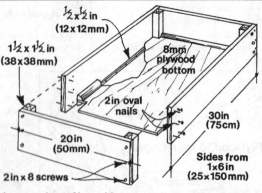

$^1/_2$ x $^1/_2$ in (12 x 12mm)

$1^1/_2$ x $1^1/_2$ in (38 x 38mm)

8mm plywood bottom

2in oval nails

30in (75cm)

20in (50mm)

Sides from 1x6in (25×150mm)

2in x 8 screws

Method of fixing plywood bottom and half-round skids; round over ends of skids to ensure smooth running. One or both drawer ends can be faced with laminate before fixing handle.

Recess screw and nail and screw heads and fill with plastic wood before varnishing whole of inside and outside.

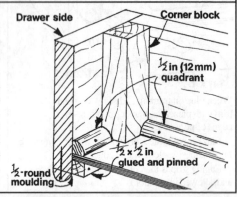

Drawer side

Corner block

$^1/_2$ in (12mm) quadrant

$^1/_2$ x $^1/_2$ in glued and pinned

$^1/_2$-round moulding

A 'marble'-top table to construct

In this case the 'marble' is a plastic laminate, but this still makes for an excellent working surface. Here's how to do it.

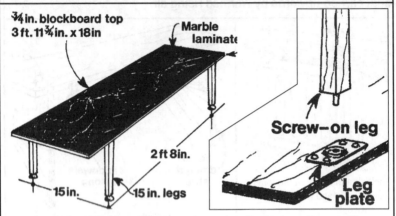

¾ in. blockboard top
3 ft. 11¾ in. x 18 in

Marble laminate

Screw–on leg

Leg plate

2 ft 8 in.

15 in.   15 in. legs

Top is made from blockboard, but is covered on face and edges with plastic laminate in marble pattern.

Length is such that laminate can be exactly 4ft long – which allows for trimming. If fixed with 'delayed-bonding'

contact adhesive it can be moved into exact position after applying to blockboard.

Ready-made, square/tapered wooden legs are used; they screw into plates screwed to underside of top.

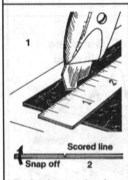

1

Scored line
Snap off   2

Cut laminate and make edging strips by scoring with knife fitted with special scoring blade.

Take several strokes across marbled face (1); then snap by pressing upwards (2).

Laminate edge strip

Guide board

Contact adhesive

Underside

Fix edging strip first. For accuracy, fit a guide board temporarily to upper face of blockboard with half-driven-in panel pins. Follow makers' instructions on adhesive.

File this direction only

Have laminate for top fractionally over-size. Fix with contact adhesive then trim all edges at 45deg with coarse file or shaping tool. Hold it at angle to edge and apply pressure on forward stroke only.

163

Constructing a radiator shelf

Apart from acting as a shelf (for light objects), the main purpose of this unit is to prevent staining of the wall above the radiator by dust carried upwards by warmed rising air.

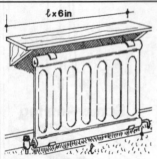

ℓ x 6 in

Shelf should be about 6in longer than radiator and fixed about 4in above it.

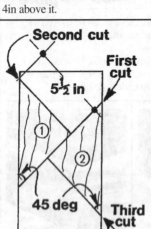

Second cut

First cut

5½ in

① ②

45 deg

Third cut

6 in

Brackets are sawn from 6in. board as shown, so that cut edges will be out of sight. If necessary, smooth sawn edges with glasspaper.

Cut notches for glass plates with chisel, and bore match-

Made from 6in-wide veneered chipboard, shelf is fixed to wall with screws, through two glass plates, into wall plugs.

A triangular bracket cut from length of chipboard is fixed near each end with dowels.

Lengths of self-adhesive foam draught strip stuck along rear edges give airtight seal to wall.

1 in

1½ in glass plate

Foam draught strip

¼ in dowels 1½ in long

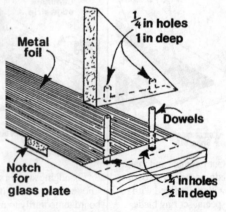

Metal foil

¼ in holes 1 in deep

Dowels

Notch for glass plate

¼ in holes ½ in deep

ing ¼in holes into underside of shelf and top edges of brackets.

After checking that dowels are not too long, assemble with woodworking glue. Cooking foil, fixed with clear adhesive, will protect shelf against heat.

Bed headboards: plain & padded

The luxury of being able to comfortably read or watch the telly in bed is greatly assisted by a good headboard. Here's how.

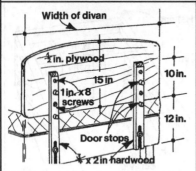

Width of divan

½ in. plywood

15 in.

10 in.

1 in. x 8 screws

12 in.

Door stops

¾ x 2 in hardwood

Simple board is made from plywood, shaped with saw and shaping tool.

Hardwood (oak, beech, etc.) 'legs', with slots, are glued and screwed to back at exact spacing of fixing screws to be found at one end of divan.

Small rubber door stops protect wall.

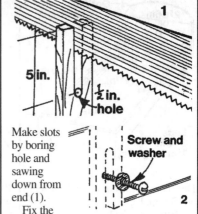

5 in.

½ in. hole

Make slots by boring hole and sawing down from end (1).

Screw and washer

Fix the headboard at suitable height by tightening screws, with large washers under heads (2).

Quilted vinyl   Braid

Thin padding can consist of ready-made quilted vinyl (sold in variety of colours/ patterns). Cut to shape and fix with a fabric adhesive.

Then cover edge with upholster's braid, secured with fabric adhesive or fancy nails. Paint or varnish board edges before padding.

Glue or tack to back

Plain vinyl

Foam

1½ in. glass plate

String

Button   2

Chipboard or plywood can be fixed to wall behind bed with glass plates.

If desired, first cover with foam and plain vinyl (1).

Buttoning can be done with string through small holes in back, and secured with glue or a small tack (2).

Making a divan base

Need a new bed? Well, making the mattress might be a bit beyond most DIYers, but a divan base is another matter.

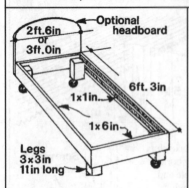

Divan is made from 1 x 6in boards and 3 x 3in legs.

Mattress can be laid over slats or on a 'sprung' base; support for either is provided by 1 x 1in ledges.

A plain or padded headboard can be added if desired.

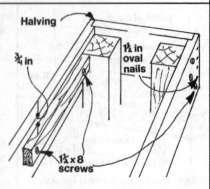

Parts are fixed together with woodworking glue and nails/screws. Boards best joined with halvings as shown, but may be butted together.

Castors or glides can be fixed to legs.

Planed, knot-free softwood such as parana pine is suitable and will measure $1/8$-$1/4$in less than nominal dimensions.

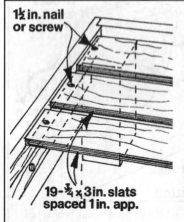

If using slats for mattress support, cut to fit from $3/4$ x 3in. planed timber, which will be about $5/8$in thick.

Lay loose or nail/screw to ledges.

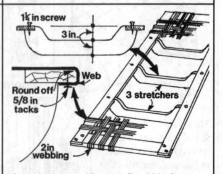

Or make 'sprung' base to fit within frame.

Shaped stretchers are from 1in block-board; cut out with coping saw, fix with glue and screws. Fix elastic ebbing, about 1in apart, lengthwise first, with four large tacks each end. Stretch tightly and evenly; then fix webs across frame, passing under and over longer ones.

Simple marquetry

For first attempts choose a simple, open picture or silhouette. Or buy a ready-prepared kit, supplied with instructions. Cut-out pieces of veneer can be laid in a sequence such as that shown, using a 'clear' adhesive. Trace picture outline and transfer to plywood with carbon paper.

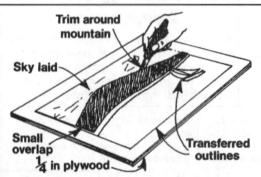

Trim around mountain

Sky laid

Small overlap
¼ in plywood

Transferred outlines

Transfer shape for sky on piece of veneer, making it slightly over-size at lower edge. Cut out with sharp craft knife and stick on plywood.

Prepare cut-out of larger hill, lay over sky and cut around it; then remove waste veneer.

Stick down and repeat. Cut away for boat last.

Make 'frame' from veneer strips. Glue down one, lay next over it and cut mitre with knife (1). Remove waste, glue down second strip and repeat for other corners. Carefully smooth edges and picture surface with No. 6/0, then No.9/0 garnet paper held around cork block (2). Finish with wax polish, French polish or clear varnish.

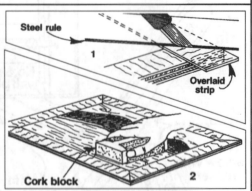

Steel rule

Overlaid strip

Cork block

NOTE: Simple method shown is not necessarily best for more advanced work. Buy selection of veneers and choose appropriate colours from them. Veneers may be secured with adhesive tape while glue sets.

A wine-bottle rack to make

A place to store wine in the home is always useful. You can keep this rack in the best environment for your wine.

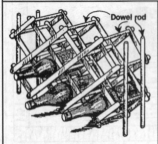

Not difficult if care is taken in measuring for and drilling holes, rack will hold up to ten bottles.

Two identical lattices, from $1/8$ to $3/16$ x 1in hardwood, are screwed to 5in lengths of $3/4$ or 1in dowel rod. Similar rod is used for uprights.

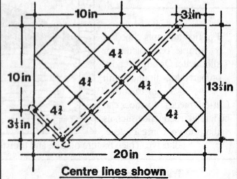

Centre lines shown

Simplest way to determine lengths of lattice strips is to make full-size drawing as shown (eg. on back of spare wallpaper), starting with 20 x 13-$1/3$in rectangle. Mark hole centres on strips and drill with $1/8$in bit; round-over all ends.

Drill $5/32$in holes in ends of dowels (below) and press in No. 6 fibre wall plugs.

Then assemble with round-head screws, brass or chrome, with washers under heads, completing each lattice in turn.

Screws drive more easily if smeared with petroleum jelly.

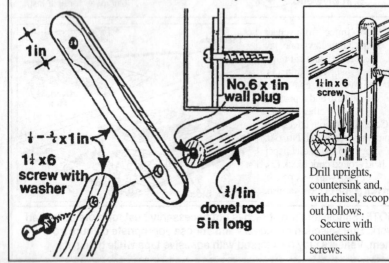

1in

$\frac{1}{8} - \frac{3}{16}$ x 1in

1¼ x6 screw with washer

No.6 x 1in wall plug

¾/1in dowel rod 5 in long

1¼ in x 6 screw

Drill uprights, countersink and, with chisel, scoop out hollows.

Secure with countersink screws.

Making an oak blanket chest

Chest has the appearance of traditional framed-and-panelled one, but is simply made from standard oak-faced chipboard.

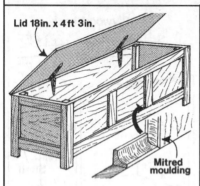

Lid 18in. x 4ft 3in.

Mitred moulding

The chest is 15 in wide for front, ends, back, and 18 in for top.

'Panelling' is formed by gluing and pinning on strips of $1/2$ in x 2in oak.

Optional, better appearance is given by fixing moulding into angles.

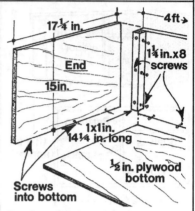

$17\frac{1}{4}$ in.

4ft

End

15in.

$1\frac{1}{4}$ in.x8 screws

1x1in. $14\frac{1}{4}$ in. long

$1/2$ in. plywood bottom

Screws into bottom

Saw front and one end, back and other end, from two 6ft lengths.

Make corner posts, drill and countersink for No. 8 screws. Fix with glue and chipboard screws. Make bottom to fit; fix with glue and screws.

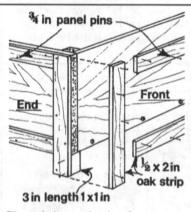

$3/4$ in panel pins

End

Front

$1/2$ x 2in oak strip

3 in length 1 x 1 in

Glue and pin on oak strips: first corner verticals, then long rails and, last, intermediate verticals.

Back is left plain.

Punch down pins, fill with oak-shade plastic wood and rub down with fine glasspaper.

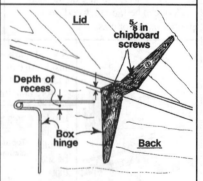

Lid

$5/8$ in chipboard screws

Depth of recess

Box hinge

Back

Four butt hinges could be used, but two box (or bent strap) hinges as shown are stronger.

Cut recesses in edge of back with saw and chisel.

Finish chest with brown-oak wood dye, followed by two-three coats polyurethane varnish.

Bathroom cabinet/medicine chest

A neat little cabinet that can be used in the bathroom for toiletries and/or medicine – which should be kept out of the reach of children.

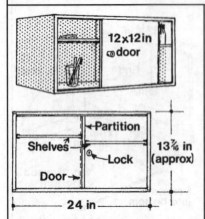

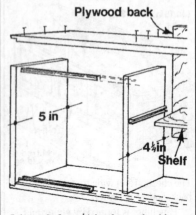

Cabinet is open on left; has lockable sliding door at other end so that medicines are safe from children.

Glass/plywood shelves and door are carried on plastics sliding-door channel.

Door can be $1/4$in plywood, sheet plastics or mirror glass.

It is made from $1/2$in plywood, with glued and pinned 4mm plywood back, and fixed to wall plugs with four $1\,1/4$in round-head screws through back.

Corners are halving jointed, secured with glue and $1\,1/2$in panel pins.

Central partition is fixed with glue and pins.

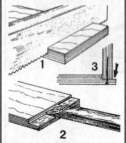

To make corner halvings saw across plywood through half number of piles (1). Remove waste with chisel, cutting away one ply at a time (2). Make joint to project slightly (3); trim later.

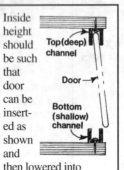

Inside height should be such that door can be insert-ed as shown and then lowered into bottom channel.

Special (glass-sliding-door) lock is fitted; bolt projects inside edge of partition when locked, preventing movement of door.

Bore hole for lock through wood or plastic with centre bit; have it drilled by glass merchant with glass or mirror door.

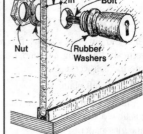

Re-seating occasional chairs

Often a good wooden frame of an upright chair lasts much longer than the seat, which can easily be rebuilt or replaced.

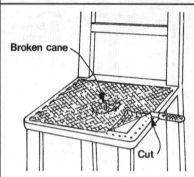

Re-caning requires skill/practice, or is expensive to have done professionally. But simpler re-seating is possible after first removing old cane as shown: carefully cut loops where they pass through holes in chair frame and strip woven cane.

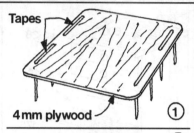

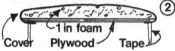

To avoid need for tacks or nails use plywood drilled with four matching holes and thread in tapes (1). Lay on foam; then fit cover tautly, fixing with fabric adhesive on under-side (2).

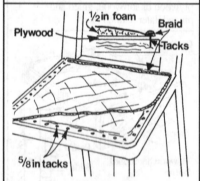

For more permanent fixing, cut plywood to shape, use $1/2$ in foam cut rather smaller than plywood.

Fix to top of chair frame with cut tacks about $1^1/2$ in apart.

Cover these with upholstery braid, fixed with fabric adhesive.

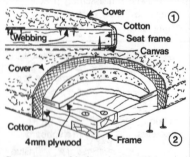

Correct way with drop-in seat (1) is to remove cover, stuffing, webbing fit new webs; then reverse the procedure, using new cover.

Easier is to strip to frame, fix plywood and use foam (2).

Fix cover at front first, draw taut and fix back; then sides, pleating corners.

NOTE: 1. Do not use nails, tacks on good, old chair; it can then be restored correctly later. 2. Round over all edges, corners to prevent chafing of cover.

Making a drawer unit

This small drawer unit could have a host of uses around the home, or even in the workshop or garage. Here's how to build it.

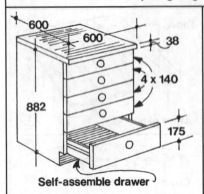

Self-assemble drawer

Principal dimensions in mm. (components are sold in metric sizes) for a '600 module' kitchen cabinet, which could also be used as a drawer chest.

Drawer fronts are in two of stock sizes, drawers self-assembly p.v.c.

Alter sizes if necessary to match existing units.

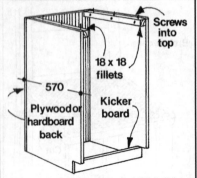

Carcass, in veneered chipboard sides sawn to size and notched for kicker (exact height determined by drawer-front sizes chosen). Cover sawn edges with edging strip. Fillets are screwed to sides and top. Kicker board can be plywood or softwood, glued and pinned, later painted black.

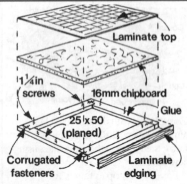

Top can be bought as preformed unit ready for fixing to fillets. Or it can be made up as shown, with simple softwood frame, corners halved, glued and secured with corrugated fasteners.

Glue and screw frame to chipboard and glue laminate top and edges.

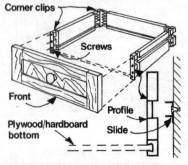

Drawers could be of almost any type, but self-assembly, with p.v.c. profile and corner clips, is easiest.

For drawers shown, 100mm profile is used for 140mm fronts; 120mm for 175mm front.

Drawer bottom is supported in groove inside front. U-shape plastic slides shown are screwed inside carcass.

Making a kitchen wall-cupboard

This job is much easier than it first looks, as it is designed for use with widely available ready-made hardwood doors.

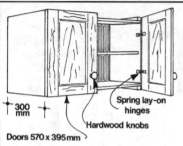

300 mm

Doors 570 x 395mm

Spring lay-on hinges

Hardwood knobs

Cupboard is planned around now-popular ready-made hardwood doors.

These come in various sizes, including that shown, and should be obtained before construction is started.

Carcass and shelf are in white melamine-faced chipboard 300mm (12in) wide. Hinges are sprung for self-closing and are surface-fitted.

Use knobs in wood matching doors.

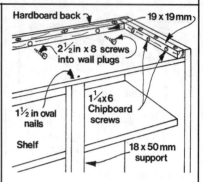

Hardboard back

19 x 19mm

2½in x 8 screws into wall plugs

1¼x6 Chipboard screws

1½ in oval nails

Shelf

18 x 50mm support

Method of construction: using 19mm square fillets fixed with glue and screws.

Top is shown, but bottom is identical.

Fix vertical central support with oval nails; punch down nail heads and fill holes. Use white-faced or emulsion-painted hardboard for back; fix it with glue and ⅝in pins.

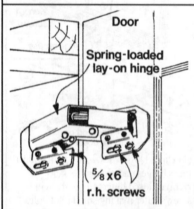

Door

Spring-loaded lay-on hinge

⅝ x 6 r.h. screws

Lay-on concealed hinge shown is easier to fix than more usual concealed kitchen-cupboard hinge (which could be used if preferred) that needs 'blind' 35mm hole in door frame.

Detailed instructions come with hinges.

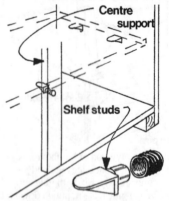

Centre support

Shelf studs

Central shelf is supported on five white plastic shelf studs and by hardboard back. Studs plug into sockets pressed into 'blind' 10mm (³/₈in) holes 10mm deep. Shelf is sawn narrower than ends by thickness of support.

Making a needlework cabinet

This is both a useful and elegant small cabinet for the home, though it could be used for other items as well as needlework.

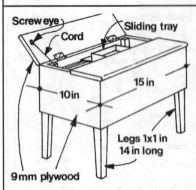

Cabinet has hinged, two-leaf top, with stop cord (nylon, silk etc.) between two small screw eyes. Sliding tray, for small items, bobbins of thread, is made from sound wooden cigar box glued to piece of plywood/hardboard.

Use same board for cabinet bottom.

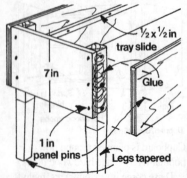

Plywood ends, sides are glued and pinned to legs; $1/2$ x $1/2$ in strips for tray slide are similarly fixed, but with $5/8$ in pins.

Make both end assemblies first, then trim and smooth before fixing two sides. Preferably, plane inside faces of legs to taper before assembly.

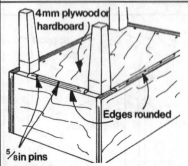

Bottom, in plywood or hardboard, is notched to fit around legs with edges projecting slightly. Fix with glue and pins. When glue has set, punch down all pin heads in bottom and sides; fill holes. Round over edges of plywood/hardboard bottom, as shown.

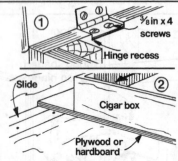

(1) Have $1^1/2$ in - 1 x $3/4$ in (open width) brass hinges and maker recess to receive closed hinge. Fix with $3/8$ in screws, after making small pilot holes or use $1/2$ in screws, nipping off tips.

(2) Use cigar box for tray, gluing it to thin plywood/hardboard to fit cabinet.

NOTE: All 9mm plywood must be seven-ply of prime grade. If this is not available, use good 12mm plywood. This is easier to use, but heavier.

A tile-top table to make

Tile-top tables make an attractive central feature in a conservatory; are easy to wipe clean, and resistant to hot coffee mugs.

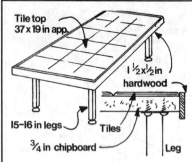

Tile top 37 x 19 in app.

1½ x ½ in hardwood

15–16 in legs

Tiles

¾ in chipboard

Leg

Simply constructed table with chipboard top and 6in tiles, edged with hardwood, later finished in p.u. varnish. chromed steel legs are screwed under top, as inset.

Size can be varied to suit smaller or different number of tiles, while alternative legs could be used if preferred.

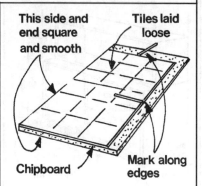

This side and end square and smooth

Tiles laid loose

Chipboard

Mark along edges

Prepare chipboard, making one side and edge at right-angles and smooth.

Lay tiles loose, allowing for spacing, if not self-spacing.

Mark size on board and trim, smooth to lines. Seal with thinned p.u. varnish.

'Well' for tiles

Dense chipboard

Smooth off-end

½ x 1½ in hardwood

Fix hardwood edging, with woodwork glue and fine pins, to form 'well' of tile thickness.

Punch down heads and fill holes with matching stopping.

Sand and varnish. Fix tiles with ceramic-wall-tile adhesive.

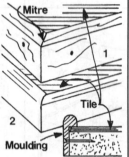

Mitre

1

Tile

2

Moulding

A more professional finish can be obtained by mitring edging (1), or by fixing mitred hockey-stick moulding over edges of tiles (2).

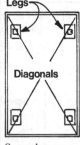

Legs

Diagonals

Screw legs on diagonals drawn on underside of top, with $5/8$in x 8 screws, or as supplied with legs.

NOTE: Chipboard should be of dense grade, or could be replaced with blockboard. If convenient, use 7mm floor tiles – rather than thinner wall tiles, which may crack or craze in time.

Add-on cupboard bookshelf unit

This combination of cupboard – with an optional sliding door – and one or more bookcases above it has many possibilities.

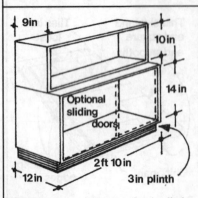

The base unit, standing on simple plinth, can be used as cupboard with or without doors, while one or more bookshelves can be added at any time.

Approximate sizes given allow any unit to be made from standard 8ft veneered chipboard.

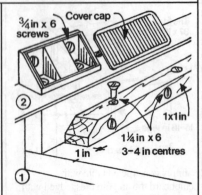

Chipboard, sawn to lengths and edged at exposed ends, can be corner-joined by using drilled, countersunk fillet (1), preferably using glue as well as screws.

Simpler is with three plastic corner joints (2) in white/brown, to match chipboard. Use chipboard screws.

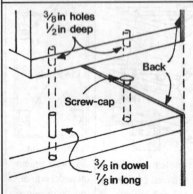

After making each unit and gluing, pinning on back of hardboard or plywood (previously painted, stained or varnished) bore shallow holes to receive loose (unglued) dowels, which serve to keep units aligned.

If dowels are not yet required, press screw caps into holes.

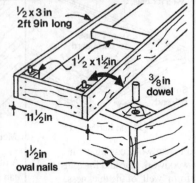

Plinth is made from $1/2$ x 3in softwood glued and nailed to lengths of $1^1/_2$in square batten.

Corner blocks are bored for loose dowels, which should fit corresponding holes in base unit.

Punch down nail heads, fill holes, sand; then coat plinth with matt black.

Desk for homework or hobbies

Yes, it looks just like that old, traditional school desk. Perhaps with good reason – it's made for working at. Here's how to make it.

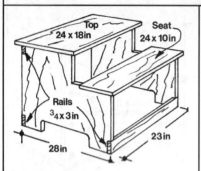

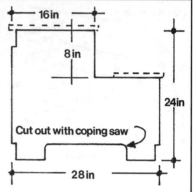

Suitable for young people of average height up to early teens, desk could be made 2in higher overall for taller person.

Sides, top and seat are in 16-18mm. blockboard, while three rails are in $^3/_4$in x 3in (18 x 75mm) softwood.

Finish with paint or, after fixing edging strip, clear varnish.

Both sides are alike. Mark out as shown, taking care that corner notches are exact size of rails.

All cuts can be made with 22in hand saw, or jig-saw fitted with 'medium-woodwork' blade.

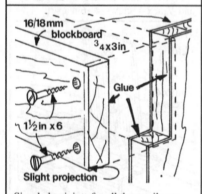

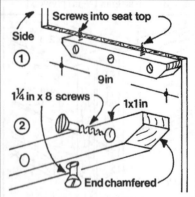

Simple lap joints for all three rails are formed as shown, allowing slight projection of rail ends for trimming when glue has set.

Saw notches in sides; drill counter-sink for screws. Assemble 'dry', check, then re-assemble after smearing with woodworking glue.

Method of fixing seat to sides (1), using 1 x 1in (25 x 25mm) planed softwood fillets. Screw holes are $^3/_{16}$in counter-sunk for screw heads (2).

Desk top is fixed in same way, but with fillets 15in long and using seven, instead of five, screws with each fillet.

Making a storage chest

Chests have been used for centuries to store all sorts of things, and they are just as useful in our modern age.

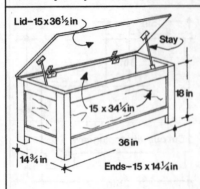

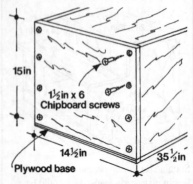

Useful as toy-box, linen chest etc., unit is made from 15in veneered chipboard: one 6ft length makes front and back; another makes ends and top.

Stripwood is glued, pinned to front and ends to imitate framing and form legs. Bottom is 9mm ($^3/_8$in) plywood.

Ends are sawn to $14^1/_2$in long, smoothed and then fixed to front and back boards with chipboard screws, driven through drilled and countersunk holes.

Corners could also be glued for greater strength.

Plywood bottom is fixed with glue and $^3/_4$in x 4 screws, 4 - 6in apart.

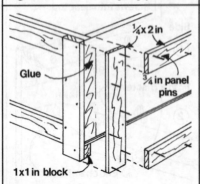

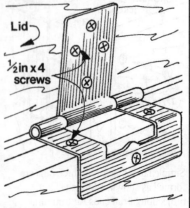

Stripwood (matching chipboard, or softwood for painting) is secured with fine pins and glue.

Fix leg strips on end first; fit 1 x 1in corner block; then legs at front and back; horizontal strips last. Slightly recess pin heads with punch, and fill holes.

Single-cranked skeleton hinges shown are easy to fit. Fix them about 4in from each end with chipboard screws. If board used is more than 16mm thick, $^5/_8$in screws can be used.

Coffee table-cum-magazine rack

This bit of furniture is a real bonus for living room, conservatory or even a large bedroom – and it's easy to put together.

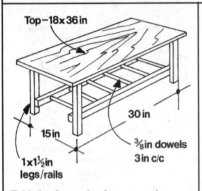

Table is of very simple construction, but more experienced workers may prefer to form conventional joints between the legs and rails.

Top is in wood-grain veneered chipboard, legs, rails and dowel (for rack) in hardwood; the hardwood should be varnished.

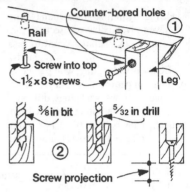

Glue and screw legs to top rail (1); set square before tightening screws.

Holes for screws are counter-bored (2): make 'blind' hole $^3/_8$ in diam, then drill screw clearance hole. 'Blind' hole should be of depth to allow screws to project $^3/_4$ in into rails $^1/_2$ in into top.

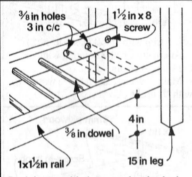

Back is assembled separately, checked for fit, then glued and screwed to legs.

Bore holes in which dowel is good fit, about $^1/_2$ in deep.

Saw dowel rod into equal lengths, fractionally too short, so that there can be slight end movement; press ends into the 'blind' holes.

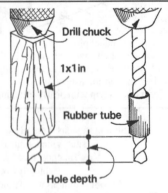

Make all 'blind' holes, using some form of depth stop of drill/bit. One can consist of square wood with hole bored through lengthwise, bottom corners rounded (1). Another, especially with twist drill, uses rubber tube or binding of insulating tape (2).

Handy portable toolbox to make

This type of toolbox is a boon to any handyman, keeping tools tidy and ready to hand for use anywhere inside or outside the home.

Made mainly in first-grade 9mm ($^3/_8$in) seven-ply, box has two sections for, small saw, hammer, screwdrivers, chisels.

Below is sliding tray, with partitions forming compartments for items such as nails, screws, wall plugs, drill bits.

After pin-heads have been punched down, holes filled, box could receive two coats p.u. varnish.

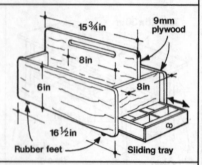

(1) Method of assembly of main case – all in 9mm plywood.

All members are made true, to ensure good butt joints, and then fixed together with woodwork adhesive and panel pins.

Fix centre shelf first, then ends; check handle/partition is good fit before gluing, pinning; fix bottom last.

Form finger-grip with nearly-touching

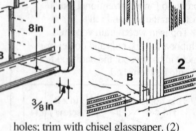

holes; trim with chisel glasspaper. (2)

Alternative, better, jointing with housings three plies deep.

Make saw cuts, and remove waste with $^1/_4$in chisel.

Sliding tray has 9mm plywood sides glued, pinned to $^3/_4$ x 1in ends, faced with thin plywood.

Bottom is thin plywood glued, pinned to sides, ends.

Partitions are halved, making slots with saw, and glued in.

Ball catch prevents tray sliding open when box is carried.

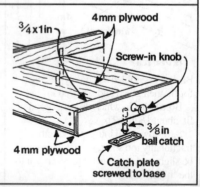

Making a mini-wardrobe

Many is the home that has a bedroom which appears to small to accommodate a wardrobe, but this scaled-down version should solve the problem.

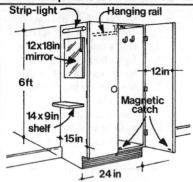

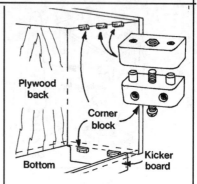

Wardrobe can be made in chipboard (melamine or hardwood-faced). Small shelf serves as dressing table; strip-light (with shaver socket?) can be connected to convenient wall socket. Inside shelf, with front-back hanging rail under, could be added for child's room.

Notch ends for skirting and, at front, for 3in. toe space. Saw top and bottom to length and fix to ends with corner blocks (white or brown) secured with 1in. x 6 chipboard screws. Fix 4mm. plywood back, also kicker board, with glue and panel pins.

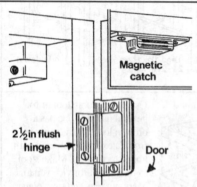

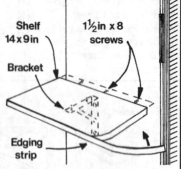

Hang each (lay-on) door with three 2 1/2in. flush hinges fixed with 5/8in. chipboard screws; these hinges are thin, do not need to be recessed into door or frame. Fix magnetic catches flush with front of top and bottom, then screw mating catch plates to doors.

Make shelf with matching chipboard or with blockboard (to be painted or stained, varnished), rounding front corner and laying edging strip. Mount on simple - say white plastic - bracket and secure with chipboard screws from inside after drilling, countersinking holes.

Three stools to make

Stools are handy to have around the house as very portable seats, whether for the bedroom, living room or kitchen.

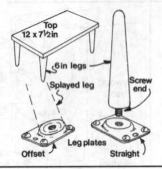

Simplest stool has top of 1/2in. plywood or veneered chipboard, with screw-on legs; choose fixing plates for splayed or right-angled legs. Attach plates with round-head screws. Stool shown is suitable for child or for use as 'step' for reaching high shelves.

Also easy to make, this larger stool is suitable for use with a breakfast bar. Prepare legs, rounding sharp edges and boring for dowel rails. Make two end frames first, fixing dowels with glue and 3/4in. pins, from inside; them fix plywood with glue and screws. Fix plywood and dowels between end frames secure 1 x 1in. fillets with glue and pins after drilling for screws to be driven into top.

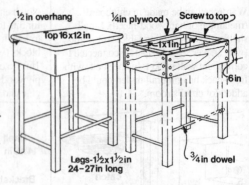

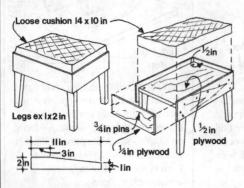

Useful as a foot-stool or for general use, this one has a drop-in loose cushion made from latex foam, covered with upholstery fabric. Make stool to fit cushion (or vice versa). Mark out legs and saw, plane bevels. Then make side frames fixing 1/4in. plywood with glue and pins. Fix ends, then 1/2in. plywood base. When glue has set, push down pin heads, fill holes and sand down ready for painting.

Small child's blackboard

Every child loves to chalk on a blackboard. Make someone you know happy with this easily constructed board and easel.

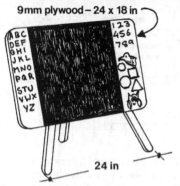

9mm plywood – 24 x 18 in

24 in

Plywood board has three legs, centre one pivoting. Whole board is evenly coated with slightly thinned emulsion paint; then centre portion is painted with special blackboard paint. Letters, figures and simple pictures can be done by hand or with transfers.

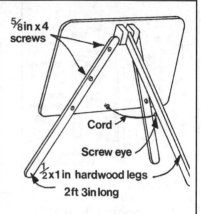

⅝in x 4 screws

Cord

Screw eye

½x1 in hardwood legs
2ft 3in long

Fixed legs are secured to back of board with woodwork adhesive and three screws - which must not pierce the front. Centre, pivoting leg closes flat and is held in open position with nylon or cotton cord tied to a pair of small screw eyes.

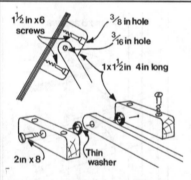

1½ in x6 screws

⅜ in hole

3/16 in hole

1x1½in 4in long

2in x 8

Thin washer

Construction of leg pivot. Softwood blocks, in 1 x 1 1/2in., are fixed with glue and screws after assembly. The are counterbored, so that screws will go full 1/4in. into plywood. Screw, with washer each side of leg, passes through countersink hole in one block, clearance hole through leg.

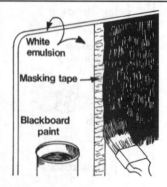

White emulsion

Masking tape

Blackboard paint

After white emulsion paint has dried fully, lay strips of masking tape and brush blackboard paint between them; remove tape when paint is touch-dry. Draw/transfer letters, figures etc. in white margins.

Handy woodwork-horse

When turning your hand to carpentry a work-horse can be as useful as a second pair of hands.

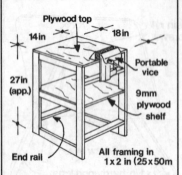

All framing in 1 x 2 in (25x50m)

Unit, consisting of strong softwood framework with plywood top and shelf, can be used as either portable bench, with clamp-on vice as shown; or, lying on its side or end, as sawing horse 14 or 18in. high. Preferably, apply clear varnish to completed unit.

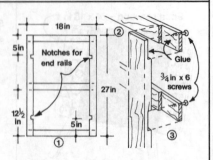

First make two identical frames to dimensions shown (1). Halving joints are used to corners (2) and T-halvings (3) halfway down side members. Mark out joints accurately and make corner halvings with tenon saw; others with saw and chisel. Also saw and chop out notches for end rails. Then, after checking joints for fit, glue and screw frames together.

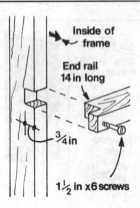

Saw notches in end rails to fit corresponding notches in upright. Secure each joint with glue and single screw through countersunk hole in rail.

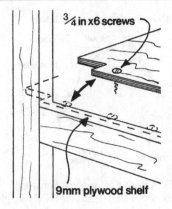

Notches to fit uprights are sawn at corners of shelf, which is fixed to centre rails with glue and screws. Plywood top, with square corners, is fixed similarly.

184

Floors
Walls and
Ceilings

Pages 186-218

Laying sheet flooring

If you have always wanted to lay your own sheet flooring but were unsure how to deal with the difficult spots like basin or lavatory pedestals, read on to find out the tricks of the trade.

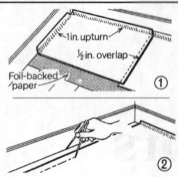

Procedure is similar for vinyl or lino. Floor must be smooth and dry. Keep roll in warm room for a few days, then cut lengths to allow upturn and overlap (1). Wood floor treated with preservative should be covered with foil-backed building paper. Always leave for ten days or so before final trimming. First trim to long, straight wall (2), moving length aside and making line parallel to wall with compass or dividers. Cut to line with scissors (vinyl) or sharp knife (lino).

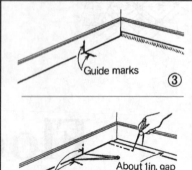

To trim ends, chalk guide marks on sheet and well (3); draw sheet forward (4), set dividers as shown and mark end; then cut. Complete trimming by cutting through centre of overlaps with knife against straight-edge.

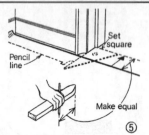

To mark around wall obstructions (5) draw right-angle lines against set square and then use dividers or pencil marker (pencil tightly through hole in pointed stick) as shown.

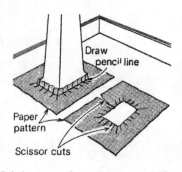

It is best to make a paper pattern (6) for base of basin or lavatory pedestal. Press into position and draw line around the angle. Cut paper to line and transfer shape to flooring material.

Staining and polishing floors

Before staining or polishing any floor, it is imperative to prepare the surface first

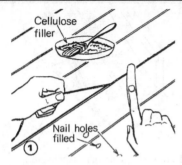

Good preparation is most important part. Fix loose boards, drive down nail heads and fill holes with plastic wood or cellulose filler. Plane off sharp ridges; then press filler into narrow cracks. For wider cracks (1) coat rough string with filler and press well in with knife blade. If floor is to be stained, tint filler with stain.

Hire a special floor sander, and, using like a vacuum cleaner (2), smooth off floor surface, following instructions supplied. Edges must be done with an edge sander (hired), orbital sander or attachment on electric drill.

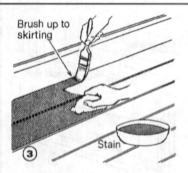

After thorough sanding, wipe surface with damp rag to remove dust. Use stain of same make as sealer/varnish to follow. Working from end to end (3) do up to skirting with brush; remainder, two or three boards at a time, with rag swab. Or brush on polyurethane varnish containing its own wood dye.

With parquet, remove all wax polish with medium steel wool and white spirit. Wipe off with clean cloth and, if necessary, smooth with orbital sander (4) or floor sander. Apply floor seal/varnish with brush. Varnish can be gloss, satin or matt as preferred.

Strip and parquet flooring

If your door bottom has to be sawn to clear the new floor you're laying, make sure to do the sawing before you begin the floor.

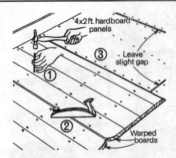

Careful preparation of floor is first essential. Re-nail loose boards, punch down 'proud' nail heads (1) and remove ridges with shaping-tool plane (2). On very rough floor, next lay hardboard panels (3); fix with 3/4in. non-rust panel pins, driven in 6in. apart from centre outwards, then from centre lines to corners.

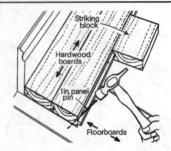

Hardwood (teak, oak, sapele etc.) tongued-and-grooved boards about 1.2 x 2in. make excellent flooring. Lay them at right-angles to floorboards and drive close together using short length with tongue removed as striking block for hammer. 'Secret' nail by driving pins at 45 deg. through angle of tongue; punch down heads.

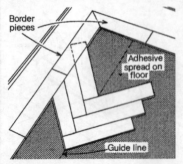

Herring-bone parquet can be formed with blocks of 3/8in. hardwood or thin plywood - both are made specially for this purpose. First fit border and draw guide line on floor parallel to edge of this. Trim ends of blocks to border. Blocks are fixed with adhesive obtained from suppliers of blocks.

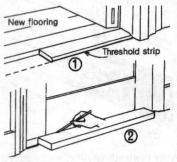

(1) Finish at door opening with shaped threshold strip. (2) Door bottom may have to be sawn to clear new floor. If necessary, do this before laying floor. Mark against edge of board rather thicker than flooring. Some parquet is in square panels and laid as tiles.

188

Laying floor tiles

Laying floor tiles has never been so easy as it is when you follow the below centre line method.

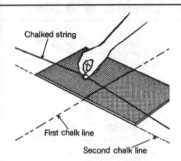

After preparing wood floor or thoroughly cleaning concrete floor (which must be free from damp) 'snap' a centre line with chalked string held taut between two temporary nails. Place two tiles on line and 'snap' second centre line at right-angles to first, as shown.

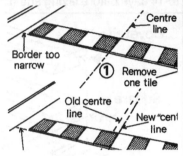

Place row of loose tiles on one centre lines and check width of borders (1). Both should be at least half-tile width (4 1/2in.) for good appearance. If border is too narrow remove one tile, move remainder and 'snap' a new 'centre' line (2). Repeat this procedure in other direction.

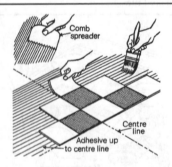

Working to new 'centre' lines, apply adhesive to floor with brush or spreader, following instructions on can. Lay five tiles against line; 'hinge' (do not slide) them into place and press well down. Add others to cover half floor, except border. Repeat on other half.

To measure and fit the border tiles, place tile (1) over a laid tile; put second tile (2) over that but touching wall. Mark line against edge of tile (2) on tile (1) and cut to line with scissors or sharp knife. Lay cut portion as border, cut edge to wall.

Repairs to parquet floors

Beware that trouble can easily arise if certain mistakes are made. Common errors include damp floors, blocks not stored in room for 10-14 days before laying and no gaps left at wall for expansion.

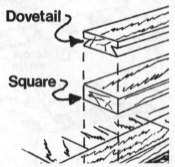

Loose parquet blocks can usually be re-fixed with a bitumen-rubber adhesive. Blocks are of two main types: dovetail and square, but some are tongued and grooved, so less inclined to lift. If several blocks are loose, suspect one of faults as above.

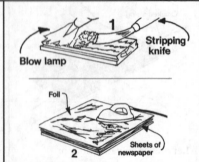

Pitch can be scraped off solid blocks after heating with blow-lamp (1). Keep flame moving; work in safe place outdoors. Adhesive on parquet tiles can be largely removed by heating over foil, newspaper with laundry iron (2). Take care with felt-backed tiles.

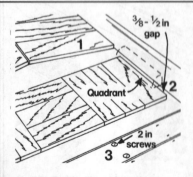

Parquet tiles/blocks may 'bulge' because they have been fixed tight against skirting (1). Cut and re-fix, leaving gap (2), which can be covered with quadrant moulding or filled with work strip. Springy floorboards can cause parquet to lift; secure with screws (3).

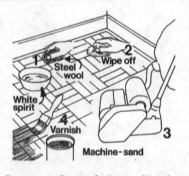

Sequence of re-surfacing neglected parquet: 1. scour with steel wool, white spirit; 2. immediately wipe off softened wax, dirt; 3. sand with (hired) floor-sanding machine - or for small areas orbital or drum sander; 4. apply p.u. varnish or two-part plastic lacquer.

Sheet floor coverings

Before laying, floor should be flat and smooth. Punch down nail heads, then sand wood floor- or cover with hardboard. Use self-levelling compound and, if necessary, damp-proofer, with solid floor.

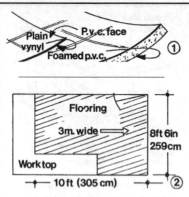

Choose less-expensive plain, or quieter cushioned, vinyl (1). To find best width (2,3,4 metres) draw simple floor plan (2); supplier can advise from this. Avoid joins if possible. 'Lay-flat- vinyl can usually be laid without adhesive.

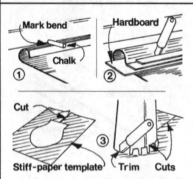

Turn back vinyl and mark along crease (1). Then cut to line with knife - (2) strong scissors. To fit around pedestal, make paper template or cut under-size and make short 'star' cuts before trimming with knife (3).

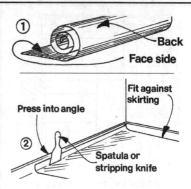

Loosely reverse-roll, even 'lay-flat', flooring (1); leave overnight. Cut to approximate shape, but 150mm. or so over-size. Lay long edge against skirting, turn up other (2); press into angle, then trim with knife, scissors.

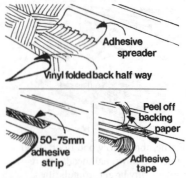

All-over adhesive may be needed, but follow makers' instructions. Fold back vinyl and treat each half floor in turn (1). For easier lifting later, applying strips of adhesive around all edges (2) or use double-sided adhesive tape (3).

Hardboard and plywood flooring

While water-resistant plywood is good for levelling and stiffening a slightly springy floor, standard hardboard provides a good surface for vinyl tiles and carpeting

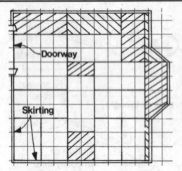

Standard hardboard provides good surface for vinyl tiles, carpet etc. Have small (say 2 x 4ft.) panels and lay in form of brick-bonding. First draw from plan on squared paper to estimate requirements. Lay whole panels first, then pieces cut to fill areas shown hatched above.

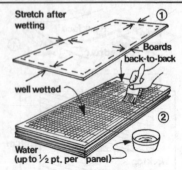

Hardboard should be 'conditioned' (stretched) before laying (1); then, after being securely fixed, it will become drum-tight as it dries. Brush, sponge water liberally over (rough) backs of board (2) and lay back-to-back on flat surface for 24-48 hours before use.

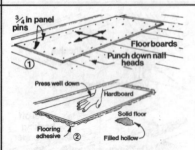

Fix hardboard to wood floor - after punching down nail heads and removing any larger irregularities - with 3/4in. non-rust pins. Start from centre, pins 8in. apart. then around edges 4in. apart (1). Panels can be fixed to cleaned solid floor (2) with flooring adhesive - without being 'conditioned'. First fill major floor depressions with mortar/exterior filler.

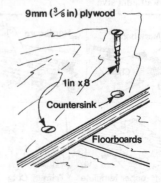

Water-resistant plywood 9mm. thick is good for levelling and stiffening a slightly springy floor. Fix with countersunk screws at 8-10in. centres in lines 16-20in. apart. Seal with diluted bonder before laying ceramic tiles.

Fixing to tiled walls

Tiles can be easily scratched and cracked by improperly applied fittings, but with a little care damage can be avoided, whatever the method of fixing.

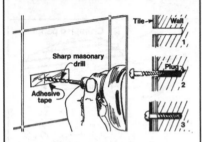

To drill for wall plugs stick adhesive tape over marked position. With hand drill, hold exactly at right-angles, apply steady pressure and rotate very slowly until glaze is pierced. With power drill (low-speed only), first pierce by rotating chuck with fingers, as shown. Drill deep enough for plug to pass through tile (1); use screw to insert plug (2); and screw on fitting (3).

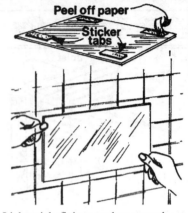

Lightweight fittings can be mounted with sticker tabs. Fix to back of mirror, peel off paper backing and press tabs against cleaned tiles. Position carefully, because later movement is not possible.

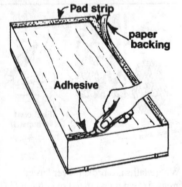

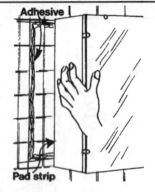

Heavier fittings, such as cabinets, can be securely mounted with special pad strip and adhesive. Apply adhesive around back of cabinet, smooth on strip immediately, and leave one hour. Apply adhesive around outline previously marked on wall; remove paper backing from strip and apply adhesive. Wait about 20 minutes, then press cabinet against wall, ensuring it is correctly aligned. Position cannot be changed once adhesive surfaces have made contact.

Repairs to lathe-and-plaster walls

If you have a large area of wall or ceiling which needs to be replastered you would be advised to call in a professional plasterer, but for small areas of damage you should be able to do the repair work yourself.

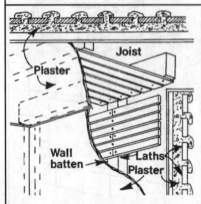

With this finish (usually only in older houses) lathes are nailed across the joints, or wall battens, and plaster is pressed through the laths so that it forms a 'key' behind them, as shown in insets. It breaks away if laths are faulty.

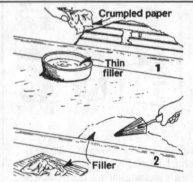

Cracks and small areas of damaged plaster can be filled with cellulose filer. But where laths are broken, first pack hole with crumpled newspaper soaked in thin filler (1).When dry, apply filler, mixed to a thick paste, with small trowel (2).

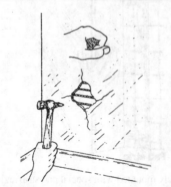

All cracked, loose plaster (test by tapping with knuckle) should be chipped away until a firm and 'solid' area is reached. Take care to avoid damaging laths.

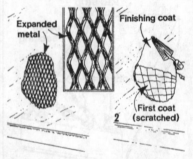

Where laths are broken over larger areas fix expanded metal over them (1), after coating cut edges with paint to prevent rusting. Then apply two coats of wall plaster. When first is nearly dry, scratch with tip of trowel; then apply second coat with large trowel or float to finish with existing plaster (2).

Simplified wall plastering

D-I-Y plastering has been made easy with various ready-mixed one-coat plasters suitable for inexperienced plasterers to apply.

For smoothing slightly rough, uneven wall, use 'skim' plaster, applied up to 1\8in. thick from tub in which it comes. Use liberal, upward brush strokes (1), Smooth with spreader supplied (2).

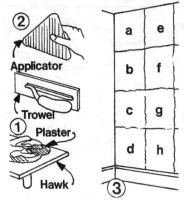

For thicker coats (up to 2in.) use special one-coat plaster; it can be applied with plaster's trowel (1) or plastic 'applicator' supplied (2). Spread upwards, covering areas in sequence shown (3).

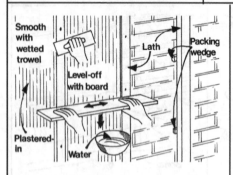

When plastering a whole wall it is helpful first to fix temporary laths about 16in. apart. If necessary, insert wedges to keep laths in same plane; check with long straight-edge. Plaster between laths, level off with edge of board, giving sawing motion, and smooth with trowel frequently dipped in water. Remove laths, fill channels when plaster has set.

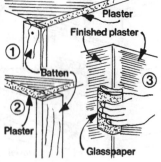

To make a neat job at exterior corners, fix temporary batten to wall and plaster up to it (1). When plaster has set, transfer beaten to other wall and repeat (2). When hard, lightly glasspaper down angle (3).

Repointing a wall

Crumbling, broken pointing can be the cause of damp. Repointing small areas does not have to be a difficult or time-consuming job.

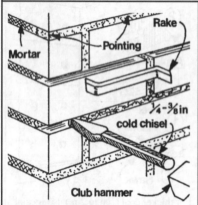

Hack out to depth of 1/2-3/4 in. with cold chisel and club hammer. Then rake, scrape out all loose material. Rake can be made from steel bar - or use edge of cold chisel or strong screwdriver.

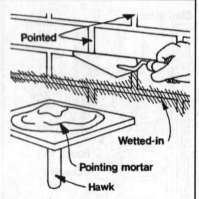

Point areas of about 1sq. yd. at a time, after brushing out dust and wetting-in joints Use dry, ready-mixed pointing mortar or make with 1 part cement, 1 lime, 6 builders' sand. Charge back of pointing trowel and press in mortar.

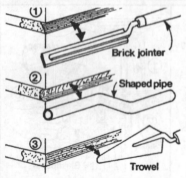

Weather-struck pointing (1) is usually best for brickwork, and is done by drawing jointer or small trowel along joint. If hollowed joints (2) are preferred use rounded jointer or pipe bent as shown. Flush pointing (3), usual with stone walls, is done with trowel.

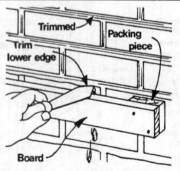

Especially with weather-struck pointing, upper edge will be straight and 'clean'. Excess mortar needs to be trimmed from lower edge, as shown. Have a board, with packing piece each end (to allow mortar droppings to fall through) and trim with putty knife, trowel.

Save it! Wall insulation

Most heat from the home is generally lost through walls which have not be adequately insulated. Although professional expertise is needed for some applications, others can be safely accomplished.

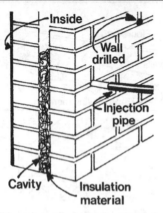

With cavity wall, shown, best insulation is obtained by injecting foam or other insulating material. But this must be done by reputable specialist firm.

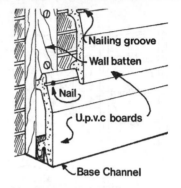

Maintenance-free insulation can be applied to outside of either cavity or solid wall by battening (use preservative-treated timber) and nailing on cellular-interior Upvc boarding. Get detailed instructions from makers.

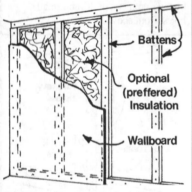

Wall insulation is easier from inside. One method is to fix battens at 24in./16in. centres and then nail on plasterboard, insulation board or other cladding. For best insulation use battens up to 2in. thick and fill spaces with insulating blanket.

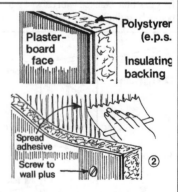

Special thermal board (1), with choice of e.p.s. thickness, gives excellent insulation. Fix to flat wall with recommended adhesive (2) one board at a time; have few screws for extra security. Use Battens on uneven walls. Study instructions before purchase.

Building a room partition

Dividing large rooms into smaller living areas may seem a daunting task, but with a bit of thought and preparation, partitions do not have to be an impossible dream.

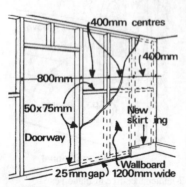

Good partition wall can be made with timber framing as shown, covered with wallboard, e.g plasterboard, both sides. If required, a door can be in any convenient position. For improved sound insulation fix glass-fibre blanket, with dabs of glue, before boarding second side.

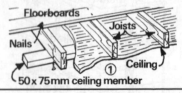

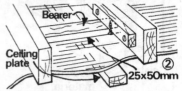

Ceiling plate is easily fixed across joists (1) but could be along one joist. When needed parallel to but between joists, fix bearers of 25 x 50mm. wood as shown (2). Joist positions can be found by measurement, or drilling small holes, from above.

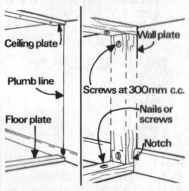

Fix ceiling plate and drop plumb line to determine correct position for floor plate. Fix floor plate with either nails or screws (later if plaster ceiling below). Cut wall plate to fit and screw to wall plugs.

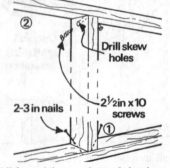

All frame joints can be made by skew-nailing (1) but to avoid risk of cracking a plaster ceiling it is better to use screws (2) driven through pre-drilled holes. Pre-drilled holes also make skew-nailing easier.

Wall redecoration problems

It is some times necessary to make running repairs to papered walls. This does not necessarily mean that the the entire room needs to be redecorated.

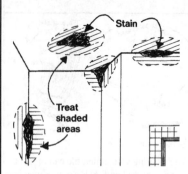

To prevent stains caused by dampness (which should first be cured) showing through new decorations: 1. strip off any paper; 2. wash area with fungicide or dilute bleach; 3. brush on two coats aluminium primer or, better, special interior waterproofing solution. Treat area well beyond stain.

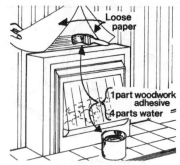

When wallpaper comes away around fire, peel back and seal wall with diluted woodworking adhesive. When dry, re-coat wall with more dilute adhesive and smooth paper back with soft duster. Better is to seal wall before.

White powdery deposit, known as efflorescence, is caused by salts from plaster etc. crystallising on surface. Remove with fairly stiff, dry brush. A few repetitions at intervals may be necessary before redecoration is 'safe'.

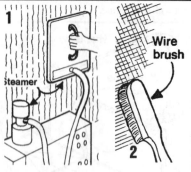

(1) When necessary, stripping of texture paint is not easy and is usually best accomplished by using a wallpaper steam stripper, from tool-hire shop. Steam will gradually soften paint so that it can be scraped off with a stripping knife. (2) Painted paper can be stripped in normal way after well scratching through the surface.

Cutting and drilling tiles

Simply cutting tiles in a straight line to fit those little nooks can look daunting to the beginner, but with a little help, shaping tiles to fit around bathroom or kitchen fittings will seem like child's play.

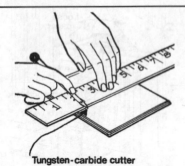

Tungsten-carbide cutter

Straight 'cuts' are easily made using special scriber/cutter with tungsten-carbide tip. This is drawn, under steady pressure, once only along the line, to scratch through glazed surface. Simply curved 'cuts' can be made in same way, but without the rule.

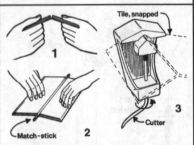

After scoring with cutter, tile can often be snapped in the hands (1). Another way is to lay it over two matches (directly under scored line) and to press firmly down at each side (2). In either case, tile will snap cleanly if correctly scored. Even better for beginners is the new tool (3) with triangular jaws which snap tile when cutter is inserted and screwed in.

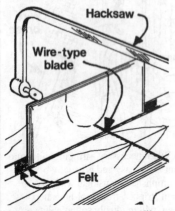

Small-radius cuts are most readily made with special blade (carbide grains welded to steel wire) held in hacksaw. Hold tile in vice and move to keep saw close to padded jaws.

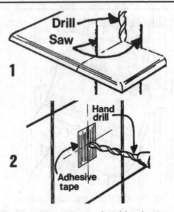

Corner cuts can be made with wire-type blade, preferably after drilling hole (1). To drill wall tiles, use masonry or glass drill held in hand-drill; adhesive tape prevents slipping (2).

Easier wall panelling

Although panelling appears to have gone out of fashion for living rooms, the fashion for all things Scandinavian has ensured its existence in bathrooms and kitchens. Nor is it an effect that requires a professional.

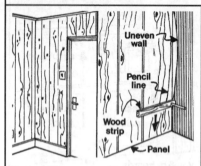

Reasonably smooth walls can be panelled without battening. Plywood or other panels are fixed with wall-panel adhesive, applied with a gun. It is best to prise off the skirting and replace later. Saw panels to length; also to width where they meet window or door. Start at corner and, if necessary, fit edge to wall. Mark with pencil through hole in wood strip; then trim with coping saw or shaping tool.

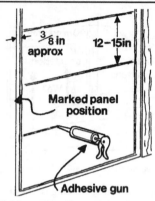

Hold panel in place and mark position on wall. then apply lines of adhesive about 3/8in. away from edge positions; also 12-15in. apart across wall. 'Hinge' panel into place and press evenly.

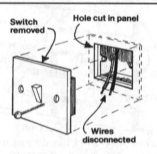

For switch socket mark position accurately and cut out hole as shown. Switch must be removed, after switching off main supply, and later replaced. If not experienced in electrical work have this done by qualified person. Check hole before fixing panel.

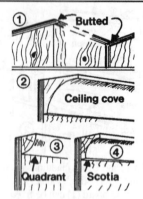

Panels can be butted at corners (1) and, at external angle, smoothed with glasspaper. Top edge can be covered with ceiling cove (2) or 1in. wood moulding (3,4).

Exterior wall-cladding

Appearance apart, wall-cladding gives extra weather protection and improved insulation. Wood, plastics and brick or stone can all be applied by the enthusiastic amateur.

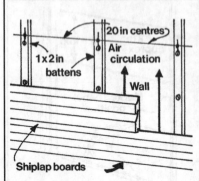

Shiplap boards

A simple method of cladding is shown, with vertical wall battens and horizontal shiplap boards. Fix battens with non-rust screws into plugs: boards with rustproof nails/pins. Allow for air-circulation behind boards.

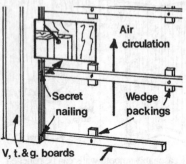

V, t. & g. boards

For vertical boarding, fix battens horizontally. Slightly tapered wedges behind battens allow for ventilation and for making flat surface on slightly irregular wall. Vee, tongued and grooved boards look well, can be secret mailed with non-rust pins through tongues (inset).

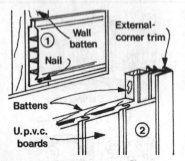

Rigid pvc. and Upvc. claddings are rot-proof and 'everlasting'. One example of cellular rigid board (1) can be fixed similarly to wood. U.P.V.C. board (2) in one of many profiles. Special edge, corner and other fixings are available for all board types.

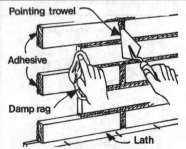

Brick, or stone-effect, tiles can match rendered or block walls to other walls. They can be applied almost as ceramic tiles over a temporary support lath. 'Butter' tile back with special adhesive; press firmly against wall; point between tiles and smooth off with damp rag.

Note: Buy preservative-impregnated battens, or treat with reliable preservative.

202

Forming a wall arch

An archway dividing a room or rooms can make an attractive feature, whether you want to adapt an opening or create a whole new look.

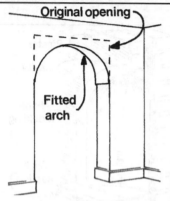

Original opening

Fitted arch

Rectangular wall opening can be arched fairly easily. But if new opening is required, seek clearance from Council Planning Officers. Support must be provided if wall is load-bearing.

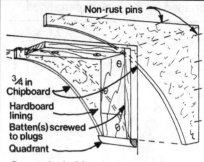

Non-rust pins

³⁄₄ in Chipboard

Hardboard lining

Batten(s) screwed to plugs

Quadrant

One method of forming an arch is to screw battens to inside of opening, fixing chipboard sawn to shape (in one, two, four sections) to these and adding curved lining of hardboard, plywood, glued and pinned. Ends are finished with quadrant moulding. Arch should be a little less than wall thickness to allow for plaster skim.

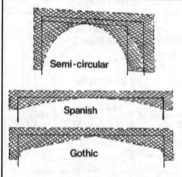

Semi-circular

Spanish

Gothic

Easier way is by using pre-formed arch in galvanised expanded metal, ready for plastering. Three of shapes available, from builders' merchants, are shown, but there are many others in various sizes. Each comes in two overlapping sections to allow for different wall thicknesses.

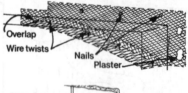

Overlap
Wire twists
Nails
Plaster

Hack away plaster

Pre-formed arch can be fixed to wall with galvanised nails or dabs of plaster. Before plastering, fix overlapping halves together with twists of rust-proof wire. On already-plastered wall, plaster is cut away to receive arch and coating plaster. Make-good when plastering expanded metal. Further instructions come with arch.

Decorative wall niches

A niche set into a wall can be an ideal way to display to their best advantage your prized ornaments. Although some methods need a certain level of skill with brickwork others can be successfully created by the less experienced.

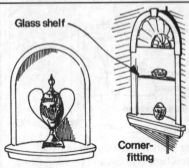

Face-fitting

Corner-fitting

Glass shelf

Two of the many types of fibrous-plaster niche that come complete and with basic installation details. The face-fixing niche requires a hole in the wall, which is not always feasible; but the corner-fitting one can be fairly easily mounted on wooden bearers.

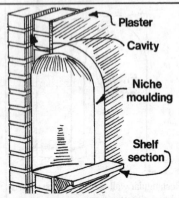

Plaster

Cavity

Niche moulding

Shelf section

Most face-fixing niches can be accommodated by cutting away the bricks of the inner layer of a cavity wall with cold chisel, hammer; with fair experience of brickwork.

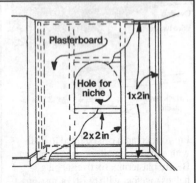

Plasterboard

Hole for niche

1x2in

2x2in

Instead of cutting away brickwork, a simple method is to make a false wall, especially as in a recess, to receive the niche. It should be set forward by the full depth of the niche, and consists of framing covered with, e.g., plasterboard.

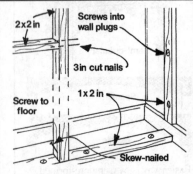

Screws into wall plugs

2x2in

3in cut nails

1x2in

Screw to floor

Skew-nailed

Fixing of softwood framing. Screw 1 x 2in. to floor and to each wall and ceiling joist(s). Fix uprights (at not more than 24in. centres) and rails to receive niche with cut nails. Saw hole in ivory-faced plasterboard and fix with galvanised nails. Use a single sheet if possible to save need to fill joints.

Building a light partition wall

A lightweight partition can help you make the most of a large room and with a grasp of the rudiments of carpentry need not be too daunting a task.

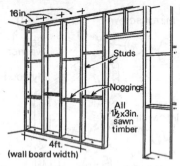

Framework of sawn timber is fixed as shown and later covered with wallboard; 2.g. plaster board. Studs (uprights) are spaced to suit width of wallboard, usually 4ft. Short cross-members (noggings) about 2ft. 6in. apart are staggered for easier nailing.

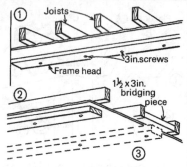

First fix frame head to ceiling, with screws into joists. It can go across joists (1) or along one of them (2). If it must go between, bridging pieces (3) are fixed to receive screws – possible only when joists are accessible.

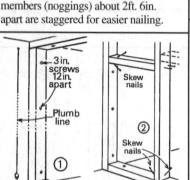

Fix side member to wall with screws into plugs, checking for vertical with plumb-line (1). Screw/nail sill to floor and fix studs (again checking with plumb-line) top and bottom with 3in. nails set as shown; then fix noggings (2).

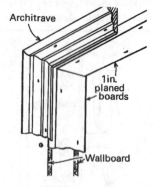

After fixing wallboards with galvanised nails, fixed planed boards around door opening with 2in. oval nails. Nail on architrave moulding in same way. Recess nail heads and fill holes.

IMPORTANT: Obtain written permission of local council before commencing work. Council surveyor's department will supply application form.

Fixing wall pictures and mirrors

What family home is complete without its gallery of pictures and mirrors? But to create clean professional finish takes more than just hammering in a tack...

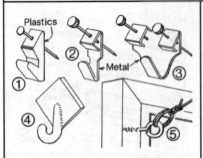

Angle hooks, in plastics or metal (1,2,3), with hardened steel fixing pins, are most convenient for hanging all except very heavy pictures or framed mirrors, provided that wall plaster gives good 'hold'. Moulded plastic adhesive hook (4) is suitable on smooth surfaces (e.g. tiles). Screw eye, with split ring (5) is usually best for attaching cord to frame.

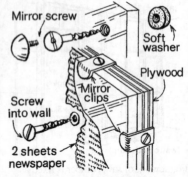

Mount drilled, unframed mirror with mirror screws, which have domed head. Insert cork or other soft washer between mirror and wall. Undrilled mirror can be fixed to plywood board with clips as shown. Fit mirror to plywood, remove, screw board to wall, refix mirror.

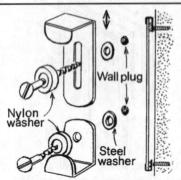

These special clips provide neat mounting for plain mirrors. Upper clip is raised to insert mirror, then depressed to hold it securely. Screws are driven into wall plugs. Fittings on same principle, but with top clip spring-loaded, are made in moulded plastics.

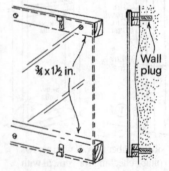

When wall is very uneven, as in some old cottages, screw battens to wall, using countersink screws and wall plugs. Battens provide a good mounting for either mirror screws or clips. They must provide flat surface for mirror and should be tapered if necessary.

Fixing adjustable wall units

Fixing shelving units to walls can provide valuable and attractive storage and display space. It is a simple task so long as the correct preparation is made and the correct tools used.

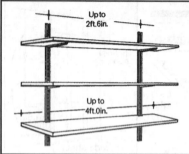

Up to 2ft.6in.

Up to 4ft.0in.

Wall units can be open shelves, as shown, or a shelf can be replaced by a cupboard. Wall supporters are slotted to allow brackets to be placed at any height. Shelves can be 3/4in. veneered chipboard or planed timber. Any length of shelving can be used by adding further supports.

Mark on wall positions for top of supports. Then, with masonry drill, mark position of top hole. Remove support and drill hole for type of plug to be used; rubber tubing on drill acts as depth gauge. Insert plug, replace support and loosely fit top screw. Set support vertical against plumb line and fix bottom end. Drill and plug other holes and drive in screws. Special fixings are needed for plasterboard walls.

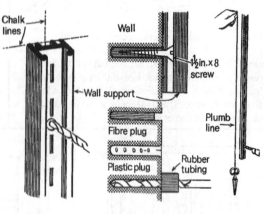

Chalk lines

Wall

1½in. × 8 screw

← Wall support

Fibre plug

Plastic plug

Plumb line

Rubber tubing

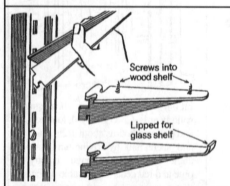

Screws into wood shelf

Lipped for glass shelf

Clip in the brackets; these are available in various lengths and should be about 1in. less than shelf width. Special type, with lip, is made for glass shelves - which should usually be 1/4in. thick. Both brackets and supports vary slightly according to make, but all are fixed similarly.

207

Panelling a wall

Whether you choose to buy adhesive-backed decorative panels or timber which needs to be affixed with nails, wooden panelling can make a world of difference to a room.

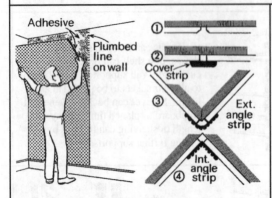

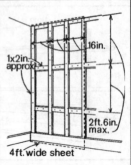

Simplest method is to fix decorative hardboard or plywood with contact adhesive; but wall must be flat and clean. Work to a plumbed line the width of the sheet (usually 48in.) from corner. Leave 1/8in. gap between hardboard sheets. Treat joints by: (1) bevelling edges; (2) fixing cover strip; (3) and (4) fixing wood or plastic mouldings over corner joints.

Panels can be fixed to battens 2in. x thickness of skirting, secured to plastered brick or block walls with masonry nails. Spacings shown are for usual 4ft.-wide sheets. Allow plywood panels to touch each other.

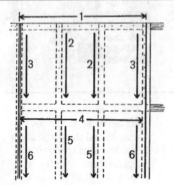

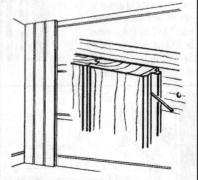

Sequence of pinning panels, with 3/4in. rust-resistant 'lost-head' panel pins to wall battens. Set pins around outsides 4in. apart, inner pins 8in. Touch-in pin heads with matching paint or punch down and fill with plastic wood.

Fit only horizontal battens when using solid boards. Choose Vee'd, tongued and grooved boards about 1/2in. thick and 'secret nail' by driving pins at an angle through base of tongue. Knotty pine and red cedar are suitable timbers.

Fixing to walls

Many projects around the home will necessitate fixing something to a wall, be it panels, pictures or a door frame. Each task will vary in its execution depending on the material of the wall and the item to be fixed.

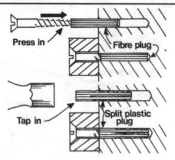

Screws into wall plugs usually give best fixing to a solid wall. Drill hole with masonry bit in hand/low-speed power drill: diameter of screw for fibre plug, larger for most plastic ones. Press fibre plug just below surface with screw; gently tap in plastic.

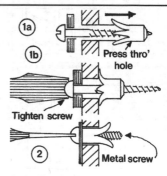

(1a, b) Simple plastic anchor for fixing to hollow wall, wallboard etc. Screw must pass through fixture, into anchor, before tightening. (2) Small plastic plug suitable for thin fixtures when space behind wall facing is small.

Adhesive tape helps prevent crumbling of wall plaster (1). If surface crumbles use plug of special fibrous plaster: roll 'cigar' (2) and press well in; make hole (3), drive in screw immediately.

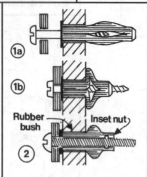

(1a, b) Hollow-wall plug with thin flange; screw is easily removed, replaced. Soft-plastic plug is shown; corresponding one is made in metal. (2) Rubber-bush anchor with inset nut that takes small bolt.

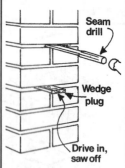

Window, door frames are often fixed with clasp nails into wedge-plug made from softwood. Hole is cut in brickwork joint with seam drill (type of narrow cold chisel).

Stone-tile wall cladding

Professional-looking stone-tile cladding, whether as a decorative feature on an internal wall or as an attractive insulator on external walls, can be achieved without professional knowledge.

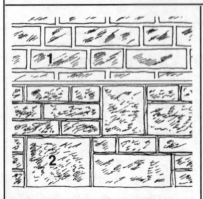

Reconstituted-stone tiles in various natural-stone colours can be bought in packs covering 1/2 or 1 sq. metre. Sizes are assorted and suitable for regular coursed tiling (1) or random effect (2). Latter come in one, two or three-tile height for standard (usually 10mm.) spacing.

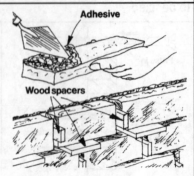

Wall – especially if rendered – must be in sound condition. Fix with special adhesive cement from tile suppliers. First arrange pattern, laying tiles out on ground; then 'butter' back of each with adhesive and press on wall, starting from bottom corner. Space equally with short lengths of wood.

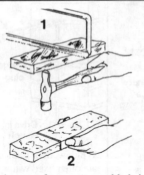

In absence of masonry-saw blade in power drill, tiles can be cut – to avoid cross-joints – by making shallow groove on both sides and edges with hacksaw and giving sharp tap with hammer.

Pointing mortar

Leave few days, protecting in wet weather, before pointing with mortar from tile suppliers or made from one part cement, one line and six sand. Mix well and make to stiff paste with water. Later, remove any on tile face with wire brush.

Installing a new ceiling

Although not a common chore about the house, installing a new ceiling is sometimes necessary to replace one that is damaged or to lower the depth of a room.

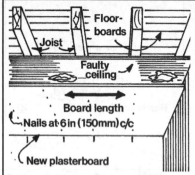

Badly damaged ceiling (especially lath-and-plaster) is best taken down and replaced with new board - a nasty and awkward job unless house is empty. If loose parts are removed, new plasterboard can be fixed over old, with galvanised nails into joists. A helper is required.

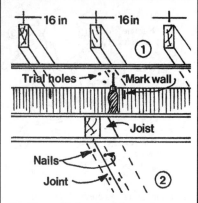

Positions of joists (at right-angles to floorboards) can be found by making trial holes with e.g. bradawl (1). Joists are normally at 16in. (400mm.) centres; mark positions on wall. Centre boards joints on joist (2).

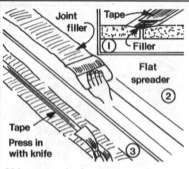

Using taper-edged, paper-covered plasterboard (1) good finish for painting, papering is fairly easily obtained. Fill joints (2), press in special jointing tape (3), apply more filler. Feather-off and smooth with damp sponge. Before starting, study free instruction supplier's booklet.

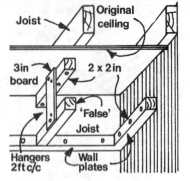

Suspended (lower) ceiling can be fixed to wall plates and joists. 'False' joist can support ceiling board, t & g, etc. Easier is to buy aluminium framed suspended ceiling kit, with ceiling panels, instructions.

Ceiling repairs

If your ceiling is starting a look a little neglected, do not despair, most can be transformed with a touch of skill and patience, without having to call in the professionals.

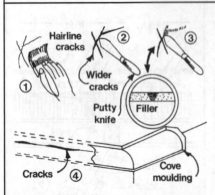

Common faults and cures: 1. Hairline cracks – brush in thin filler. 2. Wider cracks –rake out to dovetail shape, brush away dust and 3. press in filler; over-fill, level with damp cloth when nearly dry. 4. Cracks between wall and ceiling can be covered with adhesive-fixed polystyrene or plaster cove.

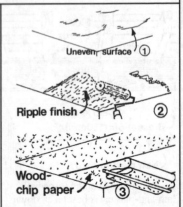

Unsightly irregular ceiling 1, can be improved without replastering by 2 applying a ripple-finish plaster/paint with roller; or 3 covering with textured or wood-chip paper. both disguise effect.

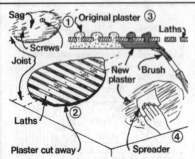

Minor sags in lath-and-plaster ceiling can sometimes be supported by carefully drilling and driving no-rust screws into joist 1. Or it may be better to cut away loose plaster 2 and repair with ready-mixed plaster skim; apply with brush forcing between laths 3; smooth with spreader.

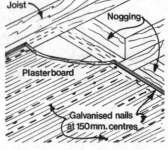

Lath-and-plaster ceiling in bad condition should be wholly or partly stripped to joists (very messy job) and made good with eg: plaster board. Nogging pieces must be fitted to support ends of boards. First study maker/supplier's free instruction booklet.

212

Fixing ceiling cove moulding

A ceiling cove an add an attractive feature to a room. It can also cover small cracks which can sometimes appear between the ceiling and walls.

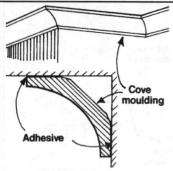

Cove comes in paper-faced plaster or expanded polystyrene. Former gives better result; latter is lightweight, easier to handle, while mitring is avoided by use of ready-made interior/exterior corner pieces. Use wall-tile adhesive for polystyrene.

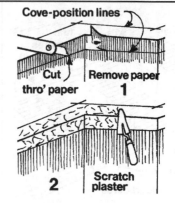

Mark cove position on ceiling, walls and, if papered, cut through (1), then wet carefully and remove paper strip. Scratch plaster to provide good key for adhesive (2) and brush off dust.

(1) 'Butter' flat sides of cove with adhesive; for plastic cove use special adhesive from cove suppliers (powder to mix with water). (2) Press firmly into position and wipe off surplus adhesive with rag; smooth off with damped brush.

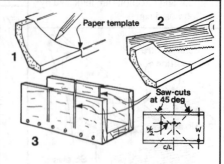

Mitres for plaster cove can be marked with free paper template (1) and then sawn to line with panel saw (2). Or make a mitre box (3) into which cove is snug fit; this gives easiest, most accurate mitring. Lightly smooth sawn edges with glasspaper. Check and, if necessary, correct all joins, square or mitre, before applying adhesive. The adhesive can also be used to fill slightly open joins.

Making fixings to ceilings

Curtain rails, room partitions and electric light fittings may all need to be secured to the ceiling. With a little forethought and preparation it need not be a difficult task.

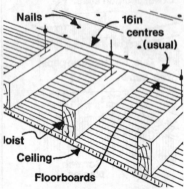

How the usual ground-floor ceiling is constructed, whether the ceiling itself is lath-and-plaster or some form of ceiling board. Screw fixings should, wherever possible, be made into the joists, whose positions and directions are indicated by the floorboard nails.

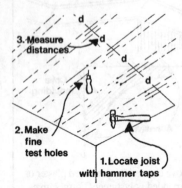

Trace joint positions by tapping ceiling with a small hammer; a 'solid' sound is heard under a joist. Make few small test holes to find centres of two joists. Locate others by measurement. Spacing at 16in. centres is customary but not universal.

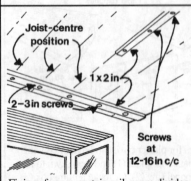

Fixings for e.g. curtain rail, room divider are provided with batten screwed either across or along joists. For intermediate fixings parallel to joists it may be necessary to combine the two methods, or to fix to boards between joists as for electric-light fittings.

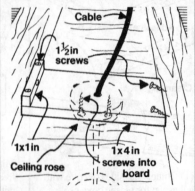

Do not attempt to fix electric-light or other fittings to ceiling itself, but to board between joists. Two fixing methods are shown: with fillet screwed to board and joist (left); with screws at angle near board end (right). Floorboards may need lifting to gain access.

Making a storage loft

An open loft or large, heavy duty storage shelf in a garage or out- building of sufficient height can provide valuable space in a family home.

A storage loft can be made in the same way as an upper floor. Joists are fitted between special galvanised-steel wall brackets and are covered with 3/4in. chipboard or floorboards. Access can be gained from a ladder at the open end.

The special joist brackets may appear thin, but they give ample support. Place them at 16in. centres for joists up to 7-8ft. long; 12in. for joists up to 12ft. Fixing to building blocks or average bricks is with masonry nails. With hard bricks it may be necessary to drill and plug wall and use screw nails.

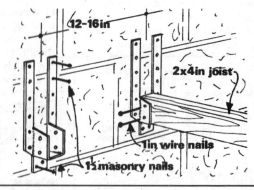

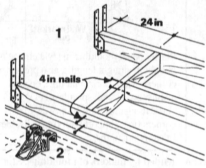

It may be more convenient to have access to loft away from the front edge. This can be provided (1) by cutting one joist short and fixing a short length of joist as shown. Stronger than nailing is to use metal joist hangers (2) which clip over one joist and support the edge of the other; secure with nails.

Using 'period' mouldings

In suitably large rooms a reinforced plaster centre piece and matching cornice mould can be very effective.

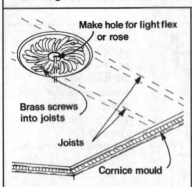

Make hole for light flex or rose

Brass screws into joists

Joists

Cornice mould

Reinforced plaster centre pieces and matching cornice moulds are both fairly easy to install and the mouldings can be sawn, drilled almost as softwood; use fine-tooth saw.

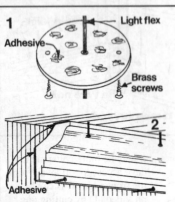

1

Light flex

Adhesive

Brass screws

2

Adhesive

Apply dabs of plaster (1) to centre piece and press into position. Give heavier mouldings temporary support with floor prop, or screw to joists. Fix cornice (2) with adhesive, support with fine nails.

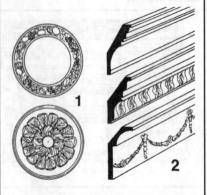

1

2

Plaster centre pieces (1) and cornice moulding (2) come in wide range of patterns and sizes: centre pieces from about 12 to 30in. diam.; cornice, 3-9in. deep. Study makers' literature in making choice of matching styles.

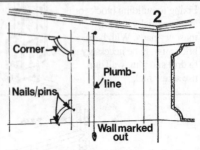

2

Corner

Plumb-line

Nails/pins

Wall marked out

Plaster panel moulding in style choice is bought in straight lengths, also pre-shaped corners. Mark horizontal lines on wall against board with spirit level (1); verticals against plumb-line (2). Fix corners first, support with fine nails, then fit straight lengths.

NOTES: Use adhesive supplied/recommended by makers of mouldings. Study makers' detailed instructions. Fill slight gaps, holes with plaster wall filler.

Lit and suspended ceilings

Make a special feature of your ceiling by installing a light above it. It is not as complicated as it might sound but, the wiring must only be undertaken by an experienced electrician.

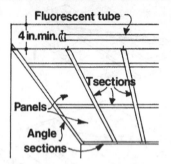

Using special extruded aluminium sections, a suspended ceiling can have translucent or lightweight acoustic panels. In the former case at least 4 in. is required above ceiling for fluorescent lights. Both types of panel are made in 2 x 2 ft.

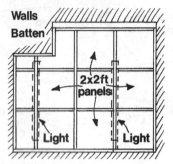

First draw scale plan of ceiling to find how best panels can be arranged. With suitable planning fewer panels need to be cut, especially if a width can be made up with a batten. Preferably have lights directly over frame members, as shown.

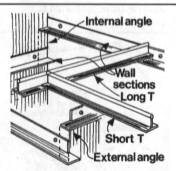

Angle sections are screwed to wall plugs, forming corners as shown and setting with spirit level. T-sections are first made to fit from wall to wall over angles; then short T-sections are fitted between. Cutting is easy with small hacksaw.

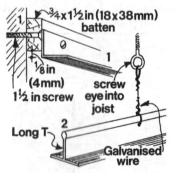

With irregular wall, or to make up to multiple of panel width, fix battens and screw angles to these (1). Or span of more than 10ft. a central support should be provided, as shown (2). Clips can be obtained to join lengths to T-section.

NOTE: Specialist firms supply materials and instructions for ceilings of any size; also suitable light fittings if required.
If in the slightest doubt have an electrician install lights.

Cutting and shaping ceiling tiles

Another popular way of decorating a ceiling is to afix polystyrene tiles, but because of the fixtures you will have to work around planning is essential to create that professional look.

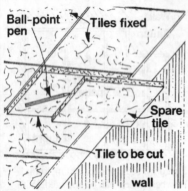

Polystyrene ceiling tiles are fixed, with all-over adhesive, from centre lines outwards. To make tiles to fit to wall first mark as shown: lay tile to be cut directly over fixed tile, place spare tile over it and slide to fit against wall, mark with ball-point pen.

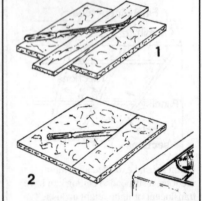

Cut marked tile with sharp knife (serrated carving knife is good) against a straight-edge (1), making several slicing cuts. Or use old table knife blade heated in gas flame (not to red-heat) (2); this will 'melt' through tile.

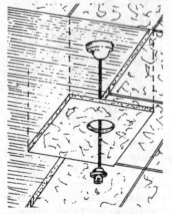

To fit over ceiling rose make cardboard disc diameter of rose and use to mark tile (Four tiles if they meet at rose). Cut with craft knife or heated blade.

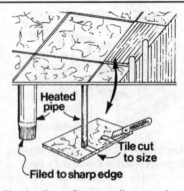

Slot the tiles to fit over wall-mounted pipes. Slots can be cut entirely with craft knife, or holes can first be made with a length of spare pipe filed to sharp edge at one end. Heat and then press through tile; complete slot with knife.

Plumbing &
Electrical
Work

Pages 220-248

Frost, and insulating water pipes

To keep icing up and frost at bay, look first to your loft when it comes to insulation and lagging pipes.

Usually most in need of protection against frost are the pipes in the loft, especially when the 'floor' is insulated; but insulation should not be laid directly under the cistern. Especially vulnerable is the rising main when it comes just inside an outside wall, as shown. After lagging the pipe, pack insulating blanket around it and well into the eaves.

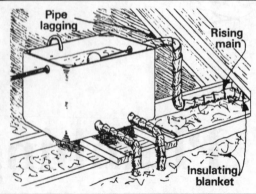

Pipe lagging

Rising main

Insulating blanket

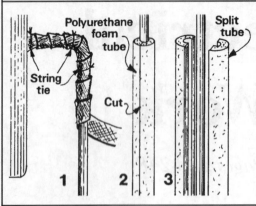

Polyurethane foam tube

String tie

Cut

Split tube

1 2 3

Lag cold pipes with strip felt or p.v.c.-covered glass/mineral fibre (1). Well overlap turns and secure with string. Easier is to use special polyurethane-foam tube with cut down one side that can be pressed over pipe (2). Hot pipes are best insulated with expanded polystyrene split tube (3) in straight and angled lengths secured with metal clips.

Exterior pipes, for garden tap or outside lavatory, can be given a good measure of frost protection as shown. It is important that the insulation should be kept dry, so cover with polythene sheet. Where not too inconvenient though, it is better to turn off outdoor water supply and drain pipes during frosty weather.

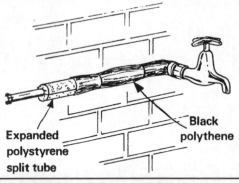

Expanded polystyrene split tube

Black polythene

Installing a bath mixer tap

Modern mixer taps are usually not too difficult to install in place of an old pair of separate taps, but see the note, below.

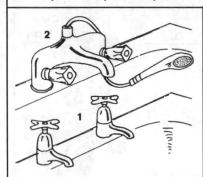

With most modern baths it is a simple matter to replace separate taps (1) by a mixer tap with provision for a shower/spray head (2).

Check distance between taps (usually 7in centres) and buy mixer of D.I.Y. type supplied with instructions.

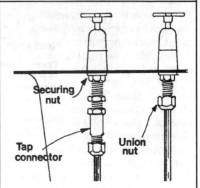

Remove bath side to gain access to tap connections and turn off hot and cold supplies. Unscrew union – also tap-connector pipe if fitted – and remove tap after unscrewing securing nut.

Correctly fitting set spanners, rather than adjustable, are desirable.

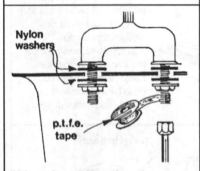

Using nylon washers where shown, or a sealant, fit mixer tap and tighten securing nuts; neatly remove excess sealant, if used.

To ensure watertight joint you can bind two turns of special (known as p.t.f.e.) sealing tape around the thread.

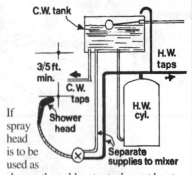

If spray head is to be used as shower the cold water tank must be at least 3ft (5ft for other than short pipe runs) above shower head.

Main problem with this job is likely to be access. There's never much room under a bath and it can be a fiddle.

NOTE: If in any doubt about suitability of supply for a shower seek advice of water supply authority before buying a mixer tap.

Curing a dripping tap

Why pay a call-out fee to a plumber to fix a dripping tap, when all you may need is a new washer. Here's how to tackle the problem.

Dripping is stopped by replacing washer. First turn off supply so that water ceases to run with tap open. With usual type (1) unscrew and raise cover, hold body firmly and unscrew gland with spanner. You may first need to remove handle after taking out screw (1,2). Combined handle/cover (3) must be taken off to reach gland hexagon, usually after prising off cap and removing screw.

Fixing screw

Cover unscrewed and raised

unscrew gland

Cap

Fixing screw

3

Screw cap

2

Fixing screw

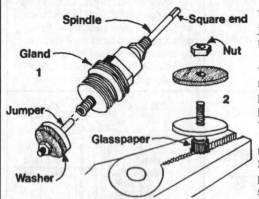

Spindle

Square end

Gland

1

Nut

Jumper

Glasspaper

2

Washer

With gland removed, jumper with washer can usually be taken out (1).

Grip spindle in pliers (2) with strip of fine glasspaper, rough side to spindle, as protection. Unscrew nut and prise off washer; fit new washer, replace nut.

Alternative, and easier, is to fit new jumper/washer. Some jumpers must be prised out of screwed spindle with screwdriver tip.

If separate cocks are not provided for taps fed from cistern, tie up ball arm and run bathroom cold taps to empty. This also saves loss of hot water when washering a hot tap. Taps fed directly from mains are turned off at stop-cock, probably under sink.

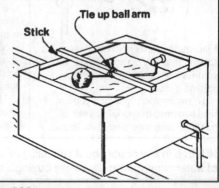

Tie up ball arm

Stick

Renovating cold water tank

Old fashioned galvanised cold water tanks need renovation at some point in their useful lives. Here's how to go about it.

Tie up ball arm or turn off stop-cock (if fitted); cold water will then be available at kitchen sink tap. Turn off immersion heater/boiler and empty tank by opening hot and cold bathroom taps. Scoop sludge from tank bottom and bale or siphon out water still left below level of supply pipe. Dry out with mop.

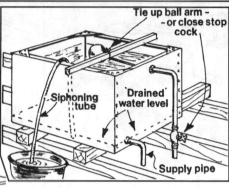

Tie up ball arm ~ - or close stop cock

Siphoning tube

`Drained` water level

Supply pipe

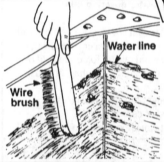

Water line

Wire brush

Scrub inside with wire brush – wearing goggles to protect eyes. If tank has weak areas, due to heavy rusting, it should be replaced with a modern plastic tank. If only scaly and pitted, renovation is possible.

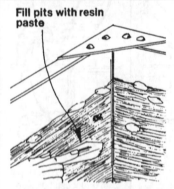

Fill pits with resin paste

When inside is clean and dry (drying can be speeded with hair-dryer), fill all pits with epoxy-resin paste, pressing well in and smoothing with putty knife or small trowel.

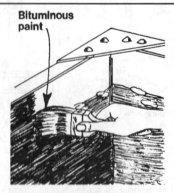

Bituminous paint

After filler is hard give three coats bituminous paint to whole interior, following makers' instructions. Paint should be guaranteed taintless and odourless. Swab with water before re-filling tank.

Clearing blocked waste pipes

Clearing blocked waste pipes can be a messy job, but when it happens it is a necessary one. Here's how.

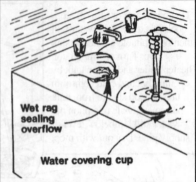

Suitable tools: (1) rubber force cup, about 4in in diameter, suitable for sinks and basins; (2) $^5/_6$in cup, with steel back plate, better for lavatory bowls; (3) special sink-waste plunger, more powerful than force cup; (4) coil-spring wire rod.

To clear bath waste, seal overflow with wet rag and, with water covering it, depress and release force cup held over waste outlet until 'gurgling' sound is heard.

Plunger-type tool can be used instead of cup.

Same method applies to basin or sink.

When sink empties very slowly, waste may be clogged with grease.

Use proprietary waste-pipe cleanser according to makers' instructions, or put down handful of washing soda and pour boiling water over it.

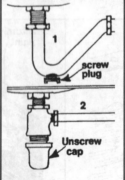

When cup does not clear waste pipe, place bowl under trap and then remove plug (1).
With 'bottle' waste unscrew cap (2).

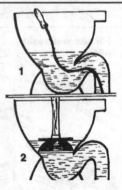

Choked lavatory-pan outlet can be cleared with spring-type rod or length of spring curtain rod (1); or with large force cup (2).

224

Insulating the cold water tank

Insulating tank is safeguard against freezing and keeps water cool in hot weather. This is how to go about it.

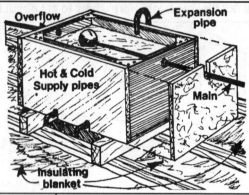

Neatest method is by using prepared kits of five expanded-polystyrene boards, bought complete with fixings for standard tanks. Alternatively, make pieces from plain 1in board, which can be cut with sharp carving knife and secured with tapes.

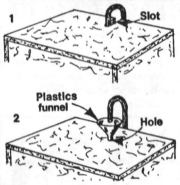

When crooked end of expansion pipe is long enough it can pass through slot in lid (1). If end is above level of tank, fit a funnel through hole so that pipe enters funnel mouth (2). It is important that pipe can discharge into tank.

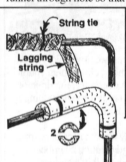

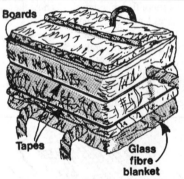

Glass-fibre quilt can also be used as insulation. Special kit can be bought; or use 16in-wide material as used for insulation between joists. Wrap around tank and bind with tapes. Lay boards across top and cover with blanket, or use expanded polystyrene lid.

NOTE: Before buying tank insulation kit measure tank carefully (length, width and height); there are over 30 standard sizes.

Lag all exposed pipes with special strip, overlapping half width and tying at intervals (1). Or use polystyrene split tube, in straight and shaped lengths (2).

Cleaning and clearing a drain

A blocked drain can be a real nuisance, but clearing and cleaning it is not that big a job. Here's how to set about it.

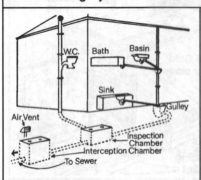

This simplified diagram shows how the services feed into the main sewer.

Waste pipes from bath, basin and sink often go to an open gulley, while the w.c. soil is taken underground direct to the inspection chamber.

The intercepting chamber is usually near boundary of property.

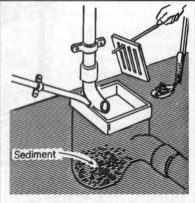

To stop smell or overflow from gulley lift out grid with a poker and remove sediment from U-trap, by hand or with an old spoon bent and bound to a stick.

Flush with hot solution of washing soda. Clean grid.

If water still does not flow readily down gulley, clean out inspection chamber. Remove dirt, paper etc. and flush with buckets of water or hose.

Put grease in groove around frame before replacing man-hole cover.

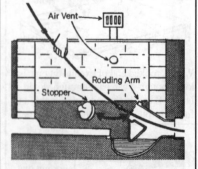

When water does not flow quickly from inspection chamber, check interception chamber and, if necessary, run drain or chimney-sweep rods through rodding arm, turning rods clock-wise while inserting.

Rodding may also be necessary from inspection to interception chambers

If fault remains call in a builder.

Hiding unsightly pipes

Pipes inside the home that run down or along an inside wall can be very unsightly. Here's a way to hide them from view.

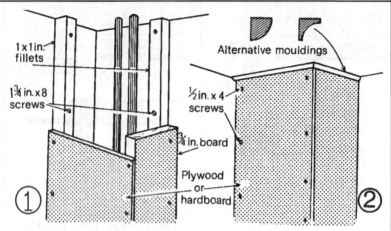

①
- 1 x 1 in. fillets
- 1¾ in. x 8 screws

②
- Alternative mouldings
- ½ in. x 4 screws
- ¾ in. board
- Plywood or hardboard

(1) Method of casing-in vertical pipes in a corner. Fix two wood fillets to walls with screws and plugs, or masonry nails.

Screw a board wide enough to clear pipes to one fillet; then complete 'tunnel' with plywood or hardboard.

This can be pinned, but screws allow easier access to pipes.

(2) Finish top with short lengths of moulding mitred at corner. Fix – to sides only, not ceiling – with contact adhesive.

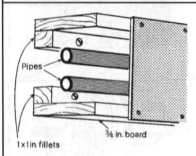

Pipes

¾ in. board

1 x 1 in. fillets

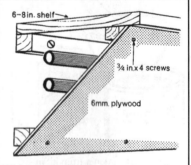

6–8 in. shelf

¾ in. x 4 screws

6mm. plywood

Corresponding arrangement for enclosing horizontal pipes, or vertical pipes away from corner.

Method of fixing is the same as before, but two boards are required. Paint with emulsion to match walls.

Do not run tunnel close to a hot boiler.

With horizontal pipes the casing can be made to serve as a useful shelf.

Chamfer two fillets and both edges of plywood with a plane before fixing to wall and shelf.

Choose dimensions so that the plywood is nicely clear of lower pipe.

Repairing a leaking water pipe

Here are two ways to repair a leaking water pipe – one is a temporary measure, and the other is more permanent.

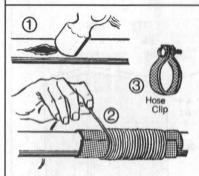

First turn off main supply to stop leakage. Then, with old lead pipe, carefully tap together edges of split to close it (1). As a temporary repair, wind strip of soft rubber or foam around pipe and bind firmly with cord (2) – or fit two or three hose clips (3), if available.

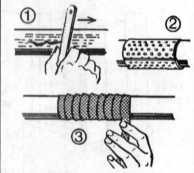

For more permanent repair close crack and clean pipe by scraping with hacksaw blade or knife (1).

You can then use a small glass-fibre repair kit. From this take piece of perforated metal (2) or glass-fibre strip (3) and wrap this around pipe, taking it beyond ends of crack. With strip, overlap the turns, as shown.

Mix resin and hardener from kit in polythene dish or old cup, using quantities as specified in makers' instructions, to produce a thick-cream consistency.

Once mixed, resin should be used within ten minutes or so.

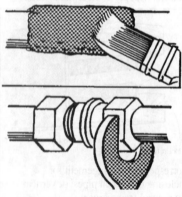

Apply mixed resin over patch with knife or brush. Put on second layer of strip and more resin.

With copper pipe, leakage will often be at union (joint). Slacken nut, press pipe well into union, then tighten.

Curing a dripping tap

If it is in hearing range, a dripping tap is infuriating. It can also end up discolouring washbasins and baths, as well as wasting water.

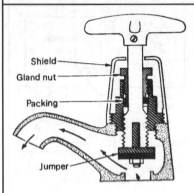

From this section through a typical tap you can see how the parts are screwed together. The tap is shown partly open, to allow water to flow.

If the washer is faulty, it will not completely stop the flow of water, even when the handle is screwed right down. Buy a new washer.

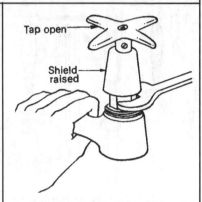

To fit a new washer, first turn off the main cock. Then open the tap and, after water stops running, unscrew and raise the shield and apply a well-fitting spanner.

Support the tap while unscrewing.

After removing the main assembly lift out the jumper. Unscrew the small nut and replace the washer; you generally need a $1/2$ in washer for a basin, $3/4$ for a bath. Re-assemble

Close the tap (using minimum force) and turn on the main cock.

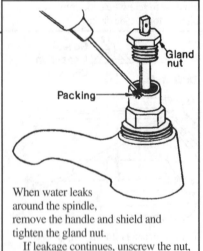

When water leaks around the spindle, remove the handle and shield and tighten the gland nut.

If leakage continues, unscrew the nut, pick out the old packing and force in some cotton wool smeared with petroleum jelly.

Replace the nut, shield and handle.

Clearing drain blockages

Here are some useful tips on the right tools and methods for clearing blocked drains.

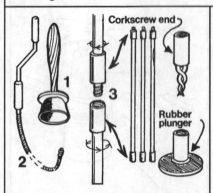

Some useful tools: 1. suction cup for clearing sink, bath or basin waste pipe; 2. drain auger – coiled wire 'rod' with auger end and handle for rotating – useful for lavatory U-bend and smaller pipes; 3. drain rods (same as chimney-brush rods; can be hired) with screw-on corkscrew and plunger for outside drains.

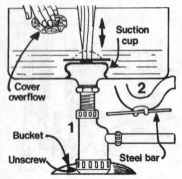

Sink, basin, bath waste-pipe blockage can often be cleared with suction cup, closing overflow outlet with wet cloth.

If that fails, unscrew base of p.v.c. bottle trap (1) or unscrew U-bend if that type is fitted.

Unscrew plug of old-type U-trap (2). Have bucket, bowl under.

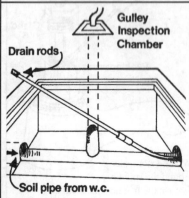

When w.c. pan is slow to empty, even after using suction cup or drain auger, remove manhole cover and check inspection chamber.

If full, use drain rods with corkscrew end to clear pipe to interception chamber.

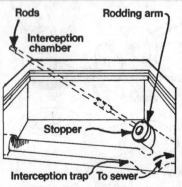

If interception chamber (between inspection chamber and sewer) does not empty, remove stopper from rodding arm and use drain rods down this.

Several rods may be required, along with plunger and/or corkscrew end.

Clearing a blocked waste

If you are faced with a blocked waste in bath, washbasin or sink, here are some methods of clearing it.

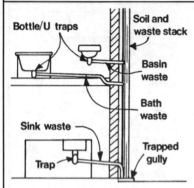

Representative arrangement of waste-pipe outlets from bath, basin and sink. Particularly in older houses, there may be separate soil and waste stacks, with upper-floor wastes feeding into a hopper-head.

Ground-floor sink usually has waste pipe running to outside gully, as shown.

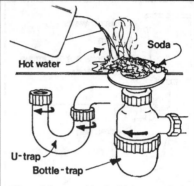

Clear sink waste blocked by congealed fat by putting in small handful of washing soda and pouring hot water over it.

If this does not clear blockage after a few minutes, place bucket under sink and remove and clean trap; two typical types are shown.

Most non-fat blockages at sink, basin or bath can be cleared by using rubber suction cup (or force cup) as shown: run in a little water, close overflow by pressing damp cloth over it; then operate suction cup. Continue for some time if obstruction is in outlet pipe.

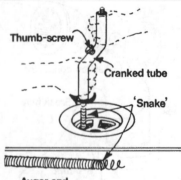

For blockage along waste pipe, 'snake' cleaner is helpful. Simplest is similar to spring curtain rod-or it may be flat, springy steel – with handle.

Better is that with cranked handle, shown, which can be moved along 'snake' as it is gradually fed down pipe.

Replacing a w.c. pan

Replacement of broken pan is not difficult, especially if exactly similar pan can be used. Here's how to do it.

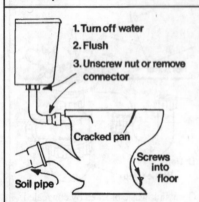

1. Turn off water
2. Flush
3. Unscrew nut or remove connector

Cracked pan

Screws into floor

Soil pipe

First turn off water supply or tie up ball arm. Flush to empty cistern; them remove flush pipe.

With plastic soil-pipe connector simply draw pan forward after removing floor screws.

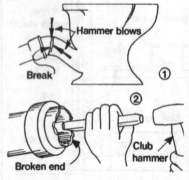

Hammer blows

Break

①

②

Broken end

Club hammer

When outlet is cemented into end of soil pipe, break bend with heavy hammer (1) and remove pan.

Next chip away broken ceramic and cement with sharp cold chisel (2), after stuffing newspaper or rag in pipe, to hold back fragments, and putting on protective goggles.

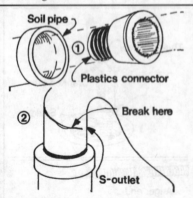

Soil pipe

①

Plastics connector

②

Break here

S-outlet

Fix new pan through flexible plastic connector (1) which comes in various patterns. Ease connector spigot into soil-pipe end, them pan outlet into connector.

When old pan has S-outlet (2), break it where shown and fit new one through connector, lowering pan into position.

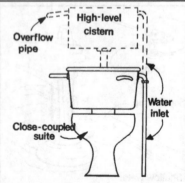

High-level cistern

Overflow pipe

Water inlet

Close-coupled suite

The job is more complicated if high-level-cistern installation is to be replaced by a low-level suite. Pipe runs need to be modified and new hole made through wall for overflow. Soil outlet may also need modification.

Check, measure carefully before deciding on procedure.

Replacing a cold-water cistern

Fitting a new cistern may seem like a difficult job, but with a bit of forethought and the help of these tips, it should be possible.

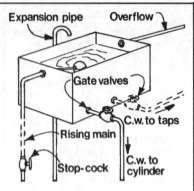

First study pipe layout; c.w. supply, shown dotted, will not be found when cold taps are fed directly from main.

Turn off heating, close stop-cock, drain cistern through cold bath tap where possible; otherwise through hot tap.

Bail-out bottom of cistern.

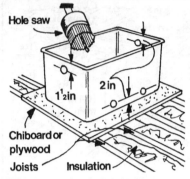

With rectangular semi-rigid plastic cistern it is often possible to keep to same pipe runs. Drill holes for ball-valve, connectors with hole saw at approximate position indicated.

Plastic cistern must be stood on chipboard, plywood etc. laid across joists.

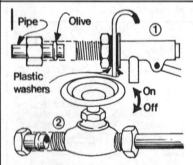

Fitting of ball-valve (1) and gate-valve (2); other connections are similar in principle.

If existing ball-valve and brass unions are old, consider replacing them; saw pipes 10in or so from cistern, making up with short lengths of new pipe.

Study instructions by the fitting makers.

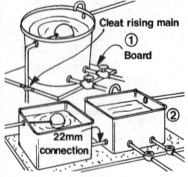

When loft entrance is small, round plastic cistern (1), which 'gives' quite a bit, may be easier to squeeze through.

Or two smaller rectangular cisterns can be used, connected together with short pipe near bottom (2).

Other fittings are as for single cistern.

Avoiding frost troubles

The ravages of freezing weather are definitely something to be avoided, so here are some tips on keeping Jack Frost at bay.

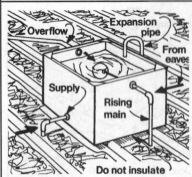

Loft, especially when floor is well insulated (as it should be) is main danger spot for freezing; but do not insulate directly under cistern.

Icy draughts can come from gaps at eaves and, sometimes, up overflow pipe. Roof itself may also be a cold spot.

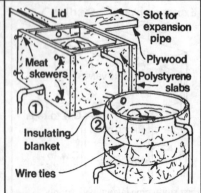

Insulate square cistern against frost by forming 'box' with slabs of expanded polystyrene (e.p.s.) and covering top with another slab of e.p.s. glued to plywood lid (1).

Or wrap insulating blanket around cistern (2) again providing lid insulated with blanket or e.p.s.

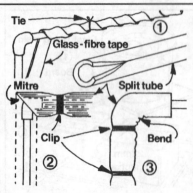

Exposed pipes are vulnerable to icy draughts, especially at elbows. Insulate by binding with special paper-backed glass-fibre tape (1) allowing good overlap.

Easier is to use: prepared split insulating tubing: some types should be mitred at corners (2); others can be bent (3).

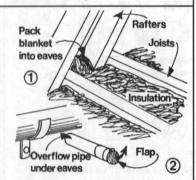

Cold draughts under eaves can be prevented by packing with insulating blanket (1); but do not seal all gaps because some ventilation is required.

Draught up overflow pipe can be stopped by fitting simple flap valve (2) from builders' merchants; it will open should overflow occur.

Adjusting float valves

What to do when the loo gets too little water to flush properly, or when the cistern is always dripping from the overflow pipe.

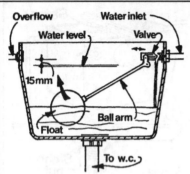

Basic principle of operation: When w.c. is flushed, cistern empties, float falls, valve opens and water enters cistern.

Valve should cut off when water reaches approximate level indicated; if not, water may run through overflow.

If valve closes too soon, w.c. may not flush.

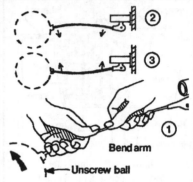

With most older types, arm must be bent slightly (1) to vary water level: bend downwards (2) to reduce level (as when there is overflow); upwards (3) to raise level. It is usually best to turn off water supply and remove (unscrew) ball float before bending arm.

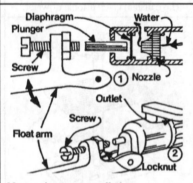

Newer cisterns generally have diaphragm-type valve (almost trouble-free) shown simplified (1).

Common method of adjustment is with screw (2). Slacken locknut and turn screw clockwise to reduce level; anti-clockwise to raise it.

Flush w.c. and check after adjustment. Then tighten locknut.

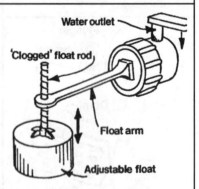

Another type of diaphragm valve, which also is made in plastic, has shorter float arm, and is fitted with float having a 'cogged' or 'notched' rod.

This can be moved upwards or downwards, and locked in correct position by the 'cogs', to provide correct water level.

When the w.c. won't flush

If your loo will not flush, here are some tips on what to do to solve the problem without calling in a plumber.

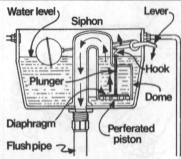

Usual siphon-type flushing cistern. When lever is operated, plunger lifts piston, with plastic diaphragm, and forces water around bend in siphon unit and down flush pipe.

Siphonage causes water to continue to flow until cistern is almost empty.

If water level is correct (adjusted by bending ball arm) failure suggests a faulty diaphragm.

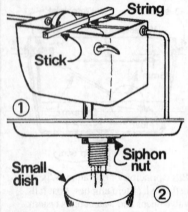

Siphon unit must be removed to replace diaphragm. First turn off water or tie up ball arm (1). Flush or empty cistern, disconnect flush pipe and unscrew siphon nut (2) with large wrench.

Have dish to catch dribble of water.

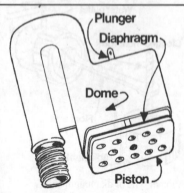

Disconnect hook from end of plunger; then lift out siphon, usually in white plastic. Withdraw piston and plunger.

Some pistons (and domes) are circular, others as shown. New diaphragm must match old one. Buy in advance, stating shape of dome and brand name.

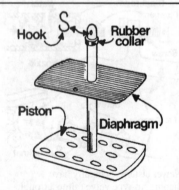

Remove rubber collar; slide off old diaphragm; fit new one (cut with scissors if too large); replace collar and insert piston in dome.

Re-assemble everything in reverse order of dismantling, taking care to replace any washers.

Concealing bathroom pipes

Unsightly pipes in the bathroom can be concealed quite easily – giving you extra shelf-space in the process. Here's how.

Where pipes run across a ground-floor bathroom or lavatory they can easily be hidden with a useful shelf.
The front is left open to give immediate access to the stop-cock and, where provided in this position the drain cock(s).
A shelf about 6in wide is usually adequate.

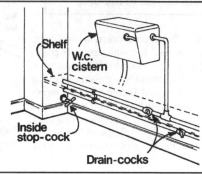

Shelf, in $^3/_4$in softwood or veneered chipboard, is carried on bearers (1). Bearer can

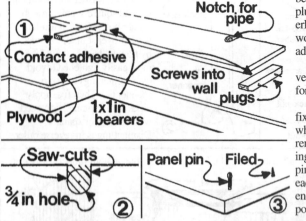

be screwed to wall plugs but not properly to thin plywood; use contact adhesive there.

Mark position of vertical pipe and form notch (2).

Shelf can be fixed to bearers – while being easily removed – by having $^3/_4$in panel pins underneath each end, head-ends filed to point (3).

Shelf behind wash-basin is in two units, ends behind pedestal (1). Pipes are hidden by vertical board (2) fixed to shelf with angle brackets. Other angles are screwed at base to keep board upright. Fixing to wall is with keyhole-slotted glass plates (3) that can be slipped over head of screws driven into wall plugs. Either left-or right-hand shelf unit can be removed after lifting plates off wall screws.

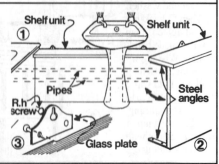

Fixing sink taps and waste

If you are thinking of replacing a sink unit yourself, here is how to fix the taps and waste of your choice to the unit.

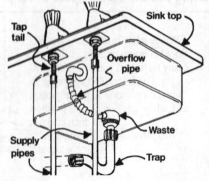

How fittings are attached to usual pressed-steel sink top, with flexible overflow pipe fitted over slotted waste connector.

Trap connects to waste pipe passing through wall. Before removing supply pipes from taps turn off main hot and cold water supplies.

Waste and trap can be disconnected without turning off.

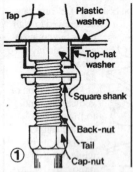

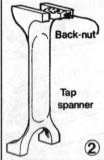

Fixing of a tap to metal sink (1). Fit plastic washer and insert tap tail and square shank through square hole. Next, fit top-hat washer over square, followed by flanged back-nut, which is most easily tightened (avoid over-tightening) with tap spanner (2). Then fix supply pipes with cap nuts, tightened with wrench or spanner. Dismantling is in reverse order.

Method of installing waste fitting (1). First seal under flange with rubber washer or plumber's mastic.

Fit first washer, followed by overflow connector and second washer. Then fit back-nut and tighten. Trap nut is made hand-tight. When tightening, loosening backnut, hold waste with pliers (2) to prevent turning.

Ease stiff tap or waste back-nut with penetrating oil.

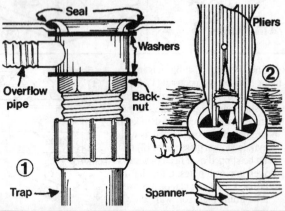

Plumbing in a washing machine

It is not too big a job to plumb in a washing machine. That usually means tapping into the hot and cold water supply in your kitchen.

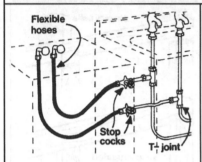

Basic requirement is to fit compression-type T-joints in cold and hot supply pipes (one only with some machines) and run short pipes from these to special washing-machine stop-cocks, to which flexible hose connectors are screwed.

Turn off h & c supplies before commencing work.

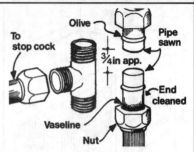

To fit T-joints cut pipe with small hacksaw, remove burrs with file.

Clean end with steel wool, slide on nut and olive, after smearing inside nut with vaseline. Screw on finger tight, then tighten further 1-1$\frac{1}{2}$ turns with spanner – two spanners used together for upper and lower nuts.

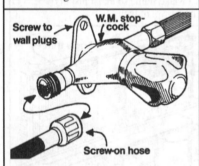

One convenient type of washing-machine stop-cock for screwing to wall after fitting new, extension pipe from T-joint. Connector of washing-machine hose is screwed on tightly with fingers.

There are other types of cock, but all are used in similar manner.

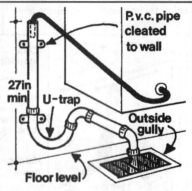

Waste hose can be hooked over edge of sink or, neater, fed into p.v.c. pipe with trap, passing through wall to outside gully.

Special pipe can be bought; it must be at least 35mm inside diameter.

NOTE: Metric fittings (15mm) suit $\frac{1}{2}$in copper pipes: types vary, so get leaflet from suppliers; also study makers' installation instruction for machine. Check best positions for stop-cock, T-joints.

Panelling a bath

If you want to install a new bath, or if you have an old-style, free standing one, here is how to box it in with panelling.

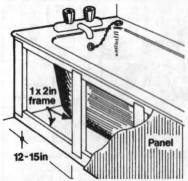

Simplest method, especially when not using a ready-made bath panel, is to form a wooden framework, as shown, and to cover this with enamelled hardboard secured to frame with eight dome-headed screws. Have four/five vertical frame members, approximately equal distances apart.

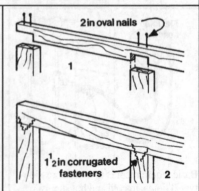

Frame members can be joined with simple halving joints made with saw and chisel and secured with 2in oval nails (1). Or vertical members can butt against horizontal ones and be fixed with corrugated fasteners (2).

Make frame so that it just fits under rim of bath.

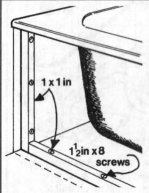

Fix bearers to wall and floor with screws and wall plugs, or with wall-panel adhesive.

Set-in bearers as indicated, so that frame and panel will go under bath rim.

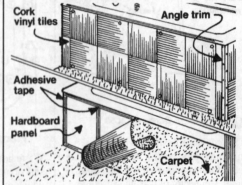

Instead of plain panel, standard hardboard can be tiled (1) to match a wall or floor; or hardwood-faced plywood may be preferred.

Another interesting affect is obtained by covering with piece of carpet similar to flooring (2); fix with double-sided adhesive tape, so that it can be peeled away if necessary to remove screws.

Curing a noisy water system

Thump, bang, rattle! – particularly in the middle of the night. It's enough to keep anyone awake. Here's how to fix it.

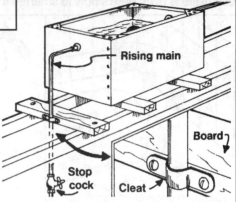

A 'humming' noise, heard when water is drawn, may be caused by vibration of the rising-main pipe near the ball valve. Prevent by making pipe firm; one method is to cleat it to a board screwed across joints, as shown.
Reducing pressure at the stop-cock may also help.

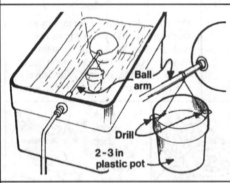

Another cause of noise – often 'hammering' or 'groaning' – is vibration of the ball valve itself. Ripples on the water cause the float, and hence the valve, to vibrate.

A simple remedy is to fit a form of shock absorber to the ball arm. Small plastic plant pot, drilled and suspended with copper wire works well.

Noise may be caused by a faulty ball valve (in c.w. tank or lavatory cistern). The usual, piston-type valve (1) is more likely to cause noise, especially if badly worn. If valve is in poor condition it can easily be replaced by the 'quieter' diaphragm type (2). This has the further advantage that the diaphragm (which serves same purpose as a piston washer) seldom needs any attention.

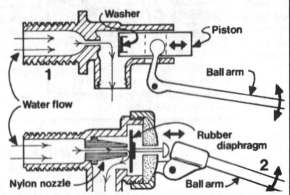

241

Bath care and maintenance

An enamel bath can get scruffy with wear and tear long before its useful life is over. Here's how to smarten it up and keep it that way.

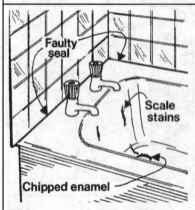

With care, many faults (eg. scale, stains, chipped enamel) can be avoided.

Important is to rinse bath and then wipe out after use; use a mild liquid cleaner when necessary.

Seal edges to prevent water seepage.

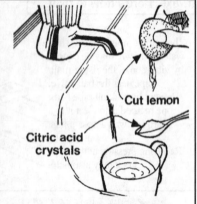

Prevent scale, stains under taps by re-washering. Remove existing marks with a special 'bath scale and stain remover'. Or rub with cut lemon; leave few hours before rinsing. Alternatively use teaspoon citric acid in cupful water.

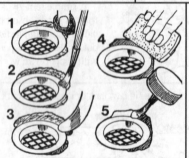

Treat chipped enamel in sequence: (1) clean with steel wool; (2) apply rust inhibitor following makers' instructions; (3) press in a resin filler (as used for car bodywork); (4) smooth with fine wet-or-dry paper dipped in water; (5) dry, then touch-in-with 'porcelain' enamel from bottle with its own brush in cap.

Burn marks, deep scratches in acrylic bath may be removed by rubbing with fine abrasive paper (1). Remove light scratches and roughness with metal polish (2).

Seal bath edge with flexible sealant smoothed with finger tip (1); or, enamelled bath, with quadrant tiles fixed with tile adhesive (2).

When the tank overflows

An overflow from either your main water tank, or the loo cistern, can be unsightly and damaging. This is how to fix it.

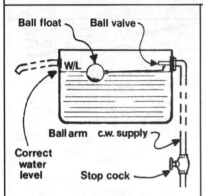

Ball float — Ball valve

W/L

Ball arm   c.w. supply

Correct water level

Stop cock

In normal conditions there is no overflow, water is approximately in line with water-level mark (in lavatory cistern) or 'tide-mark' (in c.w. tank).

If overflow occurs, turn off stop cock – at least overnight – until fault has been corrected, especially in frosty weather.

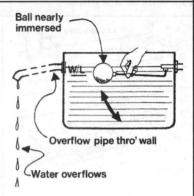

Ball nearly immersed

W/L

Overflow pipe thro' wall

Water overflows

Slight overflow may result from presence of dirt or fine grit within the ball valve.

Flush lavatory, or open a cold tap, and press ball arm hard down, then repeat; in most cases, sudden force of water will clear minor obstruction in valve.

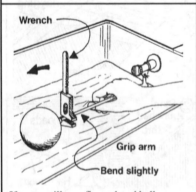

Wrench

Grip arm

Bend slightly

If water still overflows, bend ball arm (easier using wrench as shown) so that water level is made lower. Bend until water is at correct level.

If this does not effect a cure, new valve washer may be necessary, or ball float may be leaking.

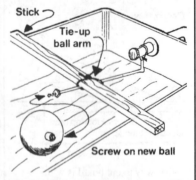

Stick

Tie-up ball arm

Screw on new ball

Should ball float be suspected, turn off supply or close valve by tying-up arm as shown. Then slacken lock-nut and unscrew ball. If ball contains water (shake to check) replace it with new plastic one. If ball proves correct, valve should be re-washered.

Access to under-floor pipes

It is sometimes necessary to go in search of pipes laid under your floorboards. To access them with the least disruption you should follow these few rules.

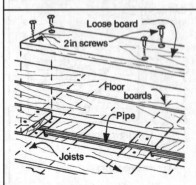

When flooring is laid or re-laid after installation of central heating, access traps should be provided and secured with screws - not nails. They can usually be found by following the pipe-run, and may be of any length, bridging two or several joists, and screwed to each.

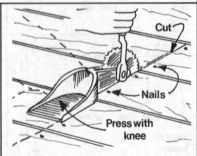

If access is not provided, prise out length of board after sawing across, also, if t. & g., along tongue. Best use (hired) floorboard cutter, or a circular saw, set to board thickness. If possible, remove nails and saw along line of holes; otherwise saw beside nail-line.

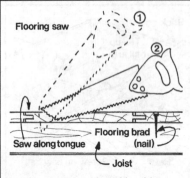

Another way to cut board is with flooring saw shown - but not directly over pipe or cable! Saw close to side of joist: (1) make hollow cut with curved tip; (2) complete with straight toothed edge. Tenon saw can be used, but not easily; or bore holes and use keyhole saw.

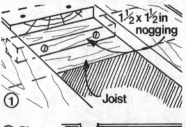

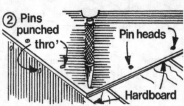

(1) When board is sawn to side of joist, fix 1 1/2 x 1 1/2in. nogging (batten) for each end of access board - to be secured with countersunk screws. (2) Hardboard covering is best freed for lifting by punching pin/nail heads through it.

Extending electrical leads

How often has the length of your wire been incompatible with the distance of the socket? It should be a problem no longer.

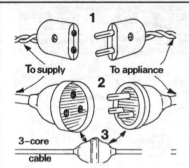

Twin flex (as for table lamp) can be joined with plug and socket (1) but new full-length flex is better. Join 3-core cable (for motor mower etc). with waterproof plug-socket (2). Plug rim is secured in socket flange(3).

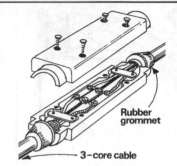

Permanent joint in flexible cable is made by using enclosed cable connector. Corresponding colour-coded wires are secured to each pair of terminal screws after preparing ends and passing cable through rubber grommets.

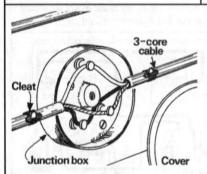

Permanent connection between two semi-rigid cables (as in house wiring) is best made by using a junction box, which should be screwed to wall plugs, skirting board, etc. Take care that corresponding colour-coded wires are securely attached to each of three terminals.

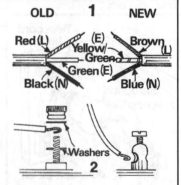

Colour codes of old and new cables (1). When using both types connect together red-brown green-yellow/green and black-blue. Methods or connecting twisted bared ends to two usual terminal types (2).

NOTE: Remember electricity can be dangerous; if in any doubt seek expert help. Never make joints by twisting wires together and binding with insulating tape.

Making a wall light fitting

Lighting is not just a necessity, it can also highlight your rooms to their best advantage.

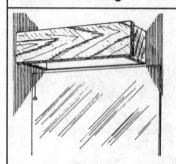

Suitable for use over a mirror or picture, the fitting takes ordinary light bulbs and can be connected to a convenient wall socket. If wiring into the lighting circuit, this should be done by experienced electrician. Paint inside flat white before fixing lamp-holders etc.

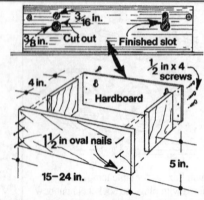

Made as a simple open box from 3/4in. wood or 1/2in. plywood. Fix front with glue and nails, punch down heads and fill holes. Hardboard back is fixed with screws after wiring. Two slots are made as shown to clip over 1in. No. 8 screws in wall plugs.

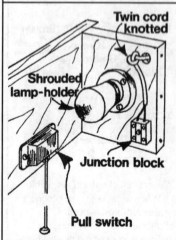

Fully insulated, shrouded lamp-holder is fixed inside each end, while plastic junction block and pull switch can be fixed where shown. Use twin lighting cord for connection to plug.

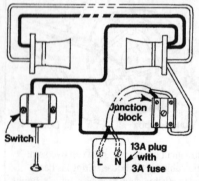

Make connections with good quality lighting flex. Fix wires across inside of front board with small cable cleats, keeping it well clear of bulbs. It is important that all components and wiring should be of good quality. If in any doubt about method of connection seek expert help. *Electricity can be dangerous.*

Two 13A sockets from one

With the plethora of household items which need electricity, who hasn't at some time wished for a few extra sockets?

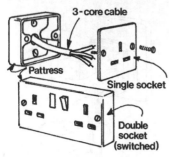

3-core cable

Pattress

Single socket

Double socket (switched)

Much better than using splitter is to replace single socket with double one (preferably switched). For surface-mounted socket shown, switch off at mains, remove circuit fuse and then carefully unscrew socket, remove cable ends and take off pattress. Drill, plug wall, fix new pattress, then double socket.

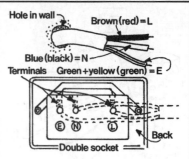

Hole in wall

Brown (red) = L

Blue (black) = N

Terminals   Green + yellow (green) = E

Back

Double socket

With colour-coded cable (old alternative colours are given in brackets) connect to socket as indicated. If cable is not coloured, note L, N, E terminals and tag each wire. With very old cable, rubber covering will have perished; best leave until circuit has been re-wired - or carefully bind with insulating tape.

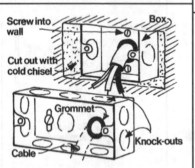

Screw into wall

Box

Cut out with cold chisel

Grommet

Knock-outs

Cable

Flush socket will be screwed to steel box. Centre new box over old, mark around it and cut out plaster each side. Take out single box and remove appropriate 'knock-out' of new box, insert grommet; pass cable through and screw box to wall plugs.

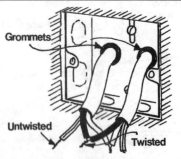

Grommets

Untwisted

Twisted

Two cables are often found in box, with ends of corresponding colour-coding twisted together. In that case, untwist with pliers before removing box. Press out two 'knock-outs' in new box, fit grommets, pass cable through and re-twist before connecting.

REMEMBER that electricity can be dangerous, even lethal. If in *any* doubt, seek expert help before touching any wiring.

Checking electrical equipment

Electrical items, because so many are in daily use, are the things that will most often need attention of one sort or another.

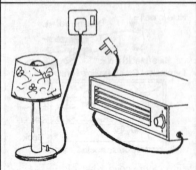

If appliance such as fan heater shown fails to work, first check socket outlet by plugging in another, such as a table lamp. Should this operate it proves that current is reaching socket; if not, fuse in consumer unit (fuse box) probably needs replacing.

When supply socket is in order check that plug of failing appliance is good fit. Move in and out while 'wiggling' it (1) and/or 'wiggle' cable near entry (2). Intermittent operation then indicates fault at plug.

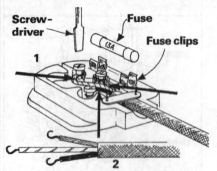

Remove cover from plug and check that all thee terminals are tight. Also see that there are no breaks in wires at points arrowed (1); if there are, re-make connections (2). If leads and connections are sound, replace fuse with new one of same rating: 3amp. (blue) or 13amp. (brown); 3amp. up to 700watts.

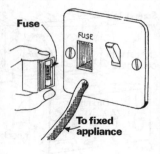

Electrical fittings, such as wall-mounted heaters, are supplied through fused outlet as shown. Holder is withdraw to change fuse. Similar outlet, without switch, is used for clocks, but fuse holder is held with a screw.

NOTE: Failure of appliance to operate after checks shown may indicate faulty cable or internal connections; or expert repair may be needed.

Some DIY Techniques

Pages 250-266

Quick woodwork fixings

The right tools can make fixing jobs, particularly if you have a lot of repetitive work, much quicker to complete.

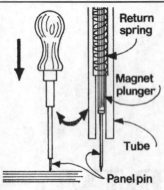

Inexpensive pin-push is useful for multi-pinning, as in fixing plywood and hardboard. It drives in and slightly recesses pin head when smart hand pressure is applied.

Hold tool at right-angles to work.

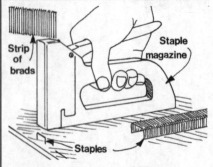

Stapling gun is excellent for light fixings, especially in awkward place or when working overhead.

It takes strips of staples, which are self-feeding. Some models receive different staple sizes. Press-button electric guns give even easier fixing; some also take special strip of brads up to 1in; or an adaptor for brads.

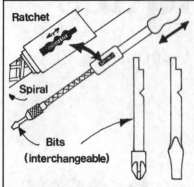

A spiral screwdriver simplifies repetitive screw-driving and is operated by pushing down, then releasing handle.

It comes in different sizes and receives a range of bits for cross-head and slotted screws.

Sliding thumb-catch gives reversal or ratchet-locking.

Make pilot holes for screws.

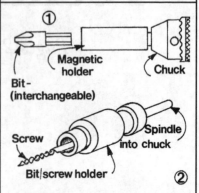

Screwdriver bits are available for use in electric drill (run at low speed). Special interchangeable bits fitting magnetic holder (1) are relatively inexpensive.

More sophisticated types have bit holder and gripper for screw (2). They are often too expensive to justify purchase for occasional use.

Using nails and screws

It's always worth looking at the basics of woodwork. Here's when and where to use nails or screws.

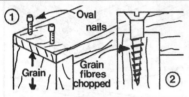

end-grain (1); screws would chop across the grain fibres (2) and give weak fixing.

Screws are better for side-grain fixings (3) and do not damage the grain fibres. In both cases shown, joints should be glued before nailing/screwing.

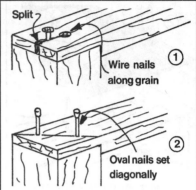

Nails, especially round wire nails shown, should not be placed along the grain (1) where they would tend to split the wood.

Arrange them on a diagonal (2) and, preferably, make fine pilot holes.

Oval nails – greater diam. along grain – are better.

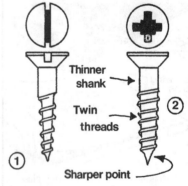

Particularly in rough (no-joints) carpentry, stronger fixing is obtained by sloping and staggering nails as shown (1).

Risk of splitting the wood in rough and in rustic carpentry is reduced by blunting nail points by lightly hammering against stone or steel.

Traditional screws (1) have shank full diam. of thread. Newer types, often vaguely called chipboard screws, have twin thread, so easier, quicker to drive, while thinner shank reduces risk of splitting.

They can have slotted or cross heads.

Making it stick

There is always a correct type of adhesive or glue for each type of job you may be faced with. Here are four examples.

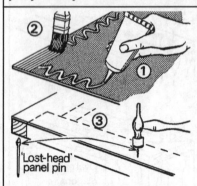

To fix hardboard to a wood frame use p.v.a (milky-white) wood adhesive.

Apply from tube or squeeze bottle in wavy line (1), and then brush out evenly (2). Glue both back of hardboard and face of frame.

Drive in 'lost-head' panel pins (3), working from centre towards each end.

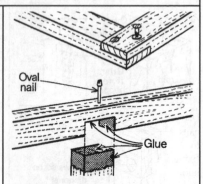

Also use p.v.a. wood adhesive for gluing joints. Brush it over meeting surfaces in thin, even coating. Keep joint under moderate pressure, with screws, nails, weight or cramp, until glue sets. Wash brush in water after use.

For outdoor woodwork use a synthetic-resin (waterproof) glue.

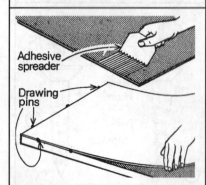

Contact adhesive is best for fixing plastic laminate (eg. to table top). Pour some on back of laminate and spread evenly with comb-type spreader supplied.

Apply similarly to table top. Wait until touch dry, then gradually bring surfaces together, after inserting drawing pins to position end and one corner.

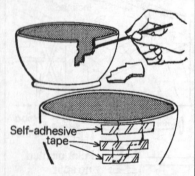

For china, glass or hard plastics apply even film of clear epoxy-resin glue to both edges with thin, pointed stick. Press pieces together and temporarily secure with adhesive tape or modelling clay.

Keep in warm place for a few hours. Excess glue, when hard, can be removed with a sharp knife.

Using lid, door and flap stays

It can be very useful to have a hinged surface that stays put when you open it, particularly upwards. Here are tips on stays.

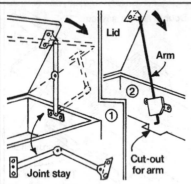

Simple brass joint stay (1) can be used for either cabinet lid, shown, or a fall-down writing-desk flap.

For audio equipment a stay with smooth, adjustable braking (2), sometimes called a hi-fi stay – or a hydraulic lid stay – is preferred.

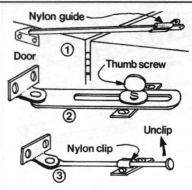

Three typical stays for hinged cabinet or wardrobe doors: (1) 'silent' type in which metal arm runs in nylon guide; (2) locking stay holds door in position when screw is tightened; (3) detachable type where arm, in nylon clip-guide, can be removed for full door opening.

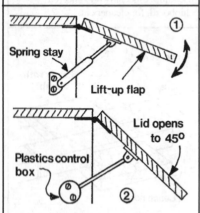

Lift-up flap stays for, eg., small cup-board doors over wardrobe:

(1) is spring loaded – spring holds door open or closed without need for catches; (2) holds door at about 45deg, locks when fully open – lift flap to release; stay shown is right-hand fixing.

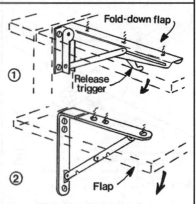

Two self-locking fold-down flap-support stays, as for kitchen table or work top 12-15in deep: (1) self-locks when raised – press trigger to release; pair will support 175lb. (2) is heavy-duty, for loads up to 285lb per pair.

Both come in white-enamelled steel.

Basic woodworking processes

Getting the basics of woodworking right is the foundation stone of all more advanced carpentry skills. Here are some useful pointers.

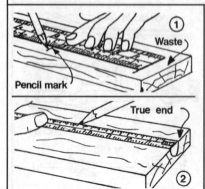

Correct marking-out is of first importance. For smaller items use steel rule along with a sharp pencil; rule with both metric and imperial divisions (1) is preferable. When measuring larger items, long boards, use steel tape (2), also with imperial and metric markings.

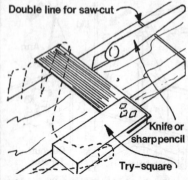

After marking lengths (double line for intermediate saw-cut) draw lines across face of wood, next down both edges, then across back.

Hold try-square firmly against wood and make lines with sharp pencil — or use knife, especially on veneered chipboard, for cleaner cut.

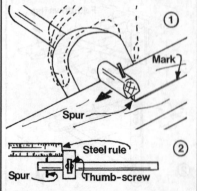

Mark lines parallel to edge of wood - for sawing, jointing, etc. – with marking gauge. Press stock against wood, tilt so that spur is at trailing angle and then press lightly forward (1). Set gauge accurately against steel rule (2); tighten thumb-screw and check setting.

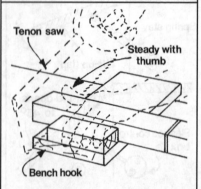

Where possible, use beechwood bench hook to support wood for sawing. Hold workpiece firmly in angle as shown, steady saw blade with thumb-tip. Start with short, light strokes; then complete with full strokes, allowing only weight of saw to apply downward pressure.

Using dowels

The elegant appearance of furniture built with 'invisible' dowel joints is not as hard to achieve as you might think.

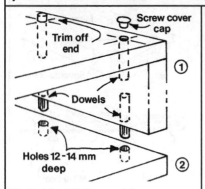

Typical dowelled corner joints:
(1) Through dowel joint, easier to make because holes through one member serve as guides when end-drilling. Dowels can have slight projection, for trimming, or recess for cover cap. (2) Stopped, invisible, dowels give better appearance.

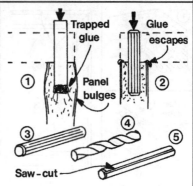

Have dowels tight press fit in holes. With plain dowel (1) panel could be damaged by glue pressure. With prepared dowel (2) excess glue can escape.
Ready-made dowels with serrations (3) or rifling (4) avoid trouble.
Or make saw-cut along plain dowels and round-over ends.

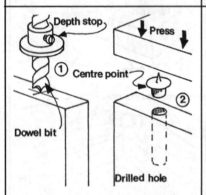

All holes can be made with twist drill of dowel diameter, but dowel bit shown (1) is better; use depth stop with either.
Simple way to mark accurately, after drilling end holes, is with centre point (2). Points are inserted, other board is carefully pressed over them.

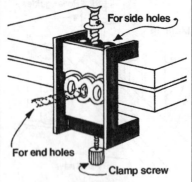

When much dowel-jointing is to be done, a good jig is well justified. One of the many types is shown; with this, both series of matching holes (6, 8 or 10mm) can be drilled with one setting of jig.
Tool comes with spacers, prepared dowels and necessary instructions.

Making mitres

A well-made mitre looks very attractive – but it also has a very practical purpose in woodworking. Here's how to do it.

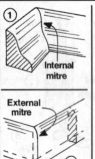
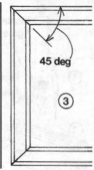

Mitres look well when correctly made; they are especially used on mouldings - which cannot be accurately corner-jointed in any other way. Examples shown are: (1) mouldings around a work top or edge of a tray; (2) edging for table-top; (3) corners of picture frame.

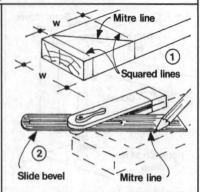

Two simple ways of setting-out of mitre: (1) Draw two lines, width of wood apart, using try-square; then draw diagonal — which is mitre line. (2) Use slide-bevel shown, set against 45deg set-square; or mitre-square, which is similar to bevel but fixed at 45deg.

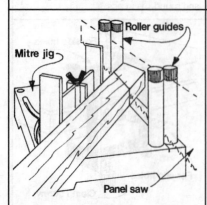

When much mitring is to be done, a mitre box is worth its cost. Easier, though, is to use a special mitring jig, such as that shown.

Using a fine-tooth panel saw, accurate mitres can be cut in mouldings (with two sides flat) up to 4in wide and 4in deep.

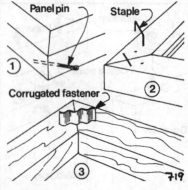

As well as being glued, mitred frames need additional support. Small and light picture frames can be secured with a panel pin (1) or staples (2), 'shot' in with a stapling gun. Heavier and 'rougher' frames can be strengthened with corrugated fasteners (3).

Sanding woodwork

Hand-sanding of other than large flat surfaces is still often to be preferred. Here is how to go about it.

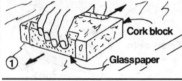

Cork block

Glasspaper

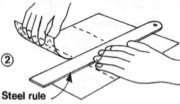

Steel rule

Use a cork sanding block (1) along with a one-sixth sheet of abrasive paper (about 280 x 230mm or 11 x 9in).

Tear the paper against a steel rule or straight-edge. (2).

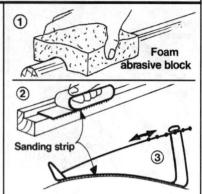

Foam abrasive block

Sanding strip

Plastic-foam sanding block (1) can be used on flat surfaces, but is better for curves. A small 'plane sander' (2) is excellent for narrow edges, while for long curves and adjustable curves sander (3) is useful. Self-adhesive sanding strips are available for both.

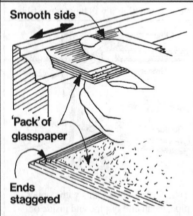

Smooth side

'Pack' of glasspaper

Ends staggered

Mouldings can sometimes be smoothed with pad of steel wool, but this could spoil sharp angles.

A better way is shown, where 'pack' of glasspaper strips, edges staggered, is used. Strips can be about 2in square.

Dust bag

Sanding belt

Orbital/finishing sander (1), excellent for larger surfaces, can be moved along or across grain, and takes $1/3$ standard abrasive sheet. For heavier duty (even on rough wood) belt sander (2) is most effective. Abrasive belt is replaceable; tool should be moved along grain.

Dust bag is advised for both sanders.

Soldering methods

Different methods of soldering are suitable for different jobs. Here are some tips on how to go about various tasks.

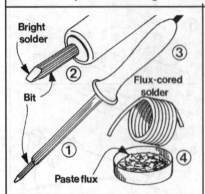

Electric soldering iron (1) is nowadays employed almost universally. Tip of bit (2) when at correct temperature should be bright, with clean solder film.

It is used with flux-cored solder (3) or plain solder and separate non-acid flux, paste or liquid

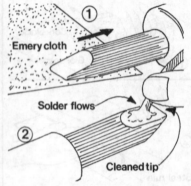

Re-'tin' bit when dirty, pitted. First clean by drawing quickly across abrasive sheet (1), then coarse rag.

Immediately apply cored solder (2) which will flow smoothly if temperature is right; if too low, solder will not flow; if too high it will have scum film.

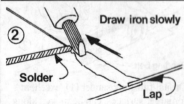

To solder wire to a tag, clean end, bend to hook in tag (1), then apply spot of cored solder with iron.

For joining tinplate (2), copper, brass, use larger iron. Move along slowly while holding solder to tip.

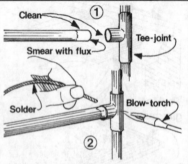

To make capillary joints with copper pipe, clean end of pipe and inside of joint (1) with emery cloth; wipe with clean rag, smear end of pipe with flux; insert it and rotate to spread flux.

Heat pipe and joint with blow-torch (2) until solder, when applied, will liquefy and run into joint.

Saw sharpening

A sharp saw will save you a lot of wasted energy. Sharpening one is not so difficult if it has non-hardened teeth.

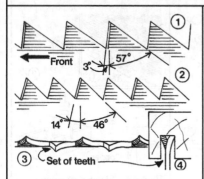

Front 3° 57° ①
14° 46° ②
③ Set of teeth ④

With practice, saws having non-hardened teeth are not difficult to sharpen.

Study tooth shape: rip saws (1) are different from other types (2), having steeper front edge. Alternate teeth in all types are set (bent) outwards (3) so that groove is wider than blade (4).

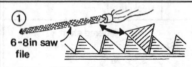

6-8in saw file ①

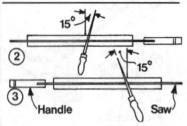

15° ②
15° ③
Handle Saw

Sharpening is done with triangular saw file (1). Give two or three file strokes on front edge of teeth pointing towards you, file angled towards handle (2).

Reverse saw in vice (3) and repeat on other teeth. Practise on old saw with not more than 10 points per inch.

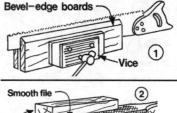

Bevel-edge boards ①
Vice

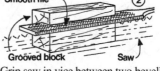

Smooth file ②
Grooved block Saw

Grip saw in vice between two bevelled-edges boards (1), edge projecting $^1/_2$in or so.

Then, before sharpening, level tips of teeth with one or two light strokes of smooth file, preferably held in wood block grooved for file (2).

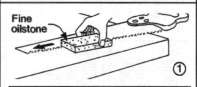

Fine oilstone ①

②

After sharpening, lay saw flat on bench and lightly run fine oilstone once along teeth, first on one side, then on other (1).

When re-setting is necessary (eg. because saw 'binds'; usually only once every 4-5 sharpening) do this before sharpening, using special pliers-type saw-set (2).

Hammers and mallets

The right type of hammer or mallet for a particular task will make the job that much easier. Here are some tips.

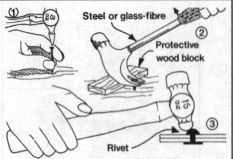

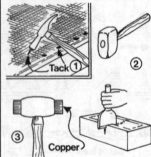

Three popular hammer types:

(1) cross pene or Warrington for joinery, especially useful when starting small nails, pins – 8oz size convenient;

(2) claw hammer (16-20 oz) with cushioned steel or glass-fibre shaft, best for most carpentry - – use claw for withdrawing nails;

(3) ball pene or engineer's hammer, useful for eg. riveting.

Always hold any type near end of handle.

Extremes: Slender, magnetic tack hammer (1) useful for upholstery;

Heavy (2-4lb) club hammer for masonry work (2);

Copper-ended hammer (3) is 'safer' because it does not produce fragments (which could injure eyes) when struck against steel chisel.

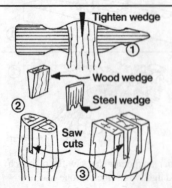

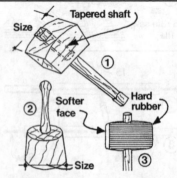

Loose hammer head can be dangerous. Secure by tightening wedge (1), driving in steel wedge or, temporary, by soaking in water. New handle can be fitted by driving wedge into saw-cut (2); two saw-cuts are generally used with large, square-ended shaft (3).

Traditional woodworker's mallet (1) is better than hammer against chisel handle or woodwork; $4^{1}/_{2}$in size is convenient. Woodcarver's mallet (2) with beech head; $3^{1}/_{2}$in size best for most DIY work. Rubber mallet (3) is useful, 'safe' general-purpose tool.

Double and secondary glazing

Double or secondary glazing not only cuts heat loss – and your fuel bills, but also can greatly reduce noise pollution.

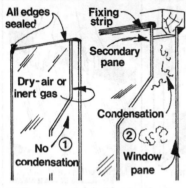

(1) Factory-sealed double-glazed unit; gap between panes if filled with dry air or inert gas, so condensation cannot occur. (2).

Secondary-glazing: normal window plus extra pane on inside. Edges are sealed but condensation can occur — so best made to open/remove.

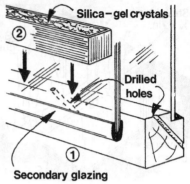

Secondary glazing

Reduce condensation with secondary glazing by drilling few (say $3/16$in) inclined holes (1) through bottom rail to admit outside air; loosely fill holes with steel wool. Another way is to put special, narrow tray of silica-gel (anti-condensation) crystals between panes (2).

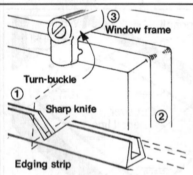

Well-tried simple secondary-glazing system uses soft plastic edging strip, V-cuts made with sharp knife at corners (1), pressed around edges of glass or clear rigid-plastic pane (2).

Special turn-buckles (3), 12in apart, secure pane and allow easy removal for cleaning.

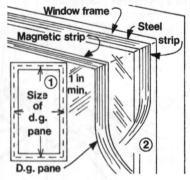

One of easiest secondary-glazing methods, with 2-4mm clear rigid plastic (not glass) held with magnetic strip.

Cut plastic to size (1) and mark around it on frame. Apply self-adhesive strip; then fix foam-backed magnetic strip around pane (2) and place in position.

Simple glass-cutting

Cutting glass is not necessarily a job just for experts. You can do it yourself, but take care – and practise first.

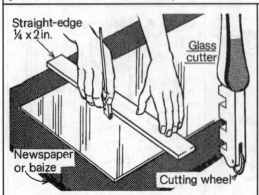

Straight-edge ¼ x 2 in.

Glass cutter

Newspaper or baize

Cutting wheel

Scratch (on under-side)

First make practice cuts on spare glass. Lay glass over sheets of newspaper or baize on smooth, flat table.

Use inexpensive wheel-type cutter as shown; this is better than a diamond except for experts.

Using a wooden straight-edge, draw the cutter once across the glass, starting right on the edge and applying firm, even/pressure.

Turn glass over, hold as shown and tap, from end to end, along back of scratch.

This makes scratch deeper so that glass will snap more easily.

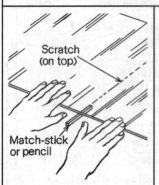

Scratch (on top)

Match-stick or pencil

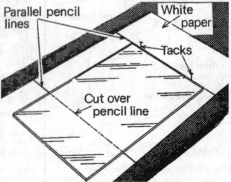

Parallel pencil lines

White paper

Tacks

Cut over pencil line

Place a match-stick or pencil under one end of scratch, and press on glass at each side of line.

If cut was 'clean' glass will snap exactly on the line.

For accurate cutting draw two pencil lines on white paper (eg. back of spare wallpaper) and lay this over newspaper.

Drive two tacks into one line and, with glass against these, cut over second pencil line, using straight-edge as before.

For windows, cut glass $1/8$in smaller than opening.

Fitting bullion window panes

The bulls-eye, or bullion, window pane can add a touch of olde worlde charm to a window or door.

One or more bullion, or bull's-eye, panes can add interest to a window or door.

In general, The panes are more appropriate to small-pane windows, but they are made – in both glass and acrylic plastics – in sizes from approximately 9 x 13in to 18 x 24in.

It is usually necessary to choose the next size larger than the opening and cut the pane to fit.

Measure the height and width of the opening, into the rebate, and have the pane 1/8in shorter and narrower.

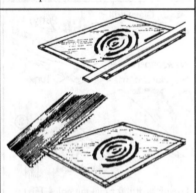

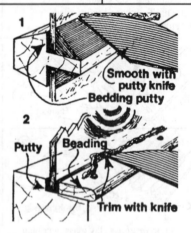

1 Smooth with putty knife
Bedding putty

2 Putty Beading

Trim with knife

Standard bullions can be made as small as 5 in sq. Have glass panes cut by the supplier. Acrylic ones are easily cut: with the bull's eye central, mark out with a sharp scriber, rub a little paint into the lines and cut with a fine-tooth saw.

Fit window bullions same as plain glass (1). With door, glass is usually secured on outside with beading (2), after laying bedding putty, pressing pane against it and running in another thin layer of putty.

Working with glass

Glass is always potentially dangerous to work with. But, by taking sensible precautions, it becomes a doable DIY job.

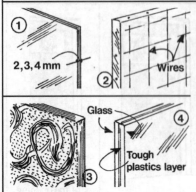

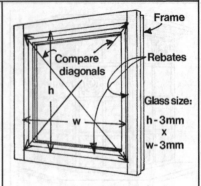

Four usual types of glass: (1) clear window glass, 2, 3, 4mm thickness; (2) wired glass, for strength in eg. conservatory roof; (3) patterned, for privacy in bathrooms etc.; (4) laminated safety glass for large door panes, shower screens. Toughened safety glass resembles plate, but cannot be cut.

When measuring for new glass, after removing old and raking out rebates, allow 3mm ($1/8$in) less in height and width than distances inside rebates.

Also check frame is square (diagonals equal) or make allowance in cutting glass.

Stout paper, thin card template may prove helpful.

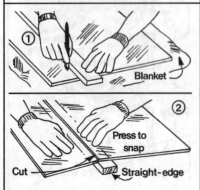

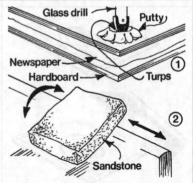

To cut, *wear gloves*, lay glass over blanket, smear turps along line, draw cutter once only against straight-edge, under steady pressure (1). With cut over straight-edge, press to snap (2). Curves can be cut free-hand over pattern; tap back of glass along scratch line with end of cutter.

Use glass drill for making holes. First form crater with putty, plasticise, put in few drops of turps and turn drill slowly under steady pressure; ease pressure as bit penetrates.

(2) Edges can be smoothed with flat, fine sandstone: keep wetted.

Repainting window frames

Both window and metal window frames can last very much longer if properly looked after – and that can mean a new coat of paint.

1. Brush with white spirit

2. Wipe wipe rag

One coat of gloss paint is usually sufficient for the interior.

Lightly sand down old paint and clean, especially in rebate, shown, by gentle scrubbing with white spirit and wiping off loosened dirt and grease. This gives better paint flow and adhesion.

Sequence of painting: first paint rebates and short members (1 and 2) for each of openings, in direction of the fine lines shown. Then paint longer members, crossing ends of previous strokes; hinge stile last. Method can be adapted to frames of different types.

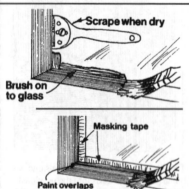

Scrape when dry

Brush on to glass

Masking tape

Paint overlaps

Rebates can be painted up to glass with steady hand. Alternatively, let paint run on to glass (1) and remove with razor-blade scraper when hard. Or use self-adhesive masking tape (2) and peel off as soon as the paint is touch-dry – not hard.

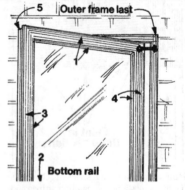

5 Outer frame last

Bottom rail

Order of painting exterior is similar to that for interior, whether metal frame, as shown, or wood. But if paint is cracked or blistered, strip and prime, or sand down well, before applying undercoat and gloss. Masking or trimming with scraper should not be necessary.

Repainting a door – panel or flush

It pays to follow a clear sequence of preparation (see note, below) before embarking on the painting of a door – panelled or flush.

Sequence of painting a panelled door, after doing the outer frame. Note that door furniture is removed. The object is to paint each frame member separately, and to work so that you paint across the ends of previously painted members.

In painting panels, work in sequence shown, doing around the moulding first (1). Then brush on slightly spaced vertical stripes (2), brushing up and down. Next brush-in (3) across the panel. Finally, 'lay-

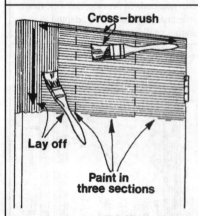

Cross–brush

Lay off

Paint in
three sections

Paint a flush door in a series of rectangles. Treat each as a panel, painting stripes and cross-brushing to ensure even coverage. Cross-brush again when the full width has been painted, and then lay-off downwards.

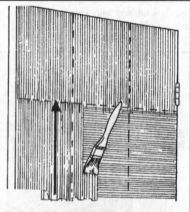

Treat the following widths in the same way, but laying-off upwards into the previously painted width. Work as quickly as possible and without interruption so that no area of paint will dry before the next is applied.

NOTE: Before painting wash well, rub down with glasspaper or, for exterior in poor condition, strip, prime and undercoat. Use exterior gloss for outside; same or silk/satin finish for interior doors.

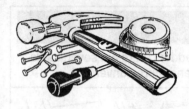

Tools and Implements

Pages 268-276

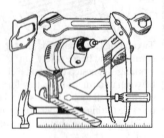

Ladder aids

Many tasks will involve the use of a ladder. There are several aids which can help make their use safer and more convenient.

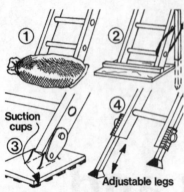

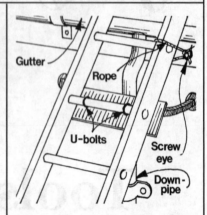

In absence of helper, ladder foot can be supported on firm ground with a heavy sand-bag (1). On soft ground, use board with ledge (2) and tie ladder to stake. Suitable for most ground is swivel foot (3). On sloping ground or steps, adjustable legs (4) can be fitted.

Top of ladder should be roped to firm anchor where possible, especially if resting on stand-off bracket shown, which allows ladder to clear gutter and down-pipes. One type has rubber cups at ends and is secured to rung with U-bolts.

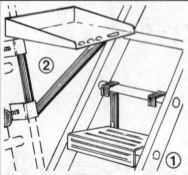

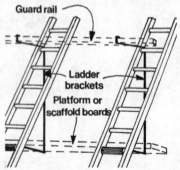

Two fittings that make for greater comfort - and hence safety - in working: (1) is step that can be clamped between two rungs; (2) is tray for paint can and small tools which is fixed to one side (string) of ladder. There are variations on those shown; buy good quality.

When not convenient to use scaffold tower, alternative is to fix a pair of ladder brackets to two ladders. Brackets are adjustable and clip over the rungs; they will support scaffold boards or staging and, preferably, a guard rail. Brackets can be hired from tool-hire shop.

Sharpening bits and drills

To achieve the very best from your tools they need to be in tip-top condition, so ensure your bits and drills are always sharp enough for the job.

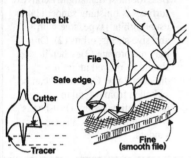

Centre bit, as used in hand brace, is one of easiest to sharpen. Lightly press point into space wood, tilt so that cutter edge is horizontal and make two or three passes with smooth file having 'safe' edge. Then file lightly on inside of tracer. Note that tracer must project beyond cutter; point beyond tracer.

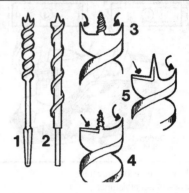

Twist or auger bits: (1) for use in hand brace; (2) for power drill. Tips vary, and are sharpened by light filing at points arrowed (3-5). Some for use in brace have screw-thread point (3, 4); for power drill, point is plain (5).

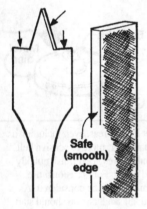

Flat or spade bit for use in power drill is sharpened by filing where indicated with safe-edge file, shown. Keep file at exact angle of cutting edges of bit.

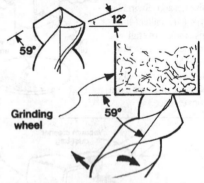

Twist drills are more difficult and practice (starting with large drill) is necessary. Angles shown are usual, but keep to those of actual drill. Using grinding wheel with tool rest, rotate drill through about 90 deg., tilting it slightly to left to produce 12 deg. 'lip' angle. cool in water frequently.

Power-tool sanding

A power sander is a valuable tool to have, but ensure you use the correct model to suit the task at hand.

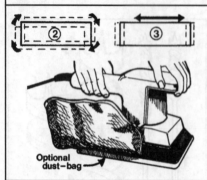

Best for most flat, slightly convex surfaces is finishing sander (1). In usual (orbital) type, sole with abrasive sheets, orbits (2). Or it may reciprocate (3), when it should be moved in grain direction only. One model can be switched from orbital to reciprocating action. Dust-bag is worthwhile option on some sanders.

Optional dust-bag

Handy and economical is disc-sander attachment with electric drill - but it can make circular scratches. With 5in. rubber-disc type (1) drill must be tilted so that only 1/3 of abrasive disc makes contact. With firm disc (2) and 'Swirlaway' type (3) smaller (4in.) disc makes overall contact and scratching is less likely. With firm-disc sander, self-adhesive abrasive discs are extra convenience.

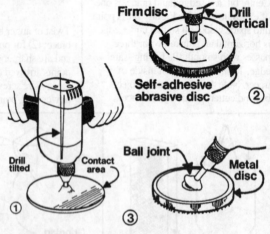

Firm disc **Drill vertical**

Self-adhesive abrasive disc ②

Drill tilted **Contact area** ①

Ball joint **Metal disc** ③

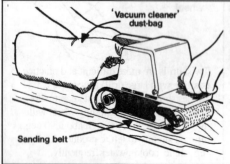

'Vacuum cleaner' dust-bag

Sanding belt

For larger areas, even including a small floor, more expensive belt sander gives good finish quickly and easily. For occasional use, hiring should be considered. As with all sanders, you should start with coarse-grit abrasive (e.g. 32-40 grit) if surface is very rough, and progress to fine grit, such as 150 - even finer for belt sander, up to 320 or over.

Working with a router

Here are a few simplified details of representative router that can be used for grooving, rebating, rounding etc, and even, after practice, for jointing.

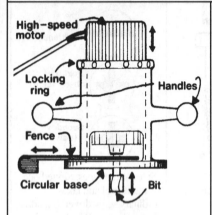

Interchangeable bits are used for different purposes and depth of cut is regulated by accurate raising, lowering of motor. Fence acts as guide at edge of board.

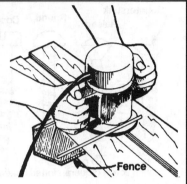

How tool is held when grooving along a board. A so-called straight bit is used and fence is held against board edge while moving router forward. For grooves much farther from edge, a lath is temporarily fixed and circular base of tool kept against it.

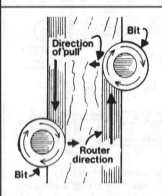

When using any type of bit, direction of working is important because bit rotates clockwise and should 'pull' towards wood and away from fence. It will 'wander' if router is moved in wrong direction.

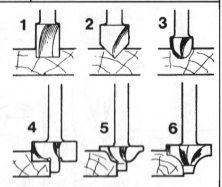

A few of many types of router bits or cutters; known as: (1) straight, (2) vee-grooving, (3) core, (4) rebating, (5) ogee, (6) rounding. Types (1-3) are used with fence or guide, except when free-hand carving; (4-6) have 'pilot' projection which serves as guide when run against edge. Traverse fairly quickly when using pilot bit.

Screws and screwdrivers

Choosing the right screws for a job is important, and so is the choice of screwdriver, if you are to achieve a professional finish with the most ease.

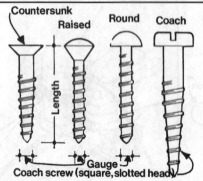

Coach screw (square, slotted head)

Main types of screw head. Screws are described by length (in inches) and gauge number representing diameter at widest point. For comparison, two centre screws are shown with Twinfast (double-spiral) thread, especially suitable for chipboard. Coach-screw gauge is expressed as diam. of shank in ins.

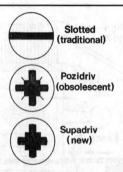

Slotted (traditional)

Pozidriv (obsolescent)

Supadriv (new)

Screw-head types. Slotted one is traditional and takes ordinary screwdriver. Supadriv is superseding Pozidriv, but also takes Pozidriv, but also takes Pozidriv screwdriver – or even driver made for Phillips (now rare) screw heads

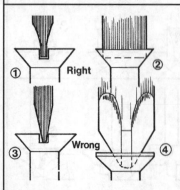

With slotted screw, driver should be good fit in slot and very slightly narrower (1, 2). If end is tapered (3) it may slip and damage screw-head. Supadriv/Pozidriv driver (4) is size-rated by numbers: e.g. No. 2 fits screws from 5 to 10 gauge.

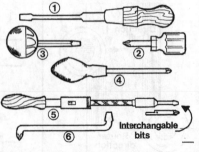

Interchangable bits

Selection of screwdriver types: (1) traditional 'cabinet' style, with hardwood handle; (2) stubby (with slot or cross-head blade) for working in confined space; (3) large-ball-handled ratchet driver (with interchangeable bits); (4) plastic-handled pattern; (5) spiral ratchet driver operated by pressing on handle; (6) cranked combined slot, cross-head driver for awkward corners.

Nails, screws and bolts

Whatever your level of skill, no one can hope to make a good job of an installation if they have not used the correct tools.

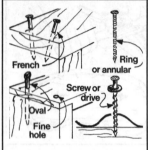

French (round) nails give strong fixing; oval look better, are less likely to split wood. Ring, annular nails are ridged to give better grip; screw, or drive, nails, suitable for e.g. corrugated roofing, grip well. Make small holes through top member and, where possible, slope nails.

For easy removal, as with carpet, furniture webbing, always use cut tacks. Panel pins are neatest for fixing e.g. plywood; 'lost-head' type drive fully into surface. Use galvanised staples for netting.

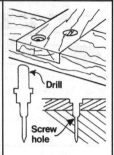

Screws give better fixing - but not into end grain, where nails should be used. make pilot and clearance holes, also countersink where required; easiest with special drill shown, of correct size for screw: e.g. 1in. x 8.

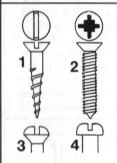

Ordinary wood screw (1) and twin-thread screw specially for use with chipboard (2). Both can have screwdriver slot or cross, and countersink (1, 2), raised (3) or round (4) head.

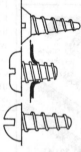

Steel self-tapping screws, for fixings to thin metal - often used on domestic appliances - can have countersink, flat or round head, slot or cross.

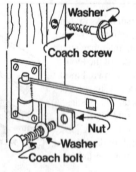

Use coach screws, with spanner, for heavier timbers, as at corners of sectional shed. Coach bolts, where possible, give even stronger fixing; also use where heavy hinges have square holes.

Five useful 'extra' tools

Here are a few tools which you might need every day, but are nevertheless useful to have around.

Blade-setting screws

Grain

Spokeshave (1) for smoothing curved edges, works, rather like a plane. With work in vice, hold tool with thumbs behind (2). Always work towards long grain (3). Use flat-faced spokeshave for concave edges; round for convex.

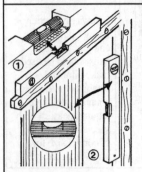

Builder's-type spirit level, with horizontal and vertical vials, 24in. long, is excellent when fixing e.g. shelf bearers (1) or vertical members for built-in furniture (2) where it usually is more convenient than a plumb-line.

Rule

Steel needles

Press against moulding

Profile copier, with series of fine steel needles passing through frame (1) is helpful when marking out e.g. floor-coverings of plywood to fit closely around a moulding of irregular shape. Simply press edge against moulding.

Small hacksaw-type general-purpose saw with interchangeable blades of the tooth-sizes shown. Finest blade is suitable for metal and plastics, second for many woodworking jobs, third for damp wood, as in tree-pruning.

Blade-tension nut

7 teeth per inch

14 t.p.i.

32 t.p.i.

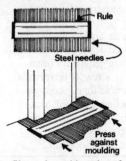

Guide

Oilstone

Honing guide for chisels and plane irons ensures accurate sharpening even by beginners. Side screw clamps blades up to about 2 1/2in. wide. Instructions on side of tool.

274

Sharpening home/garden tools

Everyday implements used around the house need as much attention as your DIY tools.

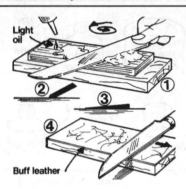

Light oil

② ③

④

Buff leather

Sharpen knife on oilstone, as used for chisels, plane irons. Rub with circular motion (1) holding blade at 25-30 deg. (2); if worn thin, hold flat to stone (3). For better finish, draw sharpened edge along buff leather glued to wood block

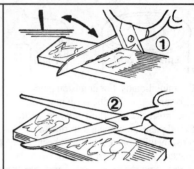

① ②

Scissors can also be sharpened on oilstone. Hold slightly tilted, ground edge flat on stone (1) and rub with circular motion, taking care to keep at exact angle. Finish by pressing flat on stone (2) and giving a few circular rubs. Wipe off dirty oil.

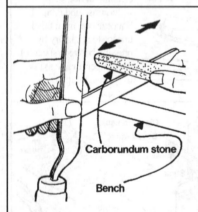

Carborundum stone

Bench

Garden shears can be sharpened with carborundum or scythe stone, used without oil. Support blade as shown and tilt to bring ground edge horizontal. Then rub backwards and forwards with stone. Better, use oilstone, hand held, on edge and then flat side.

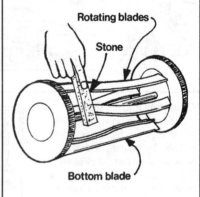

Rotating blades

Stone

Bottom blade

It is often sufficient to sharpen only rotating blades of lawn mower - which can be done with carborundum stone, carefully following angle of edge. Burrs can first be removed with fine file. Simple sharpener to clip over bottom blade can be bought.

Cleaning paint brushes and rollers

As with all your tools, decorating brushes and rollers will give best results and last longer if thoroughly cleaned after use

 Emulsion/vinyl Water

 Oil paint varnish

 Brush cleaner or White spirit

Cleaning liquids: For emulsion paint, also some gloss paints, wash in water. Use brush cleaning fluid or white spirit for oil paints; methylated spirits for most metallic paints. Always check makers' instructions if in doubt.

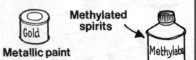 Gold — Metallic paint — Methylated spirits — Methylated

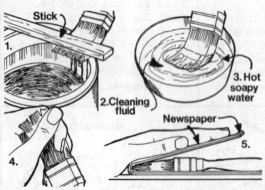

Stick
1.
2. Cleaning fluid
3. Hot soapy water
Newspaper
4.
5.

Immediately after use: 1. Scrape off as much paint as possible against edge of tin; 2. Clean by pressing bristles, one side and then other, repeatedly in cleaning fluid; 3. Repeat cleaning in hot, soapy water, rinse under tap; 4. Squeeze out, from bristle tips to stock; 5. Dry by pressing between sheets of newspaper. Leave to dry fully, then wrap in newspaper.

Clean paint roller in similar sequence as for brushes: 1. Remove as much paint as possible by scraping with stick; 2. Roll back and forth in cleaning liquid, then in soapy water. Rinse well under tap and shake out; 3. Dry by rolling over several sheets of newspaper, then hang up handle until completely dry before putting away in dry place.

Cleaning liquid, Soapy water
1. Stick
2.
Newspaper

REMEMBER: For short intervals brush-head can be wrapped in foil or polythene to keep airtight.

Woodwork
Tricks and
Techniques

Pages 278-294

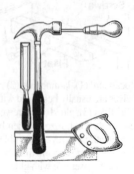

Jointing man-made boards

Many DIY tasks involve jointing boards, be it for shelving or furniture-making but the correct methods have to be followed.

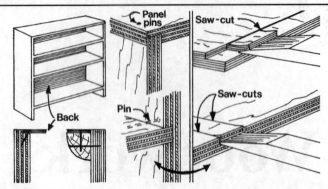

Bookshelves provide example of corner and T (shelf) joints. With plywood, glued and pinned, both types are easily made with saw and chisel, sawing to depth of exact number of plies. Plywood/hardboard back can be fixed in rebate or with glued, pinned moulding. For corner joint make saw-cut, then chip out rebate with 1in. chisel, keeping chisel edge exactly to glue-line. Groove is formed by making two saw-cuts and removing waste, along glue-line, with narrow chisel.

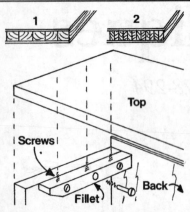

Blockboard (1), laminboard (2) corners, shelves are usually best fixed with 3/4 x 3/4in. fillet (3), glued and screwed, first to vertical, then to horizontal member. Drill countersink for screws, assemble 'dry', dismantle, remove burrs from board face and finally assemble with glue.

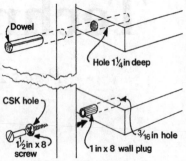

Two methods of fixing plain/veneered chipboard at right-angles (for corner of T). (1) Using dowels: drill holes through vertical and use as jig for drilling into horizontal. Glue dowels and press in. (2) Drill, countersink vertical, drill into horizontal and press in wall plug; screw together. Chipboard screws can be used without plugs, but give weaker fixing.

Making dovetail joints

One of the tricks to making your joinery look sleek and professional is to master the art of joint-making.

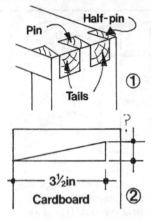

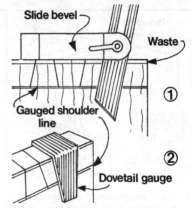

(1) Typical through-dovetail, as for corners of frame or carcase; use more dovetails on wider boards. (2) Angle of tails can be set out on cardboard template as shown.

Make out tails after planing end of board square; leave fractional waste for later trimming and mark shoulder lines around wood with marking gauge. Draw on dovetails angles against slide bevel (1) or with gauge made from strip metal (2).

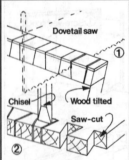

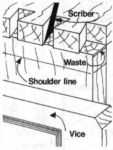

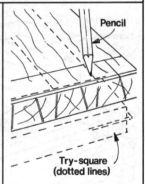

(1) With wood held at angle in vice, saw vertical, saw for tails - keeping saw-cut on 'waste' side of lines. (2) Chop out between tails with chisel; go half-way through from each side then pare smooth.

To mark out ends of pins, hold wood vertically in vice and lay tails over end, as shown. Then carefully mark along tail sides with scriber or other sharp point, such as that of compasses.

With try-square and sharp pencil draw lines from 'pin' marks to shoulder line. Then form pins in similar way to tails, sawing down to shoulder line and chopping out with sharp chisel.

Which simple joint for what?

Choosing the right joints for each piece of furniture, and each part of that article, you make can mean the difference between success and failure.

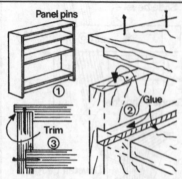

In carcase construction of, e.g., bookshelf unit (1) in solid wood, plywood or plain, dense chipboard, make lap halvings at corners, and housings for shelves (2). When using plywood (easiest to work) have groves, halvings exact number of plies deep (3). trim when glue has set.

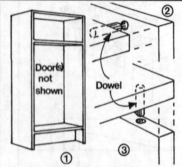

Dowel-jointing is better when using veneered chipboard as carcase of, e.g., a wardrobe or cupboard (1) - or for bookshelves. Use 8 x 30mm. dowels with 16-19mm. board. For tall cupboard have dowels horizontal (2); with shorter unit, where top is seen, have dowels vertical (3).

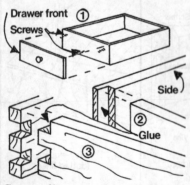

Corners of box construction, as simple drawer (1) can have half-lap joints (2), as with bookshelves, or corner-locking (sometimes called finger) joints (3). These can be made by hand with sharp saw and chisel, but more easily with power-tool jig attachments.

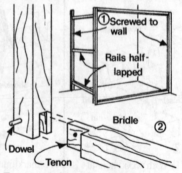

Framework for such as built-in cupboard (1) to be clad with plywood or hardboard and fitted with hinged/sliding doors. Joints at all corners could be half-lap, but bridle joint (also known as open mortise-and-tenon) is better, especially if secured with dowel as shown (2).

Furniture legs and fittings

Choosing the right legs for your handiwork can make an incredible difference to the look of the finished piece of furniture.

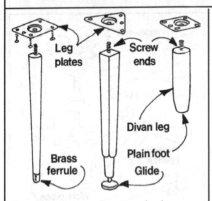

Representative screw-on wooden legs, used with leg plates, screwed to, e.g., table top. Legs, usually hardwood, are available in ebonised or 'natural wood' shade in lengths from about 6 to 28in.; divan legs 6in. only. Plates can be 'straight', shown, or 'offset' for splayed legs.

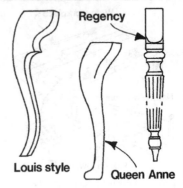

Three 'period' legs (in 4-18in.) suitable for reproduction furniture; they need to be used with jointed framing. Suitable as front legs for, e.g., occasional chairs, or all legs of foot stool/table.

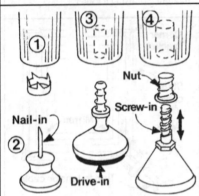

Types of glide: (1) simple metal dome-tends to indent flooring; (2) nail-in type, which spreads weight over floor surface; (3) swivel glide is self-tilting on floor and can be used with straight, splayed legs; (4) adjustable glide with drive-in nut allows height adjustment.

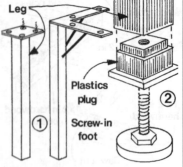

Steel lets, in either black or chrome, are sometimes preferred for modern furniture. Two patterns are shown (1); both have welded-on fixing brackets. Adjustable feet can be screwed into special plastic plugs (2) which are a drive-fit in leg. Corresponding fittings are made for circular steel legs.

Gripping woodwork

To ensure that your carpentry is all that it should be you need the correct gripping implement.

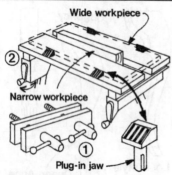

Wide workpiece

(2)

Narrow workpiece

(1)

Plug-in jaw

Apart from the usual steel one, the traditional beechwood vice (1) is specially useful when the workpiece is not parallel. The portable Workmate vice-bench (2) has similar advantages, and can also be used with wide boards/frames by plugging in the plastic jaws.

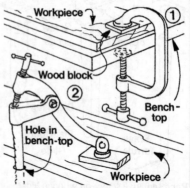

Workpiece (1)

Wood block

(2)

Bench-top

Hole in bench-top

Workpiece

A G-cramp (1) is good for securing workpiece, such as long board, to bench, and for holding joints until glue sets; 4in. is perhaps most useful size. Holdfast (2) is even better for holding smaller workpiece when, sawing, carving, edge-moulding or using a router.

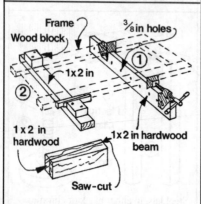

Frame ³/₈ **in holes**

Wood block

(1)

1 x 2 in

(2)

1 x 2 in hardwood

1 x 2 in hardwood beam

Saw-cut

Secure framing, wide workpieces while glue sets by use of cramp-heads (1) on home-made hardwood beam; or (2) by making up a beam, with blocks screwed on, and tightening by driving in folding wedges-made by sawing and planing, say, 7in. length of 1 x 2in. hardwood.

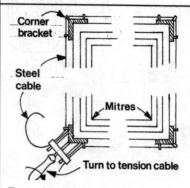

Corner bracket

Steel cable

Mitres

Turn to tension cable

For 'serious' picture-framing, special mitre cramps are well worth while. The type shown has metal corner brackets, and the whole frame is locked up by a flexible steel cable, tightened after the joints are glued and the frame set square, by rotating the handle.

Metal fixings for woodwork

Metal plates and fittings are the ideal choice for new or repaired wooden furniture, but the design has to be right.

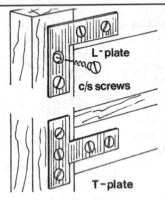

Two usual shapes of plate suitable for fixing butt-jointed framing or for repairs when, say, a tenon has broken. In steel or brass, they come in many sizes, and may be recessed for better appearance.

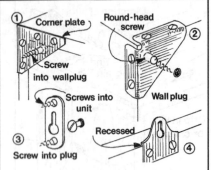

Fittings used for wall-mounting of cupboards, heavy frames, etc.: (1) Simple steel corner plate on carcase (box-type) construction; (2) corner bracket that allows 'box' to go flush against wall; (3) keyhole plate and (4) glass plate, allow unit to be securely mounted, yet easily removed, can be recessed or surface-mounted.

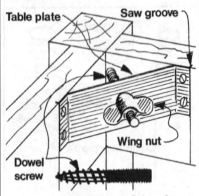

Useful K.D. (knock-down) fittings for table of which legs are detachable after removing wing nut from dowel screw driven into corner of leg. Rails are grooved with saw to receive turn-in ends of table plate. Plate, screw, wing nut are ordered separately.

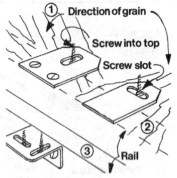

Types of so-called shrinkage plate, used for fixing table top to rails; top can 'move' on shrinkage/expansion without splitting. Types (1) and (2) are used according to grain direction - at right-angles to screw slot. (3) avoids need to recess rail and is two-directional.

Finishing interior woodwork

The smoothing and shining of a piece of carpentry makes all the difference to its appearance and longevity.

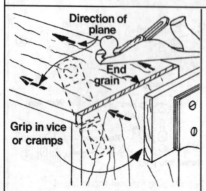

Final trimming and smoothing after construction can best be done with a finely-set smoothing plane. When planing end-grain, as in halving shown, hold plane at angle, working from each corner and planing in direction of grain.

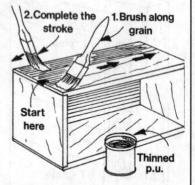

Obtain good finish with polyurethane varnish in gloss, silk, matt-clear or wood colour. Thin first coat with 10% white spirit. Brush in directions shown to avoid 'build-up' at corners. Sand lightly when dry, remove dust, give further coat(s) unthinned p.u. varnish

As alternative to complete p.u. finish, which is hard and tough, a softer, silk effect can be obtained with wax polish. After giving one (thinned) coat, rub in direction of grain with steel wool wiped over polish. Finish by buffing with muslin pad.

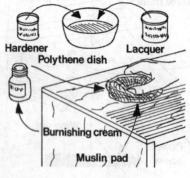

Use a two-part plastic lacquer (in clear, black, white) for heat, solvent-resisting surface. mix lacquer and hardener as directed, in polythene dish. Apply as for p.u. and rub with steel wool/wax for semi-matt, or with burnishing cream for mirror finish.

Hiding exposed pipes

Bare water or heating pipes can spoil the look of a room, but fortunately, in most cases they are quite easy to camouflage.

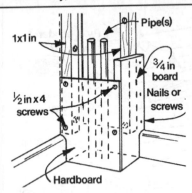

Among easiest to conceal are pipes running up corner of a room. Fix 1 x 1in. bearers with screws into wall plugs, shown, or with wall-panel adhesive. Then fix 3/4in. board at side with nails, screws or adhesive. Attach front cover with screws, for easier removal.

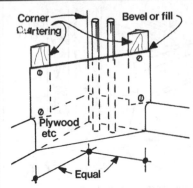

Where pipes run close to corner, or if there is only single pipe, better appearance can sometimes be obtained by covering whole corner, as shown. Front hardboard, plywood over board should have edges bevelled - and/or gaps could be closed with filler before painting.

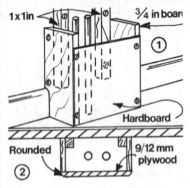

Enclose pipes running up wall face by fixing 1 x 1in. bearers and 3.4in. board each side. Then screw hardboard, thin plywood to front (1). Instead, 9/12mm. plywood, with edges rounded over (2) could be used for somewhat smoother appearance.

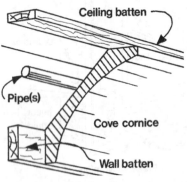

It may be possible to make a neat enclosure of pipe running along ceiling angle by using cover cornice mould - if necessary, with battens to take cornice clear of pipe(s). Later access would be difficult. Measure carefully and make scale drawing before starting.

Dealing with wood decay

Wet rot, if caught early enough, can be controlled and the timber made good.

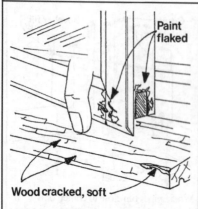

Paint flaked

Wood cracked, soft

Typical example is window sill/frame. Paint will not adhere well, criss-cross cracks are seen, wood feels spongy under thumb nail. First remove all paint, and scrub along grain with wire brush.

P.v.a. bonder: 1
water: 3

①

Cut away

Build up with filler

②

Cut away rotted edge of e.g., sill (1) and liberally brush few coats diluted p.v.a. bonder into wood - while dry; or use proprietary wood hardener. When hard, build up, also fill cracks, with exterior-grade wood filler (2); then sand flat and smooth before painting.

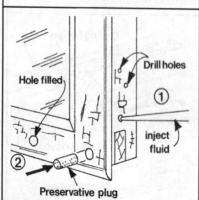

Hole filled

Drill holes

①

inject fluid

②

Preservative plug

Further decay can be minimised by liberal application of a clear, preservative fluid. Better, drill holes and inject preservative (1) with clean force-feed oil-can. Do not fill holes or paint for two weeks. Simpler is to drill and insert solid preservative plugs (2).

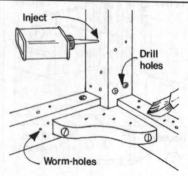

Inject

Drill holes

Worm-holes

Woodworm can be as serious as rot, especially on valuable furniture. Apply woodworm fluid with sprayer (for structural timbers) or by brushing. On furniture (often underneath) apply fluid from injector can - into worm holes or, better, into holes made with drill.

Simple gilding and ebonising

Turn a workaday piece of furniture into a work of art by the simple application of know-how.

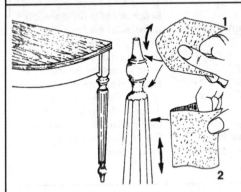

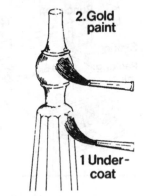

Table with period legs is example suitable for gilded legs/apron and ebonised top. Rub down top with fine glasspaper held around cork block. Turn table upside down and do legs: hollows with strip of glasspaper around first finger (1), sharp angles with paper bend as shown (2). Any old polish should be removed before proceeding as above.

To gild, apply thinned undercoating, lightly rub down and then apply gold paint. Use pencil brush for details, and avoid 'build-up' of paint in angles.

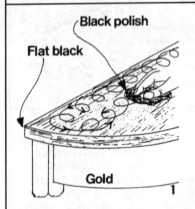

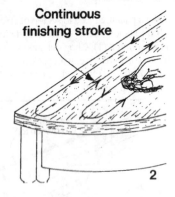

Obtain ebony finish by giving even coat of flat black or blackboard paint and then treating with black French polish. Apply with cotton wool-muslin pad in usual way: briefly, give several coats with continuous circular motion of pad (1); finish with overlapping end-to-end strokes (2). If there are sharp angles or mouldings treat these with pencil brush instead of pad. For semi-gloss finish allow polish to harden and then rub with finest steel wool and a little wax polish.

Fitting a woodwork bench vice

To get the most out of your vice, and therefore of your creations, it is necessary to fit it correctly.

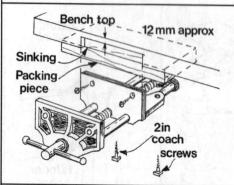

Bench vice of 6-7in. jaw width is one of the most useful woodwork tools if properly fixed to a rigid bench. Use a board as packing and recess the bench top to receive fixed jaw of vice, as shown. Vice is secured with wood screws through fixed jaw and two or four coach screws through lower flanges.

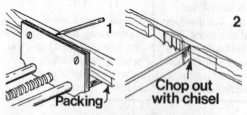
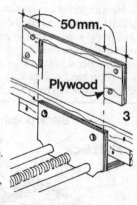

First make a packing piece to set top of fixed jaw about 12m. (1/2in.) below bench surface. hold vice in position and mark around it (1). Chop out sinking with chisel (2). Simpler way is to fix vice, with packing, against bench edge and cut shaped plywood, or exact thickness of jaw, to fit jaw, to fit around it (3).

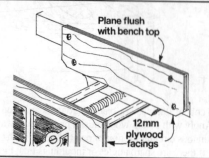

When vice is rigidly mounted, make wood facing for both jaws. Use either 18mm. planed hardwood or 12mm. plywood. Made to project very slightly above bench top and screw on after deeply countersinking holes in rear facing. Close vice and plane flush with top.

NOTE: Vices vary in detail but method shown applies to all.

Fixing shelves and shelving

Shelves, although relatively simple to erect, can look and be a total disaster unless they are fitted correctly.

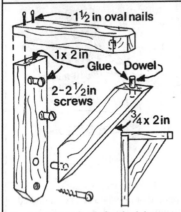

Hardwood brackets often look better than metal ones, and are easily made. Top should be about 1in shorter than shelf width and about 3/4 length of upright. Glue dowels into strut ends, then into other members.

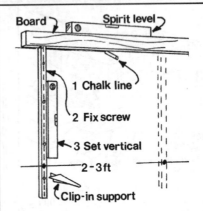

Adjustable wall brackets in various finishes are all fixed similarly: 1. mark position of tops with chalk against board with spirit level; 2. drill, plug wall and fit top screw; 3. set vertical with spirit level, mark for drill and fix other screws.

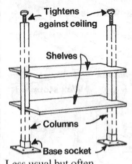

Less usual but often convenient are column shelves, which serve as room divider. Columns fit in sockets screwed to floor, while screw-adjusting fitting grips against ceiling - best positioned under a joist and screwed to it.

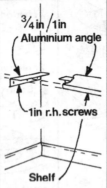

Recess shelves can be carried on aliuminium angle, set against spirit level, screwed to wall plugs. Or use 1 x 2in softwood bearers.

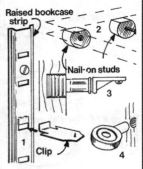

Types of bookcase- shelf: (1) perforated surface-fitting metal strip in brass/zinc finish; (2) ultra-simple studs with nails; (3) neat plastic plug, fitting socket pressed into side; (4) clear plastic stud, pressed into board hole.

Using wood fillers and stoppings

Wood can often get damaged and gouged but with the application of a filler the furniture or fitting can be saved.

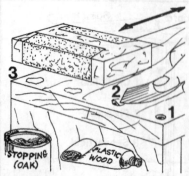

Fill nail/screw holes (1) by pressing in stopping or plastic wood (2). Leave filling standing proud; when hard, smooth with medium glasspaper on block (3). Use a filler in neutral shade before painting; in approximate shade of hardwood before straining, polishing or varnishing.

Edges of blockboard (shown), chipboard or plywood can be smoothed for painting by brushing on ordinary plaster filler thinned with water to creamy consistency. Lightly sand after filler has dried. Stir a few drops of matching water stain into filler if wood is to be stained.

Grain filling is desirable before polishing/varnishing most hardwoods. Buy paste grain filler in shade of wood and thin slightly by mixing in which spirit. Rub into surface, working across grain, with coarse rag. Wipe off excess in direction of grain with clean rag.

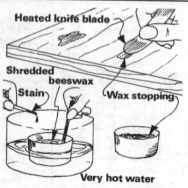

Filling of small holes in polished furniture can be done with beeswax tinted with spirit stain. Shred wax into small tin, melt in near-boiling water and add drops of stain while mixing. When cool, press in with heated blade of old table knife.

Choosing and using screwdrivers

The ubiquitous screwdriver may seem like the simplest tool in your box, but each is ideally suited to particular jobs.

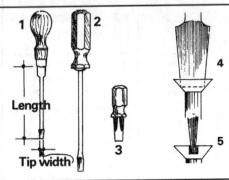

Three main types for slotted screws: (1) cabinet, with wooden handle, gives comfortable grip, must not be hammered; (2) general-purpose, with tough plastic handle, may be hammered; (3) stubby, for use in confined space. Screwdrivers are described by blade length and tip width; tip should be close fit in screw head (4 & 5).

Cross-head screwdrivers come in standard pattern (1) as well as stubby; also with interchangeable bits (2) and double-ended offset (3) with two different-size points. They are specified by points sizes 1 to 4, and size 2 (for screws 5 to 10 gauge) is most used. Size 1 fits smaller screws, size 3, gauge 12 and 14 screws. Enlarged detail of cross-head screw and points to fit (4).

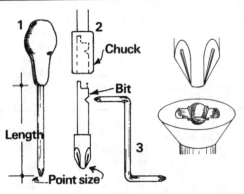

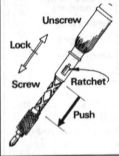

Push-type with interchangeable bits: slotted-type, cross-head screwdrivers, also small drills, stored in magazine handle. At mid-position ratchet tool acts as fixed screwdriver.

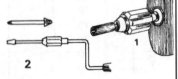

(1) Screwdriver attachment for power drill; automatic clutch prevents over-tightening, and end locates over screw-head. (2) Bits for woodworker's brace when heavy pressure is required.

NOTE: Advantages of crosshead screws: more torque can be applied without risk of screwdriver slipping; screws more easily removed. With cross-head screws, driver must be kept square to screw head.

Metrication in woodworking

The workings of the European Union, inevitably, have had an impact on DIY, particularly in the change from imperial units.

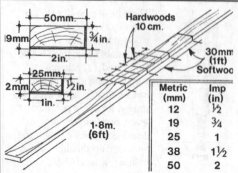

Metric (mm)	Imp (in)
12	½
19	¾
25	1
38	1½
50	2

Sawn softwood is sold in metric lengths from 1.8 metres upwards in 30 cm. steps; hardwood in 10 cm. steps. Cross-section is fractionally smaller in metric than corresponding imperial sizes, as indicated by the examples. Planed timber is about 3mm. thinner and 3-6mm. narrower than nominal (sawn) sizes. Plywood, chipboard, blockboard, etc. are sold in metric sizes; thickness is in mm., as before.

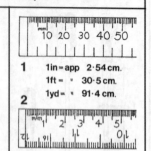

1 1in = app 2·54 cm.
   1ft = "   30·5 cm.
2 1yd = "   91·4 cm.

Metric-only rules (1) are available, but it may be preferred to have one marked in both metric and imperial (2), especially when replacing old timber by new.

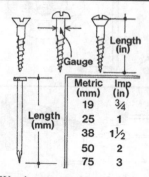

Metric (mm)	Imp (in)
19	¾
25	1
38	1½
50	2
75	3

Wood-screws, measured as shown, are generally metric, although you might find imperial still about. Nails went metric years ago.

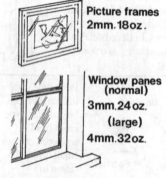

Picture frames
2mm. 18oz.

Window panes (normal)
3mm. 24oz.
(large)
4mm. 32oz.

Glass is now often sold in metric lengths/widths, with thickness stated in millimetres rather than by weight. Equivalent descriptions of most-used thicknesses are as given.

NOTE: Despite the introduction of metric measurements for most materials, merchants will be please to talk imperial if you're still uncomfortable with Euro-measure. Ask for help.

Removing tight or broken screws

Screws which have been badly inserted, have disintegrated through age or simply painted over can be retrieved.

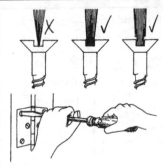

Most important is to have well-fitting screwdriver. If too pointed it will slip out of slot. If necessary, file tip with parallel sides to fit slot. Then, with screwdriver at right-angles to screw head, press firmly against handle and turn slowly at same time.

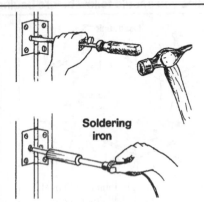

Soldering iron

Rusted-in screws can be loosened by striking screwdriver (preferably plastic-handled) with side of hammer; with tip securely in slot, give one solid blow. Alternative is to hold tip of hot soldering iron against screw head for few seconds.

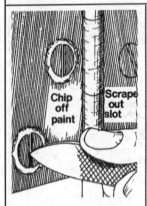

Chip off paint **Scrape out slot**

When paint is over screw head and in slot, chip it off around screw with screwdriver or old chisel and scrape all paint from shot with, e.g., nail file.

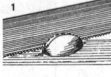

Hack–saw
Centre punch

Damaged slot in round-head screw can usually be 'repaired' by making a few strokes with a hacksaw (1). With countersink screw, try loosening with centre punch and hammer (2).

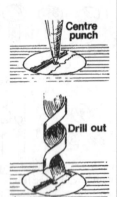

Centre punch

Drill out

If all else fails, make a centre-punch depression in middle of slot and carefully drill out screw.

Nail and screw choice

Choosing the correct nails and screws for a job is more complicated than you might have thought. Below are some general rules you should follow before beginning a job.

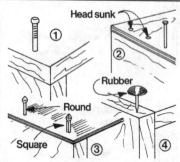

Four nails for light joinery: (1) oval-head, can be punched down, hole filled; (2) panel pin, as for fixing plywood-lengths up to 1 1/2in. or more; (3) 'lost-head' hardboard nails, round or square, rust-proofed; (4) rubber-headed nail or tack for use as e.g. small foot.

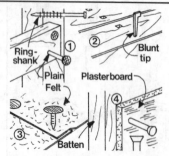

Some nails for fixing carpentry: (1) round or French nail, with plain or ring shank, gives stronger fixing than oval nail for e.g. fencing; (2) flooring brad-blunt tip prevents splitting; (3) clout nail, usually galvanised, for e.g. roofing felt; (4) plasterboard nail, has countersink head.

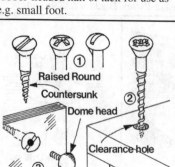

(1) Screws for most purposes come with any of three heads shown in steel, brass, chrome, zinc-plated etc. (2) Special screws particularly suitable for chipboard have sharper thread, shank of smaller diameter. (3) Dome-head screw, as used for mirror -mounting.

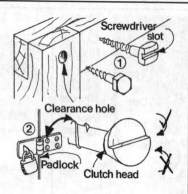

Two less-usual screw types: (1) coach screw, for heavy duty in joining e.g. frame members-can have square/hexagon head, with/without screw slot; (2) security (clutch-head) screw has slot with sloping sides so that it can be screwed in but cannot be unscrewed.

Furniture

Pages 296-306

Re-surfacing old furniture

Seen a table in a junk shop with an interesting shape, but in a terrible mess? Don't be put off. It may well be worth re-surfacing.

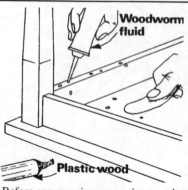

Before commencing renovation search for worm holes, especially on undersides. Inject woodworm fluid with nozzle can in which it is sold. Repeat after a week. When wood has dried fill holes with plastic wood of matching shade, pressing well in with kitchen-knife blade.

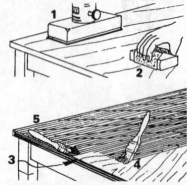

Smooth and remove old surface with finishing sander (1) using fine abrasive sheet and light pressure. Lift frequently to clear dust. Or use medium, then fine garnet paper on sanding block (2) in grain direction. Apply polyurethane varnish or two-part lacquer in sequence (3-5).

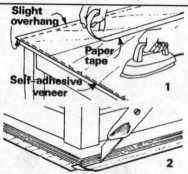

Badly damaged veneer can be sanded down or removed and new iron-on veneer (in teak and sapele) laid. When cold, damp and peel off paper tape joining veneers (1). Then trim from underside with sharp knife. Edges should be done first, when required, with matching edge veneer.

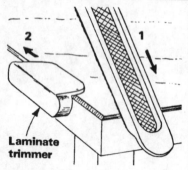

When plastic laminate is used, with contact adhesive, make fractionally over-size. After adhesive has set trim edges with very finely set plane, shaping tool (1) or (very convenient) edge-trimmer with inclined plane-like blade (2); work by drawing tool towards you.

'Leather' writing table top

A 'leather'-topped writing table is not only a pleasure to work on, but an asset that adds style to any room. Here's how to make one, or recover an old one if the leather top is badly damaged.

Remove worn or shabby leather by slowly peeling while soaking glue with very hot water. Do not over-wet but soften glue as much as possible. After removing, soften remaining glue in same way and scrape off. Mop with dry rag, allow to dry and finish with coarse glasspaper.

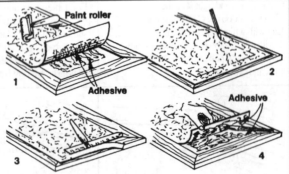

Leather top is expensive, but fabric-backed vinyl can be used instead; have piece 2-3in wider and longer than old leather. Brush (pva) woodwork adhesive mixed 1:1 with water over top and back of vinyl, leaving 1in.margin. Smooth down from centre outwards with duster or paint roller (1). Mark into angle with pencil (2); then cut with sharp knife against steel rule (3). Finally, lift edges, apply adhesive to margins (4) and smooth down.

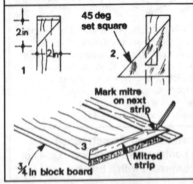

'Leather' table/desk top can be made by gluing on 'frame' of veneer or laminate. Mark mitres on two pieces, by measurement (1) or with set-square (2). Cut, then mark next length (3). Check fit and fix with contact adhesive. Edge top with matching strips.

Renovating polished furniture

Well-polished furniture is a delight. So if you have pieces that are scratched and marked, set to. It's not so hard.

Remove rings and light scratches with a polish reviver on rag (1). Scrape out scores, clean with white spirit on fine brush (2) and fill with polish allowed to thicken slightly by exposure, using pointed stick (3). Lightly rub down and brush-polish.

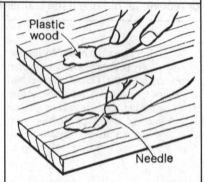

Fill depressions and burns, after scraping, by pressing in plastic wood of matching shade with knife blade. Smooth with very fine garnet paper and imitate grain with light needle scratches. Brush on thin film of polish, rub down and repolish.

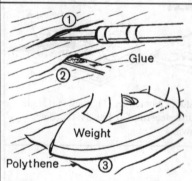

To flatten veneer blisters make inclined cut along grain with craft knife (1). Work in a little glue with strip on thin card (2). Press down, wipe off surplus glue, cover with sheet of polythene and leave with weight on it overnight.

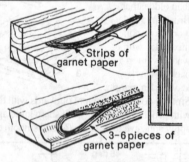

Badly damaged polish should be stripped. First remove wax with white spirit and steel wool. Then rub in direction of grain with garnet paper. Work in sharp angles with several strips of garnet paper arranged as shown (top). Do hollows with a few strips of paper curved to fit (above).

REPOLISHING can be done with inexpensive 'home' French polish kit, following simple instructions; some kits contain a polish reviver. Or – not quite as good – by applying polyurethane varnish with a brush

Re-seating a chair

How many times has an elegant wooden upright chair been consigned to the garage or loft because the seat has gone. Here's how to fix it, even if it was once a cane or rush seat.

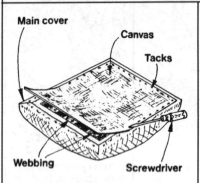

Main cover

Canvas

Tacks

Webbing

Screwdriver

With upholstered seat method is similar whether seat is loose (shown) or fixed. To replace webbing/cover first take off canvas; remove tacks by holding tip of screwdriver under head and tapping handle with hammer. Same applies to tacks holding main cover and, sometimes, an inner cotton one.

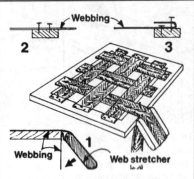

Webbing

2   **3**

Webbing   **Web stretcher**

After removing cover and padding, old webbing can be replaced as shown. Fix lengths from front to back and then 'weave' cross lengths through them. With wood block made as shown (1); tack and cut off (2); then fold over and drive in three more tacks (3).

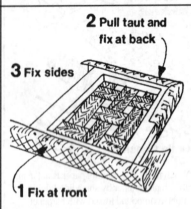

2 Pull taut and fix at back

3 Fix sides

1 Fix at front

Use old cover pattern to cut out new one. Keeping it taut, fix to front underside of frame with $5/8$ in tacks. Pull evenly taut and tack at back edge. Fold and pleat corners and, keeping taut, tack down both sides.

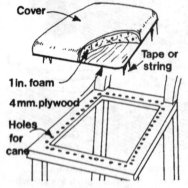

Cover

Tape or string

1 in. foam

4 mm. plywood

Holes for cane

Worn cane/rush seat can be replaced with padded one made from piece of plywood with foam padding and fabric cover. Before covering plywood fit lengths of string or tape to tie through holes in chair frame. Cover is fixed to underside edges of plywood with fabric adhesive.

Repairing leather-look upholstery

Blemishes and holes in vinyl and leather upholstery can really spoil the look of suite or chair. Here's how to repair them.

Holes and tears in vinyl and leather can be invisibly repaired by using special vinyl paste, which comes in mixable colours. First trim the edges of the damaged part with sharp knife or razor blade.

Mix colours (from small tubs or tubes) to match shade of upholstery on, eg. a tile. Put sheet of glass-fibre mat as backing flat under damaged area and fill with paste, pressing it slightly under edges.

Next put graining paper, grain side down, over paste and press flat. (Correct graining paper should be chosen before starting repair).

Set iron to 'Rayon' and apply tip only over graining paper, protecting surrounding vinyl with cardboard mask. Iron for two minutes, leave a few minutes and peel off. Do not use chair until filling is cold.

When matching graining paper is not available, make grainer by spreading liquid rubber compound mixed with hardener over undamaged part. Leave ten minutes, peel off and use in same way as paper.

NOTE: All necessary materials can be obtained as small kit, with instructions. Extra coloured paste can be bought separately.

Strengthening a chair frame

A much used, and perhaps much loved, chair gets more and more wobbly until its no longer safe to sit on. You can always throw it out, but it may be quite easy to repair. Read on ...

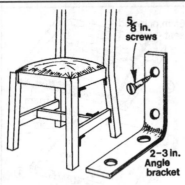

Loose joints can be strengthened without dismantling and re-gluing by fitting strong steel angle brackets at some or all of the positions indicated. If necessary, carefully bend the bracket in the vice so that it is exact fit in corner. This method should not be used on valuable furniture.

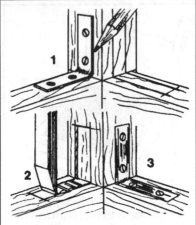

A better appearance is obtained by recessing angles into frame members. Draw around bracket (1); then make series of cuts with chisel and mallet (2) and scoop out waste. Screw on bracket (3).

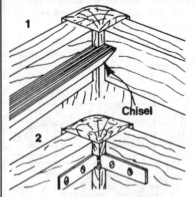

Steel angles can also be used at top between rails and legs. If rails are inset as shown, cut notch (1) so that bracket will fit closely (2). As repair will not show, recessing is not necessary.

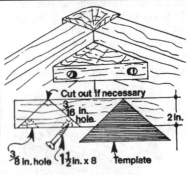

Better method of strengthening joints between legs and top rails is to glue and screw in block made from 1in thick oak. Mark out with cardboard template made to angle of corner. With inset rails, saw out corner of block. Drill shallow $3/8$in and then $3/16$in holes for No. 8 screws.

Re-seating a bedroom chair

Even simple bedroom chairs may well be worth the trouble of repairing. Here is a simple method that anyone with basic wood working tools and skills can undertake with confidence.

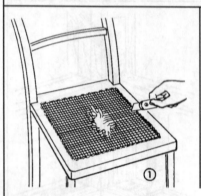

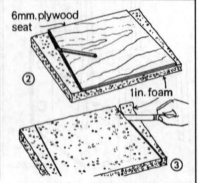

General method shown can be applied to many types of seat. Prise off a nailed-on wooden one; remove a damaged wicker seat by cutting loops around edges (1). Cut plywood to shape of seat, well overlapping the holes. Smooth edges with glasspaper and use as pattern to mark shape on foam with ball-point pen (2). To cut foam, make long slicing cuts with very sharp carving knife (3).

Have cover material (fairly thin is easiest to use) 4-5in longer and wider than plywood. Fix one edge to underside

of plywood at back, pull taut around foam and fix front edge in same way (4) – do not glue near corners yet. Fix other two edges in same way and pleat corners (5). Carefully cut away excess material to avoid several thicknesses, tuck triangular pleats under (6) and glue. Press down and hold till adhesive grips.

Fix new seat with screws just long enough to go through plywood (7). Alternative method is to use 4mm plywood, $1/4$in foam and fix with brass-head upholstery nails (8).

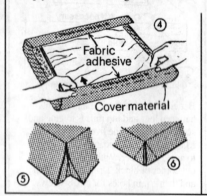

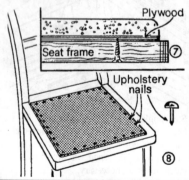

Staining, painting and polishing

Even the most battered, scuffed and neglected pieces of furniture can take on a new lease of life with new paint, stain or polish

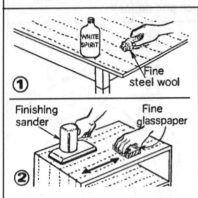

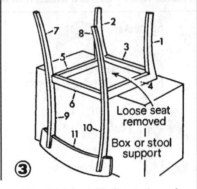

(1) On previously polished wood, first clean well with white spirit applied with fine steel wool. Wipe off with clean rag.

(2) With new whitewood, lightly moisten with damp rag. When dry, rub in direction of grain with fine glasspaper held around wood or cork block; or smooth with finishing-sander power tool. Remove dust.

(3) If staining, varnishing or painting a chair (after rubbing down) do legs and underside first, with chair inverted; complete with chair upright, following the general sequence indicated.

(4) To paint a chest, remove drawers and fittings, stand chest on two battens

and brush in sequence shown. A good treatment is: proprietary primer/undercoat; rub down; two coats gloss paint.

(5) A good furniture finish can be obtained by brushing on three coats of polyurethane varnish; rub down with fine garnet paper before last coat.

For an even better finish use polyurethane French polish. Make pad as shown and put a few drops of polish on cotton wool; lightly squeeze, then twist muslin around it. Apply several coats with circular motion, rub down with fine garnet paper and give two or three coats in straight strokes.

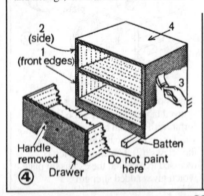

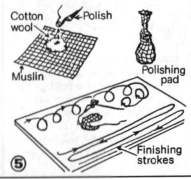

Furniture castors

Moving furniture around is much easier if it is fitted with castors, but some castors are more manoeuvrable and kinder to floors than others. Then there are those that stick and squeak ...

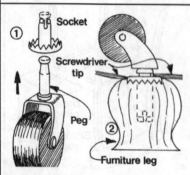

Most widely used type of castor (1) has steel peg which is press fit in socket driven into hole bored in furniture leg. For replacement, cleaning, slight lubrication, peg is levered out of socket with screwdriver. When necessary, socket can be levered out in similar way (2).

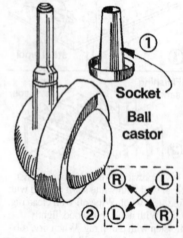

Ball castors (1), 'kinder' to flooring, give easier movement, are usually in sets of 4, often marked for left/right-hand fitting (2). Alloy socket is easy drive fit in hole.

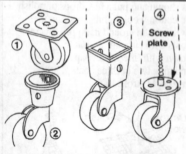

Various other types of castor fixing: (1) plate-type, screwed to side-grain; (2) round socket for thin or turned legs; (3) square socket for small-section square legs; (4) screw-plate type, mainly used for end-gain fixing. Types (2), (3) and (4) are generally in brass and used for 'quality' furniture, especially antique or reproduction.

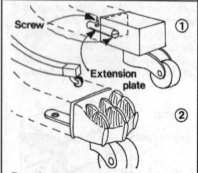

Brass box castors are used for, eg., splayed table legs, as in some Regency furniture. They can be plain (1) or in various decorative designs, including the 'claws' (2). Underside of leg is recessed to received the extension plate, which gives added strength.

A facelift for polished furniture

Well polished furniture is a delight, especially when it is kept in tip-top condition. Here's how to give it a facelift.

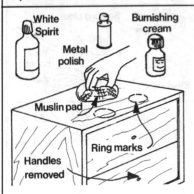

First step is to clean and de-wax with muslin pad damped with white spirit. White ring marks and the like can then be removed by rubbing with metal polish or specially-made burnishing cream. Always work in direction of grain. Remove drawers and fittings for treatment.

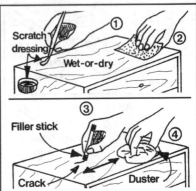

Fine scratches are removed with burnishing cream. Fill larger ones with scratch dressing (1); then smooth off with fine wet-or-dry paper (2); finish with burnishing cream. Small cracks, gaps can be filled with special wax filler stick (3) in wood shade; polish with soft duster (4).

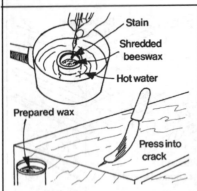

Make good wax filler for gaps, cracks by melting shredded beeswax in container standing in hot water. Mix in a spot of white spirit, then a drop of matching stain. Scrape out crack and press in stained wax with springy knife. Buff up with soft duster, along grain.

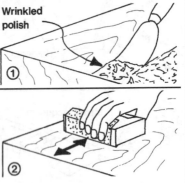

Strip bad surface to bare wood for re-coating with eg. p.u. varnish. Using chemical stripper (1) scrape after finish has become wrinkled, following makers' instructions.

Or, after cleaning and de-waxing, strip with garnet paper on sanding block (2). Easier with orbital sander.

Different furniture finishes

Here are some tips on how to apply different finishes to furniture, whether to repair old pieces or to enhance new wood.

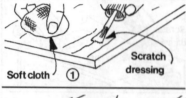

Minor scratches can often be removed with scratch dressing. One type is applied with a screw-cap brush (1), left for a few minutes then surplus wiped off. Another way is to rub in grain direction with burnishing cream or even silver polish (2); finish with soft duster.

If satin finish is acceptable, whole surface can be lightly sanded with fine garnet paper on sanding block (1) or, easier, with orbital sander, then wax-polished using pad of grade-000 steel wool (2). Or, after sanding, brush on teak oil Danish oil (3) and wipe off.

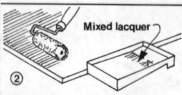

Two-part lacquers give hardest-wearing, heatproof finish. Mix lacquer and hardener in recommended proportions (1). Apply first coat (2) with roller, brush, spray-gun. Give two further coats and, next day, sand lightly, polish with burnishing cream or, for satin finish, use steel wool-wax.

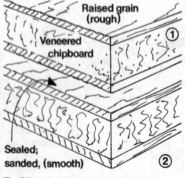

To fill grain of new hardwood, solid or veneer, first raise grain (1) by damping lightly, evenly. Allow to dry before sanding in grain direction. Then apply sealing coat of polish/varnish/lacquer to be used and again sand to produce good surface (2) for final coats.

Carpets
and
Curtains

Pages 308-314

Laying a stair carpet

Two ways to lay a stair carpet, both somewhat easier to do than would appear to be the case at first sight

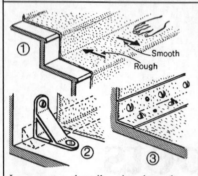

Lay carpet so that pile points down the stairs (1). It can be fixed with rods (2) or invisible gripper bar (3). The latter is usually preferred, especially when using full-stair width carpet.

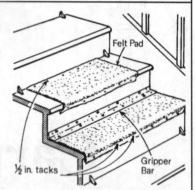

Fix underpads over treads and turning over nosing. When using gripper bar nail this over felt. Lay carpets downwards on straight stairs. Pull taut and insert rod, if used

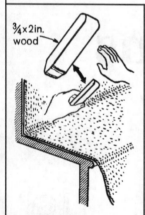

With gripper bar force carpet into angle and over spikes with piece of wood shaped as shown.

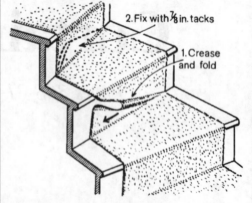

On stairs with turn work upwards and use tacks (not nails) for fixing on turn, even if gripper is used elsewhere. Pull carpet taut, form crease (1) and fold down so that it does not show.

Then secure with long tacks (2).

NOTE: Have sufficient length of carpet to allow for moving up or down half a step once a year. This equalises wear and prolongs carpet life.

Fixing curtain rails and poles

Well hung curtains can make a room, particularly at night. Part of the secret lies in the how they are hung.

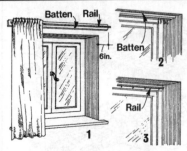

It is nearly always best to fit a batten (about $3/4$ x $11/2$ in) to which rail brackets can be screwed. If placed about 2in above the window reveal (1) curtains can be of any length. If mounted inside the reveal (2) curtains can only come down to the sill. When window frame is wide enough brackets can be screwed directly to it (3).

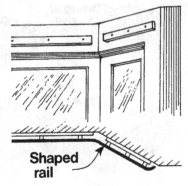

Shaped rail

With bay window use separate battens with a track of a type that can be curved to the shape shown; it can be shaped in the hands to 'easy' curves. Some tracks cannot be bent.

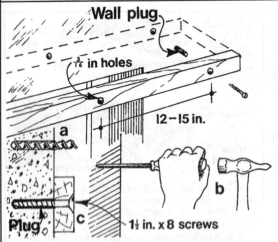

Wall plug

$\frac{3}{16}$ in holes

12 – 15 in.

Plug

1½ in. x 8 screws

Drill and countersink holes in batten. Mark position of central hole on wall and drill for plug with masonry bit (a), or with hand tool and hammer (b) in concrete lintel; press plug into hole and screw on batten (c). Mark through batten for other holes; then remove batten, drill and plug.

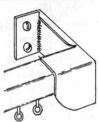

Brackets for cornice pole or extensible (telescopic) track can be screwed directly to wall plugs.

Repairing and binding a carpet

With the cost of new carpets being what they are, it is always worth considering repairing one of basically good quality.

For loose carpet, cut piece of hardboard a little larger than damaged area (1). Turn carpet over on card or board and cut around with sharp knife (2).

Using same hardboard as template cut patch from spare carpet; coat edges and half pile length with fabric adhesive (3). When touch-dry press patch into place. Coat back of carpet and a piece of hessian with adhesive and smooth down (4).

When nearly dry, lightly beat all over with hammer.

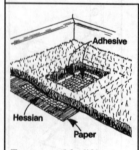

To save need for lifting fitted carpet, cut hole and patch. Put sheet of paper, then hessian, through hole. Coat half pile edges and hessian with adhesive. Fit patch when touch-dry and hammer down.

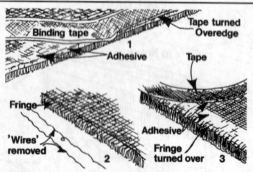

Bind Wilton Carpet by applying adhesive to back and half edge of pile. Coat one side of $1^1/_2$in binding tape with adhesive; when touch-dry press down and turn $1/_4$in over edge (1).

With Axminster carpet remove two/three 'wires' to form fringe (2). Coat back of carpet with adhesive, turn over fringe and, if desired, fit strip of binding tape (3).

NOTE: Patches can be cut from spare carpeting, or from part of carpet covered with furniture not likely to be moved. Take care to match direction of pile.

Lifting and re-laying fitted carpet

While a skilled carpet fitter is need to lay a new fitted carpet in the first instance, you can tackle the job of lifting and relaying an existing one. Here's how ...

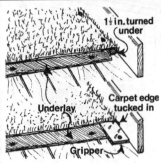

Method of lifting (eg. for room re-decoration) depends upon fixing used. Usual are: (1) tacks through turned-under edge; (2) gripper strip fixed to floor with inclined spikes over which carpet is pressed.

(1) Tacks are levered out with pincers after, if necessary, starting them with tip of broad screwdriver under head. Untack underlay in same way.

(2) With gripper strip, carpet is pressed towards wall with one hand, while edge is pushed forward and lifted with other. Avoid excessive force.

When relaying with tacks, drive in 9in apart, 1in from edge along one long wall (1). Shuffle-stretch carpet to opposite wall; put in temporary tacks; pull taut and tack along edge (2).

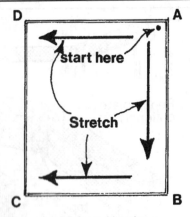

Sequence of fixing (with tacks or gripper); fix and stretch from A to B; stretch A-D and B-C; fix C-D; then B-C and A-D.

NOTE: Method is similar when laying new carpet but special stretcher is required. Initial fitting should be done by expert. Use $7/_8$ in tacks - never nails.

Making curtain pelmets

Curtains, particularly on large living room windows, have such an impact, it is worth considering the added elegance of pelmets

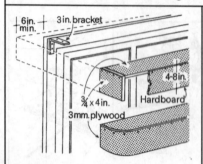

Simplest method, where window framing projects from wall face. For square ends, nail together three lengths of board; then glue and pin on hardboard or plywood front. With curved ends, radius should be 6in or more. Steam front to simplify curving. Mount pelmet on strong brackets about 2ft 6in apart.

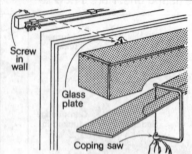

Another method of mounting, when curtain track is fixed to a wall batten. Screw glass plates to top board, hold pelmet in place to mark wall, and drive $1\frac{1}{4}$in screws into wall plugs.

Pelmet is removed by lifting to clear screw heads. Use a coping or fret saw if curved front is required.

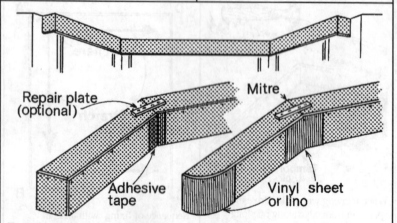

For inside a window bay make pelmet in three sections with mitred corners.

Mark for mitres with boards lying on window sill. Cover joints between front pieces with wide adhesive tape (as used for carpet laying); or, with rounded ends, glue on pieces of vinyl or lino floor-covering.

Pelmet can be mounted one section at a time before covering joints.

Paint inside of pelmet before fitting – outside after covering joints.

Fixing and patching carpets

Here is another way of patching worn patches on carpets, and making sure that they are firmly re-fixed if they work lose.

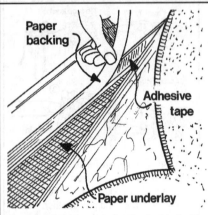

Paper backing

Adhesive tape

Paper underlay

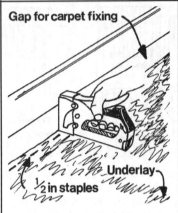

Gap for carpet fixing

Underlay

½in staples

Foam-backed carpet can be fixed with double-sized adhesive tape. Lay paper underlay in 2in from walls, fit carpet; next roll back edges and apply tape to floor.

Then work around walls, peeling off backing paper and pressing carpet over tape.

When underlay is required, for non-backed carpets, it is most easily fixed with stapling gun. Leave gap around edges for gripper or other carpet fixing. Keep underlay just taut.

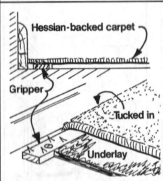

Hessian-backed carpet

Gripper

Tucked in

Underlay

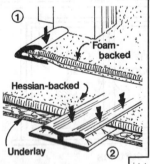

① **Foam-backed**

Hessian-backed

Underlay ②

Probably most popular method of fixing hessian-backed carpet is with spiked grippers nailed/adhesive-fixed to wood/solid floor. Stretcher must be used before pressing carpet over gripper and tucking in as shown.

Two aluminium binder-bars used at doorways, with either type of carpet: (1) for single carpet; (2) for meeting carpets. Binders for hessian-backed are spiked. All are locked by hammering, over spare wood, where arrowed.

Below: to patch thread-bare area (1) cut patch to cover; used as template to cut carpets. Fit seaming tape, coated with fabric adhesive, under and around edges (2).

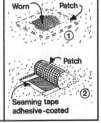

Worn **Patch** ①

Patch

Seaming tape adhesive-coated ②

Hanging curtains

Hanging curtains properly is a job that can require patience and care, but the results are really worth having.

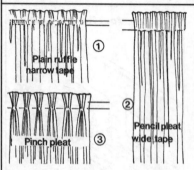

Plain ruffle narrow tape ①

Pencil pleat wide tape ②

Pinch pleat ③

Decide on type of curtain head required: (1) simple ruffle pleat; (2) pencil pleat; (3) pinch pleat. Order curtains, or buy heading tape, accordingly. In general (1) is suitable for 'chintzy cottage' room, while (2) and (3) suit long curtains in more modern, formal setting.

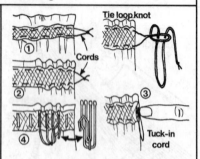

Tie loop knot

Cords ①

②

③

Tuck-in cord

④

In case of simple ruffle use narrow tape (1). Wide tape is required for pencil pleating (2). In both, first secure cord at one end; knot and pull at other. Do not cut cord, but tie into loop and tuck under end of tape (3).

Special hooks, tapes are used for pencil pleats (4).

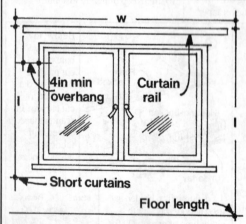

w

4in min overhang

Curtain rail

Short curtains

Floor length

With wall-mounted rail (regardless of type) allow good projection beyond window opening. Overall width of unpleated curtains should be at least $1^1/_2$ times 'w'; twice for pencil pleat.

Add sufficient to 'l' to allow for shrinkage if washed; this depends on material, but suppliers can advise.

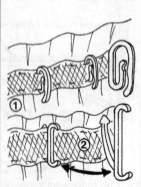

①

②

Two of the many types of plastic hooks used with popular plain plastic rails: (1) for narrow tape, hooks through glide ring; (2) for most tapes, is snapped over wide rail.